Rules for a Successful Book Club

VICTORIA CONNELLY

Victoria Connelly asserts the moral right to be identified as the author of this work.

Cover design by J D Smith.

Published by Cuthland Press
in association with Notting Hill Press.

ISBN: 978-1-910522-11-0

To my dear friend Ruth with love.

ACKNOWLEDGEMENTS

Many thanks to the wonderful team who help put my books together: Catriona, Jan, Jane and Roy. I love working with you all!

CHAPTER 1

Polly Prior was running late. That was nothing new in itself because she was always trying to do at least three things at once, but it upset her nevertheless.

'Archie!' she shouted up the stairs. 'I'm going whether you're ready or not.'

A minute later, her six-year-old son came tearing down the stairs followed by Dickens the spaniel.

'Didn't I tell you that Dickens isn't allowed upstairs?' she said, doing her best to flatten her son's dark hair with her hands.

'He sneaked up when I was brushing my teeth,' Archie said.

'Well, I hope he hasn't been on your bed again.'

'Not much,' Archie said, 'and I made it after he jumped off.'

Polly shook her head. 'I don't want to find any more paw prints on your pillow. It's not hygienic.'

Archie grinned, obviously remembering the time when Dickens had waded through every puddle in Suffolk before racing up the stairs and leaping onto his bed.

'Get your bag,' Polly told him now. 'I've put your packed lunch in it and make sure you eat your sandwiches, okay?'

'As long as you've not put a banana next to them,' he said, screwing up his face in disgust as he put his shoes on.

'I've not put a banana next to them,' she said, knowing of her son's aversion to banana-smelling bread. 'You've got grapes today. Dickens – basket! I'll be back after lunch for a good long walk,' she told the dog who cocked his head to one side, appearing to understand.

Archie bent to pat the young spaniel's head.

'Come on, Arch. We're late enough as it is.'

Polly opened the front door onto a steely grey January morning and instantly wished that she was back in bed. The first day of the spring term was always the most trying after the joy and fun of the Christmas holidays, but Christmas was long over: the tree had been recycled and the decorations had been safely packed away for another year.

'Do your coat up and put your gloves on,' she said and she opened the front door of 3 Church Green and ushered him outside. Their Land Rover was parked opposite their Victorian cottage. It was her husband's car and, after his disappearance, it had been held as evidence before being returned to them. How strange it had been to drive it knowing that the police had combed every inch of it for clues. Clues which had led them nowhere for Sean Prior was still missing.

'For over three years,' Polly said, her whisper lost to the wind.

Getting in the car now, she glanced at the glove compartment on the passenger's side, knowing that her husband's sunglasses were still in there. She hadn't had the heart to move them because doing so would seem such a final thing. It would be like admitting he was never going to come home and there was still a tiny little corner of her heart that truly believed that he might just turn up one day.

She hadn't wanted to use his car at first, but her dad, Frank Nightingale, had told her that it was a much better vehicle than the second-hand car she used to drive and she had to admit that it was perfect for days when a wet dog, a wet child and a week's worth of shopping all had to be accommodated.

'Belt done up?' she said now, turning around to check on Archie who nodded, his eyes focussed on his phone.

'Phone away, Archie. You know it's for emergencies only.'

'*Muuuum!*' he complained. 'Tiger's just texted me.'

'You're going to see him in about five minutes,' she pointed out.

Archie put his phone in his bag and puffed out his cheeks in protest.

It was only a short drive from their village of Great Tallington into Castle Clare and it wasn't long before they'd reached the primary school.

'Kiss!' she said, as the two of them got out of the car.

'Aw, Mum!' Archie protested, but he allowed himself to be kissed all the same before legging it into the playground with a wave of his little gloved hand.

Polly blinked away her tears as she got back in the car and drove on into town, parking a short walk from her brother Sam's bookshop. It was always with mixed emotions that she greeted the start of each new school term and it never seemed to get easier. There was the wrench of leaving her safe little home in which she'd cosily snuggled with Archie for the duration of the holidays with the occasional trip to see her parents and grandparents. Christmas was never complete without dinner at Campion House and this year had been extra special with the arrival of Callie Logan on the scene.

Polly smiled as she thought about Sam and how the pain of his past had finally been laid to rest with the arrival of Callie. And it wasn't just Sam who was in love; the whole of the Nightingale family was besotted with the young author especially Grandpa Joe who, at eighty-three, still had an eye for the ladies.

Now, as Polly turned the corner into Church Street, she focussed on the day ahead. As sad as she felt about returning Archie to school, she couldn't help acknowledging that there was something intensely satisfying about getting back to a real routine and the regularity of the school timetable and her duties at the three bookshops run by her family, as well as her part-time job teaching English as a foreign language in a small school in Bury St Edmunds. She'd had to take on more hours since becoming a single parent family, but she loved her job.

Today, she would be working with Sam and, bowing her head against the boisterous wind, she opened the door into the shop and hurried inside, a flurry of leaves chasing her heels.

As much as she loved working with Josh in the bookshop next door, ordering and selling new books, and helping Bryony out in the children's bookshop across the road, there was something rather special about Sam's second-hand bookshop with its endless rows of pre-loved tomes all hoping to find a new lease of life and somebody new to love them. She never tired of browsing the shelves, seeing what little gems fate had delivered into their hands, and trying to team up exactly the right book with the right customer; that was a part of the job she always enjoyed.

'Hey, Polly!' Sam said as he strode into the main room of the shop. 'It's a bit blustery out there, isn't it?'

'It is. I must tidy my hair,' she said, quickly unpinning the clip that held it neatly at the nape of her neck before brushing her hair back into place and clipping it once again.

'Archie okay?'

'You know, I think he was actually looking forward to getting back to school for the first time ever,' Polly said. 'He seems to be in thick with a boy named Tiger.'

'Yes, I've heard him mention that name before,' Sam said. 'That's not the boy's real name, surely?'

Polly shook her head. 'I believe he's called Terence,' she said.

'No wonder he goes by the name of Tiger,' Sam said with a grin. 'Do the teachers call him that too?'

'I have no idea,' Polly said as she took off her coat and walked through to the back room to hang it up in the kitchen before joining Sam again.

'So, how are you getting on with the book club arrangements?' he asked. 'We've had a few more sign-ups.'

Polly looked at the piece of paper on the clipboard which Sam kept by the till, casting her eyes down the list of names. She recognised a few of them like dear Flo Lohman and Winston Kneller. Then there was Antonia Jessop – Castle Clare's bossiest resident.

'I hope she doesn't take over things,' Polly said.

'Who?'

'Antonia Jessop.'

'Oh, she already has,' Sam said. 'She said she hopes we're doing the classics and not this modern rubbish.'

Polly tutted and continued to look down the list of names.

'Honey?' she said incredulously. 'Who on *earth* is Honey?'

'Hortense Digger. You know her?'

'She's in the WI, isn't she? I didn't know she calls herself *Honey* Digger?'

Sam shrugged. 'I guess.'

'What *is* it with people and nicknames?'

'I don't know, Parrot,' he said.

'Very funny,' she said, play-punching him in the ribs at the use of her childhood nickname. 'Anyway,' she said, placing her shoulder bag on the counter and pulling out a notebook, 'I think Antonia raises quite a good point about which books we should read and it's something I've been thinking about too. So I've made a little table of all the different genres we could choose from. What do you think?'

Sam took the notebook from her and read through the list. There were classics, historicals, biographies, science fiction and fantasy, travel, thrillers and crime.

'Ah,' Sam said.

'What?' Polly said, instantly on her guard.

'You've missed a very important one out.'

'Have I?' She looked at the list again and frowned.

'Romance.'

'You want romance on there?'

'Flo Lohman will want it.'

'Okay,' Polly said, taking a pen out of her bag and adding it neatly. 'If you insist.'

'I do,' Sam said. 'Some of the greatest novels ever written are romances. Just think: *Pride and Prejudice* and *Jane Eyre. Wuthering Heights* and *Madame Bovary.*'

'But they all come under classics,' Polly pointed out.

'Well, those ones do, but I'm sure we'll have suggestions for modern romances too like *The Bridges of Madison County* and *The Shell Seekers.*'

'Oh, yes, I do like Rosamunde Pilcher,' Polly said, 'but, generally, I prefer a good biography.'

'But the point of a book club is to get you to read outside your comfort zone, isn't it?'

'As long as it's not *too* much outside of it,' Polly said. 'And that's another thing I've been thinking about. How are we going to decide on the books we read?'

'We should probably take it in turn, don't you think?' Sam said.

'What – unchecked? Just leaving it up to an individual?'

'Why not?' Sam asked. 'Could be interesting.'

'Yes, but just imagine if somebody chooses one of those *Married to the Billionaire Sicilian Playboy*-type of books.'

'There's room for *every* kind of book in the world, Polly.'

'Maybe,' she said, 'but not at every kind of book club.'

Sam looked thoughtful. 'Maybe you're right. Perhaps we could take it in turns to suggest a book, but then make sure the rest of us – the majority of us – are happy with the choice. How would that suit?'

'That could work,' Polly agreed, scribbling all this down in her notebook. 'Now, practicalities. We're holding all the meetings in the back room here, and you've only got your old sofa at the mo. Are you sure you can borrow chairs from the village hall?'

'Yep,' Sam said,' I've checked with the caretaker. We can collect them on the day and return them the next morning.'

'Great,' Polly said, ticking something off in her notebook. 'So, seeing as you're going to all this trouble, I think we should suggest that everyone chips in a pound each time to cover costs.'

Sam's eyebrows rose. 'A pound? I can't do that!'

'Why not?' Polly asked. 'It isn't really fair that you should provide everything for free and you've got to heat the place and stay after opening hours and provide the tea.'

'Yes, but I'd feel really uneasy about taking money from anyone, especially the likes of Winston.'

Polly nodded, obviously seeing where her brother was coming from.

'Why don't we just get everyone to bring something instead?' he said. 'Flo and Antonia have already said they'd be happy to bring in a bit of home-baking.'

Polly's nose wrinkled. 'I can't vouch for the hygiene levels at Flo's cottage. She probably allows the hens and pigs into the kitchen.'

Sam laughed. 'Probably, but I'm sure Winston won't complain.'

'Okay, so venue, chairs, food and drink are all taken care of,' Polly said.

'And the first meeting is next week,' Sam said.

Polly took a deep breath. 'Are we ready?'

'I think so,' he said.

'You seem very relaxed about all this.'

'Do I?' Sam said. 'Well, that's all an illusion. I'm panicking inside.'

Polly smiled. 'I'll be there to help you.'

'I know,' he said, smiling back at her, 'and that's what's carrying me through this.'

He straightened a few books that he had displayed in front of the till.

'Hey, how's Grandma?' Polly asked, putting her notebook and pen away.

'She's good,' Sam said. 'I miss not having Grandpa in the shop with me every day, but I think he's right to spend more time with Grandma.'

Polly nodded. 'I'm still having nightmares about that afternoon she went missing.'

'Me too,' Sam said. 'I've never been so scared in my whole life. But she's got Grandpa and Mum and Dad to keep an eye on her. Lara too at the moment.'

'Lara's not gone back to university yet?'

'Next week,' Sam said.

'Blimey, students have it easy.'

'You were one too, don't forget.'

'I have forgotten,' Polly said. 'Those days seem like another lifetime.'

Sam nodded. 'Come on,' he said, 'I've got two big boxes of books to sort out.'

'Will I need a duster?'

'Absolutely,' he said, 'they arrived in the back of a trailer that also had a couple of sheep in it.'

Castle Clare's church clock had just struck one as Polly left the bookshop. She drove back to Great Tallington after picking up a few groceries from town, and opened her front door to be greeted by an exuberant Dickens who knew his walk time had finally arrived. Changing out of her neat shoes, Polly popped on her wellies and placed a woolly hat on before clipping Dickens's lead on and heading back out into the grey afternoon, breathing in great lungfuls of icy winter air. They crunched down the frozen footpath behind the church and did a circuit of the big field, and, once they were safely away from the roads, Polly unclipped him and watched as he leapt over puddles, his long brown ears flying behind him.

Of course, the very best thing about dog walking on a winter's afternoon was returning to the warmth of one's cottage afterwards and, after rubbing Dickens down with a massive towel, Polly made herself a quick cup of tea, luxuriating in its heat and sipping it whilst tidying the kitchen. She then scooted around the house with the vacuum and put a wash load on and then went upstairs to tidy up.

By the time the house was looking shipshape, it was three fifteen which meant another trip into town to pick Archie up from school. So, putting on her coat and shoes once again, she got in the car and drove the short distance back to Castle Clare. This might have been the first day back after the Christmas holidays, but Polly couldn't help feeling that the old routine hadn't ever really stopped. The familiarity of the hours were both a blessing and a curse, taking her mind off the bigger issues in her life, but numbing her from them too. And she didn't want to be numb; she didn't want to have to pack her feelings away so that she was able to get on with the day-to-day business of being a mother. She was tired of that, but what choice did she have?

When Sean Prior had gone missing on a warm September day three years ago, Polly had stopped being a wife, for what was the role of a wife when her husband had disappeared? It was as if that part of her had been erased along with all trace of Sean.

But she didn't have time to think about that now. She never seemed to have time and, pulling up at the school, she sat in the car and waited for Archie. She didn't have long to wait for the car door was soon pulled open and her son jumped onto the back seat and started his non-stop commentary about his school day all the way home.

It was after they'd parked the car and got out that the near-fatal accident happened. One minute, Archie was stood on the green, waiting for her to lock up and, the next, he was in the middle of the road. It was one of those terrible moments in life that seemed to speed up and slow down at the same time.

'Archie!' Polly shouted as she saw a motorbike turning into their lane. Dropping her bag and running out after her son, she managed to grab him by the arm and pull him to safety on the other side of the road whilst the motorbike swerved dangerously and tore up the green, leaving a deep skid mark in the soft grass before almost crashing into a tree.

'Oh my God, Archie! What did you think you were doing?' Polly cried, holding her son's face in her hands.

'I was going to pick up that crisp bag,' he said, his big eyes wide with innocence.

'What?'

'It was littering our road,' he said, pointing in the direction of the wayward crisp packet.

'Oh, Archie! No crisp packet is worth risking your life for,' she said, 'and what have I told you about crossing roads? You know you're not meant to run out into them without looking!'

It was then that Polly remembered the motorcyclist and looked up to see him wheeling his bike back onto the road. He was tall and was wearing leathers and a helmet which he took off as he approached them.

'Are you guys all right?' he asked.

'We're fine,' Polly said, taking in the handsome face with a wide mouth and messy fair hair that was blowing in the wind now that it was released from its helmet. There was something familiar about him, but Polly couldn't quite put her finger on it. 'I'm so sorry. My son wasn't thinking.'

'Jago?' Archie suddenly said.

'Archie?' the young man said. 'Are you okay? I didn't recognise you in your hat.'

'I'm fine,' he said.

'You two know each other?' Polly said.

'I'm Jago.'

Polly frowned, none the wiser.

'I came round a few weeks ago,' he continued. 'About the guitar lessons. I met Archie out on the green one morning when he was walking your dog. A spaniel, right?'

'Dickens,' Archie said. 'Dickens likes Jago, Mum.'

'Does he?' Polly said with suspicion.

'I was just leaving my house and Archie clocked the guitar I was carrying, didn't you?'

'He straps it on his back when he takes it out on his bike,' Archie said, obviously impressed.

'Right,' Polly said, less impressed than her son. 'But we don't want guitar lessons.'

'I know,' Jago said. 'You told me.'

'*I* do, Mum!' Archie piped. 'I want them!'

'Archie, we've been through this. You're already learning the piano and you're struggling with that.'

'But that's because it's boring!'

'Oh, and you wouldn't get bored with guitar lessons?'

He shook his head. 'I'd *love* guitar lessons!'

'Well, we're not going to talk about it now, okay?' Polly told him. 'Listen, are you sure you're all right?' she asked, turning back to Jago.

'No bones broken,' he said.

'And your bike?'

'Needs a good wash after all that mud, but it's fine. Don't worry about it.'

'I'm so sorry to have given you such a fright. Tell Jago you're sorry, Archie. You might have caused a serious accident.'

'I'm sorry,' Archie said, his cherubic face looking serious for a moment.

'That's all right, little man,' Jago said. 'No real harm done.'

Polly watched as he turned around with a wave of his hand and crossed the green to rescue his bike.

'Archie Prior!' Polly said, as soon as Jago was out of earshot, 'what are you doing to my nerves?'

Archie looked up at her with a face so full of innocence that she couldn't be angry with him for long.

'Can we have tea now?' he asked.

A laugh exploded from her at her son's effortless return to normality.

'Yes, let's have tea,' she said. 'As soon as you've practised that new piano piece.'

'Aw, Mum! Can't I learn to play the guitar instead *pleeeease*?'

'No you can't. Your father wanted you to learn the piano and that's what you're going to do, isn't it?'

Archie stomped angrily into the house and Polly followed him, silently cursing the guitar-wielding biker for putting such notions into her young son's head.

CHAPTER 2

Callie Logan had been staring out of the window of her study at Owl Cottage for some time now, taking in the pretty view across the green at Newton St Clare. Even in the middle of winter, it was a view she loved and she really couldn't imagine any other now, but it could be an awful distraction from her writing and she was meant to be making headway with the second book in her new series.

Callie's soon-to-be ex-husband and current editor, Piers Blackmore, had already sent her a few pertinent emails reminding her about the importance of keeping the ball rolling when you were onto a good thing and Callie couldn't help feeling anxious. She'd only just signed the contract for her first book last month and, although she'd received a handsome advance, she felt deeply uneasy about the prospect of working with her ex.

She'd known that Piers wouldn't make life easy for her if she agreed to sign a new book deal with him and, so far, she'd been proved right. Of course, she had chosen to accept his very generous advance and knew full well that there'd been strings attached. She couldn't have everything her own way, she knew that, but she couldn't help thinking that there was more to all this than just business, and it was hard to shake the image of his face when he'd visited Owl Cottage back in November and told her that he'd made a big mistake in letting her go and that he wanted them to get back together again. It was as if he'd conveniently forgotten that they were getting divorced and that Callie had made a new life for herself in Suffolk.

Her real fear was that he'd try that again. Her agent knew how she felt, but she'd casually brushed aside Callie's feelings.

'Piers is a professional,' Margot had told her. 'You won't be working directly with him anyway.'

Well, Callie hadn't believed that for a moment and, sure enough, Piers had made sure that he was her editor even though she'd been told she'd be working with somebody else.

She stood up from her desk and went downstairs to make herself a cup of tea, switching on the lamps in the living room, but leaving the curtains open for a little longer as the last few streaks of light faded from the winter sky.

She was quite determined that she wasn't going to let Piers spoil things for her. Since she'd made the decision to leave both him and London and start a new life for herself in Suffolk, she had felt a tonne of weight slipping from her shoulders, and then the most unexpected thing had happened: she'd fallen in love with Sam Nightingale. Her first Christmas in Suffolk had been spent with his family at their beautiful Georgian house deep in the countryside and how warmly she had been welcomed. If Sam's mother, Eleanor, had been surprised that Callie hadn't been spending Christmas with her own parents, she hadn't shown it. Perhaps Sam had tactfully filled her in on that subject, Callie thought as she poured newly boiled water into a mug. Her parents, who lived in Oxfordshire, still hadn't made the trip to Suffolk to see their only daughter's new home and Callie couldn't help feeling hurt by that.

Still, she thought, it was insane to dwell on things she couldn't change and she knew that her parents weren't going to change their ways now and suddenly start showing an interest in her and what she was doing with her life, and that was fine because she knew that she was leading a good and happy one.

Lighting the wood burner, Callie lost herself in reading some of the pages she'd printed out of her new novel, attacking dreadful sentences with a purple pen and making notes in the margins for additions to be made later. It was as she was coming to the end that she heard Sam's Volvo pulling up outside Owl Cottage.

'Hey,' he said a minute later when she opened the door to him. He bent his head down and kissed her and Callie couldn't quite believe that this handsome sensitive man was really in her life now. 'How are you?'

'I'm good,' she said, caressing his face. 'Come on in. It's nice and toasty by the wood burner.'

He followed her into the living room.

'Here,' he said, producing a book from out of one of the brown paper bags with the Nightingale logo on it, *For books which make your heart sing*. 'I brought you this.'

'Sam, you can't keep giving me all your stock. You'll have nothing left to sell!'

'It's just one book,' he said with a grin.

'Yes, but you've been giving me "just one book" each day for the last week!'

'I can't help it,' Sam said. 'I couldn't *not* give you this.'

Callie couldn't help but smile. She loved being spoilt especially when the spoiling came in book form, so she took the little book and looked at it.

'Conversations with my Agent,' she read.

'By Rob Long,' Sam said. He's a writer and producer in the US. It's a very funny book. I think you'll like it after what I've heard about your own agent. I think it's a universal thing that agents never listen to their clients.'

'Good to know,' Callie said with a laugh. 'I was beginning to think I might have just got unlucky.'

Sam took a step towards her and put his hands on her shoulders. 'You're not looking forward to going into London, are you?'

'I just don't see why I have to,' she said with a sigh. 'I've told Margot that everything can be done over the phone and by email these days, but she insists that I attend this silly meeting.'

'Well, it is often better to talk business face-to-face,' Sam said.

'Traitor!' she said. 'I thought you were meant to be on my side.'

'I am,' he said. 'Just tell Margot – and Piers – that this is your one exception and that you expect to be left alone to write your book in peace after.'

Callie nodded. 'I'll tell them.'

'And I can come with you if you want some moral support.'

'Really? I thought you hated London.'

'With a passion,' he said, 'but I'd come with you if you needed me to.'

'It's okay,' she said, thinking once again about how lucky she was to have found a man like Sam. 'I'll cope.'

'I know you will.' He bent to kiss her again. 'Now, what shall we have for tea?'

'I have absolutely no idea,' she said.

'I'll bring you a few cook books tomorrow,' he told her with a grin.

Polly had just tidied up the tea things when there was a knock on the door. She frowned. It was unusual for anybody to call in the evenings and she certainly wasn't expecting anyone.

'Who is it?' she called as she walked down the hallway, checking that her hair was still neatly clipped back.

'Jago Solomon,' the voice came back and she opened the door. 'I've come to see how the little lad's getting on.'

'Oh,' Polly said in surprise, 'come in.'

He bent his head under the low door frame and walked in. 'It's Polly, isn't it?' he said, holding out a large hand.

'Yes,' Polly said, shaking it.

'I can't seem to get yesterday out of my mind.'

'I hope you've not been worrying about it,' Polly said. 'I think Archie's all but forgotten about it now. You know what children are like.'

'And how are you?'

'I'm fine. It shook me up, but it's certainly made me more vigilant now. You know he was chasing a crisp packet?'

'A what?'

'A crisp packet. He's absolutely obsessed with litter!' Polly explained. 'He won a competition at school to design an anti-litter poster and it was hung in the library in Castle Clare for a month. Well, he thought that would solve the world's litter problem!'

'So, he's a young eco warrior?'

'You could say that,' Polly said.

'Can I see him?'

'He's watching TV in the living room,' she said.

'All right if I go through?' He motioned towards the door.

'Okay,' Polly said, 'but mind the–'

'Ouch!'

'–beam.'

Jago rubbed his forehead. It really wasn't a good idea to be over six feet tall in Suffolk what with all the low ceilings and beams to negotiate, Polly couldn't help thinking.

They walked into the living room together where Archie was sitting on the sofa. Dickens, who'd been curled up at his feet, was up now and eager to greet their visitor.

'Jago!' Archie said, abandoning the garish cartoon on the TV as he realised who it was. 'Did you bring your guitar?'

'Not tonight, Arch,' he said, bending to give Dickens a friendly pat. 'Maybe another time?' He turned to look at Polly who was taken aback by the unexpected offer.

'Erm, maybe,' she said.

'Oh, go on, Mum. I want to hear him play. He can play *Vixen Vibe* on it.'

Polly rolled her eyes. *Vixen Vibe* was the latest chart-topping hit that was difficult to escape if you had a child. It had been in the soundtrack of a smash hit film and was being played everywhere.

'I'm not sure I want to hear that,' she said, giving a tiny smile.

'Don't worry,' Jago said, 'it's not my only tune.'

'I want to hear them *all*,' Archie said.

Jago looked at Polly. 'Are you sure I can't persuade you?' he said, his wide mouth stretching into a grin.

'Archie – let me have a word with Jago about all this, okay?' she told her son before leading Jago into the kitchen.

'I was just going to make a cup of tea,' she said. 'Would you like one?'

'Thanks.'

She filled the kettle and cleared her throat, unsure of how to speak to the young man who seemed to be so chummy with both her son and her dog.

'You're Maureen Solomon's son, aren't you?' she said.

'The one and only.'

'I've not seen you around before,' she said.

'No,' he said. 'I've just got back from America.'

'Oh,' she said, turning to face him.

'Spent a year out there after university. Got an uncle who runs a bar in a town near Seattle. I worked there, provided a bit of evening entertainment and travelled around a bit.'

'Sounds like fun.'

'It was,' he said. 'The Pacific Northwest is beautiful. I went up to Alaska for a bit too. Awesome landscape.'

'But you came home to Suffolk?'

He nodded. 'It's funny, isn't it? I really thought I might make a go of it in the States, but – well, you know.'

She wondered what he meant by that. Had something in particular brought him home? He really was very handsome, she couldn't help thinking, with his dark blond tousled hair and his ever-present smile. He had nice eyes too. Slate-grey, she noticed. He was wearing a big bulky coat and black jeans and biker boots.

She blinked. She was paying *far* too much attention to him.

'Milk?' she asked, turning back to the tea things.

'Black. No sugar,' he said.

'Have a seat,' she said, presenting him with his tea a minute later and joining him at the kitchen table.

'So,' he said without preamble, 'what have you got against the guitar?'

Polly was surprised by the forthright question. 'I don't have anything against the guitar,' she said. 'But it isn't right for Archie.'

'Why not? He's showing a real interest in it and that should always be encouraged, I think.'

'Look,' Polly said, deciding it was best to take control of the situation once and for all, 'it's really admirable that you're so passionate about music.'

'I am passionate,' he said, a light dancing in his slate-grey eyes.

'And I admire that,' she said, 'but Archie is learning the piano and I really think that's enough to be getting on with. He's only six–'

'When I was six, I was playing the piano, the guitar and the drums.'

'Oh, please don't mention drums to him!' she said.

Jago laughed. He had a nice laugh. It was big and warm. An honest, wholesome laugh, Polly thought.

'I won't mention drums,' he said.

'Thank you.'

'On one condition.'

'What?'

'That you let me bring my guitar over,' he said.

'Look – I really don't think–'

'Just to let him see it and hear it and have a go,' Jago said. 'That's all I'm asking.'

Polly frowned. 'Why is this so important to you?' she asked.

He shrugged. 'I don't know,' he said. 'I guess I saw something of me in Archie that morning on the green. He's got a spark about him, you know?'

'Oh, I know,' Polly said with a smile.

'Then you should help that spark take light. You shouldn't be trying to extinguish it.'

Polly's mouth dropped open. 'I really don't appreciate being told how to raise my son.'

'I'm sorry,' he said quickly. 'I didn't mean to offend you. I wasn't suggesting–'

'I might be a single parent,' she interrupted, 'but Archie is the centre of my world. There's nothing I wouldn't do for him.'

'I'm sure there isn't,' Jago said, his face flushed red in embarrassment.

'And for you – a young *stranger* – to come waltzing in here and criticise the way I do things–'

'I wasn't criticising,' he said. 'Honestly I wasn't.' He reached out across the table and picked up her hand. Polly gasped at the sudden, intimate touch. 'I'm sorry. I'm making a mess of this, aren't I?'

Polly could feel that her heart was racing. She wanted to tell him to go, but the words wouldn't quite come out.

'Why don't I let you think about it for a bit?' he asked. 'Okay?' He let go of her hand, took a huge gulp of his tea and then scraped his chair back and stood up. It was then that something caught his eye.

'What's this?'

Polly followed his gaze. It was her notebook about the book club which she'd left open on the dresser table. Beside it were several felt tip pens.

'We're starting a book club in Castle Clare. I'm just putting a few ideas together.'

'With felt tip pens?' he said, raising an eyebrow.

'I'm marking all the different genres we're hoping to read.'

'Isn't that a bit OCD?'

'I am *not* an obsessive compulsive,' she said, feeling rattled once again. 'I'm just very organised and Archie happened to have some felt tips.'

He caught her eye.

'Can I join?' he asked.

'The book club?'

'Yeah,' he said with a grin.

'You want to join our book club?'

'Sure. Why not?'

'Because it will probably be full of old people who have nothing better to do with their evenings and you're–'

'What?'

'Young,' she said.

'But not too young?' he asked.

She took a deep breath. She really didn't know what to make of this young man. First he'd questioned her parenting abilities and then he'd said she suffered from Obsessive Compulsive Disorder, and now he was making fun of her little book club.

'I'd like to join,' he said. 'I studied music at uni, but I used to read all the time only I never got to talk about books much. When is it?'

'The meeting? It's at seven thirty on Wednesday at Nightingale's. You know the second-hand bookshop?'

'I know it,' he said.

'You *really* want to join?' Polly said.

'I really do,' he said and something in his smile made her believe him.

'Well, okay,' she said. 'I guess I'll see you there.' They walked out into the hallway and Polly opened the door for him.

'Promise to think about those guitar lessons,' he said.

Polly nodded.

'We can talk about it again at the book club.' He gave her another smile. 'Say bye to Archie for me.'

Polly watched as he walked across the road and over the green to his mother's house.

'Has he gone?' Archie said, suddenly appearing in the hallway.

'He told me to say bye to you.'

'When's he coming back?'

Polly looked down at her son's face which was full of expectancy.

'Don't worry,' she told him. 'I don't think you'll have too long to wait.'

CHAPTER 3

Jago Solomon walked across the green in the dark, taking care not to stumble into the deep skid mark made by his bike the day before. What a way to introduce himself to Polly Prior, he thought. Of course, he'd met her briefly when he'd called round to see Archie with his guitar, but had been told in no uncertain terms that he wasn't wanted there. Jago remembered the woman whom he'd spoken to briefly, recalling how pale she'd looked. Her brother had told him that Polly hadn't been feeling well and he'd regretted his bad timing. But she'd reacted the same way tonight.

Still, he wasn't ready to give up yet. He sincerely believed that he'd made a connection with Archie that morning on the green and there'd been more than a little of himself in the young boy. Jago wanted to reach out to him and encourage that dream. It was just a pity that Archie's mother was so protective of him although who could blame her after what she'd been through? His own mother had told him a little of what had happened to her.

'Sean Prior was his name,' Maureen Solomon told her son. 'One day he was here and the next he was gone. Vanished! Like he was never really here at all. They found his car in a country lane, but there was no sign of him. No note, no explanation. Just gone.'

Poor Polly, Jago thought, as he let himself into 7 Church Green opposite the Priors' own home. Like the Priors', it was a small terraced cottage with a living room and kitchen downstairs and two bedrooms and a bathroom upstairs. Jago's father had left when Jago was fourteen. Divorce had happened soon afterwards and the family house had been sold and 7 Church Green bought. It had stretched Maureen Solomon to the limit to get a mortgage on the little house and she'd taken a second job for many years just so they could get by. Jago would never forget those anxiety-filled days, but they'd been so relieved not to live under the shadow of Murray Solomon anymore. With his foul mouth and his high-speed fists when he'd been drinking, it was a wonder that Jago and his mum weren't more battle-scarred than they were.

'That you, Jago?' a voice came as he opened the front door.

'Yes. Just me.'

Maureen Solomon was in her early-fifties and worked as a receptionist at the doctors' surgery in Castle Clare. She had wavy fair hair which hung down to her shoulders and a pretty face with the same large slate-grey eyes and wide mouth her son had inherited, but was a diminutive five foot one in stature. Jago had definitely inherited his height from his father. Luckily, that was all he'd inherited from him.

'You been bothering that nice Mrs Prior again?' she asked him as he walked in to the living room and sat down on the sofa, stretching his long legs before him. His mother sat down in a chair opposite.

'I wasn't bothering her,' he said. 'I was just making sure she was okay.'

His mother didn't look convinced. 'You could have done that on the phone.'

He frowned. 'That wouldn't be right. Not after nearly ploughing her and her son over.'

Maureen shook her head. 'You should be more careful on that bike of yours. You've got me worried all the time!'

'It wasn't completely my fault,' he said, running his hand through his hair.

'And get your hair cut.'

'Mum!' he said with a groan. 'I should have stayed in America.'

'Don't say that!' his mum said. 'I *love* having you here. You know I do.'

'But you've done nothing but moan about everything I've done since I got back.'

'That's just my little way of showing you I care,' she said, giving him a little smile. 'I missed you so much when you were away.'

'I missed you too, Mum.'

She shook her head. 'You didn't have time to miss me.'

'Well, I kept myself busy, I have to admit.'

'You worked too hard. I got a call from your uncle and he said you were the hardest grafter he'd ever seen.'

'He's exaggerating,' Jago said.

She shook her head. 'You know my brother. He wouldn't say something just for the sake of talking.'

'He gave me a really great opportunity,' Jago said. 'I managed to travel and save up a bit too. That's why you've got to let me help out,

Mum.'

'I told you. I'm not taking your money.'

'I'm not expecting to live here rent free, Mum.'

'You're my baby boy,' she said. 'I'm not charging you rent.'

'Well, you're not going to get a choice in the matter,' he said, 'because I'm paying you.'

'But you should be using that money to launch that band of yours.'

'That's sweet of you, Mum, but I don't think that's realistic, do you?'

'*Realistic?* What's that got to do with following your dreams? You haven't given up on them, have you?'

'No, of course not,' he said. 'The band's great fun, but I just feel that I should be building something more solid.'

'What, like those jingles you keep selling?'

'There's nothing wrong with jingles. They pay good money.'

'Maybe, but that's not what you really want to do, is it?'

'What if it is?' he said, knowing that he was upsetting his mum and hating himself for doing so but, at the same time, realising that the odds of him making it as a real musician were very slim.

His mother shook her head. 'I don't believe you,' she said. 'You're a musician, Jago. You should be composing and performing, not stuck at that horrible computerised keyboard bashing out trite little jingles for second-rate television channels.'

He sighed. 'Look, I've got to earn some money. Some proper money. I know the sacrifices you made so that I could have music lessons and go to university.'

'I didn't do it so you could pay me back,' she said.

'I know that, but I want to and the fastest way to do that is to take on more tuition and write more jingles.'

Maureen didn't look happy. 'But you won't give up composing, will you?'

'I won't give up composing.'

'Promise?'

'I promise.'

She smiled. 'What did I do to deserve a son like you?'

'Just being a mum like you,' he said.

A light frost was already settling on the town of Castle Clare on the night of the first meeting of the book club. It had come round far too quickly for Sam's liking, Polly knew, but she was there to make sure he had everything in place.

'You ready?' she asked him as he counted the chairs for the umpteenth time.

'As ready as I'll ever be,' he said.

'Okay, let's open the door,' she said. The two of them walked through to the front of the shop and saw that somebody had already arrived but, when they saw who it was, they weren't totally surprised.

Sam opened the door.

'Come on, come on,' Antonia Jessop said, bustling into the shop with a large wicker basket and an umbrella on her arm before anybody could give her a proper greeting. 'Fancy keeping people freezing on the doorstep!'

'You're *very* early,' Polly said, deciding not to mince her words.

'I am perfectly punctual,' Antonia replied. 'I fully intended to arrive early to make sure that everything was under control.'

'That really isn't necessary,' Sam told her. 'Everything's in place.'

'Well, we'll see about that, won't we?' she said, her tall wiry frame moving through the shop at alarming speed.

'I told you she was going to take over,' Polly whispered to Sam.

'Let her have her moment,' Sam said.

'I would if I could be assured it was just going to be *one* moment but she's like a bossy headmistress and, if you give her so much as a nod, she'll have us all strutting about and bowing down to her orders in no time.'

'That's not going to happen,' Sam said calmly.

'Yeah? Well, I guess we'll see, won't we?'

Polly and Sam walked through to the back room. Antonia was standing in the middle and Polly couldn't help noticing that she'd placed her basket on the chair that was clearly meant for Sam as it was out on its own facing the others.

'I told you!' Polly said.

Sam shushed her with a flap of his hand. 'Miss Jessop?' he began uneasily. 'Is there a problem?'

Antonia, who was in her mid-seventies with steel-grey hair pulled tightly into a rather severe-looking bun, simply shook her head.

'All these chairs need rearranging,' she said.

'There's nothing wrong with the chairs,' Polly said.

22

'They're all facing the wrong way,' the old woman went on.

'What do you mean, Miss Jessop?'

'They should be facing into the room not towards the door.'

Sam puzzled this over for a moment.

'Don't give into her,' Polly whispered.

'That's so we can see any latecomers arriving,' Sam said at last.

'*Late*comers?' Antonia Jessop cried. 'Latecomers should *not* be admitted at all!'

'Don't you think that's a little severe?' Sam said. 'I mean we're not the Old Vic here, are we?'

Antonia seemed to bristle at this statement. 'Well, perhaps they could come in during the tea break.'

'The door will remain open during meetings,' Sam said. Polly was glad to see that her brother was taking a stand against the old tartar.

Antonia Jessop's thin mouth was a straight line of disapproval across her pale face.

It was then that the shop bell tinkled.

'I'll see who that is!' Polly said, eager to get out of the bossy woman's presence if only for a brief moment.

'Jago!' she said as she walked into the front room. 'You came.'

'You didn't think I would?' he said, eyebrows rising. He was holding his bike helmet under his arm and ran a hand through his messed-up hair.

'No, I didn't.'

'I'm a man of my word,' he told her.

'So I see.'

'How's Archie?'

'He's good. He's at a neighbour's. They have a cockatoo so he loves going round there.'

Jago grinned. 'I'd have loved pets growing up.'

'You didn't have any?'

'Nah. My dad–' he paused, 'wasn't into them.'

'That's a shame,' Polly said. 'We grew up with a house full of dogs. The occasional cat too, and Lara's rabbits which somehow always got into the bedrooms.'

'Sounds great fun!'

'It was,' Polly said, 'except when Tabitha the French dwarf lop ate my favourite hat.'

He grinned. 'So, have we got a good crowd?' he asked.

'Not yet. Just Antonia Jessop.'

'I don't know her.'

'Best you keep it that way too,' Polly told him.

'Oh, do I sense some group tension already?' he asked.

'You could say that,' Polly said, keeping her voice low. 'She's a crabby old bossy boots.'

'Exactly the sort of person I love to spend an evening with,' he said.

'But she has brought some home-baking.'

'Ah, well, that restores her reputation then, doesn't it?'

'Oh, look – it's Flo,' Polly said, watching as a woman in her sixties with shoulder-length white curls crossed the street and entered the shop.

'Hello, my dear,' she said as she saw Polly.

'Flo, this is Jago. Jago – Flo.'

'Very pleased to meet you, Flo,' Jago said. 'How are you?'

'All the better for meeting you, young man!' she said with a smile, 'although my left shin is howling a bit today. Peony the pig backed me into a corner at teatime.'

'Oh, dear! Are you okay?' Polly asked.

'Just a bit bruised, that's all. She means well, that pig, but she doesn't realise how strong she is,' Flo said, rubbing the bruised shin. 'I've brought some goodies.' She held up an old carrier bag which was more hole than bag. 'Some apple slices. Had a huge glut of apples this year. More than I can eat on my own.'

'I'm sure they'll be very welcome,' Polly said, leading Flo and Jago through to the back room where Sam and Antonia were preparing a tray of Antonia's orange and lemon cookies.

'Don't break them,' Antonia barked at Sam. 'They're very delicate.'

'Can I introduce you to Jago and Flo, Antonia?' Polly said.

Antonia looked up, her eyes widening at the wild biker hair of Jago and the even wilder curls of Flo Lohman.

'Hello, my dear,' Flo said, coming forward to shake Antonia's hand. 'I see you've been at the baking too. 'I've brought some of my apple slices.'

Polly watched as Flo delved into the holey carrier bag and brought out a battered tin and began to place her apple slices on top of Antonia's delicate biscuits.

'*Careful* with my biscuits!' Antonia shrieked.

'I'll get another plate,' Sam said, disappearing into the kitchen and coming back with one. 'Flo, how about we put your slices on here? They look absolutely delicious.'

Flo nodded. 'Good idea,' she said, picking up two of the slices which oozed gooey filling onto the orange and lemon biscuits below.

'Well, really,' Antonia complained.

'Extra flavour,' Flo said with a cheeky little smile.

Antonia Jessop pursed her lips in consternation.

The shop bell sounded again and, a moment later, Callie Logan walked into the room.

'Hey!' Sam said, walking towards her and kissing her cheek.

'I hope I'm not too late,' Callie said.

'Nope,' Sam said, 'perfect timing. We're just dishing out some sweet treats.'

'Oh, how lovely,' Callie said.

'Help yourself,' Flo said.

'These look wonderful,' Callie said, taking an apple slice. 'Thank you.'

Flo beamed with pride. Antonia tutted and turned away in disgust.

'Is Winston coming?' Callie asked. It was at that very moment that the bell on the door rang and the old man shuffled through to the back room with his old chocolate Labrador, Delilah, in tow.

'Evenin',' he said, tipping his felt hat.

'Good to see you, Winston,' Sam said. 'Do you know everyone?'

'Oh, aye,' he said, looking around the room. 'Apart from this young 'un.'

'Jago,' Jago said, coming forward and the two men shook hands.

'And who's this beauty?' Jago said.

'Oh, that's Flo Lohman,' Winston said with a wink at Flo.

Everybody laughed. Except Antonia Jessop who tutted again.

'Oh, you mean the dog?' Winston said. 'That's Delilah. Had her since she was a mere slip of a thing. Goes everywhere with me does Delilah.'

'But I'm not sure a book club is the right place for a dog,' Antonia pointed out.

'Why not?' Winston asked.

'Well, she's erm–'

'What? *What* is she?' Winston asked.

'She's erm – a bit *old*, isn't she?'

'She'd be about the same age as you in dog years, I reckon,' Winston said, winking at Polly who had caught his eye, 'and *you're* not too old to be here, are you?'

Suitably chastised, Antonia pulled a chair out and sat down. 'I think we should begin, don't you?' she said, addressing the question to Sam.

Sam looked at his watch. 'We're just waiting for one more,' he said. 'Honey Digger.'

Antonia frowned. 'Don't you mean *Hortense* Digger?'

'I believe she goes by the name Honey,' Sam said.

'Well, it doesn't surprise me that *she's* late,' Antonia said.

'Shall I go and see if there's any sign of her?' Polly asked and Sam nodded.

Polly walked through to the front of the shop and looked out of the window. A woman was walking up the street, but could this be the mysterious Hortense 'Honey' Digger whom Polly had yet to meet? Polly watched her, taking in the fluffy white-blonde hair that looked so bright under the street lighting, and the long frilly skirt that flounced as she moved.

Sure enough, she entered the shop.

'The book club *is* here, isn't it?' she asked, her glossy pink mouth smiling at Polly.

'Honey?'

'Yes!'

'Very pleased to meet you,' Polly said, noticing the thick make-up and the lilac eye-shadow Honey was wearing. She really didn't need either for, despite being in her mid-sixties, Polly guessed, Honey was still a very beautiful woman.

'Am I the only one?'

'Oh, no,' Polly said. 'We're all in the back. Come on through.'

'I'm afraid I'm horribly late,' Honey said.

'Not at all,' Polly assured her. 'We were only just about to begin.'

Polly led the way into the back room. 'Can I introduce Honey to everyone?'

Honey followed her in and beamed a soft smile around the room.

'Charmed!' Winston said, instantly on his feet, tipping his hat with one hand and shaking Honey's with his other.

'Good to meet you,' Callie said. 'I'm Callie.'

'Flo!' Honey cried. 'If I'd known you were coming, I would have brought back my egg boxes.'

'Just drop them off when you're next passing,' Flo said.

'And you know Sam, of course?' Polly said.

'Hello, Honey,' Sam said.

'And you know Antonia, I believe?' Polly asked.

'Yes. *We've* met,' Antonia declared.

'Yes,' Honey said, her smile fading a little. 'Antonia and I are old friends.'

It was then that Honey saw the biscuits and apple slices.

'Was I meant to bring something?' she asked, her face falling in dismay.

'It isn't compulsory,' Sam said. 'But you're very welcome to.'

'Then I will next time for sure.'

Winston beamed his approval. He'd already eaten one apple slice and two biscuits.

'Please help yourself,' Polly said.

Honey approached one of the plates. 'Ah!' she exclaimed. 'Antonia's orange and lemon biscuits. Now, they're an *old* favourite, aren't they?'

'At least I brought *some*thing with me,' Antonia said.

Winston guffawed from the sofa whilst Sam cleared his throat.

'What's going on with those two?' Jago whispered to Polly.

'They're a couple of Titans from Castle Clare's WI,' Polly whispered back. 'Life-long rivals, I hear.'

Jago smiled. 'Should be interesting.'

'Fasten your seatbelt,' Polly said with a grin.

CHAPTER 4

'Right, we'd better make a start,' Sam said. 'Everybody take a seat.'

It was then that Polly noticed that, whilst she'd been watching for Honey's arrival, the chairs had been rearranged, obviously after the instruction of Antonia Jessop. But she had to admit that the little circle they now made looked friendly and inviting.

Winston was the only one on the sofa and Delilah lay on the floor by his feet. Everybody else had chosen one of the rigid wooden chairs borrowed from the village hall and Polly had somehow ended up in between Antonia Jessop and Jago Solomon. She looked at the little assembly and hoped that it was the start of something rather wonderful both for Sam's bookshop and for Castle Clare. It was exciting to be at the very beginning of a new venture, she thought, and she sincerely hoped that it would be a successful one.

As people shuffled in their seats to get as comfortable as was possible on the old chairs, Honey Digger unbuttoned her coat to reveal a candyfloss-pink cardigan over a white lacy blouse and a flaring skirt which Polly had only got a brief glimpse of under the street lighting. Now, it was revealed in all its splendour. With its bright green background littered with flowers in every colour, it was like a little glimpse of summer in the middle of the Suffolk winter.

'What a pretty skirt,' Polly couldn't help saying, suddenly feeling very drab in her utilitarian black one.

'Oh, thank you!' Honey said with a smile.

Antonia glanced at the skirt in disdain before stroking her hands down her own hairy Tweed one.

'Right,' Sam said, 'welcome, everyone, and thanks for coming out on a particularly gloomy winter night. It's lovely to see so many of us for this first meeting. Now, I want to keep things fairly informal because tonight is really all about what we want from the book club. Polly and I have a few ideas, but we're open to suggestions and would love to hear everyone's thoughts.'

Polly bit her tongue. Everybody's thoughts *except* Antonia Jessop's that was.

'Then we can all talk about books: what we like, what we don't like – that sort of thing. How does that sound?' Sam continued.

Everyone nodded.

'Good. I don't want to scare anybody off at this stage, but I do think we should lay a few ground rules about the book club just so we all know what we're doing. Everyone happy with that?'

'First rule of book club,' Jago said. 'You must *not* talk about book club.'

There were a few titters around the room and Polly caught Jago's eye and he grinned at her.

'*What's* he talking about?' Antonia Jessop cried. 'Of *course* we've got to talk about book club. How else are we going to spread the word?'

'He's referencing a film,' Polly explained. 'It's a line from a film.'

'Well, it's not a film that *I'm* aware of,' Antonia said.

'That doesn't surprise me,' Jago said under his breath. Polly shot him a warning glance.

Sam cleared his throat. 'So, first things first. Are we all happy to meet every other month? Any thoughts on that?'

'We thought monthly meetings would be too much,' Polly joined in.

'I'm a very slow reader,' Flo said. 'I know I couldn't manage a book a month. Not unless they were those nice slim Mills and Boon novels.'

Antonia tutted. 'We won't be reading *that* kind of novel!'

'There's nothing wrong with those kind of novels,' Honey said. 'They've given me much pleasure over the years. You should try some, Antonia. A bit of romance in *your* life certainly wouldn't go amiss.'

Antonia's thin lips got even thinner at this comment whilst Winston chuckled from the sofa.

'So, are we all agreed on every other month for a meeting? January, March, May etc?'

'Sounds good to me,' Winston said. 'Although I'll miss these nibbles in the other months.' He leaned forward from the sofa and took another of Flo's apple slices.

'There are some of my orange and lemon biscuits here,' Antonia said. 'Not many of you are eating them.'

Flo allowed herself a little smile.

'How are we going to choose the books?' Honey asked.

'That was my next point,' Sam said. 'I think it would be a great way to get to know each other, and to keep things fair, if everyone had a choice. Of course, to make sure we're all happy, we'd all need to be in agreement with the choice of book.'

'Yes,' Antonia said, 'because if it was down to the individual, we'd end up reading some dreadful Barbara Cartland novel.'

'There's nothing wrong with a bit of Barbara Cartland,' Flo Lohman said, realising that the barbed comment was aimed at her.

'That's right,' Sam said diplomatically. 'There's room for every book in the world.'

'Well, I prefer the classics,' Antonia said. '*Hard Times, Jude the Obscure—*'

'Oh, how dreary,' Flo said. 'Isn't a classic just a book in which everyone dies and *nobody* has a happy ending?'

'I can think of lots that have happy endings,' Sam said.

'Well, can we please make sure that *our* books have happy endings, Sam, dear?'

'I think some of them will and some of them won't,' he said. 'I think it might be good for all of us to read outside our comfort zone.'

'And that's why I've prepared a list of genres we should look at,' Polly said, taking the list out of her handbag together with a notebook.

Jago took a look. 'Ah, the felt pen chart,' he said.

Polly glanced up at him. He was smiling; she wasn't.

'What's johnres?' Winston asked.

'*Genres*. It's the categories books are placed in,' Sam explained. 'Polly?'

'I've made a list to include non-fiction genres like biography and history, and the fiction genres include crime, thrillers, classics—'

'Romance?' Flo asked.

'Yes, romance,' Polly confirmed, remembering that her brother had told her that Flo would be on the lookout for it.

'What about children's fiction?' Callie asked.

'Children's? Are we to read *children's* books?' Antonia said.

'I don't see why not,' Sam said. 'They're a very important part of literature and many of the great classics are children's books. Just think of *The Secret Garden, Little Women* and *Swallows and Amazons*, and the modern classics like *Goodnight, Mister Tom* and *War Horse*. That's a very good suggestion, Callie.'

Callie smiled. 'I know I may be biased,' she said, 'but I really think some of the best stories are those written for children.'

'Including your own of course,' Sam said with a proud little smile.

'Well,' Callie said, blushing furiously, 'I couldn't possibly say!'

'You're a writer?' Honey asked. 'How exciting. I must have a chat with you. I've written a little story for my grandchildren and they simply love it! Perhaps you can help me get it published.'

'Oh, no!' Antonia said with a groan. 'Not that *thing* about the haunted Wendy House that you read out on the WI picnic?'

'And what's wrong with it?' Honey asked.

'Ladies, ladies,' Sam said. 'Let's get back to book club business, shall we?'

Winston chuckled again from the sofa. 'I'm loving this,' he said with a little shake of his head. 'It's better than anything on the telly.'

'So, meetings every other month during which we take it in turns to choose a book agreed upon by the group as a whole. Okay?' Sam said.

Everyone nodded.

'Who chooses first?' Antonia asked.

'I think it only fair that Sam has the first choice,' Polly said, 'seeing as he's organised everything.'

'Quite right,' Winston said.

'Choose a nice romance,' Flo said. 'I do like a nice romance.'

'We know,' Antonia said.

Sam pushed his glasses up his nose and cleared his throat. 'Well, I have had a few thoughts and I've come up with both a classic *and* a romance. A novel that has proved its worth over several readings of mine over the years and one which TV and film directors turn to again and again.'

'Oh, no,' Antonia said, 'not that Mr Darcy book!'

'No, not *Pride and Prejudice*,' Sam said, 'although that would make a very good choice at some point.'

'I don't like Jane Austen,' Antonia said, to shocked gasps from Flo and Honey. 'She's too sickly saccharine for *my* taste.'

Polly resisted saying something, knowing that she could never have any sort of a happy relationship with somebody who denounced Jane Austen in such a way.

'Which book were you thinking of, Sam?' Flo asked.

'Thomas Hardy's *Far From the Madding Crowd*.'

'Oooh!' Flo said. 'That's just been made into a film, hasn't it?'

'It has indeed,' Sam said.

'And Gabriel Oak was to die for!' Honey said with a little giggle.

'Is that the one with that Julie Christie?' Winston asked. 'I've always had a soft spot for her.'

'That's the film version from the 1960's, silly,' Honey said.

'Is it? I lose track of time these days,' he said.

'How does everyone feel about reading it, then?' Sam continued.

'Doesn't everybody always die in Hardy's novels?' Flo asked, a frown etched across her forehead.

'Mostly,' Callie said, 'but this one has a happy ending.'

'After just a *few* deaths,' Sam said.

'Oh, dear,' Flo said. 'I'm not sure I'm going to like that.'

'Well, *I'm* happy to read it,' Antonia said.

'I'd love to,' Jago said, and everyone else mumbled their approval.

'We'll make sure the book choice after that has fewer deaths, Flo,' Sam said.

'Good,' she said. 'Life's too short to be reading about death.'

'If anybody would like to order a new copy of the book, I'll be happy to arrange that with Josh next door. As far as I'm aware, there are two second-hand copies here in the shop, but one's a bit tatty so I'd be happy to give that to anyone who'd like it.'

'I'll tek it,' Winston said. 'I don't mind tatty.' He lifted up the corner of the coat he hadn't yet taken off and pointed out the holes in it.

'I'll get it for you in the break, Winston,' Sam said. 'So, if we're all happy with that, why don't we kick things off with what we all like to read? We can go round the circle and each of you can tell us your favourite book or author–'

'Anthony Trollope,' Antonia interrupted. 'You can't beat a good Trollope.'

Jago gave a chuckle and Polly did her best not to join in for fear of never being able to stop.

'His Barchester novels are some of the finest literature,' Antonia went on.

'I think I've read one of his,' Flo said. '*The Rector's Wife*? I did enjoy it.'

'That's *Joanna* Trollope!' Antonia said.

'And a relative of his, I believe,' Callie said.

'Winston?' Sam said.

Winston's head jerked up as if he'd been about to doze off. 'What's that?'

'Do you have a favourite book or author?'

He screwed his eyes up. 'Let me see,' he said. 'Favourite book. Favourite author.'

The group waited patiently.

'Nope,' he said at last. 'Not really.'

'Well, let's hope we can introduce you to some favourites here,' Sam said, and then his eyes rested on the young man next to him. 'Jago, isn't it?'

Jago nodded. 'Erm, a favourite? I read a lot of non-fiction as part of my music studies, but I managed to read a few of the classics too like Dickens and some Conan Doyle. I read some plays as well – some Arthur Miller.'

'He was married to Marilyn Monroe,' Honey pointed out.

'I don't think *that* has anything to do with Arthur Miller's writing,' Antonia said.

'Actually,' Sam said, 'Arthur Miller wrote *The Misfits* for Marilyn Monroe.'

Honey seemed delighted by this information.

'Which plays did you read, Jago?' Sam asked.

'I didn't get on very well with *The Crucible*, but *A View from the Bridge* was fantastic.'

Polly looked at Jago with renewed respect. 'Maybe we should add plays to our list of books?' she said.

'That's not a bad idea,' Sam said.

'What about poetry?' Flo asked.

Sam frowned. 'Probably not a great idea. Poetry tends to divide readers.'

'Even love poetry?' Flo asked, hope in her voice.

'Especially love poetry,' Sam said. 'Now, where did we get up to? Polly, I think.'

'Favourite books?' she said, twisting her hands together in her lap. 'Well, since having Archie, I haven't had much time to read which is an awful confession for somebody who works in a bookshop, isn't it? But I read whenever I can. Everything really. The classics, the latest book club favourites, books recommended by friends, and children's books with Archie. But I suppose I enjoy biographies the most.'

Sam nodded. 'Now, we all know that Antonia likes a nice Trollope.'

There were a few titters around the room at that.

'Flo – we know you like romance, but do you have a favourite title or author?'

'Well, I've just finished reading *In the Prince's Arms* which was very good,' she said.

Antonia shook her head in dismay.

'It's a sequel to *Lost with the Prince* which kept me up all night wanting to know what was going to happen.'

'That's always a sign of a good book,' Sam said.

'But not necessarily a sign of a *quality* book,' Antonia said.

'Perhaps that's something we can talk about,' Sam said. 'The difference between popular fiction and literary fiction.'

Polly scribbled his idea down in her notebook.

'And Honey? Any favourites?'

'I like a good thriller,' she said. 'Lots of intrigue and a nice handsome hero to make the world a better place. Lee Child and Scott Mariani are unbeatable. I often take Jack Reacher or Ben Hope to bed with me!'

Flo gave a giggle and Polly couldn't help smiling.

'Well, it looks as if we've got a really wide range of interests in the group,' Sam said at last. 'Shall we break for a cup of tea and some more of these nibbles?'

Winston leaned forward and helped himself to another of Flo's apple slices and Jago bent forward and took one too. Antonia, who was watching, didn't look pleased.

Polly followed Sam into the tiny kitchen and helped with the tea things, filling the kettle and putting it on to boil.

'It's going really well,' she told him.

'You think?'

'Don't you?' she asked, noticing the two little creases of anxiety above his nose.

'Antonia worries me,' he said.

'Oh, you mustn't let her.'

'Nothing seems to please her – whatever anyone says or does.'

'I know. I did warn you. But that's just it – she *likes* being displeased.'

'But that doesn't make any sense,' Sam whispered as he placed a teabag in each of the mugs.

'It does if you're Antonia Jessop,' Polly said. 'She's one of life's miseries, that's all. Let her have her grumbles but, whatever you do, don't let her get to you.'

Sam placed several mugs on a tray. 'I'll do my best,' he said as he left the kitchen with the mugs of tea.

'So,' Flo was saying to Antonia through a mouthful of one her own apple slices, 'where did you say you lived – Great Tallington?'

'No!' Antonia said indignantly. '*Little* Tallington. Not *Great* Tallington.'

Polly did her best to stop herself from saying something she might regret. It was a very snobbish belief, but not an uncommon one, that anywhere prefixed with the word 'Little' was far superior to those prefixed with the word 'Great'.

'I was in Great Tallington this morning,' Antonia went on. 'Have you seen the state of the green there? Shocking. Some drunken motorcyclist has cut it all up.'

Polly caught Jago's eye and they exchanged tiny smiles.

'Well, Little Tallington's very pretty,' Flo said, 'but there aren't any facilities, are there?'

'Of course we have facilities,' Antonia said. 'We have a post office counter in the village hall once a week and the mobile library stops there.'

'I can never keep track of that mobile library,' Flo said. 'When is it? Every other Wednesday afternoon unless it's cloudy or something? How am I to remember that what with all my animals to take care of?'

'How are they all?' Polly asked her.

'Well, one of the hens got an egg stuck yesterday so it was off to the vets with her. She was standing on the table after the vet had worked his magic and out plopped the yellowest yolk you've ever seen in your life. I was quite tempted to take it home for tea.'

Antonia had turned an alarming shade of green.

'I've got a little poodle,' Honey said. 'She's called Princess, but she doesn't act like one. She likes to attack my balls of wool. Do you have any pets, Jago?' she asked, beaming a smile at him, obviously thrilled to have a handsome young man in the group.

'Er, no,' he said. 'It's just me and my mum.'

'I think everyone should have animals,' Flo said with a nod

towards Delilah who was still sleeping. 'I couldn't live without mine.'

'Right,' Sam said, deciding to take charge of things again before the conversation veered too far away from books, 'so we're all happy with the book choice for next time?'

'What was it again?' Winston asked from the sofa where he was slurping the last of his tea.'

'*Far From the Madding Crowd*,' Sam said. 'I'm going to get you a second-hand copy, remember?'

'That's right,' Winston said.

'What's it about again?' Flo asked.

'Knowing Thomas Hardy,' Honey said, 'love and death.'

'And sheep,' Winston said. 'There's something about sheep in it, isn't there?'

Sam smiled. 'I believe so,' he said.

The group talked for a while longer, finishing all the tea and nibbles. Delilah snored her way through the entire meeting and, remarkably, Winston stayed awake.

At last, it was time to leave and Polly held the door open while everyone made their way through the darkened shop into the cold January night.

'See you in March!' Honey said.

'*I'll* see you before then,' Antonia said ominously to Sam as she left.

'She's bringing some books in,' Sam explained to Polly as she closed the door. 'She wants my advice on what they're worth.'

'Well, don't let her bully you into buying them if they're worthless,' Polly warned him.

She watched as Sam disappeared in to the back room where Callie was waiting to have a quiet word with him and that's when Jago appeared.

'That was fun,' he said with a smile.

'Really?' Polly said. 'You enjoyed it?'

'What? You don't believe me?'

'I'm not sure what to make of you,' she told him. 'Shouldn't you be down a pub with a nice young girl keeping you company?'

He narrowed his grey eyes at her. 'Are you stereotyping me? I thought somebody as well read as you would be beyond that.'

'No!' she cried. 'I just think–'

'What?'

'I'm not sure you fit in here.'

'You don't want me here?'

'I didn't say that,' she said, 'I only wanted to make sure you're happy here.'

'I am,' he said. 'I really am.' He paused. 'Hey, are you okay getting home?'

She nodded. 'My car's just down the road.'

'Want me to walk you to it?'

'I'll be fine, thank you.'

He hesitated for a moment as if he was about to say something else. 'Okay then,' he said at last. 'I'll see you soon.'

'Okay. Night.'

She watched as he left the shop and then Sam and Callie entered the room.

'Jago's an interesting young man,' Sam said. 'You two friends now, Poll?'

'He's a neighbour,' Polly explained.

'Good to have him here. Nice to have a young member.'

'Yes,' Polly said. 'He's very young, isn't he?'

When Polly left the shop, Sam locked the door and turned to Callie.

'I hope you weren't thinking of leaving,' he said.

'Not just yet,' she said, snuggling into his embrace.

'How did tonight compare to your old book club in London?' Sam asked her.

'Funnily enough, it was very similar what with all that rivalry going on between Antonia and Honey.'

Sam took a deep breath. 'Yes, I hope that's not an ongoing problem.'

Callie smiled. 'It was quite funny though, wasn't it?'

'Winston certainly had a good evening and Delilah's behaviour was impeccable,' Sam said. 'But I couldn't help being on edge through the whole meeting as I awaited a wave of nauseous dog gas!'

'Me too!' Callie said. 'At least you were sat on the other side of the room.'

'I could have been sat next door and I still would have got wind of it. Pun intended!'

'Very funny!'

'You were quiet tonight,' he said. 'Not worrying about that trip to

London, are you?'

She shook her head. 'I'm just not very good in group situations.'

'Do you work better in a couple?'

'Depends on the other half of the couple,' she said with a coy smile.

'What about this half?' he said, bending down to kiss her.

'It certainly has potential,' she said a moment later.

They were about to kiss again when there was a loud rapping at the door.

'Oh, no,' Callie said. 'What does *she* want?'

Sam unlocked the door and opened it. 'Miss Jessop? Are you okay?'

'I left my umbrella,' she said, charging through the shop to the back room, reappearing a moment later with the weapon-like item. 'You still here?' she said to Callie.

'Callie and I are a couple,' Sam said.

Antonia's narrow eyes widened at this piece of news. 'Really?' she said. 'Well, may I suggest you take whatever you were doing into the back room? It really isn't seemly to be doing *couple* things in a bookshop.'

Sam and Callie watched as Antonia left, slamming the door behind her and causing the bell to jangle loudly. They then burst out laughing.

'*Couple things?*' Callie cried.

'I like the sound of that,' Sam said, 'and I think we should take her advice, don't you?'

Callie stretched up to kiss him again. 'Yes,' she said, 'I think we should.'

CHAPTER 5

Since moving to Owl Cottage in September, Callie Logan could count the number of times she'd left Suffolk on one hand. Her friend Heidi would have told her that was not a statistic to be proud of, but it made Callie intensely happy.

As she left her home now and caught the train that would take her into Liverpool Street Station, she thought about the last few months and all the joy they had brought her. When her marriage to Piers had ended and she'd chosen to leave London, she'd been quite determined that she'd never make the mistake of falling in love again. She was a practical woman and love simply hadn't worked out for her so she'd decided that she could live without it, throwing herself into her writing instead.

Well, fate always seemed to laugh at people who made such resolute plans, she thought with a smile as the train left the green fields of rural East Anglia behind, and it hadn't been long before she'd had not one but two men vying for her attention.

Callie couldn't help blushing as she thought about local forager, Leo Wildman, with his long dark hair and irrepressible grin. As much as she'd wanted to resist his charms, she had fallen just a little bit, but there'd been something in her that had been holding back with him. Something that was beginning to let go now she was with Sam Nightingale.

There was something so special about Sam, Callie thought. She'd never met such a sweet and gentle man before. Like her, he'd just come out of a marriage which had left him shaken and uneasy with the opposite sex but, together, they were learning that love was worth taking a risk for and Callie had never been happier in her life.

Sam's family had made her feel so welcome too and she adored his mother, Eleanor, and his sisters, Polly, Bryony and Lara, and was especially fond of Grandpa Joe who had been instrumental in bringing her and Sam together. Yes, Suffolk had been a very good decision indeed. However, as the train pulled into Liverpool Street Station and she hopped on the tube, her lightness of mood left her and a feeling of gloom replaced it.

Her publishers' office was a large modern building in the west of London and Callie didn't really want to be there at all. The large open foyer always made her feel nervous and she felt so tiny sitting there whilst waiting for somebody to come and greet her. She had much rather be in her cosy little study overlooking the green at Newton St Clare. Still, she had a living to make.

Looking at her watch now, Callie realised that Margot was running late which was nothing to be overly concerned about as her agent was always running late. Only Callie really didn't want to have to face her ex-husband alone.

'Callie?'

Too late, she thought, as Piers Blackmore strode across the foyer from the lifts.

She stood up and stretched out a hand towards him, but he ignored it and went straight in to kiss her cheek.

'How are you? You look wonderful.'

'I'm fine,' she said, doing her best to remain calm and trying not to remember the fact that Piers had tried to persuade her to give him another chance even though they'd separated and she'd bought a new home.

He placed a hand on her arm. 'Shall we get a drink whilst we wait for Margot?' He led her through to the ground floor cafe which both staff and visitors to the publishing house used. It was always a fun place to try and spot famous authors and celebrities, but Callie was too nervous to do either and her eyes were too busy trying to avoid Piers. In his navy suit and crisp white shirt, he looked every inch the professional, and she couldn't help thinking how handsome he looked. His neat brown hair was as immaculate as ever and his green eyes never let her out of his sight.

'You okay?' he asked.

'I'm fine,' she said.

'You seem—'

'I said I'm fine.'

'Okay!' He held his hands up as if defending himself.

'Sorry,' she said. 'I'm just a bit—'

'What?' he asked, examining her with unnerving intensity.

She took a deep breath. She didn't want to admit to him how nervous she was and so she shook her head.

'Nothing,' she said.

'You sure?' he said, leaning in close to her. Much too close for her liking.

'Piers—'

He nodded and took a step back as if realising his mistake.

'I'll get the drinks,' he said.

He was just ordering when Margot entered the cafe at a mad dash, a huge royal blue cape flowing out behind her. She looked like a cartoon character, Callie couldn't help thinking, but at least she was there now and Callie didn't have to sit awkwardly with Piers on her own.

As Piers was bringing their drinks over to a table Callie had chosen by a window, Margot eyed Callie.

'Have you told him?' she asked. She wasn't one for wasting time with pleasantries; it was always straight down to business with her.

'Told me what?' Piers asked as he sat down opposite them.

'Tell him your ideas for the next two books,' Margot prompted.

'There are more books planned?' Piers said, sitting forward in his chair.

Callie nodded. 'Only in note form at the moment, but I want to explore the sister's story – follow that through. She's just a subplot character in the first book, but I think there's a lot in her background that could be really interesting.'

'Yes,' Piers said thoughtfully, 'I can see that.'

'There might even be scope for a series. Callie's done it before,' Margot said, her sharp eyes narrowing at Piers across the table, 'and series are hot right now and you know it.'

'They are,' Piers said. 'Publishers are always trying to find the next big one too and Callie could really be on to something.'

Callie looked at him. He was wearing what she used to call his business smile – the one that stretched across his face when he could hear the *kerching* of a cash register.

'It's not a series yet,' she reminded him. 'It's just an idea.' She wanted to make it quite clear that she wasn't going to be bullied by her agent and editor. She'd only agreed to work with her ex-husband on one book. That might be all she had the courage for. She certainly had no intention of tying herself into a long-term contract.

'This is very exciting, Callie,' he said. 'You should have told me.'

'There was nothing to tell,' she said honestly. 'It only occurred to me recently.'

'You're so clever,' he said, his eyes holding hers. 'I adore your imagination.'

She swallowed hard, turning her attention to her coffee.

It was then that Margot's phone beeped. She took a moment to read the message and then stood up abruptly.

'Well, you two don't need me anymore,' she declared.

'You're going?' Callie said in panic.

Margot bent to air kiss her. 'Got to rush, darling. Call me!' And she left in a sweep of cape.

It was as if Piers had been waiting for that very thing to happen and, for a moment, Callie wondered if he'd fixed the whole thing with Margot, because his hand reached across the table to hold hers as soon as Margot's back was turned.

'I'm glad she's gone,' he said.

'I'd probably better get going myself,' she said, making to stand up. Piers didn't let go of her hand.

'But you've only just got here,' he said. 'We were going to talk about our marketing plans for your book. Don't you want to hear our ideas?'

'I really think—'

'Callie – don't be crazy.'

She looked at him, her heart racing. 'This isn't going to work,' she said in a quiet voice that belied her anxiety.

'What do you mean?'

'I don't think I can work with you.'

He frowned. 'Are you serious?'

She nodded. 'I was told I'd be working with one of your colleagues.'

'I know, but that seemed ridiculous. Don't forget it was me who discovered that first book of yours and brought you to the place you are now. We're a great team, Callie.'

'How can you say that?' she asked, her expression genuinely baffled.

'How can you not?'

'Because we're getting divorced!' she said. 'Have you forgotten that?'

'Of course I haven't forgotten,' he snapped. 'I remember it every single day you're not there in my bed with me.'

'Piers!' she cried, flapping her hands for him to lower his voice.

'Letting you go was the stupidest thing I've ever done, Callie, and I regret it every single day and, if I could go back or change the way you feel now, I would in an instant.'

'And this is why we can't work together,' she said.

They stared at each other for a silence-filled moment.

'I shouldn't ever have signed this deal,' Callie said at last, looking into her lap.

'You're not thinking of paying the advance back, are you?' Piers said in panic. 'You signed a contract, Callie!'

Callie blanched at the tone of his voice. The businessman had awoken once again and seemed quite determined not to lose her as an author even though he'd managed to lose her as a wife.

'I want a new editor,' she said, 'otherwise I'll tell Margot to get me out of this contract.'

'You wouldn't,' he said. 'I know you Callie. You simply don't do things like that.'

'Don't try me on this, Piers,' she said, 'because I *will* surprise you.' She stood up, pushing her chair out behind her with a severe squeak which made several people in the cafe turn around to stare.

'Please,' he said, 'sit down. We can work this out.'

'Can we?'

He sighed. 'Yes,' he said. 'Who do you want as your editor?'

'I don't mind,' she said.

'Just as long as it isn't me?' He gave the tiniest of smiles and Callie sat down again.

'Pretty much,' she said, 'although I do get on well with Sara.'

'Sara it is, then,' he said.

She blinked in surprise. 'Just like that?'

'If it keeps you happy and with us,' he said.

'I hope it will,' she said.

Piers nodded. 'I don't suppose I can persuade you to come to lunch with me,' he said.

Callie shook her head. He didn't give up easily, did he?

'You can't,' she said, 'but I'd be delighted to have lunch next time I'm in town. With Sara.'

Piers sighed. 'Right,' he said. 'Understood.'

And Callie really hoped that he did.

The nightmare was always the same. Polly was running through the house trying to find him. But, as in so many dreams, the house wasn't quite her house: it had sort of stretched and elongated. The hallway seemed to be half a mile long and the rooms had grown out of all proportion, turning into cold, unfriendly places which echoed eerily when she cried out. On she ran, shouting his name into the empty rooms, searching on and on as panic rose in her chest.

She would wake up at different points in the dream, but her heart would always be racing.

Sitting up in bed now, after the same dream had awoken her, she switched on her bedside lamp. She hated waking up in the early hours especially in the winter months when there were still hours and hours of darkness ahead of her and she would feel so helplessly alone.

She got out of bed, putting her slippers on and wrapping her dressing gown around her. The house was cold now and, more than anything, she wanted the comforting warmth of another human being next to her.

Leaving her room, she put the light on and tiptoed along the landing, pushing the door open into Archie's bedroom. He was fast asleep and nothing in the world would make her disturb him, no matter how lonely and insecure she felt. Luckily, it was often just enough to stand there for a few moments and watch him sleeping.

But, as much as the sight of her sleeping son comforted her, the questions would start too, haunting her and hounding her. How long could she keep the truth from him? When would he start questioning her in earnest about his father and what on earth would she tell him when he did?

Polly shook her head. These were questions that she wasn't going to answer tonight and so she walked downstairs to the kitchen where she made herself a cup of tea. She was used to her lonely wanderings around the house at night by now. The cottage was so quiet and, although Dickens would often get up and pad across the floor to give her a friendly nudge, he'd soon return to his basket and Polly would be left to her thoughts. Thoughts such as: Will there ever be an end to this? Why did this happen to me? What am I meant to do? She sighed. These were pointless, unanswerable questions which ate away at her sanity and she had to stop them, but how could she when every moment of her life was full of Sean? His clothes were still in the wardrobe and drawers upstairs, his favourite mug stood unused in the kitchen cupboard and she drove his car every single day. Of course, every time she looked at Archie, Sean looked right back at her. How could she run away from all that?

She was just finishing her tea when something caught her eye: the brand new copy of Thomas Hardy's *Far From the Madding Crowd* which she'd ordered via Josh's shop. It was the new film tie-in featuring the romantic image of Bathsheba Everdene and Sergeant Troy embracing in a misty woodland. Polly looked at it now, wondering if she'd ever be embraced by a man again or if her time for love had ended with the disappearance of her husband. And then something occurred to her. If she read, she *could* escape from her relentless thoughts – even if it was just for a few moments. As she'd told the book club, her reading habits had changed since she'd become a wife and mother; her time wasn't her own anymore.

'But it is in the middle of the night,' she said to herself now. There was nobody to answer to. The hours stretched ahead of her with no chores to do and nobody to keep an eye on, and how much better it would be to fill those hours with the sublime words of a writer like Thomas Hardy than it would be to dwell on the wretched thoughts in her own head? Sam had chosen a wonderful novel and Polly was really beginning to see why Sam was such a huge fan and, if she wasn't able to sleep, she might as well do something worthwhile. So she picked up the book, taking it through to the living room where she switched on a lamp and curled up on the sofa, pulling a woollen blanket over her knees, and turning to one of the most beautiful opening sentences ever written.

"When Farmer Oak smiled, the corners of his mouth spread till they were within an unimportant distance of his ears, his eyes were reduced to chinks, and diverging wrinkles appeared around them, extending upon his countenance like the rays in a rudimentary sketch of the rising sun."

How glorious an introduction that was to one of literature's greatest heroes, Polly thought. And then she thought of the foolishness of the heroine for not being able to see Gabriel Oak's fine qualities. Of course, if Bathsheba had said yes to Gabriel's proposal in the early pages, there wouldn't have been a story to tell, but how frustrating it was for Polly to witness Hardy's heroine making mistake after mistake. She hadn't read the book before but she'd seen at least three film and TV adaptations of it, and the heroine still managed to irk her. But wasn't that part of the comfort of literature too? Wasn't reading about other people's mistakes a welcome relief from living your own? To know that countless other people out there – even if they were fictional – were making great fat miserable mistakes was wonderfully reassuring because it meant that you were not alone.

Polly read. And read. She was quite a fast reader and the hours slipped by as she read of Bathsheba's rejection of Gabriel Oak and how fate — the great theme which threaded its way through each one of Hardy's novels — treated Gabriel so cruelly. She read on, watching the fate of the sheep and the hiring fair, and had just met Liddy Smallbury and Mr Boldwood when tiredness overtook her, a great yawn persuading her to put the book down. It was after five in the morning and she now hoped that she could sleep soundly for at least two hours before getting up to start the day properly.

Switching the living room light off, she walked through to the kitchen to check on Dickens. He was still fast asleep, his front paws twitching as if he was chasing rabbits in his dream.

Polly headed upstairs, looked in on Archie and then went into her own bedroom, walking across to the window. She looked out into the darkness that enveloped the green and, for one strange, awful moment, thought she saw somebody standing out there by one of the big trees. She blinked and looked again, but couldn't see anything. Her imagination must have been playing tricks on her, she thought. But, as she got into bed, she couldn't shake the feeling that somebody was watching the house.

CHAPTER 6

Bryony Nightingale wasn't her usual buoyant self. Polly watched her younger sister as she stropped around the children's bookshop she ran, tearing books from the shelves and stuffing new ones in their place without her normal care and attention.

'Bryony!' Polly cried at last. 'What on *earth* is the matter with you?'

'Nothing,' her sister snapped. 'Why should anything be the matter when I've only been on yet another terrible blind date and wasted an entire evening listening to a total loser telling me about his collection of baked bean cans?'

'Baked bean cans?'

'Oh, yes,' Bryony said. 'I heard all about them. Baked bean cans through the ages, he said. He's got decades and decades of them. He even plans holidays to countries just so he can bring home a few cans.'

'Does he actually eat them all?' Polly asked.

Bryony nodded. 'Yes. But I don't even want to think of the implications of all those beans he gets through.'

'I take it you didn't go home with him?' Polly said with a grin.

'Of course I didn't,' Bryony said, 'and I'm going to kill Fiona when I see her. What did she think we'd have in common, for pity's sake?' Her sister flopped down onto a baby beanbag. 'Isn't there a single decent man out there for me? I mean, I'm not asking for perfection. Just somebody who doesn't make me want to take off at eighty miles an hour in the opposite direction. That would be a start.'

'What about Colin?' Polly asked. 'He likes you and seems pretty normal. He's cute too.'

'I know,' Bryony said. 'But that's all a bit too easy, isn't it?'

Polly frowned. 'What do you mean?'

'I mean, I know he likes me and he's a really nice guy and everything.'

'Then why not go out with him?'

Bryony sighed. 'Well, we're kind of seeing each other but not officially. It wouldn't be fair on him,' she said. 'I don't think it would work.'

Polly shook her head. 'I don't understand you.'

Bryony got up from the beanbag and brushed down the long red-and-blue-checked skirt she was wearing. Worn with a large silver metal belt from which hung dozens of little charms, it was a typical Bryony bohemian look that Polly had always secretly envied. Not that it would have suited her. Polly was far more conventional with her straight, clean-cut lines and conservative colours, but there was something wonderfully free about Bryony which she couldn't help admiring.

But she wasn't thinking about clothes now; she was thinking about men. 'Do you like musicians?' she asked her.

'What sort of musicians?' Bryony asked.

'Guitar players.'

'In theory,' Bryony said. 'Why?'

'One of my neighbour's sons has just come home. He's a music graduate. He's quite young, but he's handsome.'

Bryony cocked her head to one side. '*How* handsome?'

'Oh, you know – tall with that messy artistic sort of hair that musicians seem to have. He's got a nice smile too.'

'You mean he's always smiling at *you*?' Bryony said.

'He's a smiley kind of person is what I'm saying.' She shrugged. 'Anyway, he seems decent enough. I could have a word with him if you want.'

'What – tell him you've got a hopeless little sister who can't find a man herself?'

'I wouldn't phrase it like that,' Polly said. 'I'd just say that I'm much better at choosing men for you than you are yourself.'

Bryony stuck her tongue out at her sister, but quickly rearranged her face into the features of a normal, professional adult when a customer came through the door. They were after the latest young adult dystopian trilogy that was racing up the charts. It was a genre which Polly and Bryony disapproved of. Why such grim stories of children struggling for life in an apocalyptic society were so popular was a complete mystery to the Nightingale sisters.

'They should be reading something romantic and wonderful like *I Capture the Castle*,' Bryony said. 'Actually, I'm going to order some more copies of that and do a window display. "Love Lovely Books" or something.'

'Good idea,' Polly said, 'and what about some Madeleine Forrest novels?'

'Brilliant idea,' Bryony said. 'Her high school series is really popular and the covers are to die for. They'll look gorgeous in the window. Just what we need to brighten things up in the winter and, more importantly, they have real heroes in them too. No vampires or werewolves or shape-shifting weirdoes. Just good old-fashioned flesh and blood heroes.'

Polly immediately got busy with a piece of paper, mapping out her ideas for a window display whilst Bryony ordered the books themselves. One of the great joys of being an independent bookshop was being flexible and being able to make such spontaneous decisions about your stock and how and where you were going to place it.

'I've lost count of the number of vampire hero books we've sold over the last few years, but I think it's time that teenage girls realised that there's more to a hero than a pair of fangs,' Bryony said.

Polly laughed. 'Heroes are a curious business, aren't they?' she said. 'Just think about it for a minute. There's the abusive Heathcliff who beats his wife and hangs dogs. There's moody Mr Darcy and Edward Rochester who lies and tries to commit bigamy. It makes me worry about the state of the female mind that we find these men so attractive.'

'Yes, if these are the heroes women wish their real-life partners to be like, then there's no hope for us really.'

'Poll,' Bryony said after flipping through the order book by the counter for a moment.

'Yes?'

'Have you ever thought about dating again?'

Polly looked up from her sheet of paper. 'How can I? I'm married.'

'I know, but–'

'But nothing.'

Bryony chewed her bottom lip. 'You can't wait around forever and nobody expects you to, and they wouldn't judge you if you started dating again.'

'I'm not worrying about people judging me because I'm not going to start dating again, okay?'

'Okay,' Bryony said.

Polly checked her watch. 'Look, I'd better get going.'

'But it's so early.'

'I've got some lessons to plan for my students before I pick Archie up.' She got her handbag from the stock room.

'Polly! Don't go like this,' Bryony said. 'I didn't mean to upset you.'

'You didn't upset me,' Polly said, charging straight for the door. 'I've just got to go.'

'Polly?' Bryony shouted after her, but Polly didn't stop. She had to get out of there – away from her sister and her probing questions.

She walked into the market square and stood there as shoppers hurried past her. She didn't really have any lessons to plan, but she hadn't been able to cope with Bryony. It hadn't been the first time Bryony had approached that subject, but it had been the most direct. Little hints had been dropped in the past as to whether Polly was moving on from the idea that Sean would return. Her whole family had lost faith, hadn't they? Even her mother had recently asked her if she wanted to bring anyone to Campion House for Sunday lunch and she hadn't meant a girlfriend. No, she thought, she was the only person who hadn't given up on Sean. Well, there were two other people as well.

With that thought, she got out her phone and rang the number she'd had programmed in since Sean's disappearance.

'Alison?' she said a moment later. 'Yes, it's Polly. Good, thanks. No. No news, I'm afraid.' It was the usual routine. Every time Polly rang her parents-in-law, they'd foolishly hope that it was with news about Sean. 'He's well, thank you,' she said a moment later when Alison Prior asked after Archie. 'Yes, we'd love to. Tonight would be great. We'll come round after tea. See you later.'

Alison and Anthony Prior lived in a large modern house a few miles from Castle Clare. It was in what had once been a small village but was getting larger every year with the building of new properties, and now had a mix of old thatched cottages along the original main road and new houses clustered into cul-de-sacs at each end. The Priors lived in one of the cul-de-sacs. It was called Constable View but Polly didn't think that John Constable would recognise anything at all if he came back from the afterlife to capture the landscape on canvas.

'Is Granddad going to make me sing again?' Archie asked from the back seat.

'I doubt it,' Polly said.

'He made me last time,' Archie complained.

'He's very interested in your musical prowess,' Polly said.

'What's that mean?'

'It means that he likes to see you doing well.'

'If he likes music so much, why did he give us his piano?'

'It was a wedding present to me and your dad.'

'Can we give it back?' Archie said.

'No we can't,' Polly said. 'That would be ungrateful and you wouldn't be able to learn to play it then.' She caught his eye in the rear view mirror. 'Oh, I see,' she said. 'You're not giving the piano up, Arch.'

His mouth set in a firm, narrow line just like his father's used to when he didn't get his own way. He was so like Sean sometimes that it hurt.

Parking on the road outside the Priors' house, Polly got out of the car and opened Archie's door.

'I hate the piano,' he said. It was about the hundredth time he'd said that since he'd met Jago and Polly was sick and tired of hearing it.

She let her son ring the bell and the door was opened a moment later by her father-in-law. Anthony Prior was a tall man with the kind of broad shoulders and stern eyebrows which used to make the younger Archie run for cover.

'Hello, Archie boy,' he said now. 'Polly.'

'Hello,' she said with a little smile.

'Hi Granddad,' Archie said as his grandfather placed a large hand on his shoulder and led him into the hallway.

Polly and Archie removed their shoes and left them neatly side by side on the front door mat before walking through to the living room. The house was a symphony of white from the painted walls to the wooden furniture and soft furnishings. It was a total nightmare to bring a young grandson to and Dickens the spaniel had been told that he was no longer welcome after he'd brought muddy feet in from the back garden the previous Easter.

Archie knew the routine and, after removing his shoes, he washed his hands in the white sink in the cloakroom before making his way to the large white sofa where he sat down.

'So then, Archie!' Anthony bellowed down at his grandson,

making him jump. 'How are the piano lessons going?'

'Okay,' Archie said in a small voice.

'Playing Beethoven yet, are we?'

Archie looked at his mum for help.

'No, not yet,' Polly answered for him.

'I want to play the guitar,' Archie said. Polly threw him an angry look.

'The guitar?' Anthony said. 'No, no, no. You don't want to play the guitar. Long-haired layabouts play the guitar.'

Once again, Archie looked to his mum. 'Jago's got long hair, hasn't he? Is he a layabout too?'

Polly cleared her throat. 'No, he's not.'

'Who's Jago?' Alison asked, entering the living room from the adjoining kitchen. She was a small woman with a pretty face and a halo of white-blonde hair.

'He's a friend,' Archie informed her. 'He's got long hair and Granddad says he's a layabout.'

'You know him?' Alison asked her husband.

'He plays the guitar,' Anthony explained.

'Oh, I see,' Alison said. 'Your granddad's a bit of a snob when it comes to musical instruments. I remember when your father wanted to learn to play the guitar and wasn't allowed.'

'Sean wanted to play the guitar?' Polly asked.

'Oh, yes,' Alison said, 'but Anthony didn't like the idea. He said nobody of any consequence plays the guitar.'

'So Eric Clapton and Jimi Hendrix aren't of any consequence?' Polly said.

'Exactly!' Alison said with a tiny smile.

Anthony just shook his head. 'Exceptions to the rule. Exceptions to the rule.'

'Does that mean I can play the guitar?' Archie asked.

'No, it doesn't,' Polly said and watched as her son slumped back into a pair of white cushions.

'Polly,' Alison said. 'Come and help me make some tea.'

Polly followed her mother-in-law through to the kitchen and had to admit that it even put her own very neat and tidy one to shame. There wasn't a single breadcrumb out of place and every surface gleamed and shone. The window above the sink looked out onto a tiny fenced garden which was visible in the light from the kitchen.

There was a lawn and neat borders full of evergreen shrubs. In the summer, Alison filled it with prettily patriotic red, white and blue bedding plants.

'You look tired, Polly,' Alison said as she joined her by the sink. 'Are you okay?'

Polly nodded.

'You been sleeping all right?'

'Not really,' she admitted.

'Oh, dear. You still having the nightmares?'

Alison was the only one she'd admitted to about the nightmares. 'On and off,' she said.

Alison nodded. 'Polly, dear – have you thought about seeing somebody.'

Polly swallowed hard. Had she heard her right? Was her mother-in-law joining in with everybody else and seriously suggesting that she started dating again?

'What?' she asked, unable to hide her horror.

'A counsellor or someone.'

'Oh,' Polly said, relief flooding through her. 'God, no.'

'It might be good to talk to somebody.'

'But I talk to you,' she said.

'Yes, but, I mean *really* talk.'

Polly shook her head. 'I don't need that,' she said.

Alison sighed. 'Polly, you're an amazing woman and our Sean was so lucky to find you. You're strong and you're a wonderful mother to Archie, but nobody expects you to go through all this on your own. I really think–'

'I don't need a counsellor,' Polly snapped. 'I don't need a psychiatrist or a social worker, and I certainly don't need a boyfriend.'

'But I didn't say anything about a boyfriend,' Alison said, perplexed. 'Polly?'

But Polly had left the kitchen and was grabbing hold of Archie's hand and dragging him up from the white sofa.

'Get your shoes on, Archie. We're going home.'

Archie seemed to recognise his mother's tone of voice and didn't argue or question as he was hauled out into the hallway.

'What's going on?' Anthony asked, following them through.

'Polly!' Alison cried, but Polly already had the front door open.

'What did you say to her?' Anthony asked his wife.

Polly could hear the tears catching in her mother-in-law's throat as she tried to explain and she felt truly awful for leaving like this, but she had to. She just had to.

CHAPTER 7

Polly and Archie had a spot of supper in silence in the kitchen. Archie seemed to sense that his mother wasn't in the mood to talk and got on with the business of shovelling his scrambled eggs into his mouth.

After taking Dickens out across the green for a quick lap and tucking Archie in bed, Polly sat with a cup of tea in the living room, watching the fire in the wood burner as it slowly fizzled out. She didn't have the energy to chuck another log on. She'd be going to bed soon and, hopefully, she'd sleep right through after the emotionally draining day she'd had.

She took a deep breath. What was wrong with her that she was so tetchy and teary with everyone? They meant well, after all, and she should be able to cope with all this by now, she told herself.

'But I'm not,' she said into the quiet room.

As soon as they'd got home from her in-laws, she'd rung and apologised to Alison, but hadn't given the poor woman any sort of explanation beyond that she was tired. Alison had been so soothing and sweet that Polly had felt herself close to tears again.

'Stupid, stupid!' she berated herself and that's when she heard a light knock on the front door.

She looked at the clock. It was after eight on a cold January evening. Who would be calling then, she wondered, getting up from the chair?

A second knock sounded – a little louder this time.

'Who is it?' she called, putting the chain on the door.

'Me,' a man's voice came.

'Who's *me*?' she asked in annoyance.

'Jago,' he said, 'from across the road. From the book club.'

She shook her head. He hadn't needed to say more than "Jago". After all, how many Jagos were there in Great Tallington, for goodness' sake?

She opened the door, removing the chain.

'It's getting late,' she told him, forgetting to say hello first.

'Yeah, sorry about that. I called round earlier, but you were out.'

'Yes,' Polly said, not giving anything away. 'What did you want?'

'You forgot something the other night at the book club,' he said.

'Did I?' she said.

'Aha,' he said. 'You forgot to tell me your decision about Archie having guitar lessons with me.'

'Oh,' she said. 'Well, I've not given it much thought to be honest.'

'But what's there to think about?' he asked. 'He wants them and I'm happy to give them to him. For free, don't forget. I'm not charging.'

'No, I know,' she said. 'That's very kind, but—'

'But what?' he asked. 'Look, can I come in? It's freezing out here.'

'Oh,' Polly said. 'I suppose.'

He bowed his head so as not to crack it on the doorframe and Polly led him through to the living room and Dickens came through from the kitchen to greet him.

'Hey, boy,' he said, bending to stroke the dog's head. 'Want me to liven that fire up? It's not looking too happy.'

'I can do it myself,' Polly said, 'if I want to.'

'Okay,' he said. 'Now, you were going to tell me the amazing excuse you have for not accepting free guitar lessons for your very enthusiastic and bright boy.' He gave her a lopsided smile, but Polly wasn't going to let that steer her off course.

'I just think he's got enough on with the piano. It's what his father wanted him to learn. Archie's got his grandparents' upright,' she said, nodding towards it. 'It's a beautiful instrument.'

'I'm sure it is,' Jago said, 'but doesn't Archie hate it?'

'Oh, sure,' Polly admitted. 'Like all boys. But he'll come round. He'll thank us in the long run.'

'Are you sure about that?'

'Yes,' she said. 'I'm sure.'

Jago looked at the piano and then glanced around the room. 'You haven't got a cup of tea going, have you?'

Polly placed her hands on her hips.

'Please?' he added with a smile.

She walked through to the kitchen and he followed, his big boots loud on the kitchen floor.

'We mustn't talk too loudly,' she said. 'Archie's in bed.'

Jago nodded. 'Black, no sugar,' he said.

'I remember,' she said, amazed by his brazenness.

'I can make it if you like. If you wanted to sit down. You look tired.'

'I'm perfectly capable of making tea in my own kitchen,' Polly said.

'Okay,' he asked. 'Just wanted to help.' He took a seat at the kitchen table. 'Are you sure you're all right?'

'I'm fine,' she said. 'Why shouldn't I be?'

He studied her closely. 'You look pale and your eyes are a little red. Have you been crying?'

She glared at him, her mouth falling open. 'What business is it of yours to ask me questions like that?'

'No business at all.'

'That's right.'

'So, what's the matter?'

She sighed. What was it with this guy? 'I'm just a little tired,' she said, trotting out the old lie so quickly that she could tell he didn't believe her. 'I had a fight with my in-laws. Well, not a fight, really. It was my fault. I was mean and I snapped and I shouldn't have.' She bit her lip. She hadn't meant to say all that.

Jago nodded. 'In-laws are tricky, aren't they?'

'You have some?'

He laughed. 'No,' he said. 'Not yet. But I have eyes. I've seen in-laws before.'

'I guess I'm lucky with mine. They've been good to me...' Her voice petered out and she concentrated on the tea things before her.

'I'm sorry,' he said.

'What for?' she asked, placing his mug of tea before him and sitting down with her own.

'For what happened to your husband.'

'Oh, you know?'

'Mum told me.'

Polly took a deep breath. 'I guess everyone knows. Not that's there's much to know.'

'That must be tough on you.'

'You could say that,' Polly said, rubbing her eyes. She really was feeling tired now.

'And on Archie,' Jago said. 'How much does he know?'

Polly circled the rim of her mug with a finger and then she got up and closed the kitchen door before returning to the table. 'He knows what I tell him which isn't much. He thinks his father's working away from home.'

'For over three years?'

'I'm very convincing,' she said, her face deadly serious.

'But what about his birthdays and Christmases? Doesn't that get tricky?'

'Of course,' she said and then she cleared her throat. 'I've been sending him cards and presents.'

Jago's eyes boggled. 'Really? What – in a different hand writing?'

Polly could feel herself blushing as she nodded. 'I didn't know what else to do. I couldn't tell him the truth and so I made up a story.'

'But surely he knew something was wrong at the beginning,' Jago said. 'I mean, weren't the police involved?'

'He was so young then. His grandparents stepped in and helped. He was away from the action, really. I needed to protect him.'

Jago sucked air through his teeth.

'What?' Polly asked. 'You think that was wrong of me?'

He shook his head. 'I don't think that's for me to say,' he said. 'I think you did the best you could at the time.'

'I did,' she said. 'How could I tell a three-year-old boy that his father's gone missing? That we don't know if he's ever coming back or if he's dead or alive? How could I expect him to handle that when *I* barely could?'

Jago took a sip of his tea and then put it down on the table, wrapping his hands around it.

'My father left when I was fourteen,' he said.

'I'm sorry. I didn't know.'

'It was for the best,' he said. 'He – erm – wasn't a nice man. He made us miserable.'

'Do you keep in touch?'

Jago gave a hollow-sounding laugh. 'No way,' he said, 'and he'd better not show his face around here ever again if he knows what's good for him.'

Polly saw a look of pure anger sweep over Jago's face like a dark cloud over a landscape, shutting off all the light and warmth for a brief moment.

'Look,' he said, scraping his chair back and getting up, 'I'm not going to keep hassling you with this guitar business.'

'Good,' she said.

'You've got enough to worry about without me adding to everything.'

'Yes,' she said, wishing she didn't sound quite so harsh. She didn't mean to but, sometimes, the words came out before she had a chance to think and soften them.

She followed him out into the hallway and watched as he opened the front door. A blast of cold air greeted them, stealing as much warmth from the house as was possible.

'Okay, then,' he said, ducking his head and raising a hand in farewell.

Polly rested her hand on the door before closing it, feeling strangely dithery which wasn't like her at all. She watched the young man as he crossed the road towards his home on the other side of the green. He was leaving. Right now. And a little voice inside her said, "Stop him!"

'Jago!' she shouted. He stopped and turned back. 'Come back tomorrow, okay? After school.' She paused. 'And bring your guitar.'

That night, Jago lay awake staring at the ceiling. He couldn't stop thinking about Polly Prior. Her beautiful dark hair that had partially escaped from her hair clip, her rose-bud mouth, her sloe-dark eyes, and that luminous pale face filled with all the anxiety in the world.

When he'd thought about coming back home to Suffolk after his stint in the US, he'd imagined quickly falling into a routine of writing his jingles, of setting up his tutoring business, hooking up with a few schools, and getting his old band together. But now, all he could think about was this woman and her little boy.

Perhaps there was something about Archie that reminded him of himself at that age. Although Jago's father hadn't left until Jago was fourteen, he might as well have never existed for all the time he spent with his family. His father's job as a salesman had involved a lot of travelling and he was absent for long periods at a time which had suited Jago and his mother just fine because he was a complete jerk whenever he was around.

Jago couldn't remember when he'd first become aware of his father's violent streak; it had always seemed to be a part of his life. He could remember lying awake in bed listening to his parents' raised voices – his father's angry and aggressive and his mother's frightened and sad. Jago came to know the routine. The shouting would come first, waking him up, then there'd be the awful silence which seemed to fill the house with a strange malevolence. Then the front door would slam and Jago would watch from his bedroom window as his father would stalk away into the night. Where he went, he had no idea. Probably to some old crony of his where he could get himself drunk in peace. Jago would wait until he knew for certain that his father wasn't coming back and then he would tiptoe downstairs. He was usually about half-way down when he'd hear the sound of his mother crying. He'd open the door into the kitchen and she'd make a hurried effort to dry her tears and throw him an unconvincing smile.

'Couldn't you sleep?' she'd ask, never acknowledging the fact that he might have been woken up by the high decibel fighting going on. 'Let me get you back to bed.'

It wasn't until he was older that he'd started to get involved – that he'd come into the kitchen whilst the fighting was still going on and yell at his father to back off. Jago had always been tall for his age, but it wasn't until he was fourteen that he'd really started to look as though he could defend himself and his mother properly and his father seemed to have known that he would too.

All those old feelings about his father had been stirred up again tonight. Not that they were ever far away even after all these years. They were only a memory away. Old dead feelings that were still so very much alive.

He rolled over in bed and switched his bedside lamp on. It was no use trying to get to sleep so he swung his legs out of bed and pulled on a T-shirt and a pair of jogging bottoms. The heating had been off for hours and the bedroom was chilly. He picked up his guitar and started to strum. Some people drank a cup of hot milk or a tot of whiskey to help them relax; Jago strummed. His mother didn't mind. She said she liked it and so his fingers idled the midnight minutes away, finding the first few tentative notes of a new song. It was a sweet, melancholy sound that reminded him of Polly which wasn't that surprising really because it was her face he was seeing as he was strumming.

CHAPTER 8

Polly was in Bryony's shop the next morning, sorting out the mess her sister had made in the stock room with the boxes of new arrivals.

'Honestly, Bryony, you've got to get this room organised.'

Bryony stood in the doorway looking bemused. 'It *is* organised,' she said. 'I know exactly what's in each mess heap.'

Polly, who was kneeling on the floor, looked up at her sister. 'How you can bear to have a stock room that looks like a tip, I really don't know.'

'Just comes naturally,' Bryony said with a grin. 'Besides, customers don't see this room.'

'*I* see it,' Polly said.

'Yes, but you don't matter,' Bryony said with a teasing wink. 'Hey, come and see this.'

Polly got up from the floor and dusted her skirt down. 'I'm bringing my vacuum cleaner in with me next time,' she said as she followed Bryony out into the shop. There was a box on the shop counter which Polly had noticed when she'd come in, but she hadn't liked to pry even though she could tell it was from Well Bread, the bakery next door.

'Open it,' Bryony told her. Polly did so and her dark eyes widened at the contents.

'From Colin?' she asked.

'Who else?'

'Is that raspberry jam?'

'Oh, yeah,' Bryony said. 'He knows I have a thing for raspberry jam.'

'Seedless?'

'Of course.'

Polly looked at the exquisite, very large, biscuit. It was like an incredibly ornate jammy dodger, but the most striking thing about it was that it was heart-shaped.

'He's definitely got a thing for you,' Polly said.

'You think?' Bryony said, tutting. 'What am I going to do?'

'Eat it?'

Bryony sighed. 'I mean about Colin.'

'Tell him you're on a diet?' Polly couldn't help giggling.

'I love how you can laugh at my misfortune.'

'Being the centre of attention of a cute and talented baker isn't exactly a misfortune, is it?' Polly said.

Bryony's whole body seemed to sag.

'If you're not interested in him, you shouldn't be seeing him at all. You should tell him how you really feel,' Polly said, 'and sooner rather than later. It's cruel to keep him hoping. And baking.'

'I know,' Bryony said. 'I just haven't got the heart.'

'Yes you have,' Polly said, pushing the box towards her.

'Very funny.'

'Seriously, if you know he's not for you, it's mean to keep him dangling.'

'But how do I know if he's not for me? It's an age since I had a proper relationship. I've forgotten what it's all about.'

'Then go out with him.'

Bryony screwed up her mouth. 'I'm not sure.'

'Then go out with somebody else,' Polly told her. 'You know, I saw Jago last night? The guy who lives opposite?. He's going to give Archie guitar lessons.'

'That's great,' Bryony said.

'I hope so,' she said. 'I don't want him taking on too much, but he really seems to like this Jago and—' Polly stopped.

'What?'

Polly took a deep breath. 'I'm just aware that he hasn't got a male role model. I mean, there's Sam and Josh and they're great, but they've got their own lives. And Archie really seems to look up to Jago.'

'You're thinking of Jago as a father figure?' Bryony said, surprise in her voice.

'No!' Polly cried in horror. 'Just as a good male – man – role thing,' she said.

'A male, man, role thing,' Bryony repeated. 'I'm sure he'd be very flattered to hear that.'

'You know what I mean,' she said. 'Anyway, I could put in a good word for you with Jago.'

Polly had Bryony's full attention now. 'Tell me about him again.'

'Well,' Polly said, straightening a pile of books on the counter. 'He's tall. He's very tall. Too tall for Suffolk. He has to duck to get into our house.'

'I could go for tall,' Bryony said.

'He's got dark blond hair which is kind of messy in that way creative types have – as if they've got more to think about than their personal appearance.'

'Messy can be good,' Bryony said.

'And he's – well – he's really sweet with Archie,' Polly said with a smile, 'and that's probably the best thing I can say about anyone.'

Bryony narrowed her eyes at her sister. 'Are you sure you haven't got a thing for this guy yourself?'

'Of course I haven't,' Polly snapped.

'Because you sound sweet on him.'

'I am *not* sweet on him. I'm simply listing his attributes to my sister in the hope of making her a good match.'

Polly picked up an armful of books and took them to the shelves.

'How old is he?' Bryony asked.

'He told me he spent a year in America after graduating so that would make him about twenty-two, I think. Is that too young for you?'

'It's only six years younger than me,' Bryony pointed out. 'If he's mature, it shouldn't matter. Is he?'

'He seems sensible enough,' Polly said, finding homes for all of the books and turning her attention to plumping up the baby beanbags.

'And you're sure you're not – you know – interested yourself?'

Polly turned and glared at her sister. 'I really wish you'd stop–'

'Sorry!' Bryony said. 'I just want to make absolutely sure before I fall head over heels.' She reached up to the top shelf and took down a book and examined it as if she'd never seen it before. 'It would be nice, wouldn't it?'

Polly watched her sister for a moment. Today, she was wearing a long skirt in silver and purple and a purple velvet blouse and a long string of amber beads. Yet, for all her vibrant colour, there was a sadness that was never far from her.

'You miss him, don't you?' Polly said.

Bryony's head jerked up. 'Don't say it,' she said, replacing the book she'd taken down and returning to the till where she busied herself with some invoices.

'How long has it been?' Polly asked, thinking of the day that Ben

Stratton had left Castle Clare and had never returned.

'I can't remember,' Bryony said, not looking up, 'and I don't want to be reminded, okay?'

'Okay,' Polly said, feeling a great swell of love for her. 'It's good that you're not dwelling on the past. That's really healthy.'

'I know it is,' Bryony said in a kind of monotone.

'And it's good that you want to move on.'

'Yes.'

It was a kind of unspoken rule between them that conversations were not to be had about Mr Ben Stratton or Mr Sean Prior – the two men who had broken the Nightingale sisters' hearts. Enough tears had been shed over them in the past.

'Maybe Jago will be the one for you,' Polly said now.

'Who knows?' Bryony said, looking up at last. 'He might well be.'

Polly smiled at her. 'That's the spirit. Now, let's make a cup of tea and get to work on that oversized jammy dodger.'

It was half-past four and Polly couldn't keep the secret any longer.

'I've got a surprise for you tonight, Archie,' she said as she placed a plate of toast in front of him. 'So you're just having toast now and then something more substantial later.'

'What's the surprise?' he asked, his bright eyes looking up at her.

'Someone's coming round to see you.' She looked at the clock. 'In about an hour's time.'

'Who?'

Polly couldn't help smiling. 'Jago.'

'Really?'

'Really.'

'With his guitar?'

'I hope so,' she said.

'Am I having a lesson?'

'We'll have to see if you're good. I think he only teaches pupils who do all their homework and eat all their tea.'

Archie took an extra-big mouthful of toast.

'Don't eat *too* fast now,' Polly said with a little chuckle.

'I'm going to be the best pupil he's *ever* had!' Archie declared.

'Well, let's see how this first lesson goes. You might not like the guitar.'

'I'm going to love it, Mum!'

Polly couldn't help but be touched by her young son's enthusiasm and she had to admit that she was looking forward to the lesson herself.

After the tea things had been cleared away and they'd walked Dickens around the village, Archie was like a jack-in-the-box as he kept getting up from the sofa and crossing the room to peep out of the window.

'It's after half-past five,' he announced. 'He's late.'

Polly glanced at her watch. 'Sit down, Archie. You're making me all jittery.'

'Sorry,' he said, slumping down on the sofa.

'Can't you read your book or something whilst you're waiting?'

'I can't think about books, Mum,' he said. 'Not right now.'

She tried not to laugh at her son's earnestness and was mightily relieved when there was a knock at the door a moment later.

'Jago!' Archie said, leaping off the sofa and causing Dickens to bark heartily.

Polly followed him into the hallway, trying not to trip over the excited spaniel.

'Hey, Arch!' Jago said as the door was opened. He was carrying a guitar case and was wearing his big biker jacket.

'Come in,' Polly said.

'It's a cold night, isn't it?' he said, bending to stroke Dickens who was sniffing the guitar case.

'Come and warm up in the living room.' Polly led the way and the four of them were soon sitting down by the wood burner. Jago took his coat off and opened the guitar case, removing the beautiful wooden instrument.

'Wow!' Archie said. 'Can I hold it?'

'You'll have to if you want to play it,' Jago said.

'Is that full size?' Polly asked.

'Half-size,' Jago said. 'It's the one I learnt on.'

'So, how do you normally do things?' she asked.

'Whatever suits you really,' he said. 'Every house is different. At one place, I teach in the garage so as not to disturb anyone. Another house has its own music room.'

'Cool!' Archie said.

'It is cool, Arch,' Jago said. 'Imagine a whole room just for music.'

'So you're okay in here?' Polly said, suddenly feeling that their

65

modest living room wasn't up to the job.

'It's great,' he said.

'Can I stay and watch?' Polly asked. 'Just for a few minutes?'

'Sure,' he said.

Polly sat on a chair on the other side of the room. Dickens, who had been sitting at Jago's feet, refused to move. He wanted to be as close to the action as possible.

'Now, the first thing we want to think about, even before we pick up the guitar, is your posture,' Jago said to Archie. 'You know what posture is, right?'

'Yeah, sure – Mum's always telling me to sit up straight at the table.'

'Well, your mum's right. Posture is very important. We don't want you growing into a bent-backed beast, do we?'

Archie screwed up his nose and shook his head and sat up straight.

'So, now you're sitting right, we can pick up the guitar. See how it's got a lovely curve in the middle of its body? Well, that's going to sit over one of your legs. We'll go with your right leg for now, okay?'

'Okay,' Archie said, grabbing hold of the guitar as if it was the most precious thing he'd ever been given.

'See that big hole in the middle? That's the sound hole, and that's the bridge at the far end, and up this end are the keys which I'll tell you about later. Okay – your turn to tell me something. How many strings have we got on this guitar? Do you want to count them for me?'

Archie nodded enthusiastically and counted the strings, mouthing each number. 'Six,' he said.

'That's right,' Jago said. 'Give the top one a pluck.'

Archie did as he was told.

'What does that sound like?'

'Deep.'

'Yeah,' Jago said. 'It's a low note, isn't it? How about the one at the bottom?'

Archie plucked the bottom string. 'It's high.'

'Good,' Jago said. 'Both those strings are E, but we'll go through the names of the others later on.'

'It can't be as hard to learn as the piano,' Archie said.

Jago laughed. 'You might be surprised.'

Polly smiled. She liked the way Jago was around her son, making him feel at ease and asking him questions. As a fellow teacher, she could appreciate how Jago was involving Archie in his own learning rather than just talking *at* him like his first piano teacher had done. They'd had to get rid of Mr Crosby, she remembered. He'd simply barked instructions at Archie for a full hour and Archie had walked out of the living room looking completely crushed. But Jago was sweet and giving and Archie was responding well.

Polly watched for a moment longer before quietly slipping out of the room unnoticed. She felt she shouldn't intrude anymore, but should give them a little bit of privacy.

In the kitchen, she washed up and then took a couple of jacket potatoes out of the cupboard to prepare for tea. Placing them on the worktop, she paused and then returned to the cupboard and took a third potato out of the bag. It was the least she could do to thank Jago for his time with Archie.

For the next half an hour, she prepared tea, listening to the happy sound of voices and strumming coming from the living room. When the time was up, Archie came running into the kitchen.

'Mum, Mum!' he cried. 'I played a tune. Did you hear?'

'That was you?'

'Did you think it was Jago?'

'I did,' she said. 'I really did.'

'It was me, wasn't it, Jago?'

'It certainly was,' Jago said, popping his head into the kitchen, a grin as broad as her son's on his face.

'I'm impressed,' Polly said. 'I didn't think he'd be quite so advanced after just one lesson.'

'It was a nice simple open-stringed tune,' Jago said. 'I like to give them something that feels like proper playing. Keeps them interested.'

'Mr Crosby never kept me interested, did he, Mum?'

'No, he didn't,' Polly said, thinking about the awful piano teacher again.

'Well, I'm glad you enjoyed it, Arch,' Jago said.

'When are you coming again?' Archie looked first at Jago and then at his mother.

'What suits you?' she asked him.

'How about the weekend?' he said.

'But that's *ages* away!' Archie said.

'Jago has other pupils and other commitments,' Polly told her son.

'I suppose,' Archie said resignedly.

'If any free slots come up, you'll be the first to hear,' Jago said and Archie grinned.

'Would you like to stay for tea?' Polly asked.

'Yes, stay for tea, Jago!' Archie said.

'Oh, well that's very kind,' he said, coming into the kitchen properly.

'It's nothing fancy. Just a jacket potato and some green beans.'

'Green beans from our garden,' Archie said. 'The freezer's full of them.'

Jago laughed. 'Ours too. It was a good summer for them, wasn't it?'

'Too good,' Archie said. 'Mum kept giving me carrier bags of them to give away at school. It was really embarrassing.'

'Archie! You were helping other people out.'

'But nobody wanted them. *Every*body had their own,' he said.

'Well, I for one am a fan, so pile my plate high,' Jago said.

'She really will,' Archie said.

A moment later, all three of them were sitting around the small square table in the kitchen, tucking into their food.

'This is good,' Jago said. 'I always seem to be eating on the move. You know, a sandwich here or a hot dog there between lessons. It's really nice to sit down and enjoy a meal.'

'You should look after your digestion,' Polly said and then winced. How old did she sound? That was something her mother, Eleanor, would say. 'I mean, you should eat properly.' She sighed inwardly.

'I know and I do try,' he said. 'It's just easier not to sometimes.'

'You're young. You can get away with it, but it will catch up with you,' she said. Goodness, where was all this advice coming from? He'd think she was about a hundred years old. She'd be checking if he needed help with his washing next.

But he merely nodded and smiled like the polite young man he was.

'How are you getting on with the Thomas Hardy?' she asked him.

'Erm, I haven't actually started it yet.'

'Are you going to read it?' she asked.

'Of course. I've joined the book club to read,' he said.

'Good,' she said. Now she sounded like his teacher, she couldn't help thinking. She had to relax. She took a deep breath. 'Nice beans, huh?'

'Yeah,' Jago said. 'They sure are.'

Polly was aware that her son was watching them both, his eyes darting between them as they spoke.

'I like baked beans,' Archie said. 'With ketchup.'

'Archie eats a lot of ketchup,' Polly said.

'I do,' Archie confessed.

'I do too,' Jago said, and the two of them smiled at each other like old friends. Polly liked that.

When the meal was over, Jago started to clear the table.

'You don't have to do that,' Polly told him.

'It's the least I can do,' he said.

'Well, you can come again,' she said and then bit her lip.

'Can I?' he said and he winked at her.

'Yes – come to tea *every* day!' Archie said.

'Archie, I think it's time for your piano practice, isn't it?'

'Awww, Mum!' he groaned.

'If you want to continue with guitar lessons, you have to promise me to keep up with the piano. Go on. Twenty minutes – that's all.'

'But that's like *forever*!' he said, his shoulders slumping.

'Learning the piano will make playing the guitar much easier,' Jago told him.

'Will it?'

'It sure will,' Jago said.

Archie sighed. 'Okay then. See you, Jago.'

Jago raised his hand in a wave.

'Thanks for that,' Polly said once her son was out of the room.

'You're welcome.'

'Will the piano really help him with the guitar?' she asked.

'Well, physically, the guitar is one of the hardest instruments to learn but, as he's already learning one, that makes it a lot easier to learn another. It's kind of the same way with learning foreign languages, I think.'

'That's good to know.'

There was an awkward pause as both of them glanced at each other, but didn't quite know what to say.

'Thanks for tea,' he said.

'You're welcome.'

'Well, I'd better be off.' He nipped into the living room to retrieve his coat and guitar.

'Jago?' Polly said as he headed to the front door.

'Yes?'

'Listen,' she began, clearing her throat, 'before you go, can I ask you something?'

'Sure,' he said.

'It might seem a bit strange.'

'Now you've got me interested,' he said. 'What is it?'

'Well,' Polly began slowly, making sure that Archie was still engaged in his piano practice and wouldn't be eavesdropping, 'it's about my sister.'

'Your sister?' Jago asked.

Polly nodded. 'She's going through a difficult time at the moment.'

'I'm sorry to hear that.'

'Oh, it's nothing serious,' Polly said, 'just – you know – man trouble.'

'Right,' Jago said warily.

'And I thought – I wondered – if you could help. If you might be interested.'

Jago frowned and then realisation seemed to dawn on him.

'You want me to go out with your sister?'

'You have a girlfriend already?' Polly asked.

'Erm, no,' Jago said with a tiny grin, 'but what makes you think I'm looking for one?'

'Well – I thought you might–'

'It's okay,' he said. 'It's nice of you to think of me.'

'Bryony's really lovely,' Polly said quickly.

'Is she like you?' Jago asked.

'Not really,' Polly said.

'You mean you're *not* lovely?'

Polly looked confused.

'I'm teasing!'

'Oh, right,' she said. 'Well, we're different. 'I mean, we look a bit alike. You know, hair and eyes – that sort of thing. But she's kind of a free spirit.'

'And you're not?'

Polly shook her head. 'I'm the hemmed-in one.'

'Hemmed in?'

'I know my limitations.'

'That's a very interesting thing to say,' Jago said.

'Look, I'll give you her number. Ring her. Or not.' She returned to the kitchen followed by Jago and scribbled her sister's number down on the pad on the dresser and tore the sheet out for him. 'She works in the children's book shop in Castle Clare.'

Jago nodded. 'Maybe I'll swing by,' he said.

'You should.'

He held her gaze for a moment. 'Have you match-made for your sister before?'

'Once or twice,' she said.

'Yeah? And how did it work out?'

'Terrible,' she said and they both laughed.

'I'll bear that in mind,' he said, folding the piece of paper with Bryony's number on and putting it in his jacket pocket.

CHAPTER 9

'Here, Callie – sniff this!'

Callie looked up from an illustrated copy of *Pride and Prejudice* she'd found in Sam's shop. She thought that Mr Darcy looked rather foppish and so wasn't going to be adding this particular edition to her collection.

'What is it?' she asked as Sam approached her with a large hardback book about gardening.

'Take a good long sniff,' he said, making Callie laugh. He sounded like some kind of addict who was trying to corrupt her too. Luckily, though, she was already corrupted when it came to the secretive world of book-sniffing.

Callie bent her head and took a little sniff.

'Go on – inhale properly!' Sam said.

This time, she took a good long breath like a true connoisseur.

'Good?' he asked her.

'Very good,' she said. 'It's kind of like an autumn day which is ever so slightly damp around the edges. It's almost earthy.'

Sam nodded. 'I thought that too. It's just come in.'

'Are you going to sell it?'

'That's generally the plan with books that come in,' he said.

'Ah, but I know you smuggle a good proportion upstairs to your own private collection.'

'It has been known,' he said with a chuckle. 'Perks of the job.'

Callie returned the copy of *Pride and Prejudice* she was still holding to Sam. 'I should get on. I've still got to go shopping.'

'Don't go yet,' Sam said, putting his arms around her. 'I thought you were going to keep me company for a bit.'

'I should be working.'

'Work *later*.' He bent his head to kiss her and Callie was just beginning to see the sense in working a lot later than she'd planned when the shop bell sounded and in walked Hortense Digger.

'Honey, good to see you,' Sam said as he and Callie sprang apart.

'Oh, will you look at you two lovebirds!' she said, her pink-lipsticked mouth rising in a smile. 'All passionate like Sergeant Troy and Bathsheba Everdene.'

'I hope not *quite* like them,' Sam said.

'No spoilers!' Honey said, flapping her hands in the air in panic. 'I've not finished the book yet!'

'My lips are sealed,' he said. 'Can I help you with anything, Honey?'

'Actually, you might well be able to,' she said. 'I spotted a book when we were here the night of the book club and I'm hoping you still have it.'

Callie watched as Sam and Honey walked through to the back room. Today, Honey was wearing a long cerise raincoat and a turquoise beret with a large daisy brooch pinned to it. Callie wondered where Honey did her shopping because she'd never seen anything like Honey's ensembles for sale in Castle Clare.

As she listened to Sam and Honey's voices drifting in from the back room, Callie perused the shelves some more. How she loved coming to Sam's shop, she thought. Not only had she fallen in love with the shop itself that very first time she'd opened its green-painted door back in September and heard the merry tinkle of the old-fashioned bell, but she'd fallen madly in love with the owner too.

How lucky she felt to have found this place. It was as if some unseen force – fate, Thomas Hardy would say – had led her here, taking her by the hand after her marriage to Piers had fallen apart and had welcomed her to the town of Castle Clare and to the bookshop where she would fall in love.

How she loved having this place to come to on a wet, dreary winter's day when the writing wasn't quite going at the pace she'd like. A quick drive down the country lanes, a kiss from Sam and a peruse around the shelves was often enough to kick-start her creativity.

She was just musing on this further when Honey and Sam appeared.

'Did you find the book you wanted?' Callie asked.

'I did indeed,' Honey said, holding it out for Callie to see. '*Sweet Treats that will Wow the Crowd*,' she read.

'I used to have a copy, but a naughty neighbour borrowed it and never gave it back. There's a recipe in here I'm going to bake for the next book club meeting. It'll knock the spots off anything Antonia will bake,' she said with a little giggle, her painted pink cheeks flushing even pinker.

'I detect some rivalry between you two,' Sam said.

'All good and healthy, I assure you,' Honey said. 'Well, it is on my side at least.'

Sam ran the book through the till and popped it into a paper bag before handing it to Honey.

'I look forward to sampling the goods,' he said.

'They will be second to none,' she said. 'Right, I'll leave you two lovebirds. I've got an appointment at the hairdressers although I don't know why I bother in this dreadful winter weather. I seem to spend all my time wearing a dreary hat!'

'It's far from dreary,' Callie said.

'Sweet of you, Callie darling!' Honey said, waving to them as she adjusted the far-from-dreary hat and left the shop.

'Alone at last,' Sam said, coming round from behind the till and wrapping his arms around Callie.

'Do you think we should check the street just in case anybody else is due to pop in?'

'Let them catch us,' he said. 'What have we got to hide?'

Callie smiled, liking his unapologetic attitude.

'So,' he began, 'anything you want to tell me?'

'What do you mean?' she asked.

'I mean, you still haven't yet told me how your trip to your publisher went.'

'But I rang you as soon as I got home.'

Sam nodded. 'Yes you did,' he said, 'and you said absolutely nothing.'

'I told you it was all fine.'

'And I have the feeling you're holding out on me, Callie Logan. What aren't you telling me?'

The intensity of his gaze made her feel nervous. She'd never met a man who looked at her in quite the way that Sam did – so full of compassion and understanding. It was a little unnerving.

'I don't know what you want to know.'

'I think you do.'

'It really wasn't that interesting a meeting. I was in and out in no time,' she said evasively.

'So you didn't run into Piers, then?'

'Why would I run into Piers?'

'Because, from what I know of things, he's still very much interested in you and would more than likely get himself involved in this new book of yours.'

Callie swallowed hard.

'Callie?'

'Okay, okay. I saw Piers. He made it his business to be there.'

'As I knew he would,' Sam said. 'Why didn't you tell me?'

'Because I thought you'd get upset.'

'I'm not going to get upset. Not unless you're upset.'

'Well, I'm not upset. I was mad, but I wasn't upset.'

'What were you mad about?' Sam asked.

'The way he assumed I'd just go along with whatever he suggested. That I'd be happy with him being my editor. I told him that I wanted a new editor.'

'And what did he say?'

'He said that would be arranged, but I had to threaten to pay the advance back first.'

'Good for you,' Sam said. 'So, is that all?'

'What do you mean?'

'Is that all he said to you?' Sam placed a finger under Callie's chin and tipped her head up so that she couldn't avoid eye contact.

'He said he regrets letting me go,' Callie whispered.

'Of course he does,' Sam said. 'He'd be a fool not to see what he let slip through his fingers. Why didn't you tell me he said that?'

Callie looked into Sam's warm brown eyes that were filled with such tenderness. 'I didn't want to worry you.'

He bent and kissed her forehead. 'Hey, I'm a big boy, I can take it!'

She gave a nervous laugh.

'And I want you to be honest with me, Callie, and you can't be honest if you're going to hide things from me.'

'I'm sorry,' she said softly. 'I didn't tell you because I didn't want to upset you and now I have by not telling you!'

'It's okay,' he told her. 'You know, I'd tell you if Emma rang and said she'd made a huge mistake in walking out on me and all my dusty old books.'

Callie smiled at that.

'Of course, that's never going to happen, but you'd be the first person I'd tell if she ever did make that call.'

'I know,' Callie said and they kissed. 'How did I get so lucky finding you?'

'It wasn't luck,' he said. 'It was fate.'

'Like in Thomas Hardy?'

'Oh, no. Ours was definitely the *good* kind of fate.'

It was a cold and wet Sunday in January and there was a big fire roaring in the living room at Campion House. Frank Nightingale had filled the log basket that morning and the family were sitting around the fire whilst the roast cooked for lunch. Eleanor had switched two lamps on to help chase the winter blues away and the Christmas poinsettia plant, which hadn't lasted nearly as long as Eleanor had expected, had now been composted and replaced with some beautiful evergreens which Frank had collected from the garden.

In one of the rare moments between peeling, parboiling, roasting, setting the table and sorting out drinks for everyone, Eleanor was sitting in her favourite armchair, cosily ensconced by a heap of cushions as she enjoyed a pre-lunch glass of wine. Bryony was taking care of dessert and there was nothing more to do for a blissful half an hour.

'Grandma,' Archie said from his home on the floor where he'd been lying on his stomach reading a comic.

'Yes, Archie?'

'Mum's letting me have guitar lessons.'

'Really?' Eleanor looked across the room at Polly who was sitting on the sofa flipping through a copy of *The Bookseller*.

'With Jago,' Archie continued. 'He's really cool. He's got long hair and wears huge boots.'

'Sounds like a biker,' Josh said from the sofa next to Polly.

'He's got a motorbike,' Archie said. 'I'm going to ride it.'

'Oh, no you're not,' Polly said. 'Isn't it enough that I'm letting you have guitar lessons?'

'Not really,' he said, causing a ripple of laughter around the room.

'So who's this Jago, then?' Eleanor asked, watching her eldest daughter carefully.

Polly shrugged. 'He's Maureen Solomon's son from across the road.'

'The doctor's receptionist?'

'That's right.'

'I've always liked her,' Eleanor said. 'She makes time for people. What's her son like? I mean other than his long hair and biker boots?'

'He's nice,' Polly said. 'He's a good teacher, isn't he, Archie?'

'He's *really* good. I can play the guitar already and I've only had two lessons.'

'You'll have to play something for us next Sunday, then,' Grandpa Joe said.

'Archie's not got his own guitar yet,' Polly said.

'Are you getting him one?' Frank asked.

'I'm not sure,' Polly said. 'Let's see how he does over the next couple of months.'

'But I'd *love* my own guitar, Mum!'

'We'll see,' Polly said.

It was then that the front doorbell sounded and Brontë, Hardy and Dickens, the three Nightingale dogs, tore down the hallway to a volley of excited barks.

'It's Sam and Callie!' Lara said, springing up from the other sofa. Eleanor smiled at her youngest daughter's enthusiasm as she left the room in a blur of wild curly hair. It was good to have Lara back for the weekend from university and she'd really taken a shine to Callie and a lovely friendship was blossoming between the two of them. How wonderful that was, Eleanor thought, to see new friendships being formed under one's own roof.

'Hey, everyone!' Sam called from the hallway after Lara had let them in.

'We're through here, son,' Frank called back and Sam, Callie and Lara entered the living room together. Everyone was on their feet to give the new couple a hug, all except Grandma Nell whose only concession to their arrival was to look up from the socks she was knitting.

Polly used the opportunity of Sam and Callie arriving to escape into the kitchen where she knew Bryony was.

'Hey,' her sister said as she walked in. 'Did you talk to Mr Guitar Player?'

Polly nodded. 'I did.'

'And?' Bryony said.

Polly looked behind her, checking that nobody was about to burst into the kitchen. Finding a private place at Campion House was about as difficult as finding a room without a book in it.

'I gave him your number. Numbers. He has your home, your mobile and the shop. I was hoping he'd ring you straightaway, but he didn't say anything when he came round for Archie's second guitar lesson yesterday and I didn't want to sound desperate by pushing things. But I'm sure he'll call you. I guess he's just busy with his pupils and his band which he's getting back together.'

'What's going on in here?' Josh asked, walking into the kitchen.

'Just girl stuff,' Bryony said.

'That must mean you're talking about men,' he said, rolling his eyes as he got a couple of wine glasses out of the cupboard.

'You'd love to think that, wouldn't you?' Bryony said. 'You'd love to imagine that we have nothing better to do than stand around and talk about men all the time.'

'Oh, so I'm right, am I?' Josh said, filling the glasses with white wine before leaving.

'Do brothers ever get any less annoying as you grow up?' Bryony said, turning to Polly.

'Nope,' she said.

'I thought not,' Bryony said, sighing in defeat.

As a pale sun began to show its face from behind the great bank of grey cloud that had been hanging over Wintermarsh all day, it was deemed a perfect afternoon to walk off the Sunday lunch. What was not quite so perfect was the battle which ensued in the boot room at the back of the house as the entire Nightingale family jostled and elbowed each other in an attempt to secure the best pair of wellington boots. There was a vast array in different colours and different stages of decrepitude and nobody could ever agree on which pair belonged to whom.

'Josh – they're mine!' Lara declared.

'You're kidding, right? Those horrible pink things over there are yours.'

'I've never worn pink wellies in my life!' Lara cried in outrage. 'Anyway, they've got a big split across the toe. I'll get soaked if I wear them.'

'Wear those burgundy ones,' Eleanor said.

'But they're not even a pair, remember?' Bryony said. 'The left one mysteriously went missing and was then teamed with a purple one that Brontë found in the pond.'

'I don't want it if it's been in the pond,' Lara said, wrinkling her pierced nose in disgust.

'It might have frogspawn in it!' Archie said.

'Then you'll have to hobble around the countryside in one boot,' Josh said, instantly acquiring an elbow in his ribs.

Somehow, the Nightingales managed to leave the house with their two spaniels and pointer in tow.

Frank, Josh and Lara led the way, setting a cracking pace which nobody else bothered to keep up with. Sam and Callie were next, walking hand in hand, and they were followed by Archie who was splashing in every single puddle he passed, Dickens on a lead beside him. Eleanor, Polly and Bryony watched from behind and Grandpa Joe and Grandma Nell followed them at a more leisurely pace.

'This Jago,' Eleanor began as they walked out into an open field, linking arms with Polly, 'Archie sounds very taken with him. Maybe you should invite him to Sunday lunch.'

Bryony glanced around at Polly.

'What is it?' Eleanor asked. 'Is there something you aren't telling me?'

'No, of course not, Mum,' Polly said a little too quickly to be convincing.

'Have you coloured your hair, Mum?' Bryony asked. 'It looks really lovely in the sun.'

'No, I haven't coloured my hair. Come on, tell me what's going on.'

'Nothing's going on,' Bryony insisted.

'Bryony, love, I always know that something's going on with you because you always try to change the subject when I'm getting close. So, I'm guessing that whatever it is that you two have got cooking is related to this Jago person. Am I right?'

Polly heaved out a sigh. 'You're right,' she said, receiving an angry glare from Bryony. Polly simple shrugged as if to say, what could I do, which made her mum smile. There was never any point in trying to hide something from her and the girls knew that.

'Okay,' Eleanor said. 'Are you going to fill me in?'

'Archie!' Polly suddenly shouted. 'Keep Dickens away from that big puddle. We can let him off the lead once we're around the corner.' She shook her head. 'I sometimes wonder if I should still have Archie on a lead.'

'Don't you try to change the subject too,' Eleanor said. 'Now, what's going on with this guitar chap?'

'You might as well tell her,' Bryony told Polly. 'She'll wiggle it out of us one way or another.'

'I certainly will,' Eleanor said.

'There's not much to tell, really,' Polly said. 'I've given Jago Bryony's number and she might be going out on a date with him.'

'Might be?' Eleanor said.

'He hasn't rung yet,' Bryony said.

Eleanor frowned. 'So, you're match-making for your sister?' she said to Polly.

'I just think he's a nice young man,' Polly said.

'And I'm fed up of dating websites,' Bryony said.

'I really do wish you'd stop using those,' Eleanor told her daughter.

'I think I will,' she said.

'But aren't you seeing Colin the baker?'

'No, Mum, I'm not.'

'Oh, I thought you were.'

'She isn't officially,' Polly said, 'but he thinks she is.'

'That's sounds like an awful muddle,' Eleanor said.

'Yes,' Polly agreed, 'and one she needs to sort out.'

Bryony shook her head. 'What is this? Beat up Bryony Day?'

'Of course it isn't, darling,' Eleanor said. 'I'm just trying to get an idea of what's going on. So, tell me more about this Jago.'

'Polly says he's really cute,' Bryony said.

'I didn't say that!'

'Well, not in so many words,' Bryony said.

'You don't mind long hair, then?' Eleanor asked.

'As long as it's not longer than mine,' Bryony said. 'That would just be weird.'

'I remember when your father used to have his hair long in the seventies. I loved it.'

'Sounds horrible, Mum!' Bryony said.

Eleanor laughed. 'It was very manly.'

'What was very manly?' Sam asked.

'Have you been eavesdropping on us?'

'No,' Sam said, 'but I couldn't help overhearing that last bit.'

'We were talking about your father's long hair,' Eleanor said, raising her voice so that Frank would hear. He did and he stopped.

'I've never had long hair,' he said.

'You did too!' Eleanor said. 'You let it grow really long. I've got photos of that holiday in the campervan down in Cornwall.'

'Oh, right,' Frank said, obviously remembering.

'Dad with long hair?' Josh said.

'I'm going to grow my hair long,' Archie said as he unclipped Dickens's lead, 'so it's just like Jago's.'

'Oh, no you're not,' Polly said and everybody laughed just as Dickens did a flying jump over a stile and landed smack bang in the middle of a gloriously muddy puddle.

That night in bed, Polly couldn't help wondering if she'd made a terrible mistake in trying to match-make Bryony and Jago. Her mother had taken her to one side after they'd returned from their walk and had asked her how much she knew about the young man. Bryony, Eleanor had warned, was in a vulnerable position after all the recent let-downs and Eleanor was understandably concerned.

Jago, though, seemed like a really decent young man. He was certainly the nicest she'd met in a long time, but how sure could you be of anyone? She was simply trying to help her sister out and, if it all went wrong, then it wouldn't be the end of the world, would it? But, even more worrying than things going wrong was what if things went right? How would she feel about that?

Polly couldn't help acknowledging that there was a part of her that felt a little proprietorial when it came to Jago and she was beginning to wonder how she'd really feel if Jago and Bryony became a couple.

CHAPTER 10

It was Monday morning when Jago took the little slip of paper out of his jacket pocket and unfolded it. Since seeing Polly and Archie on Saturday, he'd been run off his feet with other pupils and band stuff and he'd hardly had time to think about Bryony Nightingale, but here he was now, looking down at Polly's neatly written note with the phone numbers staring back up at him: coaxing him, teasing him.

He had to admit to being curious about Polly's sister and wondered what had made Polly think that Bryony was right for him, and so he'd waited for his mum to leave for work and then he'd showered, shaved and breakfasted before donning his biking gear and heading into Castle Clare.

It was a beastly morning – just the sort of Monday that turns employees into wild exaggerators who suddenly find that their little sniffle of a cold is actually flu and they'd better go back to bed immediately, just to be on the safe side. It was also the sort of slick, wet morning in which Jago took no joy in riding his bike. Still, he thought as he put his helmet on, it was a better option than the bus which seemed to amble around every single village in a fifty-mile radius before reaching its destination.

The ride into town wasn't too bad and Jago parked his bike outside the children's bookshop and took off his helmet. He hadn't ever really looked at the shop properly before, but he did now, admiring its bow window and pretty door painted in a jolly yellow. It was like something out of a Beatrix Potter illustration and must be a magnet for children, he thought.

Leaving his bike, he walked to the door, the shop bell tinkling above his head as he opened it, giving him just enough of a warning to miss crashing into it.

'Hi,' he said as he entered the shop. A dark-haired woman was standing on a stool reaching up to the top shelf, but it was obvious that, even on the stool, she was struggling.

'You want a hand with that?' he asked, coming forward and taking the book from her. 'Where do you want it?'

'Oh, in between *Mermaid Cove* and *Oscar's Night*.' She turned to face him and almost toppled off the little stool. 'Jago?'

He caught hold of her shoulders as she steadied herself. She pushed her dark curls away from her face revealing the fact that she was beautiful.

'Hi,' he said again. 'Bryony?'

'Yes,' she said, shaking the hand he offered her as she jumped off the stool. 'Sorry, I don't usually make a habit of falling onto customers.'

'That's good to know,' he said, 'only I'm not really a customer, am I?'

'No,' she said, her face flooding with colour. 'I don't suppose you are unless you have a secret love of children's books. Many adults do you know. I think a lot of my customers choose the books that they want to read and simply use their children as an excuse.'

Jago smiled at this.

'Sorry, I'm gabbling, aren't I? I always gabble when I'm nervous. Can I get you a cup of tea?'

'Okay,' he said and watched as she scuttled into a room at the back of the shop. 'Can I help?

'How do you like it?'

'My tea?' he asked, following her into the stock room where there was a tiny sink and a kettle. 'Black, no sugar.'

'That's a serious cup of tea.'

'I guess,' he said.

'You're going to make me nervous if you watch me.'

'Will I?'

'Yes. Go and poke around the books or something,' she told him.

'Okay,' Jago said, amused at how very honest and direct this woman was.

He turned and walked back into the shop, his eyes scanning the shelves of candy-coloured books. Why were children's books so much more beautiful than adult books, he wondered? They were all so lovely to look at and very enticing, making the fingers itch to reach out and pull them down from the shelves.

'How are you getting on?' Bryony asked a moment later as she came out with the two teas.

'Good,' he said.

'Seen anything you like?'

Jago smiled, 'I think so,' he said and watched as Bryony blushed.

'Sorry,' he added quickly.

'Look, I hope you don't feel awkward about this,' she said.

'Why should I feel awkward?'

'This whole business of being set up.'

'People have to meet somehow,' he said.

'That's a good way of looking at it.'

'And your sister's as good a judge of character as any, isn't she?'

'Oh, yes,' Bryony said.

'Then at least we're not likely to bore each other to death.'

'She told you about the baked beans guy, then?'

'What?'

'Nothing,' Bryony said, shaking her head and taking a sip of tea.

Jago took a sip of his own, wondering what to say next as he took in the vivid green and red striped dress Bryony was wearing, hung with a metal belt and teamed with a pair of bulky biker-style boots. She was wearing large gold hoops in her ears and a scarlet ribbon in her hair. He could honestly say that he'd never seen anyone quite as striking as Bryony before.

'So,' he said at last, 'what do you want to do about this?'

'I suppose we should go out,' she said.

Again, he liked her directness. That always made things so much easier in life, didn't it?

'Good,' he said. 'Any ideas?'

'You're musical, right?'

'Right. You want to do something musical?'

She nodded. 'Well, not a guitar lesson or anything obviously.'

'Obviously,' he said with a grin. 'Listen, my band's playing at a pub near Sudbury on Friday night if you're interested.

'You'll be playing?'

'And singing.'

'Oh, wow,' Bryony said.

'You're up for it?'

She nodded. 'I'd love to see you. It. The band.'

'Great!' he said. 'The only thing is, I don't have a car.'

'Oh, well, I do,' Bryony said. 'Do you need a lift?'

'I've got my bike,' he said.

'But isn't that silly us both travelling there separately?'

'Well, you probably won't want to hang around whilst we set up and pack away.'

'Won't I?' she said.

'Will you?' Jago asked, surprised.

She nodded again and he laughed.

'All right. Do you want to pick me up at six on Friday? That'll give us time to get there, have a bite to eat and set up. I'm opposite Polly's house – 7 Church Green.'

'Okay,' she said.

'You don't mind driving?'

'Of course not.'

'Great.'

They smiled at each other and Jago raised a hand as he made to leave the shop. 'I'll see you then.'

'See you,' Bryony said.

As soon as Jago had left, Bryony turned round the hand-painted sign on the yellow shop door which read *Back in a mo* and locked it. She crossed the road and opened the green door into Sam's shop.

'Sam?' she called. There weren't any customers in the front room and so she took a chance that there weren't any in the back room either. 'Get in here – quickly!'

'Bry?' His voice reached her before he did. 'What if I'd had someone in the back there?' he said as he appeared.

'What, like Callie?' Bryony said with a teasing grin.

'No, like a customer.'

'But you didn't.'

He shook his head.

'I wanted to tell you who's just been in my shop.'

'Go on then,' he said. She paused, loving the look of rapt attention on Sam's face. 'Come on – I haven't got all day!'

'Yes you have,' she said. 'It's a cold wet day in January and nobody's got any money to spend after Christmas.'

'Great – rub it in, why don't you?'

'So there's nothing to do but make your sister a cup of tea and settle down for a gossip, eh?'

'Shouldn't you be manning your own shop?'

'No I shouldn't,' she said, turning Sam around by the shoulders and pushing him into the back room.

A couple of minutes later, tea served with a plate of coconut cookies, they sat down on the sofa together.

'I drink too much tea,' Bryony said, remembering the cup she'd just had with Jago.

'Occupational hazard,' Sam said. 'We get through gallons of the stuff here especially in winter. Staves off the cold.'

'It does.'

'You didn't come here to talk about tea, did you?'

Bryony shook her head. 'You know Jago?'

'Jago Solomon?'

'I don't think there are any more Jagos near Castle Clare, are there?'

'I know him,' Sam said. 'He's part of the book club.'

'Is he?'

'Which, as a Nightingale, you really should be a part of too, by the way.'

'You don't need me – you've got Polly.'

'That's not the point,' Sam said. 'You should make an effort and come and support it instead of spending all your evenings surfing internet sites for weirdos.'

'Is that what Mum's been saying?'

'No,' Sam said. 'It's what I'm saying.'

'Well, maybe I won't need to go out with any weirdos anymore.'

'You're seeing Jago?'

'We might be going out,' she said.

'Really?'

'Don't sound so surprised! I'm not a completely hopeless case yet.'

'I didn't mean that,' Sam said. 'It's just—'

'What?'

'It's funny.'

'What's funny?'

'I thought there was something going on between him and Polly. They kept swapping these little glances at book club.'

'Yeah? Well, she told me she's not even *remotely* interested in seeing anyone. You know how she feels.'

Sam nodded. 'So how did this happen between you and Jago?'

'Polly set it up actually.'

'She did?'

'Sisters are doing it for themselves,' Bryony said.

'They certainly are. You'll have to set up your own dating website.'

'Don't talk to me about those,' she said. 'I've had my fill of them over the past few months.'

'Good,' Sam said. 'I'd be happier if I knew you'd stopped using them altogether although I'd miss your stories about your bizarre dates, I have to say.'

'Not everyone's as lucky as you, Sam.'

'Me – *lucky*?'

'Yes, *you*! To have someone as wonderful as Callie just walk right into your shop and fall in love with you.'

Sam grinned. 'Yes, that was pretty lucky,' he said, 'but I had to get through an Emma before I got to a Callie.'

'True,' Bryony said. 'And I've had to get through a Ben–' she stopped and cleared her throat. She wasn't going to go there. She wasn't even going to give him headspace. 'Anyway, Jago–'

'Yes,' Sam said, equally up for a change of subject, it seemed.

'Could be good,' she said.

'You'll let me know how it goes?'

'We're going out on Friday night. His band's playing at a pub.'

'Make sure you've got me on speed dial if you need rescuing.'

'Oh, Sam! I don't need rescuing anymore, okay? I'm a big girl now.'

'Yeah, well, you'll always be my little sister.' He gave her a smile which warmed her heart. One thing you could always count on was Sam to look out for you.

'Listen, I'd better get back to the shop,' she said, grabbing a coconut cookie.

'Okay,' Sam said, getting up from the sofa with her. 'Back to the grind.'

'Yes, the grind of an empty shop on a wet winter's day.'

'I don't mind an empty shop,' he confessed.

'I know,' she said. 'You'd be quite happy to have the shop all to yourself, wouldn't you?'

'Until I remember the bills stacking up.'

'Whenever I think of bills, I pick up a novel immediately and stick my nose right in it,' Bryony said.

'Isn't that like burying your head in the sand?'

'A bit, but it's a much more pleasant experience.'

Polly was parking the Land Rover when Archie cried out.

'Jago!'

She turned to see Jago on his motorbike turning into the road and watched as he pulled over and took his helmet off to say hello.

'Careful of the road, Archie,' she said as her son unbuckled his belt quickly.

'Yes, Mum,' he said as they both got out of the car together.

'Hello there, Arch,' Jago said as he came across the road to greet them. 'How are you getting on with that little tune we were learning?'

'Okay,' Archie said, 'but my fingers keep tripping over each other.'

Jago and Polly exchanged a smile.

'My fingers never stop tripping over each other,' Jago said.

'You don't make mistakes,' Archie said. 'You can't. You're a teacher.'

He laughed. 'I'm a musician first,' he said, 'and musicians make mistakes all the time. It's part of how we learn.'

'Is it?'

'You should never stop learning, Arch,' he said. 'No matter how old you get.'

'You mean I have to go to school *forever*?'

'Not *school* school,' Jago said.

'Oh, phew!'

'But you must always push yourself and learn new things.'

'I don't mind that if it's cool things like football and the guitar.'

'Good.' Jago turned to look at Polly, 'I went to see Bryony this morning.'

'Oh?'

'We're heading out together on Friday.'

'That's great,' Polly said, swallowing hard.

'She seems nice.'

'She is,' Polly said, 'although I may be biased.'

'I think we'll have a good time.'

Archie was watching the two of them. 'Is he talking about Aunt Bryony?'

'Yes,' Polly said.

'She is nice,' Archie confirmed, nodding his head.

'I agree,' Jago said.

Polly cleared her throat, suddenly feeling awkward.

'Hey,' Jago said, 'I've had a cancellation tonight if you want me to come over.'

'Can he, Mum?' Archie asked.

'Haven't you got an awful lot of homework, Archie? Mrs Brancaster always sets you loads on a Monday.'

'I can get it done,' he said, a huge grin on his face.

'Well, if you're sure.'

Archie nodded enthusiastically.

'And if *you're* sure, Jago,' she said.

'Sure I'm sure,' he said.

'He's sure, Mum.'

Polly shrugged. 'Okay then.'

'Brilliant!' Archie said.

'Run on inside, Archie. It's cold out here.' Polly gave him the house key.

'See you later, Jago.'

'Will do.'

Polly waited until her son was inside before she turned to Jago again. 'Are you really sure you want to spend your free time teaching Archie the guitar when we can't pay you?'

'I've told you – it's not about the money.'

'I know,' she said, 'but I can't help feeling bad about not paying you.'

'Please don't. I really like it and–'

'Why don't you stay for tea?' Polly blurted, the idea suddenly coming to her. 'It would make me feel better about not paying you.'

'Really?'

She nodded.

'Okay, great. How would six o'clock suit you?'

'Fine,' she said.

'I'll see you later, then.'

She watched as he put his helmet back on and drove his bike the short distance to his home, waving as he arrived. She waved back.

Promptly at six, Jago arrived holding two guitars. Archie, who'd been hanging around the kitchen and getting under Polly's feet, tore to open the door, crying, 'He's here!'

She pretty much left the two of them to it, returning to the kitchen where she made a start on tea. It was a nice habit to get into, she thought, preparing tea for three again. She'd missed that and, for months after Sean's disappearance, she had cooked far more food than she and Archie could manage on their own. It had been a hard habit to break. Now, as she looked at the pasta boiling in the pan, she worried that she'd not done enough. Maybe she should cook an extra pepper and onion, just to be on the safe side.

When the lesson was finished, Archie ran into the kitchen.

'Slow down!' Polly warned him. Her son seemed to do a lot of running when Jago was around.

'Did you hear me?' he asked. 'Did you hear what I played?'

'It was very nice,' Polly said, having been half-aware of the strumming from the living room as she'd stood at the cooker.

'I'm getting better, aren't I?' Archie said.

'Of course,' Jago said as he entered the kitchen. 'You're learning something new with each lesson.'

Polly turned and smiled at him. 'Have a seat.'

'Thanks,' he said as Polly served the food.

'I hope pasta's okay?'

'It looks great.'

'I want twice as much to eat, Mum,' Archie announced.

'Why?' Polly asked.

'Because I want to be as big as Jago when I grow up.'

Polly smiled and Jago laughed.

'I'll make sure you're well-fed,' Polly said. 'Don't worry about that.'

They ate in silence for a few moments, but Polly was aware that Archie was watching Jago's every move. How he must miss having a father, she thought, feeling awful that life had thrown her young boy such a cruel curveball. But then she wondered if Archie would give admiring looks to his own father if he was here. Sean had been – what was the word – *reserved*. He had never been the kind of father to laugh and joke around with his son. His role had been more of a disciplinarian if she was honest. He'd shown Archie the boundaries, taught him things, monitored his behaviour, that sort of thing. But she couldn't actually remember her husband and son just playing together. Of course, Archie had been so young at the time and maybe their relationship would have changed. It was impossible to know now.

'You look thoughtful,' Jago said.

'Do I?' She looked up, a little startled at being caught. 'It's nothing.'

'Mum thinks a lot,' Archie said, surprising her.

'Do I?'

Archie nodded. 'You're always looking out of windows or staring into nothing.'

'No I'm not,' she said, genuinely shocked at her son's observation and quite determined to quash it.

'She is,' Archie told Jago. 'I think she misses Dad.'

Polly swallowed hard. 'Eat your tea, Archie,' she said. 'You'll never get as big as Jago if you spend mealtimes talking.'

He looked up at her and there was something mutinous in his expression. Polly held her breath, willing him not to say anything more and, thankfully, he didn't.

'Well, that was great,' Jago said a few minutes later as he finished his plate of pasta.

'Don't go,' Archie said as Jago made to leave the table.

'I can't bother you all evening,' he said.

'Why not? We never do anything.'

'Archie!' Polly said, a blush colouring her face.

Jago laughed. 'I'm sure your mum's got plenty to do without me hanging around.' He looked at her as if for confirmation.

'She hasn't,' Archie said. 'She'll just stick her head in a book or something boring.'

'Archie Prior – you are being very cheeky this evening!'

'But it's true!'

'Whether something's true or not doesn't mean you go and blurt it to some stranger.'

'But Jago's not a stranger,' Archie said.

'Sorry,' Polly said, 'I didn't mean any offence.'

'None taken,' Jago said.

'Well, maybe you'd like to stay for a cup of tea?' Polly said.

'Make him a cup of tea, Mum,' Archie said. 'We'll be in the living room.'

Polly watched in amazement as Archie grabbed hold of Jago's hand and led him out of the kitchen. There was nothing else to do but to make the tea and go and join them.

'Hope you don't mind,' Jago said as Polly entered the room with the tea and saw him looking through her and Sean's CD collection. 'I'm always fascinated to see what music people listen too.'

'Oh, they're mostly Sean's,' she said. 'We don't really listen to many of them.'

'No?'

She shook her head.

'But there's some pretty good stuff in here.'

'Is there?' she asked, watching as he pulled a CD from the rack and held it out to her. 'I don't know that one.'

'It's Shostakovich,' he said.

'Right.'

He grinned. 'You've really not listened to it?'

'That's right,' she told him.

'Well, we'll have to remedy that.' He looked around the room for a CD player.

'It's upstairs,' Polly told him. 'As I said, we don't listen to much music.'

'But Archie's got to listen to music if he's expected to play it,' Jago said.

'Oh, he listens to his own thing in his room,' Polly said.

'But not classical, I'm betting?'

'Not for a while. Not since Sean—'

'Dad used to play that sort of music really loud,' Archie said. 'It used to scare me.'

Polly caught Jago's eye. 'So we don't really play it anymore.'

He nodded. 'Okay,' he said, 'but will you let me play this for you now?'

Polly took the CD from him and looked at it. It seemed harmless enough. 'All right,' she said. 'I'll get the player.'

A few moments later, CD player plugged in, Jago popped the disc inside.

'This is called Waltz Number 2,' Jago announced as he hit the play button and the strange, rich music filled the room.

Polly could feel Jago's eyes upon her as she listened to the piece for the first time. She, in turn, looked at Archie who was looking back at Jago as if for guidance. It was as if the young boy wasn't going to make his mind up about the Russian noise until Jago said something first.

When the piece ended, Jago cleared his throat. 'Well, that wasn't really loud enough.'

'What do you mean?' Archie asked.

'You need to listen to it really loud so you can pick up all the instruments when they come in. Okay with you? I promise it won't be scary, Arch.'

Archie nodded and Polly gave her consent too and Jago replayed the track.

At first, the music was gentle with strings and a horn playing softly together. Then percussion came in, then more strings joined, creating a louder sound.

'We'll have Mrs Letchworth next door banging on the wall!' Polly warned.

'So let her bang!' Jago said, cranking up the volume even louder.

Polly laughed and Archie joined in.

'What's it like, Arch?' Jago asked. 'Go on – tell me!'

The music swelled and Polly found that she was rocking side to side as if she were about to waltz right across the room.

'Polly?' Jago said. 'How's it making you feel?'

'I feel like I'm dancing and flying at the same time!'

Archie laughed and Polly took her son's hands in hers and the two of them were actually dancing right there in the front room, tripping over Archie's toys and knocking into the book cases.

Dickens, who'd been sleeping in the kitchen, came in to see what all the fuss was about and started to bark, leaping around the room after the two of them as if he'd been injected with helium.

'It's the kind of music that makes you want to run across an enormous field, leaping over streams and kicking dandelion clocks, isn't it?' Jago said. 'How's it make you feel, Arch?' he tried again.

'It makes me want to kick a football really, really HARD!' Archie shouted above the music.

They all laughed and then, at last, the music came to an end with a final flourish of beautiful sound, and the three of them stood grinning at each other. Polly was the first to speak, her cheeks flushed.

'I can't believe I've never heard that before,' she said.

'And you won't be able to *un*hear it now,' Jago said. 'It's rather like reading a book. Once you've read it, you can't believe there was a time in your life when it didn't exist.'

Polly gazed at him, her heart still racing from her little waltz around the living room. 'That's a very astute thing to say.'

'Well, don't look so surprised,' he said. 'I can be astute, you know.'

She smiled at him.

'What does astute mean?' Archie asked.

'It means smart,' Polly said.

'Your mum thinks I'm smart,' Jago said, ruffling Archie's hair.

'Of course you are,' Archie said.

Jago laughed. 'You see – I wanted to show you both the magic of music. It can exalt us and energise us. It can give us a whole *world* of emotions from just a few notes. Not bad for less than four minutes worth of music, is it? It always amazes me how music can evoke so many different emotions all at once. So you've always got to play it. Every day if you can, okay?'

'Okay,' Polly said. 'We will, won't we, Arch?'

Archie nodded enthusiastically.

'Listen, I'd better get back,' Jago said, checking his watch. 'I don't want you to think I still have to report in to my mum, but–'

'She doesn't want us hogging you all evening,' Polly said. 'I'll walk you out.'

'You really liked the Shostakovich?' he asked her.

'I loved it! It was romantic and melancholic at the same time and ... so full of energy!'

They'd reached the front door and Polly hesitated.

'I really enjoyed this evening,' he said.

'Me too.' Polly's hand hovered for a moment before she opened the door into the cold night. 'Perhaps you can introduce us to another composer next time.'

'I'd like that,' he said.

'Continue my education. I mean Archie's education.' She smiled. '*Our* education.'

'I'll bring some of my own CDs over.'

'Okay.'

They stood looking at each other, an awkward silence hanging between them.

'Have a good night with Bryony.'

Jago nodded. 'I'll see you at the weekend, okay?'

'Absolutely.'

'Night, Polly,' he said, his voice warm and gentle as he shoved his hands in his jeans pockets and hunched his shoulders against the bitter cold.

She watched as he crossed the green to his house and then she shut and locked the front door, walking through to the living room which still seemed to hum with the music that had filled it that evening.

Archie was sitting on the sofa stroking Dickens's long ears. The spaniel really shouldn't have been up on the sofa, but Polly barely noticed.

'You know, I really like Jago,' Archie said.

'I know you do,' Polly said, sitting down next to him.

'Do you, Mum?'

Polly didn't answer for a moment. Her mind was racing over the evening that had just happened – the fun they'd had, the moments they'd shared. She couldn't remember the last time she'd had so much pure fun.

'Yes,' she said at last. 'I like Jago. I like him a lot.'

CHAPTER 11

It was funny to pull up to Church Green and not be calling in on her sister, Bryony thought, as she reached number 7. She wondered if she should call in at Polly's first – just to touch base before her date with Jago but, after taking so long choosing her outfit and the struggle she'd had trying to tame her hair, she really didn't have time.

She pulled her handbag across from the passenger seat and found her compact inside, checking her appearance and powdering her nose. She'd worn her hair loose and it waved down over her shoulders in its curly, unruly way. She'd picked out one of her favourite dresses – a midnight blue velvet one – and had teamed it with a burgundy jacket which was smothered in tiny violets. Then there were her boots which she'd agonised over, finally settling on a knee-high, lace-up pair with a modest heel. One couldn't be too careful when there was ice around.

Tooting her car horn, she waited for a moment, wondering if she should actually get out and ring the bell, but Jago had texted her and told her to just honk the horn. Sure enough, a minute later, his tall figure emerged from the door of number 7, guitar case in hand and a slither of light from the hallway behind revealing his long trench coat, giving him the look of a hero from an historical romance. Bryony swallowed hard.

'Hey,' he said as he opened the car door.

'Hey yourself,' Bryony said and then grimaced at how that sounded.

'You look nice,' he said as he popped the guitar in the back and bent to get into the passenger seat.

'Thanks. You do too.'

'Know where we're going?'

'I think so,' she said and she started the engine and headed out into the dark Suffolk countryside.

'I saw Polly and Archie again this week,' he said as they drove through a village where the church windows were lit up, turning it into a lantern.

'How's Archie's guitar lessons going?'

'Really good. He loves to learn.'

'He does. I love choosing books for him. He's always so excited. Not all kids are, I'm afraid.'

'No?'

Bryony shook her head. 'Just today, I had a mother come into the shop and she practically had to drag her daughter in. I have never seen such a miserable face on a kid before. It was quite disturbing actually. And she didn't even cheer up when I showed her the latest Lucy Lamont book. Now *that's* a problem child!'

Jago laughed. 'Oh, dear.'

'I really tried my best with her, but that kid wasn't giving an inch. But Archie – now Archie always has a smile for me, and I don't think that's because I'm his aunt and he knows he's in for a freebie or two.'

'No, you're right,' Jago said. 'Archie's one of life's happy souls, isn't he?'

Bryony smiled. 'He's a special boy. Polly adores him.'

'Of course.'

'He's the centre of her world now. You know about Sean, don't you?'

'Little bits,' Jago said.

'Nobody knows what really happened,' Bryony said. 'It's awful. How Polly gets through it, I don't know.'

'Having Archie and the rest of her family must help. You're all pretty close, aren't you?'

Bryony nodded. 'We poke into each others' business on a regular basis,' she said with a grin. 'Do you have family?'

'Not really. It's just me and Mum.'

'Oh,' Bryony said.

'It's fine. It's what I'm used to.'

'Did you ever know your father?'

'Oh, yeah,' he said in the sort of world-weary voice that instantly warned Bryony that that particular subject might be painful. 'He – he wasn't a good man.'

Bryony sighed. She couldn't imagine how horrible it must be for somebody to say that about a parent and she realised how very lucky she was to be a Nightingale and to have experienced nothing but love and support her whole life because not everybody did.

They drove round the outskirts of Sudbury and then took a back road out into the Stour Valley to where the pub was.

'You know, I've always had a secret ambition to be a groupie,' Bryony confessed.

'Really?'

'Truly.'

'Well, don't get too excited. We're never likely to hit the charts and go on tour.'

'You never know,' she said. 'Have you ever thought of auditioning for one of those TV talent shows?'

Jago grimaced. 'Not my style. I prefer obscurity.'

'Really?'

'I don't want to be rich or famous,' he said. 'I just want to make a living from what I love doing.'

'Sounds like me and my family. People rarely work with books for any other reason than for the love of them.'

'I think having a passion for what you do is more important than having a full bank account, isn't it?'

'Of course,' Bryony said. 'That's what I tell myself every time I go overdrawn.'

'Me too,' Jago said with a laugh. 'Ah, here it is. The King's Head.'

Bryony looked up at the swollen head of Henry VIII on the pub sign and pulled into the car park. Judging by the blackboard outside the door, it was kind of place which had something going on almost every evening from darts tournaments to karaoke evenings, pub quizzes to live music, and there was already a good crowd inside when they entered.

'I'll get us some drinks and then we can order some food,' he said, taking his coat off and helping Bryony with hers.

Bryony chose a table near the roaring fire, warming her hands by the flames. Jago joined her a moment later with a couple of menus and it didn't take them long to place their orders.

'Tell me more about Sean,' Jago said once the meals had arrived. 'I mean, if you don't mind.'

'I don't mind,' Bryony said. 'He was—' she looked thoughtful for a moment, 'an acquired taste, I'd say. I never really gelled with him and I did try. But I could see that Polly adored him and I did my best to get along with him as you do with in-laws.'

'What didn't you like about him?'

'I didn't dislike him exactly,' she said. 'It was more of a feeling that he wasn't to be trusted, you know? I mean, I never had any reason to mistrust him, but I still couldn't shake the feeling that there was something about him – something he wasn't telling us all.'

'Did you ever find out what it was?' Jago asked.

Bryony shook her head. 'Perhaps he's got another wife somewhere and he's gone back to her.'

'You think?'

'No, not really,' she said, taking a sip of a drink. 'I don't even want to try and guess what's happened to him. It's too awful to think about.'

'I don't how Polly coped with it all.'

'She didn't in the beginning. Mum wanted her to move back to Campion House, our family home, but Polly insisted on staying where she is in case Sean came back. We all kept an eye on her, of course, but you could see that she was in a real state. I've never seen her like that before. She was always the strong one in the family. The one you turn to if you're in trouble.'

'I wish there was something I could do,' Jago said.

'If you're encouraging Archie with his music then you're already doing the very best thing ever.'

Jago smiled.

They finished their meal, rambling easily from subject to subject and then Jago got up from the table just as three young men entered the pub.

'Bryony – these are the other members of the band. Mike on keyboard, Davy on guitar and Briggs on drums.'

Bryony stood up and shook the hands of three attractive young men. Of course, they weren't as attractive as Jago, but you could do a lot worse on a Friday night in rural Suffolk.

'I don't even know what your band's called,' she suddenly said.

'One More Song,' Jago said.

'That's unusual,' she said. 'I like it.'

'We'd always get to the end of a session – whether in rehearsals or playing a gig and it might have been us who said it or a member of the audience, but they are the words we always hear: *one more song*. It kind of stuck. Anyway, we'd better get to work.'

Bryony smiled as the four young men made their way to the far side of the bar which had been left empty for them. She watched them setting up, fascinated by the amount of equipment that was needed in order to play a few songs.

By the time they were ready to start, there wasn't a spare seat left in the pub and everybody soon got into the spirit of things as the music started. It was really very good indeed, with the four men playing and singing together in perfect harmony. It was a nice mix of gentle songs and toe-tapping numbers and the audience was very appreciative. Bryony couldn't remember when she'd last enjoyed an evening out so much. This, she thought, was a definite improvement on the calibre of dates she was getting from the dating agencies she'd joined.

After about forty minutes, the band stopped and was greeted by rapturous applause as the lads made their way to the bar where drinks were handed to them. Jago then wove his way through the crowd to join Bryony at their table.

'Wow!' she said. 'That was really brilliant.'

'You liked it?'

'I loved it!'

'Good, well, we do what we can.'

'You're so modest,' she told him. 'Everyone was absolutely rapt.' She leaned forward across the table. 'I think you could have your pick of the women here tonight.'

'Oh, really?' he said with a grin. 'You're offering me up, are you?'

Bryony laughed. 'Just making an observation.'

'You're not getting rid of me that easily.'

'I wasn't trying to get rid of you,' she told him.

'Good,' he said, and his eyes locked with hers.

'So, you guys write your own songs?'

'Of course.'

'That's impressive.'

'It's what a band should do.'

'Yes, but it's often easier for new bands just to regurgitate old favourites, isn't it?'

'It is, but not us. What's the point of that? I mean, we've done requests for special occasions and it's fine if you want a familiar, fun warm-up, but there's no real joy in that as an artist, is there?'

'I suppose not,' Bryony agreed. 'It would be like a writer just copying out somebody else's book.'

Jago nodded and that's when Briggs, the drummer, motioned at him from across the pub.

'Better get back to it,' he said. 'You okay here?'

'I'm fine here. I'm loving it. Now, get on with the show. Your public demands you!'

She watched him cross the room with that tall grace of his, gaining several admiring glances as he went.

He's with me, Bryony thought to herself, wondering if she could sneakily take a photo of him with her phone as he was singing or if that would be a little weird.

Jago cleared his throat and then switched his microphone back on.

'I'd like to dedicate this song to the lovely woman who came here with me tonight,' he said.

Bryony nearly fell off her chair in surprise and felt several pairs of eyes turn to glare at her. Was her face heating up? Very likely. Was that her heart hammering in her chest? Most definitely.

She listened intently to the words which Jago sung. They were about a girl that was trying to find her way. A girl who seemed a little lost. Had he chosen that song especially for her? She swallowed hard. Was that how the world saw her? As a lost soul? She took a sip of her drink.

It was rather special to be sung to, Bryony thought. He had one of the warmest voices she had ever heard and she loved the way he closed his eyes to sing some of the lyrics, as if he was really living and feeling the emotions he was singing.

She liked the shape he made as he sang, his shoulders slightly hunched. She liked the way he held his guitar. She liked the way he occasionally nodded his head in time to the music or tapped his foot. His whole body was involved in the process of singing a song, not just his voice. She liked the way he would sometimes lift his right shoulder and, because he sang so much with his eyes closed, when he opened them, the impact was great indeed. Bryony could see several women in the pub had forgotten the partners they'd come in with and that there'd be an almighty scrum at the bar to buy Jago a drink once he'd finished. Poor Mike, Davy and Briggs didn't stand a chance.

But Jago's with me, Bryony said to herself, pride warming her wonderfully.

When the song was over, Bryony swallowed hard and smiled as Jago opened his eyes and his gaze met hers full on. Then the spell was broken as Briggs's drumsticks beat out a rhythm and a new song began.

When the evening was finally over and they'd driven back to
Great Tallington, Bryony pulled up to 7 Church Green and cut the
engine. What was the protocol, she wondered, when a woman
dropped a man home? Did she get out of the car and walk to the
door with him? She didn't think so.

'I've had a brilliant night,' she told him, deciding to stay inside the
car.

'Me too,' he said. 'I'm glad you enjoyed it. You did, didn't you? I
mean the music? You're not just saying you did to be polite?'

'Jago – you're one of the most talented people I've ever met,' she
told him honestly. 'You've got an amazing voice. You must know
that.'

He simply shrugged. 'I get by.'

'You could really make a go of things if you tried.'

'You think so?'

'I do.'

'Wow, thanks. That means a lot.'

'Thank you for my song,' she said.

'You're welcome.'

'Do you sing to all your dates?'

'Nope,' he said. 'Just the ones I like.'

'You're a bit of a charmer, aren't you? My sister didn't warn me
about that.'

'No? What did she say?'

'I'm not going to betray that sisterly trust,' Bryony said with a little
smile.

'Fair enough. I'll just have to imagine.'

'Jago?'

'Yes?'

'That song – did you choose it for me? I mean, the words–'

'The Lost Girl?'

'Is that how you see me?'

'A little,' he said. 'You seem – you seem a little unsure of yourself.
As if you're on the verge of something, but aren't quite there yet.'

Bryony twisted her fingers together in her lap. 'I do?'

Jago nodded. 'You do.'

'I – erm – I guess...'

Jago's hands reached across and folded around her own. She
looked up at him in the darkness of the car and wondered if he was

going to lean across and kiss her, but he didn't.

'I'll call you, okay?'

She nodded. Her throat had gone dry and she didn't trust herself to speak. Instead, she watched as he got out of the car and opened the back door to retrieve his guitar. He raised his right hand in a wave, his long coat blowing around him in the cold night air.

Bryony sat in the car for a little while longer, wondering if she should call round to Polly's and tell her about the evening, but it was pretty late and she didn't want to wake Archie who would have been in bed a long time ago.

There were so many questions buzzing around her brain. Did Jago really like her? If he did, why hadn't he tried to kiss her? Had the hand-holding thing been a gesture of affection or just kindness? He'd said he would call her, but when?

And how did she feel about him? He certainly made her heart beat faster, that was for sure. He'd made her feel special by singing to her, but his song choice had made her feel a little apprehensive too because it was as if Jago had seen something in her that all of her recent disastrous dates just hadn't even noticed – that she was lost.

But was Jago the man to help her find herself again?

CHAPTER 12

When Polly came off the phone from Bryony, something inside her felt numb which was crazy really because shouldn't she have been happy for her sister? After all, it had been Polly's idea that Bryony went out with Jago. Surely she should be pleased that the date had gone so well. But she wasn't and it took her a moment to identify the emotion she was feeling.

Jealousy.

She cursed herself. Ridiculous. Who was she to be jealous? She was a married woman, for goodness' sake. She had no business to feel jealous that Jago was seeing her sister. Even if she *was* available – which she most definitely was not – Jago wouldn't look at her in a million years. She was a middle-aged mother. Well, nearly middle-aged. As good as middle-aged in Jago's young eyes, she told herself. Besides, she wasn't looking to get involved again even if she was available and even if she thought Jago would consider her. Jago was a sweet young man who had shown her son great kindness, that was all. He'd made her smile and laugh. That was all, wasn't it? She didn't really harbour romantic feelings for him, did she? The idea was absurd.

The phone went again, making her start.

'Hello?'

'Polly, it's Jago.'

Polly gasped at the coincidence.

'Are you okay?'

'Of course,' she said.

'You sound out of breath,' he said.

'I'm fine. What is it?'

'I was wondering if I could come over early for Archie's lesson today – say in half an hour. Would that be okay?'

Polly looked at her watch. 'I don't see why not.'

'Great,' he said. 'I'll be with you shortly. Oh, and thank you.'

'What for?'

'For suggesting I see Bryony.'

Polly swallowed hard. 'You had a good time?' She forced the

question from herself out of politeness.

'I did. We did. At least, I hope she did.'

'Oh, she did.'

'You've spoken to her?'

Polly sighed inwardly. Now why had she gone and said that? 'Erm, yes. She really enjoyed ... your music.' There, that was all he was going to get out of her.

Jago laughed. 'Good. Well, I'll see you in half an hour, okay?'

'Okay.'

When she hung up the phone, she ran up the stairs to the bathroom and grabbed her hairbrush, unclipping her hair and brushing it.

'Who was on the phone, Mum?' Archie asked, appearing in the doorway.

'Jago. He's coming round in half an hour.'

'Cool!'

'Make sure you're ready.'

Archie nodded and returned to his bedroom and Polly looked in the mirror at herself as she retied her hair. Her pale face stared back at her, her dark eyes large and with a slightly startled expression.

Don't go there, she told herself. You do not have feelings for Jago Solomon. You love your husband. Your long-missing husband. You can't forget about him. You mustn't forget about him.

She opened the bathroom cabinet and reached in for her make-up bag.

It's to make yourself feel better. She nodded at the lie as she reached in for the foundation she rarely used. She was lucky in having a very good complexion which didn't really warrant make-up at all and she never usually wore anything more than a lick of lipgloss and a tickle of mascara, but something in her today wanted more and she squeezed some of the creamy foundation onto her fingers.

'What are you doing, Mum?' Archie asked a moment later.

'I thought you were getting ready for your lesson,' she said as she went over her face with her make-up sponge which had to be immersed in water for a good minute to revive it. She couldn't remember the last time it had been used and it had shrivelled and hardened into a walnut.

'I am ready,' Archie said.

'Is your room tidy?'

'We're not having the lesson in my room.'

'That wasn't what I asked you, was it? Go and tidy it.'

He sighed and made a big thing of turning around and stomping back to his room.

Polly resumed the work on her face, adding a touch of powder, the merest hint of blusher and the usual delicate application of mascara and lipgloss. It was barely enough to be noticeable, she told herself, and yet she felt so much better for having made an effort. It had been so easy to slip into the role of Archie's mum and pay very little attention to her own needs especially since Sean had left them. Polly hadn't had the energy to do anything other than the basics and so the no-make-up-hair-scraped-back Polly had emerged.

It might just have been her imagination, but she was quite sure that Dickens the spaniel gave her a double-take when she entered the kitchen and Archie peered at her closely when he entered a few minutes later.

'You look all red,' he told her.

'I do not,' she said. 'I've just got slightly higher colouring than normal.'

'I don't like it,' he said. 'You look kind of funny.'

Polly chose to ignore him and busied herself with the laundry.

By the time Jago came round, she'd almost forgotten she was wearing make-up until he stared at her intently as he entered the house. 'You look different,' he said.

'Do I?'

He nodded. 'You've got more colour in your cheeks.'

'She's wearing make-up,' Archie said as he joined them in the hall.

Polly felt herself die inside at her son's traitorous revelation.

'Well, you look very nice,' Jago said. 'Going somewhere?'

'Nope,' Archie answered for her.

Polly placed her hands on her hips. 'I might be.'

'She never does,' Archie said.

Jago laughed and then caught Polly's shocked expression. 'Sorry,' he said. 'From out of the mouth of babes.'

'I think you two had better start the lesson, don't you?'

Jago, who was holding both guitars, handed the smaller of the two to Archie and followed him through to the living room whilst Polly returned to the kitchen. She stood aimlessly for a moment, not quite sure what to do. Of course, on a Saturday morning, there was always plenty to do. She could prepare something nice for lunch, sort out Archie's bag for the school week ahead, tackle the mountain of ironing or give Dickens a good old trim.

She started with the ironing, working her way through shirts, skirts and trousers. She then got hold of Dickens and, much to his alarm, went to work with a pair of scissors, neatening his ears and tail before trimming the beautiful feathering on his legs which was a complete mud magnet at this time of year.

Then it was time for Archie's bag. Leaving a stunned Dickens to sleep off his shock, she went upstairs to her son's room where she found his little rucksack. Taking it back downstairs, she unzipped it, finding his homework diary and checking that everything was in tiptop order. It was as she was returning the diary and taking out some of the rubbish that had accumulated in the bag that she found a letter from the head teacher. It was dated the week before and it was about something that was happening today.

Without thinking, Polly walked through to the living room.

'Archie?' He looked up from his guitar. 'What's this?'

He looked at the letter as though he'd never seen it before. 'Don't know.'

'Your school's having a "Bring and Bake" today at the village hall in Castle Clare.'

'Is it?'

'Yes, it is.'

He was still looking blankly at her as if to ask how an earth did that affect him.

'So that means I have to get a move on.'

'You're going to bake something?'

'Of course,' Polly said, feeling that it was her civic duty. 'We all have to support the school.'

Jago got up from the sofa.

'Oh, don't let me disturb you,' she said, suddenly realising that she'd interrupted them.

'It's okay,' Jago said. 'We're pretty much done.'

'Make your chocolate brownies, Mum, and leave plenty for us to eat,' Archie said as he and Jago followed Polly through to the kitchen, guitar lesson forgotten.

Polly rifled through the cupboards, checking that she had enough ingredients.

'Can I do anything to help?' Jago asked.

'You sure you've got time for this?'

'Yes. My next pupil sent a text whilst I was with Archie. They've had to cancel their lesson this morning.'

'Oh, I see.'

'So I'd love to stay and help.'

'Okay, then,' Polly said. 'Can you bring out that nice big bowl from the dresser cupboard?'

Jago walked across the kitchen and found the big mixing bowl, placing it on the kitchen table.

'Thanks,' Polly said as she buzzed from cupboard to cupboard assembling the ingredients which included a wonderfully unhealthy assembly of butter, muscovado sugar, cocoa powder, chocolate and icing sugar.

'Did you want to chop the chocolate?' Polly asked Jago.

'Sure thing,' he said, moving across to the sink and washing his hands before drying them on a towel. Archie followed suit and then Polly handed Jago a chopping board and a large block of dark chocolate. 'Archie, you can sift the flour and the cocoa powder into the bowl.'

Polly got on with melting the butter in a big pan before adding the sugar and stirring with a wooden spoon. She turned around from the cooker to see Jago and Archie working together at the kitchen table.

'Erm, Archie, at least *some* of that chocolate has got to make it into the brownie recipe,' Polly said with a warning glare.

'Yep,' Jago said. 'A brownie without chocolate would taste pretty foul.' He popped a square of chocolate into his own mouth and Archie giggled.

Polly shook her head. 'You're not being a very good role model,' she said to Jago, but her voice was an inch away from laughter.

'I can't remember the last time I baked anything,' Jago said. 'It was probably at school.'

'Now you're making me feel old,' Polly said.

'I was pretty lazy at university,' he confessed.

'Isn't everybody?' Polly asked with a grin.

'I didn't even cook properly, let alone bake,' he said.

'I like baking,' Polly admitted. 'It helps me relax.'

'I like you baking, Mummy,' Archie said. '*Especially* chocolate brownies.'

Slowly, the ingredients were assembled together with only the smallest amount of flour wafting up into Archie's hair from the sieve and the tiniest amount of chocolate smearing his mouth.

Soon, the kitchen was filled with the warm chocolatey aroma of the brownies.

'That,' Jago said, 'is the most glorious smell ever.'

Polly beamed him a smile. 'It's pretty good, isn't it?'

'Mum's are the best brownies in the whole world,' Archie said. 'They always sell as soon as she puts them on the table.'

'I can believe it,' Jago said. 'I can't wait to try one.'

'Mum will probably charge you for it,' Archie said.

'Oh, Archie! I wouldn't do that.'

'Well, what if I make a donation when we drop them off?' Jago asked.

'That would be very kind,' she told him. 'Cup of tea whilst we wait?'

'Thanks,' he said. He walked across to the sink and washed his hands again. Archie joined him and Polly watched in amusement as they had a mini play fight in the warm water.

Jago then surprised her by making a start on the dishes, washing up all the bowls and spoons that had been used in the brownies' creation.

'You don't need to do that,' she told him as she made them both a cup of tea.

'It's okay,' he said.

She watched him as he dried his hands on a tea towel. She liked his hands and she couldn't help wondering what it would feel like to hold them. She imagined that they would be warm and strong and that her own small, cool hands would feel safe and secure inside them.

She shook her head and turned away quickly, horrified that such a thought had entered her mind.

'Polly?' he said. 'You okay?'

'I'm good.' Her voice sounded croaky and nervous. She cleared her throat. 'I'm good,' she said again as if trying to convince herself.

They took their tea into the living room and Archie immediately picked up Jago's guitar and started strumming.

'Is he meant to be playing that?' Polly asked in alarm as she sat on the sofa and was joined by Jago.

'He's okay,' he told her.

The picture of her small son holding the grown-up sized guitar touched her deeply.

'Have you thought any more about buying him his own—?'

'I'll get him one,' Polly said.

Archie looked up at her. 'You're going to buy me my own guitar?'

Polly smiled. 'Yes,' she said, suddenly realising that it was absolutely the right thing to do. She didn't care how much it cost or how many belts would have to be tightened or how many extra classes she'd have to teach in order to do it. Archie would have his own guitar.

'Thanks, Mum!' Archie said, placing the guitar carefully on the chair behind him and flying across the room to hug his mum.

'Careful of my tea!' she cried.

'I'm going to have my own guitar, Jago!' he said.

'That's great, Arch!'

'Is it for my birthday?' Archie asked.

'No,' Polly said. 'This is just something you're going to have as soon as possible.'

'When's your birthday, Arch?' Jago asked.

'Not until March.'

'Will you help me choose one for him?' Polly asked Jago.

'It would be my pleasure,' he said.

'Because I've not got a clue what I'm doing.'

'Wow, Mum! This is brilliant.'

She cupped Archie's beaming face in her hands and kissed him loudly on the cheek, making him squirm and giggle like the baby he'd once been.

The cooker timer interrupted them and Polly leapt to her feet, her mug of tea in her hand. Jago and Archie followed her through and watched as she opened the oven door and brought out the two trays of brownies.

'Oh, yum!' Archie said, sniffing appreciatively.

Polly placed them onto the kitchen worktop to cool for a moment and then popped them onto a cooling rack and gave them a dusting of icing sugar. They looked splendid and the three of them looked at their creation with nothing short of lust in their eyes and greed in their bellies.

'Are they cool enough to eat yet, Mum?'

Polly gave one a little nudge with her forefinger. 'I think so,' she said, 'but just one each, okay?'

Jago and Archie nodded.

Nothing could come close to the taste of an oozey chocolatey brownie fresh from the oven on a cold winter's day when the rain was pattering against the window, Polly thought. The three of them stood in the kitchen without the ceremony of plates or napkins, stuffing their faces with the chocolate brownies and, at that moment, none of them could think of a greater pleasure.

'We'd better get these delivered,' Polly said at last, washing her hands in the sink whilst Jago and Archie licked their fingers clean.

'What about lunch, Mum?' Archie asked and Polly realised how late it was.

'We've got to get straight out with these, darling.'

'How about stopping off at the chippy in Castle Clare once we've delivered them?' Jago suggested.

'Fish and chips?' she said.

'Why not?'

'Oh, can we, Mum?' Archie begged.

'I don't see why not,' Polly said. 'But you don't have to come with us, Jago. I'm sure you've got other things to do on a Saturday.'

'Nope,' he said.

'And you're sure you want to come into town to deliver some brownies to a village hall and then have fish and chips with us?'

'Sure. Why not? It sounds good fun to me.'

Archie was smiling from ear to ear at the idea.

'Well, okay I guess,' Polly said, feeling just a tad anxious at how easily Jago slipped into their lives. It all felt so wonderfully natural, but she couldn't help worrying about it too because, since Sean had disappeared, she'd got used to the fact that life was just her and Archie. She'd adapted. It hadn't been much fun, but she'd got on with things. She'd managed. And now here was this kind young man with his passion and enthusiasm for all life had to offer. Why he wanted to spend quite so much time with them was baffling to Polly and yet she didn't want to question him too closely for fear of driving him away.

The truth was she liked having him there. Perhaps she liked having him there a little bit too much because the feelings that were growing inside her were beginning to scare her.

'I'll get my handbag,' she said. 'Put your coat on.'

'I will,' Jago said.

Polly laughed. 'I meant Archie, silly!'

He winked at her. 'And here was me thinking that you cared about me.'

Polly felt momentarily stunned not just by the wink, but by the emotions she was beginning to feel for this young man.

CHAPTER 13

They drove to Castle Clare in Polly's Land Rover, finding a parking space outside the church which was very handy for the chip shop later. They walked the short distance to the village hall which was bustling with people even though it had only just opened for business. Tables with pretty cloths had been laid out with cakes, flapjacks, pies, jams and chutneys made by parents, neighbours and friends of the school. Boxes of jumble were being plundered by bargain hunters and there was a brisk trade at the two rails of clothing set up on the village hall stage.

'I really missed this sort of thing when I was in America,' Jago told Polly. 'There's something a little bit special about a small English community, don't you think?'

'I do,' she said. 'I love the way that you can see home-baking next to hand-knitted clothing and pots of jam and jumble. All life is here.'

Polly handed over her brownies to the lady in charge of the home-baking table and watched as they began to sell almost immediately. She looked at the splendid display of baking, her mouth watering at the caramel squares and the Victoria sandwich, and she bought a box of jam tarts in jewel-like colours which she knew would go down well with Archie come tea time.

Archie tugged his mother's sleeve. 'It's Tiger,' he said, nodding across the room towards his friend. 'Can I go and see him?'

'Okay,' Polly said, 'but don't forget we're going for fish and chips soon.'

She watched as her son wove his way through the crowds to get to his friend and that's when she saw Winston Kneller. He waved to her and ambled over, holding up an old carrier bag.

'Just got the last of Honey Digger's triple chocolate chip cookies,' he said. 'Going to have them with my tea.' He looked up at Jago who was a good foot taller than him. 'Hello, young man.'

'Hello, Winston,' Jago said.

'You two together, are you?' Winston asked, looking from one to the other and back again.

'No!' Polly all but screamed. 'We're here together.'

'Righty ho,' Winston said and he tipped his hat at them and made his way towards the door and home with his chocolate chip cookies.

'You okay?' Jago asked her.

Polly nodded but she was feeling far from okay. She felt flustered. 'I think we should eat,' she said.

'Don't you want to look around first?'

'No,' Polly said shortly. She did not want to look around, not when she felt as if everybody was looking at her and Jago and making the assumption that they were a couple.

'I'll round up Archie,' Jago said, going off in search of the boy.

She watched as he made his way through the room. He was so much taller than everybody else and it didn't take him long to find Archie and bring him back.

'Tiger's bought a really cool robot. It's really old. It's like *ancient*,' Archie said.

'An ancient robot? Isn't that an oxymoron?' Jago asked with a laugh.

'No, I think it's a Transformer,' Archie said in all seriousness which made Polly laugh.

'Come on,' she said, placing her hand on his shoulder, 'let's get something to eat.'

They left the village hall together and Polly was aware that the likes of Honey Digger and Antonia Jessop were watching their every move. Oh, the curse of living in a small community, Polly thought. But she had to admit to being just as bad herself when it came to people watching. Didn't she like to examine and speculate? Wasn't it fun to imagine what might be going on with one's neighbours? It really did go hand-in-hand with living in such a place.

Castle Clare's chip shop was a takeaway and it was much too cold to think about eating outside on a bench so, grabbing their piping hot packages which smelled wonderfully vinegary, they made their way back to Polly's car.

'You don't mind eating them in here, do you? We can crank the heating up,' Polly suggested as they all got into the car.

'Sounds good to me,' Jago said. 'That village hall was bloody freezing.'

'I was bloody freezing in there too,' Archie said.

Jago cleared his throat as he realised his mistake. 'Erm, sorry,' he said to Polly whose mouth was hanging open. 'You know, you really shouldn't swear, Arch.'

'But you just swore,' Archie pointed out from the back seat behind them both.

'I know I did and it's an appalling habit and I'm going to stop right now,' Jago said, his tone deadly serious.

The car windows were soon foggy with the steam from the food. Polly couldn't remember the last time she'd had fish and chips. It had been something that would never have crossed Sean's mind and he certainly wouldn't have enjoyed the experience of eating them in his pristine car. His Land Rover had been his pride and joy and Archie hadn't even been allowed to unwrap a mint humbug inside it. She wondered what Sean would make of the scene now and then felt instantly guilty at being there with a Jago. But what was it everyone kept telling her? *Life goes on.* Oh, how she hated that platitude and yet she knew she needed to come to terms with it because life was pretty lonely without a partner and she'd come to love Jago's company even if it was wildly inappropriate to admit that.

She looked at him now as he half-turned in the passenger seat so he could talk to Archie on the back seat. She wasn't really listening to what they were saying, but how she loved the comfort of their voices which were always so happy together. They fitted together, she thought. Like melody and harmony; the one perfectly balanced and complemented the other.

'What do you think?' Jago asked, suddenly turning his eyes on her.

'Sorry?' Polly said, almost swallowing a chip whole.

'Mum was zoned out again,' Archie said in a sing-song voice.

Jago waved his hand. 'It wasn't important.'

'No, what was it?' Polly asked.

'Don't worry about it.'

'Tell me!' Polly said, anxious to hear it now.

'Jago wants to know if we'd like to go and hear him sing sometime.'

'Oh,' Polly said. 'Like Bryony did last night?'

'No, not exactly,' he said. 'I was thinking more of an audience of two.'

Polly frowned. 'Just us two?'

Jago nodded. 'I've got a new song I want to try out.'

'Oh, so we're your guinea pigs now, are we?'

He laughed. 'If I can get away with it.'

'What do you think, Archie?' Polly asked, turning around to face her son. 'Do you want to hear Jago singing one of his own songs?'

'Yeah!' Archie cried. 'Can we hear it now?'

Jago shook his head. 'Got to have my guitar.'

'Can't you sing without it?' Archie asked.

'Not confidently,' Jago said as he finished off his chips.

Polly studied his face and found it hard to imagine that the Jago she had come to know over their brief time together could be anything *but* confident.

He looked up and caught her staring at him. Polly looked away.

'Have you had enough to eat, Archie?' she asked him.

'I'm still eating,' he said.

'Well, don't be too long about it,' she told him, suddenly feeling awkward sitting there in the small space with Jago next to her. But things were about to get even more awkward.

The timing couldn't have been worse. As Polly unwound her window to let out some steam, she saw Antonia Jessop marching along the pavement, heading right towards them. Of course, Antonia saw Polly and noted that her window was open and so thought nothing of sticking her head through it.

'Antonia!' Polly said, shocked by the intrusion.

'Polly,' Antonia said with a tight little nod. Her eyes which, by nature, were narrow, narrowed even further as she saw Jago in the passenger seat.

'We've just had fish and chips,' Archie blurted from the back seat.

Antonia looked at the heaps of vinegary paper which they all held in their laps.

'I see,' she said, glancing down into the foot well and up onto the dashboard as if looking for evidence that it was more than fish and chips that was going on in the steamed-up Land Rover.

'Been to the village hall?' Jago asked politely.

'I have,' Antonia said sharply.

Polly saw the basket she was carrying. 'Buy anything nice?'

'I don't think so,' Antonia said. 'I bought a pot of mulberry jam which looks much too runny and flapjacks which look much too hard.'

'Oh, dear,' Jago said, unable to hide his amusement.

'But one has to support these things, doesn't one?'

'Absolutely,' Polly said.

'Right,' Antonia said, fixing the brown hat she was wearing more securely on her head and giving Jago one last glare, 'must be off.'

'Goodbye,' Polly said, quickly winding her window up before they were assaulted by anybody else. 'I have never met anybody quite as disagreeable as Antonia Jessop. To be able to find fault in a pot of mulberry jam and a batch flapjacks is quite remarkable.'

Jago laughed and Archie joined in.

'Shall we go home?' Polly asked and they nodded.

They drove back to Church Green and, after parking, Polly didn't even ask Jago if he wanted to come in because she just assumed that he'd follow them inside and that was fine.

They all took their coats and shoes off. Polly let Dickens out in the back garden and then put the kettle on whilst Jago and Archie went into the living room. When Polly joined them, she saw that Jago was rifling through the CD collection again.

'I thought you were going to bring some of your own CDs over,' she said.

'I was, wasn't I?'

She nodded. 'You should. We'd love to hear them.'

'What's this?' he asked as he turned his attention back to the collection.

Polly looked at the CD he was holding up. 'It's the Travelling Wilburys.'

'The *what*?'

'*Please* tell me you've heard of them, Mr Music Student.'

'Erm, no,' he said.

Polly's eyes were almost out on stalks at his admission. 'Jago Solomon, you should be ashamed of yourself. The Travelling Wilburys was one of the first super-groups. Now, I'm guessing you've heard of Bob Dylan?'

'Yeah, of course.'

'Well, he's in it along with Tom Petty, George Harrison from The Beatles and – I'm going to play you *Rattled*, okay?'

'I'm all ears,' Jago said.

Polly popped the CD in the player and went straight to her favourite song and the infectiously happy music filled the room.

'Hey, that's a pretty good sound,' Jago admitted.

'Of course it is!' Polly said. 'You're not the only one who knows about music.'

'I can see that.'

'You should borrow the album. You'd like the Wilburys – they're five really cool guys and their guitars.'

'Mum – stop talking and do the conga!'

'Oh, Archie, no!'

'You do the conga?' Jago said. 'Can you do that with two people?'

'You'd better believe it!' Polly said.

'I'll lead,' Archie said and Polly grabbed hold of her son's tiny waist.

One, two, three, kick! One, two, three, kick!

'Come on, Jago! Join in,' Archie hollered.

As they passed Jago, he placed his hands on Polly's hips.

One, two, three, kick! One, two, three, kick!

'Is the beat in this song right?' Jago asked.

'What do you mean?' Polly asked.

'The rhythm doesn't feel quite right!'

'It feels right to me. Anyway, this isn't a music exam, Jago!' Polly cried above the music. 'Just conga!'

'Yeah – just conga, Jago!' Archie shouted from the front of the shortest and possibly the longest conga line in Suffolk that day.

Jago laughed, and the three of them did the conga as best as they could round the small living room with Dickens the dog joining them from the kitchen.

'Mum?' Archie cried. 'MUM!'

'What?'

'I can hear banging!'

'What banging?' Polly asked, stopping the dance so abruptly that Jago crashed into the back of her.

'Sorry!' he said, quickly removing his hands from her waist.

'Oh, it's old Mrs Letchworth. We'd better turn the music down,' Polly said as the CD ploughed unapologetically into the next track.

'She's such a spoilsport,' Archie said with a frown.

'Hey – maybe we could do it really quietly?' Jago suggested.

'Yeah!' Archie said.

And so they did, Jago replacing his hands on Polly's waist and the three of them doing the quietest version of the conga ever.

'I've got to stop!' Polly said at last.

'Oh, Mum!' Archie complained, trying to get hold of Dickens to see if spaniels could conga.

'I'm not as young as I once was,' she said, aware that Jago's hands were still upon her. She turned to face him.

'That was fun,' he said.

'Yes.' She pushed a strand of hair out of her eyes but it fell right back again. Jago's hand reached out and gently brushed her hair back. Polly swallowed hard, almost flinching at the touch of his skin on hers.

'Mum – you're all red again,' Archie said, taking his eyes off Dickens who took his opportunity to leg it to the relative sanity of the kitchen.

'I'm not used to dancing, that's all,' she said, turning away from the two of them and taking the CD out of the player and returning it to its case, hoping that her face would calm down quickly.

'Hey, Arch – how about we have a little strum?'

'Brilliant!' Archie said.

'Okay with you?' Jago asked Polly.

Polly nodded. 'I'll be in the kitchen.'

She left the living room and stood at the kitchen sink, wondering what on earth was happening to her. Oh, dear, she thought. She really was beginning to have feelings for this wonderful young man and, the curse of it was, she couldn't confide in anybody about it. Normally, with things like this, Polly would turn to Bryony, but how could she do that when she'd match-made her sister and Jago? What a horrible, horrible muddle.

But not an unfixable one, she told herself. She would just have to stop feeling this way. For a moment, she thought it might be best to cancel Archie's guitar lessons, but how could she do that to her son when she'd just promised him that she was going to buy him his own guitar? She couldn't do that nor did she want to. No, she'd just have to distance herself from Jago and do nothing more than answer the door to him in the future. Fish and chips in the car, supper in the kitchen and conga lines in the living room would have to end. It was as simple as that.

Trying to put the fact that Jago was just in the next room out of her mind, Polly picked up her copy of *Far From the Madding Crowd* and turned to the chapter where Gabriel Oak warns Bathsheba to be "more discreet" in her dealings with Sergeant Troy. Polly gave a shiver as she read the words, thinking of the glances she and Jago had received at the village hall and the disapproving look that Antonia

Jessop had landed them with. Thomas Hardy's novel had been published in 1874 and yet women were still expected to handle themselves with decorum – perhaps not to such an extent as back in Victorian times, but Polly had felt the full weight of her neighbours' curiosity when she'd been seen with Jago.

She wasn't aware how fast the time passed when she read and got a genuine shock when Jago's head appeared around the kitchen door.

'Hey,' he said. 'It's time I was off.'

Polly looked up from her book and was surprised to see the kitchen clock read five.

'Oh, we've kept you all day!' she said, getting to her feet.

'No you haven't. I've chosen to be here.'

'I can't think why,' she said as they walked down the hallway, reaching the door a moment later.

'Can't you?' he whispered. She turned from the door to look at him and, not for the first time since Jago had arrived, Polly didn't trust herself to speak and so said nothing.

'Polly, I–'

'Can I have a go on your guitar next time, Jago?' Archie said as he suddenly ran into the hallway.

'Well, we'll have to see about that,' he said as Polly opened the door. 'It's been a great day.' He turned his attention back to her. 'I've really enjoyed it.'

'Me too,' Polly managed to say.

'See you, Arch!' He waved a hand at the boy and Archie waved back and Polly shut the front door, feeling her heart racing as she did so.

Archie ran upstairs to his bedroom and Polly stood in the silent hallway. She thought about the little details of the day like the way Jago had poured the salt and vinegar on all their portions of fish and chips and then carried them to the car before handing them out. She thought about Archie's smile as he'd walked back with Jago across the village hall, and she thought about the weight of Jago's hands on her hips as they'd danced in the front room.

And she knew what it was. She knew what was making her feel so breathless and confused. It wasn't just the stirring of romantic love she was feeling for Jago. It was something much more powerful than that. She was beginning to feel secure around him, happy and contented. That's what it was, she thought. The strange little unit which the three of them had formed was beginning to feel like a family.

CHAPTER 14

Maureen Solomon was sitting in the living room flipping through one of the rather tired magazine which she was in the habit of bringing home from the doctor's surgery she worked at. Jago really wished that she wouldn't. They were probably full of germs.

'You've been out a while,' she said as he came into the room. 'I thought you were just giving that Prior boy a guitar lesson and then coming back.'

He raked a hand through his hair. 'I kind of spent the rest the day with them,' he said. He found it hard not to be honest and there was no point hiding the truth from his mother. She would be bound to hear it from one of her friends who'd seen him at the village hall or at the chip shop. Castle Clare was that kind of place.

'We baked some brownies and took them to the "Bring and Bake" sale in town.'

'You baked brownies with Mrs Prior?'

'And Archie.'

Maureen raised her eyebrows. 'What *exactly* is going on with you and them?'

'What you mean?'

'I mean you're seeing a lot of them.'

'No I'm not.'

Maureen put the magazine on the coffee table in front of her and stood up. 'Yes, you are.'

'I don't see what the problem is,' he said but, even as he said it, he knew the direction his mother was going in.

'I thought you were seeing her sister. What's her name?'

'Bryony,' Jago said. He'd been right about his mother's direction. 'I am seeing her.'

'And yet you're spending all this time with Mrs Prior.'

'What are you getting at?'

'I'm just making an observation.'

'Mum, you never just make an observation.'

She shook her head. 'You're young, but you're not foolish, Jago. I don't want you getting hurt and I certainly don't want you going around breaking the hearts of as many Nightingale women as you can.'

'I'm not going to break any hearts,' he said with a frown. 'How on earth would I do that?'

'By doing exactly what you're doing at the moment. You're playing a dangerous game.'

'I'm not playing any game.'

'Besides, Mrs Prior is a married woman. Her husband might be missing, but what if he turns up tomorrow? What would happen then? I just don't think you should be involved with her.'

'I think it's up to me who I'm involved with, Mum,' he said with a sigh, leaving the room and going upstairs.

Shutting his bedroom door, he couldn't help pondering on his mother's words. What exactly *was* he doing? He'd certainly never planned any of this and the speed at which it had all happened was quite overwhelming.

He tried to think back to when he had first started having feelings for Polly. It certainly hadn't been on his first call there when she had as good as thrown him out. His relationship had been with Archie. Polly had been cool and aloof, but there had been a gradual warming of her manner towards him and he had caught her little looks and seen her little gestures.

But then she had persuaded him to go out with Bryony. What was that about? If she was beginning to have feelings towards him then why would she set him up with her sister? And where did that leave him now? He certainly didn't want to come between two sisters, but he had a feeling that that was exactly what he was going to do if things continued the way they were. And he liked them both, didn't he? He liked Bryony's vivacity, her openness and the fantastic colours she wore which seemed to be an extension of her personality, and they'd got on so well the night before. But she wasn't Polly, was she?

Jago had to admit that he was drawn to Polly's quiet sweetness, and admired her so much for the way she was raising Archie. And he could definitely feel that there was something between them even though she seemed to be doing her best to deny it.

He shook his head. He had never been in such a situation before. His time in America had been full of nothing more than light flirtations. He hadn't met anybody whom he'd thought he could really get to know and yet he'd only been back in Suffolk a short time and was already embroiled with two amazing women. How crazy was that?

His phone went and Bryony's name came up on the screen.

'Hey, you!' she said as he answered it.

'Hey!' he said, stunned by the timing of her call. It was as if she knew he'd been thinking about her.

'Listen,' she began, 'I know we only just went out together last night, and I know we don't really know each other properly, and I know this might seem really strange and you have every right to say no and I won't blame you if you do–'

'Bryony?'

She sighed. 'I'm babbling. I'm too nervous to ask you, but I really want to.'

'Ask me what?'

'If you'll come to Sunday lunch tomorrow at my parents' house.'

Jago wasn't sure how to react, after all, it could be extremely awkward if Polly was there.

'Jago?' Bryony asked. 'You still there?'

'I'm still here.'

'I've shocked you, haven't I?'

'No, of course you haven't shocked me!'

'I've gone and ruined things. I always push, you see? I always go and push and spoil things.'

'Bryony – I'd love to come to Sunday lunch with you and your family.'

'You would?'

'I really would.'

'You're not just saying that to be polite because you don't need to be. You can be honest with me, Jago.'

Jago swallowed hard. He very much doubted if complete honesty at that moment would go down well at all.

'How about you give me the address and I can bike over there?'

Bryony gave him the address together with directions and he scribbled it down, promising to be there for eleven thirty the next day.

When he hung up, he knew that it would be in his best interests not to tell his mother what his plans were for Sunday other than saying he wouldn't be around for lunch. To be fair, he was still trying to work it all out himself. But one thing was for sure: when he'd accepted Bryony's invitation, he wasn't thinking about her which he knew was wicked of him. He was thinking of the fact that he'd get to see Polly again.

The road to Wintermarsh was slick with rain which turned it a wondrous silver when the sunshine hit it. Polly's Land Rover splashed through the puddles. How fed up she was of winter and how she longed to see the primroses coming up in the garden and the first jolly bunches of daffodils. For some reason this winter seemed to be a particularly long one and she couldn't help feeling that they were locked in some Narnia-like curse and would never see summer again.

She slowed to take the turn into the driveway of the family home, parking in her usual space.

'Jago's here!' Archie cried from the back seat.

'Don't be silly,' Polly said, thinking that her son had Jago on the brain and that she'd have to calm him down a little on the subject of the young guitar player. Heaven only knew that she was finding it difficult enough to keep him from her own mind.

'But that's his bike,' Archie said and Polly looked at the old motorbike that was standing to the right of the front door of Campion House. It certainly looked like Jago's bike, but what would he be doing there?

They got out of the car with Dickens in tow, the cold wind instantly wrapping itself around them as they headed for the front door. Polly's father had planted two great terracotta pots with evergreens and pink and white cyclamen and the tiny spots of colour made Polly smile. She knocked on the door before opening it.

'Hello,' she called down the hallway and heard the responding barks of Hardy and Brontë as they ran to greet Dickens. She closed the door behind them and instantly felt the wonderful warmth of the house as she unwrapped her stripy scarf and took her coat and boots off. Archie did likewise and bent to give Hardy the pointer a fuss. Brontë and Dickens, had long since vanished, legging it into the kitchen where they were no doubt causing endless mischief.

'Is that you, Polly?'

'It is, Mum!'

'Come on through. You'll never guess who's here.'

'It's Jago!' Archie said. 'I told you he was here, Mum!'

Polly walked towards the kitchen, not yet believing it but, as soon as she entered, she saw that Archie was right and that Jago was there, surrounded by most of the Nightingale family.

'Jago!' she said in genuine surprise. 'What are you doing here?'

'Bryony invited me,' he said with a grin.

Polly looked at her sister who came forward and gave her a hug.

'I took a chance asking him,' Bryony said, but we got on so well on Friday night, didn't we? And you guys already know him so he's practically family already.'

Polly could feel herself blushing on behalf of her sister.

'And, of course, he already knows Sam and Callie from the book club,' Bryony continued and Polly smiled across at her brother and his partner.

'We're just relieved that she's not brought anyone home from one of those awful dating sites,' Josh said. 'How did you meet Jago, Bry?'

'Polly introduced me,' Bryony told her brother.

Josh's eyebrows rose. 'I never took you for a match-maker, Poll.'

'I'm not a match-maker,' she said, quickly walking over to the sink where she took control of a large cabbage.

'Who's this match-maker, then?' Grandpa Joe asked as he shuffled into the room in his slippers.

'Polly,' Bryony said, grabbing hold of Jago's arm.

Grandpa Joe eyed up Polly before turning to look at Bryony and Jago. 'You've done a pretty good job, I'd say. Very handsome couple they make.'

Bryony laughed.

'Right, everybody!' Eleanor declared. 'Give me some space otherwise this lunch will never be ready.'

The family began to vacate the kitchen, taking glasses of wine and bowls of nibbles into the living room where the fire was roaring.

'Nice cabbage, Mum,' Polly said from the sink. She usually gave her mother a hand in the kitchen and stayed behind to help now.

Eleanor approached her. 'Haven't you got a kiss for your mum?'

'Of course,' Polly said, turning round to kiss her cheek.

'You okay?'

'Yes,' Polly said, turning back to the sink to finish washing the cabbage.

'You seem rattled.'

'Rattled?' Her mother's use of the word struck her in the solar plexus. *Rattled.* It was the name of the song they'd congaed to just the day before.

'Polly?'

'I'm fine.'

'Anything to do with your guitar player being here as Bryony's guest?'

'No.'

'You're sure? Because you didn't look overly pleased to see him.'

'I was just surprised, that's all.'

'I know Bryony's only just started going out with Jago,' Eleanor said, 'but we've already heard so much about him from you and Archie that I thought it was about time the rest of us met him. She rang yesterday and asked if she could bring him and you know I hate turning down a guest. You're not angry are you, Polly?'

'Don't be silly. Why should I be angry?' She gave a smile which felt horribly tight and fake to her and, if it felt that way, she knew it would look that way to her mother too.

'Well, you seem angry to me. Is there something you're not telling me?'

'What do you mean?'

Eleanor shrugged. 'I don't know. Like maybe you've got feelings for this young man yourself.'

'Don't be ridiculous.' Polly moved away from the sink and wiped her hands on the checked tea towel hanging on the red Aga. 'Do the carrots or parsnips need to be turned?'

'Polly, stop talking about root vegetables.'

'Is Lara coming?'

Eleanor shook her head. 'She said something about having a pretty heavy Saturday night and I didn't enquire for fear of worrying too much. And you've just tried to change the subject again.'

Polly took a glass from the cupboard and walked back to the sink to fill it with water.

'Polly?'

'What?'

'Will you talk to me?'

'What about?'

'You know what about. I have eyes, you know. I can see what's going on here.'

'Well, if you can see it, we don't need to talk about it.'

Eleanor sighed. 'I want to hear it from you.'

'Hear what, Mum?'

Eleanor closed the space between herself and her daughter and looked her directly in the eye. 'What exactly is going on between Jago and Bryony. Is he really interested in her?'

'He went out with her, didn't he?'

'He did.'

'And he's here as her guest now,' Polly pointed out.

'Then why does he keep looking at you?'

'He doesn't.'

'Yes he does, Polly, and you're all nervous and fidgety around him.'

'You're imagining things. Have you been at the wine already?' Polly took a swig of water, refilled her glass and made her way out of the kitchen.

'I'm not finished with you, Polly!' Eleanor called after her, and Polly knew her mother was speaking the truth.

As was the custom at Campion House, guests were seated next to the person who had invited them and so Jago sat next to Bryony which worked out well because that was Lara's usual place so there was plenty of room in her absence. Polly and Archie were opposite and Archie had begged his mum to let him sit next to Jago, but she'd said no.

Despite Lara's absence, the table was wonderfully full with not only Jago but Callie as a guest too. Callie was now a regular and very much a part of the Nightingale family and Polly couldn't have been happier for her brother, Sam.

'So,' Frank Nightingale said from the head of the table once everyone was settled and the food was being passed around, 'who likes these carrots? I grew a new variety this year and I'm not convinced by them. They're bigger than last year's, but I don't think the flavour's quite there.'

Josh chuckled. 'Dad, a carrot is a carrot, isn't it?'

'It most certainly is not,' Frank said, 'as well you'd know if you ever tried to grow anything yourself.'

'My husband's done his best to get this lot interested in gardening over the years, but to no avail,' Eleanor explained to Callie and Jago.

'Hey!' Polly piped up. 'I grew runner beans last year.'

'So many runner beans!' Archie said and everyone laughed.

'I once attempted to grow a basil plant on my windowsill, but all the leaves turned brown and it started crawling with disgusting little creatures,' Josh confessed.

'He didn't even grow it from seed,' Bryony said. 'I got it for him from Sainsbury's.'

'Gardening is not for the fainthearted,' Frank said. 'Anyway, back to these carrots. What do you all think?'

'Very nice, Frank darling,' Eleanor said.

'Mum?' Frank said to Grandma Nell.

'They taste like carrots to me,' she said.

'Well, that's all you can ask really,' Grandpa Joe said with a little smile as he squeezed his wife's arm.

'Do you have a garden, Jago?' Frank asked

'Just a small one at the back of the house. Like Polly's.'

'He's opposite me, Dad,' Polly said.

'Oh, of course.'

'He's giving me guitar lessons,' Archie piped up.

'Yes, we know, Archie,' Eleanor said with a smile.

'And he has his tea with us too,' Archie said.

Eleanor and Bryony both stared hard at Polly.

'Only sometimes,' Jago said.

'And he dances in our front room,' Archie continued.

'Only sometimes,' Jago said again.

'He's very good at the conga,' Archie added, causing Grandpa Joe to splutter.

Baffled looks were exchanged around the table.

'It's all to help Archie with his music practice,' Polly said. 'Rhythm.'

'I see,' Bryony said, but she didn't look totally convinced.

Sam, who was sitting to Polly's right, cleared his throat. 'I think these are superb carrots,' he said. There was a moment's pause and then everybody laughed, breaking the tension.

Dessert was apple cake served with home-made custard and everybody had second helpings.

'Now, these apples,' Frank began.

'Are every bit as good as your carrots,' Eleanor said, winking at him from her end of the table.

'I was going to say that they're from the tree we planted together when we first moved here. Remember?'

Eleanor's expression softened as her memory journeyed back through the years.

'We didn't have any spare money then because there was so much work to be done on the house,' Frank continued, 'but I insisted that we started to plant an orchard.'

'I'm so glad we did that,' Eleanor said.

'It took a few years to provide as much fruit as it does now, mind,' Frank said.

'Is that the tree Sam carved his girlfriend's initials into?' Josh asked.

Sam glared across the table at his younger brother and Callie stared at Sam.

'Stop making trouble, Josh,' Eleanor warned.

'Who was she?' Callie asked.

'Nobody,' Sam said.

'Pippa Evans, wasn't it?' Josh went on.

'That's right,' Bryony said. 'Her initials were P E.'

A ripple of laughter sounded around the table.

'It was a long time ago,' Sam said patiently, picking up Callie's hand and squeezing it.

Once everyone was quite sure that they couldn't manage another mouthful even if there was enough apple cake left for a third helping each, Polly helped her mother clear away the dishes. Jago got up to help too.

'No, no, Jago,' Eleanor said. 'You're our guest.'

'I don't mind, really,' he said, following Polly out of the room with an armful of dishes. They got to the kitchen ahead of Eleanor.

'Polly?' he began. 'Look, I didn't mean to make you uncomfortable by being here, but I really wanted to see you.'

'You saw me yesterday,' Polly said, rinsing the bowls before putting them in the dishwasher.

'I know,' he said, 'but that was twenty-four hours ago. That's a lot of hours.'

Polly smiled in spite of herself, cursing him for being such a wit.

'May I remind you that you're here with my sister?'

'Yes, I know.'

'So what are you doing flirting with me in the kitchen?'

'Is that what I'm doing – *flirting*?' he asked, a grin on his face as she turned to look at him.

It was then that Eleanor walked in with a tray loaded with glasses.

'What a shame Lara couldn't make it,' she said. 'I do love a table full to its capacity.' She stopped as she saw just how close Jago was standing to her daughter. 'I'll leave these here,' she said, putting the tray down on a worktop and leaving the kitchen.

'Now, look what you've done!' Polly cried.

'*Me?*'

'Yes, you!' she said. 'You really shouldn't have come here today.'

He took a deep breath. 'I know. But I came because I wanted to tell you something.'

'You wanted to tell me something so you come to Sunday lunch as my sister's guest, surrounded by Nightingales where there's no hope of getting a single moment to yourself?'

'We've got a moment now,' he said. 'Listen—'

'What's going on?' Bryony asked as she breezed into the kitchen.

Polly gave Jago a look as if to say, *I told you so.*

'Jago's just helping me with the dishes,' she said, busying herself with the glasses her mother had placed on the worktop.

Bryony looked from one to the other and back again. 'What were you talking about?'

'Nothing,' Polly said. 'We were just—'

'Archie's next guitar lesson,' Jago finished.

'Oh,' Bryony said. 'Well, I missed you.' She took hold of Jago's arm in an act that Polly couldn't help thinking was far too familiar after only one date.

'We'll talk later,' Jago said, allowing himself to be led out of the room.

Polly sighed. She hated feeling like this, but she just couldn't seem to control her emotions when Jago was around and she couldn't deny the little glances he'd given her across the dining room table throughout lunch. She only hoped nobody else had noticed them although she suspected her mother had.

'Is that fire still going?' Eleanor's voice came from the hallway. 'We don't want to freeze having our tea.' She entered the kitchen again. 'All clear?'

Polly gave a little smile. 'It will be in a minute.'

'I'm not talking about the dishes. I was wondering which of my daughters was monopolising that handsome young man.'

'He's with Bryony, Mum.'

'Is he?'

'Yes.'

'Does he want to be?' Eleanor asked.

'What do you mean?'

Eleanor shook her head. 'I'm not going to push you, Polly, but it seems to me that there's something going on between the two of you.'

'There really isn't—'

'And that you're not quite ready to admit it yet,' Eleanor said, 'but don't leave it too long, darling. We all want to see you happy after all you've been through. You mustn't be afraid to move on and Jago seems really lovely although he needs to be honest with Bryony if he's not interested in her, and the sooner the better. And Archie adores Jago, doesn't he?'

'He's teaching Archie the guitar. That's all. We're just friends,' Polly said.

Eleanor nodded. 'Okay,' she said, 'just promise me one thing?'

'What?'

'That you give me a call as soon as you acknowledge what's going on in the heart of yours.'

CHAPTER 15

Tea was served in the living room. Eleanor had brought out her prettiest china cups. After a lifetime of servicing the Nightingale family, her china collection was a wonderful mismatch of different sizes and designs, but it was all the more fun for that and the women in the family always looked forward to seeing which pretty cup they would get. Would it be the delightfully round yellow and white one rimmed with gold? Or the sweet blue and white one with the image of a songbird? Or the elegant cup in turquoise and gold? The men would have been happy with a chunky mug with chips and tea stains, but Sunday was a day for fine bone china.

Polly sat nursing her cup in front of the fire. She had been given the little white and green cup smothered in pale pink roses. There was a tiny hairline crack inside it and Polly remembered the day that they had bought it at the church fete, discovering it in a tatty cardboard box that had been filled with old pipes and pipe cleaners. The little cup had been screaming to be rescued by an appreciative woman and Eleanor had been delighted with her purchase.

Polly glanced across the room to where Jago was sitting on one of the sofas in between Bryony and Archie amongst the heaps of floral cushions. He was holding one of the blue and white teacups and it looked so tiny in his great big hands that Polly almost laughed. But then she thought about those great big hands holding onto her waist as they'd danced in her living room and she suddenly didn't want to laugh anymore.

She got up from her chair by the fire. 'Anyone up for a walk?' she said.

'I don't know,' Sam said, 'it's pretty cold out there today.'

'Well, the dogs deserve a stretch,' Polly said. 'I won't hear the last of it if I don't take Dickens out.'

'Bryony?' Jago asked. 'Fancy going?'

'You seriously want to go out?' she asked him, looking out of the window at the grey and decidedly wet afternoon.

'Sure,' he said. 'I don't often get to walk a pack of dogs in the country.'

'Knock yourself out,' she said and Jago got up from the sofa. Bryony then caught Polly's eye. 'Actually, I will come,' Bryony said. 'I need to walk some of that cake off.'

Polly wondered if Bryony's decision was really about cake or if she just didn't trust her and Jago on their own after catching them in their tête-à-tête in the kitchen.

'Grandpa?' Polly asked as she headed into the hallway.

He waved a hand at her. 'I'll stay here with Nell,' he said and Polly looked across at her grandmother who was taking a nap in her favourite chair. After the fright she'd given them just a few months before, Grandpa had been keeping a special watch over her.

'I'll come,' Josh said.

'Come on, Sam,' Callie said, standing up. 'I need to walk that cake off too.'

'No you don't,' Sam said. 'I like that you've put a bit of weight on since moving to Suffolk.'

Callie gasped and Eleanor and Bryony gave cries of surprise too.

'I didn't mean—'

'Did a son of mine just comment on a woman's weight?' Eleanor asked.

'It came out wrong—' Sam said.

'I haven't put any weight on, have I?' Callie asked, her hands flying to her tummy.

'I just meant that you're absolutely perfect,' Sam said.

'I wouldn't say another word if I was you,' Josh said, chuckling at the predicament his brother now found himself in.

'Callie – I really didn't mean it to sound like that.'

Callie's expression was one of half-amusement and half-shock. 'I might have enjoyed a few Sunday lunches, but I don't think I'm in the danger zone yet!'

'Of course you're not,' Sam said, standing up and reaching out for her hands. 'It's just, you were such a skinny stick when you first arrived from London.'

Bryony gasped.

'A skinny stick? I'm not sure that's less of an insult than calling me a porky heifer!' Callie said.

'I didn't call you a porky heifer!' Sam said.

'Can you actually have a porky heifer?' Frank asked. 'I mean, pork and heifer are different animals, aren't they?'

'I don't think we need to concern ourselves with that,' Eleanor told her husband.

'Perhaps I should jog around the footpaths instead of walking around them with you,' Callie said with a wry grin. 'It sounds as if I need to burn off all these extra calories!'

Grandpa Joe was chuckling from his armchair and the noise woke up Grandma Nell.

'What's going on?' she asked.

'Our Sam's just insulted Callie,' Grandpa Joe said.

'I *didn't* insult her!' Sam said.

Callie play-punched him and shook her head. 'I forgive you,' she said.

'But I didn't–'

She leaned forward and kissed his cheek.

'That is one forgiving woman,' Grandpa Joe said as he began cracking walnuts with an old silver nutcracker. 'Keep hold of her, Sammy.'

'Yes, all ten tonnes of me!' Callie quipped.

The members of the Nightingale family who were going walking made a slow progress of putting on hats, scarves, gloves and boots, gathering dogs together and making sure that they had all the paraphernalia needed for a muddy country walk in the middle of winter.

A gunmetal sky greeted them as they left the house and Bryony pulled a face. 'What are we doing?' she asked.

'We'll enjoy the fire all the more when we get back,' Callie said. 'I've come to love country walks in all weathers since moving to Suffolk.'

'You are a strange one,' Bryony said with a smile that showed she was teasing.

The party walked down the lane, crossing the wooden footbridge over the ford.

'This place always makes me shudder now,' Sam said, thinking of the time he'd found Grandma Nell in the road there.

Callie squeezed his hand in her gloved one. 'I don't think Grandpa Joe is ever going to let her out of his sight again.'

'And I'm not going to let you out of mine,' Sam said.

'It would be pretty hard to considering how huge I am!' Callie teased.

Josh, who was walking just behind them, laughed out loud.

'You're not going to let me forget this, are you?' Sam said.

'Nope!' Callie said.

'Quite right too,' Bryony said, linking arms with Jago.

Polly, who was walking just behind with Dickens, tried not to look.

They left the lane, taking a footpath through a wood where they let the straining dogs off their leads and watched as they chased each other through the undergrowth. Archie ran after them, but didn't stand a chance of keeping up.

'It's beautiful here,' Jago said, turning round to include Polly.

'We used to play here as children,' Bryony said. 'I used to try and climb all the trees with Sam and Josh, but Polly would always be making funny little dens.'

'You liked dens?' Jago asked Polly.

'I guess I was always trying to find a space to call my own,' she said. 'In a household full of brothers and sisters, it was sometimes hard to find a peaceful little corner.'

'Ah, you see, I had the opposite problem,' Jago said. 'There was just me.'

'I think it must be sad being an only child,' Bryony said.

'It wasn't really,' Jago said. 'It's what I was used to and it's probably what drove me to write music.'

Polly watched as Bryony looked up sympathetically at Jago. Had Bryony kissed him yet, Polly couldn't help wondering? Not that the thought should bother her. She'd set them up, after all.

The wood opened out into a field and the dogs raced ahead of them, startling a pair of partridges who flew up and over a hedge. The recent rain had left the field boggy and sticky and, as they came out onto a narrow country lane, they saw that it was flooded up ahead.

'Oh, no,' Polly said. 'We're not going to get through that.'

'We don't really want to double back, do we?' Josh asked.

'The dogs will get filthy if we go this way,' Sam said.

'They're filthy already,' Josh said and, sure enough, they were, their legs and bellies splattered with mud long before they reached the mammoth puddle.

'We're all wearing boots, aren't we?' Bryony said. 'It's not likely to be too deep.'

The group approached the puddle. Archie was the first one in and the water was soon threatening to spill over the tops of his boots.

'Archie – wait for me!' Polly cried.

'Hold on there, little guy,' Jago said, swooping in and hoisting the youngster onto his back. Archie laughed.

'I was kind of hoping he'd carry me across,' Bryony whispered to Polly, 'like when Angel Clare carries Tess across the flooded lane in *Tess of the D'Urbervilles*.'

'That kind of thing never happens outside of a novel,' Polly said. 'You should know that by now.'

'But I'm a romantic,' Bryony said, 'and continually live in hope.'

'Then you'll always be left disappointed,' Josh said.

'Have you been listening to us?' Bryony said, glaring at her brother.

'Nothing else to do out here,' he said with a shrug before wading across the puddle.

'Only one thing for it,' Bryony said, grabbing hold of Polly's arm. 'Sisters are doing it for themselves.'

The two of them walked through the water together, making it to the other side safely. Archie was still riding on Jago's back and it looked as if Bryony wasn't going to be able to claim his attention back anytime soon.

'Polly?' Bryony began.

'Yes?'

'I wanted to thank you for this whole Jago thing.'

'That's okay,' Polly said, hoping that her face wasn't heating up in discomfort.

'I – erm–' she lowered her voice, 'I just wanted to make sure that you're all right about me being with him.'

'What do you mean?'

Bryony shrugged. 'You two seem close to me.'

'We're friends, that's all,' Polly said quickly.

'Yeah?'

Polly nodded. 'He's a fan of Archie's.'

Bryony looked ahead to where Jago was zigzagging across the little country lane like a show pony to whoops of joy from Archie.

'And Archie's certainly a fan of his,' Bryony said.

Polly watched the two of them larking about and, once again, felt a great pang in her heart at all that her son had missed out on in his years of growing up without a father.

It was dark by the time they got back to Campion House. Boots were kicked off and neatly stacked and each of the three muddy dogs got a good rub down with a towel. It was as Polly was refilling the water bowls in the boot room that Jago managed to corner her again.

'Hey,' he said.

She looked up and smiled briefly at him.

'I'll come round later, okay?' he said.

'No, don't,' she said, panic rising in her voice.

'We've got to talk about this.'

'I'd rather not.'

'Polly – I'm coming round.'

Josh came into the kitchen. 'Any food around?' he asked. 'I'm starving!'

'How can you be starving after that massive lunch?' Polly asked him, pushing passed Jago.

'We've just been on a long walk. A guy needs to keep his energy up,' Josh said.

Jago nudged Polly gently as Josh popped his head into the fridge.

'I'll see you tonight,' he said.

The knock at the door came just after eight o'clock that evening. Polly and Archie were in the front room watching a BBC drama that was a little too dark to be enjoyable on a Sunday.

Archie looked at his mum. 'There's someone at the door,' he said, baffled that she wasn't already answering it.

'Leave it,' she said.

'Can I answer it?'

'No, Archie,' she said. 'Anyway, it's late. You should be in bed.'

'But it might be important.'

'It isn't,' she told him.

He got up from the sofa and walked to the window, opening the curtains a crack.

'Don't do that,' she told him.

'It's Jago.'

'Draw the curtains.'

'But it's Jago.'

'Just ignore it.'

Archie looked totally stunned by this request and Polly knew that she was being unreasonable in not explaining things properly to him, but what could she say? That she was a married woman developing a ridiculous crush on a man much younger than her who just happened to be going out with her sister? That wouldn't do at all.

Another knock sounded. Jago obviously knew that they were at home and wasn't giving up. Polly muted the sound on the TV.

'I want to answer the door,' Archie said.

'It's your bedtime, Archie.'

'Awww, Mum!'

'Go upstairs now.'

'That's so unfair. I want to see Jago.'

'You spent the entire day with Jago,' Polly said.

They stood facing one another as if about to do battle, but then a strange noise greeted them and they looked at each other in bafflement.

'Is that—'

'It's a guitar,' Archie said. 'He's playing his guitar.'

Polly frowned. She could definitely hear a guitar being played on her doorstep, but things got even stranger when the singing started.

'What's he think he's doing?' Polly asked as Jago's voice got louder. It was the first time she'd heard Jago singing and she had to admit that he had a nice voice, but that wasn't the point, was it? He was manipulating her into opening the door and she wasn't going to do that.

In the time it took her to have these thoughts, Archie had torn out of the living room and unlocked the door.

'Archie – no!' she cried as she followed him, but it was too late. The door was open and there stood Jago, his guitar slung around his body like a happy accomplice.

'Mum wouldn't let me answer the door,' Archie said.

'It's late,' Polly said.

'I didn't mean to disturb you,' Jago said.

'So you sing at the top of your voice on our doorstep?' Polly said. 'You'll have old Mrs Letchworth ringing the police.'

'Well, you said you wanted to hear me sing one of my songs,' he said with a grin.

'Yes, but not after eight o'clock on a Sunday evening,' Polly said.

'It was brilliant,' Archie said. 'Play it again!'

'I don't think your mum wants me to, Arch.'

'Just ignore her,' Archie said.

Polly glared at her son.

'Actually, Arch, I would like to speak to your mum about something in private. Would that be all right with you?'

'Sure,' Archie said, not even attempting to put up a fight. 'I have to go to bed anyway.'

Polly watched in amazement as her son kissed her good night, gave Jago a wave and then headed up the stairs.

'As impressive as you are at getting Archie to go to bed,' Polly began, 'I really don't think you should be here at all.' She walked through to the living room and Jago followed her, closing the front door behind him. She turned to face him but, before she could say another word about why he shouldn't be there and how he should leave immediately, he'd closed the space between them and captured her face in his hands and kissed her.

Polly didn't move and she certainly couldn't say anything – not with Jago's mouth upon hers – but she could have made some sort of protest if she'd really wanted to. Only she didn't.

'There,' he said, when he released her.

She looked into his slate-grey eyes, noticing the tiny flecks of green there for the first time.

'We shouldn't have–' she began.

'Yes we should,' he interrupted. 'We should have done that ages ago. You think too much, Polly. You try and rationalise everything, but some things aren't neat and ordered. They're messy and complicated.' He smiled at her as he reached out to tuck a lock of stray hair behind her ear. 'And wonderful.'

'But I'm married,' she whispered.

'Yeah? Well, I don't see a husband anywhere.'

'Don't be cruel.'

'I'm not being cruel. I'm being honest. Sean's been gone for over three years and you need to learn to live again. This half-life you're living isn't any good. It's not making you happy, is it? Don't you want something more? Don't you want to have some fun? I know there's something between us, Polly. Something good. And I think we should grab it.'

'I can't.'

'Why not?'

'Because, if you haven't forgotten, you're involved with my sister.'

'We went on one date,' Jago told her.

'And she invited you to Sunday lunch. That's a big deal in our family. You'll probably have to marry her now.'

'I'll explain things to her.'

'She likes you, Jago, and I won't hurt her.'

'But if I talk to her,' Jago began, 'if I sort things out with her, will you think about seeing me then?'

'I don't know,' Polly said. 'This is all so–'

'Kiss me,'

Her eyes widened at his demand.

'Stop thinking and just kiss me.'

Polly could feel her heart racing. Her head was telling her to end this now – to throw Jago and his guitar out of the front door and refuse to ever see him again, but her heart was telling her something else entirely and she gave into it, throwing herself towards him and kissing him with a passion that had been so deeply locked away for so long that she'd forgotten its existence.

When they parted, Jago laughed and it was such a warm, wonderful sound that Polly joined in too.

'Woah!' he said. 'I knew you had hidden depths, but I never imagined anything like that.'

'Are you teasing me?'

'Of course not,' he said, stroking her right cheek. His hand was warm and she felt wonderfully shivery at his touch. 'You're amazing, Polly.'

'This is crazy,' she said.

'Why?' he asked, his head tilted to one side.

'Well, for a start, I'm so much older than you,' she said.

'Really? I hadn't noticed,' he said.

She shook her head. 'You hadn't noticed that I'm middle-aged?'

'You're not middle-aged.'

'I'm thirty-five,' she protested.

'That's not middle-aged!' he said with a laugh.

'It is compared to you,' she said. 'What are you – Twenty-one?'

'Twenty-two,' he corrected.

'Exactly. I could almost be your mother, Jago.'

He looked astonished at this declaration. 'A thirteen-year-old mother?'

'It happens.'

'You're just making excuses,' he said, 'and I'm not going to let you do that.'

'Oh, aren't you?'

He shook his head. 'Nope. I'm going to shake things up around here.'

'Really?'

'And you're going to love it.'

'But what will people say? I mean, if we do go out together.'

'So you *are* considering it?' he said with a little grin.

'I'm just hypothesising.'

'You don't want to do that. Anyway, who cares what people think? If they have a problem, it's *their* problem, not ours.'

'I don't like gossip and I certainly don't want to be at the centre of any,' she told him.

'You're not giving your friends and neighbours much credit, Polly. They're probably all so busy with their own lives that they won't even notice us together.'

'But they have already. The village hall yesterday and Antonia Jessop–'

'God, do you *really* care what somebody like her thinks?'

'Yes, don't you?'

'No, of course not! And, if you've got any sense, you won't either. Would you really stop yourself from enjoying life because of a fleeting thought that might or might not go through somebody else's mind? That's crazy!'

Polly blinked. He was actually making a lot of sense to her. Why was she so worried about what other people thought? It was just a part of her character, she supposed. She was always very aware of conventionality and of playing a good and proper role in society and that didn't involve going out with a much younger man when her husband might still be alive somewhere.

'Listen,' Jago said, 'we don't need to rush into things. You don't need to be seen on the back of my bike, and I promise I won't kiss the living daylights out of you in the middle of the next book club meeting. But I really like being with you and Archie. I can't remember the last time I was this happy. It just seems so natural to be with you two.'

'I feel the same way.'

He nodded and stroked her cheek again. 'You're really special.

You know that, don't you? And I want to be with you. Will you let me do that?'

Polly reached a hand up to his face, mirroring his action, and nodded. He gave a smile worthy of Gabriel Oak and it didn't come as any surprise to her when they kissed again and, at that very moment, she believed she wouldn't care if the whole of Castle Clare came barging into her front room to watch them. She and Jago were kissing and it was wonderful. Truly wonderful.

After he'd left, Polly walked upstairs to check on Archie and was surprised to see him sitting up in bed with his lamp still on.

'Archie – you should be asleep!' she told him.

'What did Jago want?'

'He wanted to talk to me.'

'I know. But what about?'

Polly sat on the edge of the bed, wondering how best to answer his question. 'Adult stuff,' she said.

'He likes you, Mum.'

Polly leaned forward to plump Archie's pillows. 'He might do. Would that be all right with you if he did, and if I liked him back?'

Archie snuggled down under his duvet cover. 'Yes,' he said. 'It would be good. I like Jago.'

'I know you do, and he likes you too. But–'

'What, Mum?'

'But what about your dad?' she dared to ask, watching her son's face, anxious to hear his response.

'Dad's gone, isn't he?'

Polly felt tears pricking her eyes. 'I think so, yes.'

'Then it's okay.'

She bent to kiss her son's rosy cheek. 'I love you, Archie.'

'Love you too,' he said and she switched his bedside lamp off and left the room.

Polly spent the rest of Sunday evening tidying around the house. She let Dickens out in the garden, prepared Archie's school bag for the next morning, read some more of *Far From the Madding Crowd* and then got ready for bed.

It was only after she'd turned her light off and got into bed that she allowed herself to cry. They were great, warm silent tears of both joy and relief because, for the first time since Sean had disappeared, Polly could see a little glimmer of happiness in her future.

CHAPTER 16

Bryony was plumping a beanbag when Jago entered the shop on Monday morning.

'Hey,' she said.

'Hey,' he said back.

'This is a nice surprise,' she told him, standing up and pushing her hair back. She was wearing a broad hair band patterned with fuchsia and turquoise swirls and a deep pink dress in crushed velvet. 'I called you on Sunday evening. Were you out?'

Jago swallowed hard. He'd seen her name flash up on his phone shortly after he'd got back from Polly's and hadn't been able to talk to Bryony, not after he'd just been kissing her sister.

'No, sorry. I was working,' he lied. Well, he had had a bit of a strum that evening.

'I wanted to make sure you were okay after the Sunday lunch onslaught.'

He smiled. 'It was fun.'

'I was worried we all might have scared you off.'

'I had a great time.'

'Good,' she said. 'I did too. In fact, I was wondering if you'd like to make it a regular–'

'Bryony,' he interrupted, 'can we talk?'

She stared at him, her beautiful eyes wide in her pale face. 'It always sounds ominous when somebody says that.'

He took a deep breath. 'Is there anywhere to sit down?'

'Well, if we both want to sit down at the same time, there's only the bean bags, I'm afraid.'

He nodded and chose the red one, his long legs folding as he collapsed almost to the floor. Bryony followed suit only a little more elegantly. It was obvious that she'd done this many times before and looked far more comfortable than he felt.

'Bryony,' he began, clearing his throat.

'Jago,' she said with a tiny laugh that sounded nervous.

There was a pause, but it was one of those awkward ones rather than one between friends who might be comfortable just sitting in silence on a pair of bean bags together.

'I – erm – don't really know how to say this.'

'Quickly?' Bryony suggested. 'Because you're making me nervous.'

'Sorry,' he said. 'I should have told you on Saturday. It was selfish of me not to.'

'Wait,' Bryony said, surprising him when she held her hand up. 'I think I know what you're going to say.'

'You do?'

She nodded and her fingers circled inside a pair of silver bangles she was wearing, making them clang together. 'It's about Polly, isn't it?'

His eyes widened in genuine surprise. 'Yes.'

'You like her, don't you?'

Jago raked a hand through his hair and sighed. 'Is it that obvious?'

'Just to the whole world,' Bryony said. 'I was kind of trying to ignore it. I kept telling myself all day yesterday that you were just friends or that maybe it was a passing crush on your part or something.'

'I don't think it is,' Jago admitted.

'No, I had the feeling it wouldn't be.'

'I'm really sorry. I never meant to hurt you.'

Bryony swallowed hard. 'You very nearly did,' she said, 'but I think I'll survive. Now, had you taken me out on a second date and sung me another song, you'd be tied to me for life.'

He looked down at the floor.

'I'm teasing you,' she said. 'Let's not make things awkward between us, eh? That would be really uncomfortable. I mean, if you're going to be spending future Sundays with us – as Polly's guest, not mine – I really don't want to feel like this around the table.'

'Me neither,' he said and he stood up. 'You're really great, Bryony, and you'll find that special someone soon.'

'You reckon?' she said as she got up from the bean bag. 'He's taking his time getting here.'

'He's on his way.'

Bryony gave a wry smile. 'I hope so.'

Eleanor was returning from a short walk with Hardy and Brontë, Grandpa Joe and Grandma Nell. They'd taken a circular footpath around one of the big fields, breathing in the frosty morning air and puffing it back out like a trio of dragons. The walk was about as much as Nell could manage these days.

'You mustn't fuss over me,' she'd told her daughter-in-law as she'd helped her over a small stile. 'I can still walk.'

'I know you can. You're fitter than a lot of people a quarter of your age,' Eleanor told her. Still, she was keeping a closer eye on Nell these days. Nell's forgetfulness was worrying. The doctor had told Eleanor to keep in touch and the family always made sure there was somebody with Nell.

As they walked in via the back door, shedding their boots, coats and scarves and giving the dogs a rub down, the telephone rang.

'I'll finish Hardy,' Grandpa Joe said, taking the towel from Eleanor as she went to answer the phone.

'Hardy won't let me have his back paws,' Eleanor called back.

'Don't worry, I'll get them,' Grandpa Joe said.

Eleanor picked up the phone. 'Hello.'

'Mum?'

'Bryony? Are you okay?'

There was a big sigh on the other end of the line. 'I'm not sure.'

'What's wrong?'

'Jago's just been in the shop.'

'And?'

'We've broken up.'

'Already? But you've only been seeing him since Friday, haven't you?'

'I think this must be a new world record,' Bryony said with a sad little laugh.

'Has this got something to do with Polly?' Eleanor asked.

'You knew too?'

'I kind of guessed.'

'I kept seeing them exchange these little looks,' Bryony said.

'I kept catching them having tête-à-têtes,' Eleanor told her daughter. 'I thought there was something going on, but Polly kept denying it.'

'She told me she wasn't available,' Bryony said. 'She said she wasn't interested in seeing anybody.'

'I think she's been trying to convince herself by saying those things.'

'I think you're right.'

There was a pause.

'Are you okay, my love?' Eleanor asked.

'Yes,' Bryony said. 'I'm okay.'

'Polly will need our support in this.'

'I know,' Bryony said, 'and she'll have mine once I've cleared my head.'

'You are *so* special, Bryony, and you *will* find the right man for you.'

'Jago said the same thing.'

'And he's right.'

'Thanks, Mum! Okay, gotta go. There's a customer cracking spines!'

'Go stop them!' Eleanor cried, shaking her head at the outrageous behaviour.

Grandpa Joe walked into the hall as she hung up from her daughter. 'I got his feet,' he said.

'Pardon?'

'Hardy. I dried them all. Six of them, right? At least, he seems to have six paws whenever there's mud around.' He chuckled. 'You okay?'

'That was Bryony. Jago called into her shop this morning to say he was seeing Polly.'

'One Nightingale girl not enough for him?'

'I think he got a bit confused as to which one he liked best,' Eleanor said.

'I'd be confused too if I was him,' Grandpa Joe said. 'It's a good job Lara wasn't here on Sunday to make matters even worse.'

'Don't even joke about it,' Eleanor said and then she shook her head. 'No, Polly's the one for Jago.'

'You sound very sure of that.'

'I am,' she said with a smile. 'I just hope Polly is too.'

Polly wasn't working her usual Monday morning shift at Sam's bookshop. She'd called him earlier, knowing that Jago would be seeing Bryony and not wanting to be in such close proximity in case her sister had the urge to flatten her with the hefty children's encyclopaedia which had just come in.

No, she'd made her apologies to Sam, saying she had to wait in for someone. Well, that was kind of true wasn't it? She was waiting for

Jago and, sure enough, as she peeped out of the living room window for the twentieth time, there he was, pulling up on his bike and taking his helmet off. He saw her and waved and she ran to the front door.

'Did you tell her?' she asked as he walked towards her.

He nodded. 'Yep.'

'Is she okay?'

'She said she'll kill you the next time you're in town, but she's fine.'

Polly's mouth dropped open. 'Oh, no.'

'I'm kidding!' Jago said. Polly clouted him. 'Ouch! That went right through my bike leathers.'

'Good,' she said, storming into the house. He followed her inside and closed the door.

'Polly, wait!' he said.

She was in the kitchen now.

'Hey,' he said as he joined her by the sink. 'What's the matter?' She felt his hands on her shoulders. 'Polly? Why are you crying?' He gently turned her around to face him.

'This is big,' she said.

'I know.' He closed his arms around her.

'I feel like I'm spinning.'

'I've got hold of you.'

She gave a light laugh and hugged her arms around his waist. 'You've still got your leathers on.'

'I wasn't sure if you wanted me to hang around.'

'Of course I do.'

'Plus I wasn't sure you wouldn't hit me again.'

'I won't hit you again. I promise.'

He stroked her hair.

'I hope Bryony's okay with all this,' Polly said. 'I feel really bad doing this to her.'

'She's fine, I promise you.' He kissed the top of her head. 'You know, I don't normally get you all to myself, do I?'

'What do you mean?'

'I mean, Archie's normally here. Not that I begrudge his company,' Jago said.

'You'd better not,' Polly said. 'Not if you want to be with me.'

'I realise that you come as a BOGOF.'

Polly laughed. 'That's right. We're a package deal.'

Jago smiled and took his jacket off, placing it over a kitchen chair. 'Come here,' he told her. 'I want you right where you were a moment ago.'

Polly took a step towards him and put her arms around him once again. How she could get used to this, she thought as she rested her head against his shoulder and sighed.

'How long have we got?' he asked her.

'I have to leave just after three to pick Archie up.'

Jago looked at the kitchen clock. It was just after half past ten. 'So, I can hold you for another four and a half hours?'

'Won't you want a break for lunch?'

'No, no. I'm good here. I'm just going to stand on this spot with you in my arms for as long as I can.'

Polly giggled.

'I like it when you laugh,' he said. 'You don't do it enough.'

'What do you mean? I've not stopped laughing since I met you,' she told him.

They stood there in silence for a moment, the sound of Dickens snoring in his basket.

'Bryony's probably told Mum what's happened by now,' Polly said.

'Probably.'

'Mum knew anyway.'

'Did she?'

Polly nodded. 'She was trying to winkle it out of me all day yesterday.'

'Will you ring her?' Jago asked.

'Not yet,' she said. 'I want to tell Archie first.'

'What are you going to say to him?'

'Well, I kind of sounded him out about it last night.'

'Did you?'

She nodded, her head going up and down on his chest. 'He really adores you.'

'He's a great kid. I love spending time with him.'

'Are you going to tell your mum?' Polly asked.

'I think she might have guessed as well.'

'Really?' Polly looked up at him, her cheeks colouring. 'Does she approve?'

'She approves of you, but I'm not sure what she'll think about me seeing you. She'll probably say I'm not good enough for you. She's very protective of you,' he told her, stroking her hair. 'I think everyone is.'

'What do you mean?' she asked, genuinely puzzled.

'I've noticed the way people look out for you here. They care about you. It's nice.'

Polly nodded as she realised what he meant. 'Everyone's been so kind since Sean left. It's one of the wonderful things about living in a small community. Not just the village, but Castle Clare too. People really do care about you. I got so many lovely messages from people and offers of help. I'll never forget it, but I can take care of myself, you know.'

'I know that,' Jago said, 'and you do an amazing job with Archie too.'

She smiled up at him. 'It was so hard at first. I felt lost. I'd always had Sean there with me and suddenly it was just me and this little boy. I probably made so many mistakes.'

'I'm sure you didn't.'

They were quiet again for a moment, contented to just stand there in each other's arms. Then, Polly began to giggle.

'What is it?' Jago asked.

'I was just wondering what Archie would think if he came in and found us like this.'

'Do you think he'd mind?'

'No,' Polly said, 'but he might be momentarily disgusted. He's going through the "I hate girls stage".'

'I don't think I ever went through that,' Jago said.

'Have you always had a thing for older women then?'

'I don't have a thing for older women,' he said with a laugh. 'But I do have a thing for you.'

'I'm worried about you coming to Sunday lunch again in case you switch affections to my mum.'

'Polly! You don't seriously think that, do you?'

'Well, you seem to be working your way around the Nightingale women.'

'But it was *your* idea that I went out with your sister!'

Polly laughed. 'I know!'

It was then that Dickens suddenly sat up in his basket, his eyes alert and his ears forward as a low growl vibrated in his throat.

'What is it, boy?' Polly asked.

Dickens got out of his basket and ran to the back door and started barking.

Polly looked at Jago. 'I'd better take a look.'

She followed the dog to the back door and unlocked it, stepping out into the garden and checking the side gate, but everything was as it should be. However, Dickens seemed quite sure something was amiss and Polly watched as he zigzagged around the small garden in that manic way which spaniels have.

Finally, Polly got fed up of waiting for him to come back in and whistled for him.

'It must have been a cat,' she said to Jago who was standing in the doorway watching them. 'It's freezing!'

'Come back in and get warm.'

Polly nodded and rubbed her arms with her hands.

'Hey, I can do a pretty good job of that,' Jago said, closing the door and then enfolding Polly in his arms again.

'I could get used to this,' she told him.

It was then that Jago's phone beeped in his pocket. He took it out, looked at the message and groaned.

'It's Briggs.'

'From your band?'

'Yep. Bit of a crisis,' he said. 'I should shoot over to his.'

'Okay.'

'But I don't want to leave you,' he said, hugging her again.

'I don't want to be the cause of some great musical disaster,' she said, 'so perhaps you'd better go. I've got a heap of ironing to do anyway.'

'And so real life intervenes,' Jago said.

Polly smiled. 'Oh, yes.'

'Can I call you later?'

'I hope you will.'

They kissed. 'This is good,' he said.

'Very good,' she told him and they walked to the front door hand in hand.

'I'll call you.'

'Do that.'

He gave her a wink and she winked right back at him which made him laugh, and she watched as he donned his helmet and rode off on his motorbike.

Polly was floating on air for the rest of the day. She didn't grimace whilst doing the ironing, she didn't groan whilst taking the rubbish out and, during the cold muddy walk with Dickens, she had a huge smile on her face because she was thinking warm thoughts about Jago.

Driving into Castle Clare to pick up Archie from school, she wondered how she was going to tell her son. Should she just come right out with it? Or should she just take things slowly, letting Archie see things for himself?

Pulling up near the school, Polly got out of the car and waited by the school gates with the other parents, nodding to a couple of her friends. She didn't socialise with many of the other parents; she found that juggling her two jobs as well as raising Archie was enough to fill her time, but there was always a certain amount of toing and froing with children's parties and she'd have to get herself organised with Archie's fast approaching, she thought.

And there he was – her little boy – running towards her as if he was still three years old rather than nearly seven. Still so excited to see her and tell her all about his day. Long may it continue, she thought, greeting him before walking back to the car as he rattled on about how he'd managed to score a whole nine out of ten in his maths test.

'That's certainly more than I ever got,' Polly confessed, remembering her hatred of maths.

It was as they were driving home that she first spotted it. She caught sight of Archie in her rear view mirror as she reached a junction. He was holding something in his hand that she couldn't quite make out.

'Archie? What's that?'

'A boat.'

'Hold it up.'

He did as he was told and Polly squinted at it, noticing that it was a model of a little ship. 'Where did you get that?'

'A man gave it to Tiger to give to me.'

'Where? When?'

'Tiger said he was outside the school gates at lunch time and the man told Tiger to give the boat to me.'

'Archie, what did this man look like?'

He shrugged. 'I didn't see him.'

'Are you sure?'

'I didn't see him, Mum.'

Polly felt quite faint. 'Give me the boat.'

He handed it to her, but a honk on a horn from the car behind them meant that Polly had to move on and so she dropped the little boat into her lap, but she could feel her heart had begun to race.

How Polly managed to make it home without glancing down at the model boat, she'd never know, but she did, parking the car and placing the boat in her coat pocket.

'Can I have it back, Mum?' Archie said as they went indoors.

'No, Archie. I need to keep it for a while, okay?'

He looked at her, obviously bemused, but then Dickens ran into the hallway and distracted him.

'Change out of your uniform.'

'Okay,' he said and, once he was safely upstairs, Polly took her coat off and reached for the boat in her pocket.

The similarity was striking.

'*Oystercatcher*,' she whispered. The *Oystercatcher* had been Sean's boat. Was it just a coincidence? Had some random person been hanging around the school with a model of a boat to give away to some child they didn't know? It didn't seem very likely. And why pick out Archie to give it to? No, Polly thought. This wasn't a random act. The boat was a clear message, wasn't it? A message sent not to her son but to her.

'Sean's back,' she whispered.

CHAPTER 17

'I've got a boat,' a man's voice said.

Polly turned around, the summer sunshine dazzling her eyes. The man who greeted her was tall with short sandy hair and startling blue eyes. He was wearing a T-shirt and shorts and had an athletic look about him that made him look right at home there on the harbour.

'She's called *Oystercatcher*. Just over there.' He pointed to a pretty yacht in the marina. Compared to its harbour companions, *Oystercatcher* was a modest little boat, but a very pretty one.

'It's lovely,' she said.

'Would you like to go out in her?'

Polly laughed at his forwardness although she had to give him marks for originality. It wasn't every man who had the luxury of approaching a woman with that particular line.

'Polly?' It was Georgia, one of the friends whom she'd arrived with. Georgia was followed by her boyfriend, Alex, and a couple of others from the gang. Polly had spent the few years since graduating teaching abroad, but now she was back home and had met a small group of friends for lunch down by a pub on the River Orwell.

'We lost you!' Georgia said.

'I was just taking a stroll,' Polly said. 'I wanted to see the view.'

'It's better from the water,' the man said. 'Nothing beats the view of the land from the water.'

Polly smiled. 'This man has just asked me to go out in his boat with him,' she told her friends.

'Is that right?' Georgia said.

Alex did a double take as he stepped forward. 'Sean?'

'Alex?'

The two men lunged for each other and did the old backslapping routine, laughing heartily.

'Georgia, Polly, everyone – this is Sean Prior,' Alex announced. He's the guy I sailed round the Greek islands with a couple of years ago.'

'Really?' Georgia was instantly impressed and stepped forward to shake the man's hand.

'How's the boat doing?' Alex asked.

'Had to sell her,' Sean said. 'But just bought this little one,' he said, nodding to *Oystercatcher*.'

'She's a little beauty,' Alex remarked.

'But little for sure,' Sean said. 'I don't think I'll ever own another like *Zephyr* again.'

'Ah, she will be missed.'

'She will,' Sean said. 'Listen, I've just asked Polly to come on board. That's okay, isn't it?'

Polly's eyes widened at his use of her name before they had been officially introduced.

'Sure thing,' Alex said. 'Go right ahead.'

'What if I don't want to go?' Polly said.

'You're turning down a sail with Sean Prior?' Alex asked incredulously, giving a shrug.

'I'll go!' Georgia said.

'Oh, no you won't,' Alex said. 'You're staying on dry land with me.'

She pouted. 'You'll have to go now, Polly,' she said, 'so I can live the experience through you.'

'Well?' Sean prompted. 'How about it?'

Polly looked out onto the water which was a stunning blue today and thought how wonderful it would be to venture out there. The fact that Alex knew Sean made it seem a little less risky to accept the offer.

'Okay,' she said at last.

Georgia clapped her hands. 'We'll watch!'

'No we won't,' Alex said. 'We're going back to the pub. Catch up with us there, okay?'

'I won't keep her long,' Sean said.

Georgia waved goodbye as if Polly was off on some transatlantic journey instead of a tootle along the River Orwell.

'Have you been sailing before?' Sean asked as he led the way.

'No, never.'

'Well, we won't be using the sails today. We'll use the motor as it's a short trip.'

They reached the *Oystercatcher* and Sean hopped nimbly aboard, turning to face Polly and holding his hand out to help her.

'Thank you,' she said, her eyes widening when she realised how small the cockpit was. They were going to be in very close proximity for the duration of their journey.

'Life jacket,' he said, handing it to her and putting one on himself. She watched how to do it. A life jacket was a new experience for a landlubber.

He started up the engine and carefully guided the boat out of the marina and into the River Orwell, taking the tiller and looking ahead with those amazing blue eyes of his. Polly crossed the tiny space and looked down into the cabin.

'Four berth,' Sean said.

'Do you sleep on the boat?'

'All the time,' he said. 'It's great for all-night parties.' He grinned. 'You can find a mooring and make as much noise as you like. But I don't really do that sort of thing these days. I'm more likely to keep her to myself and enjoy the solitude.'

'Can I take a look?'

He nodded and Polly carefully walked down the steps into the cabin and immediately started swaying.

'Oh!' she gasped, quickly coming back up into the cockpit.

'Don't have your sea legs yet?' he said. She shook her head. 'Look out towards the horizon. That'll settle you. Take some deep breaths.' She did as she was told. 'Better?'

'Thank you.'

'Perhaps we shouldn't go out to sea today,' he said.

'You weren't planning that, were you?' she asked in horror.

'Only teasing. We're not going to go far. Just up to Pin Mill.'

Polly felt mightily relieved. She hadn't realised quite how useless she would be out on the water. It was always one of those things in life that one imagined one would be good at. Whenever Polly had thought of sailing in the past, she'd had a vision of a self-assured, Grace Kelly-style woman, standing at the tiller with her hair blowing in the breeze. Instead, she was a nervous wreck with her hair not so much blowing as knotting angrily across her face.

'Relax!' Sean cried.

'I'm trying!' she cried back, and she really did, looking out from the boat as the light sparkled like a thousand brilliant-cut diamonds on the water. A huge black cormorant took off from a moored boat, its enormous wings dark against the blue sky, and Polly gasped as she saw tantalising glimpses of beautiful homes by the waterfront which would be impossible to see from any road. Secret worlds, she thought. Worlds only visible by boat. Worlds this man knew all about.

She turned to look at him as he stood at the tiller. He was wearing a navy cap now to shield his eyes and his face was bronzed from exposure to the sun and his arms were gloriously tanned too.

'Enjoying the view?' he asked with a grin.

Polly looked away, feeling herself blushing. 'Yes,' she said, pointing to a church.

'Levington,' he said and she felt the full weight of his eyes upon her. 'Come here.'

She turned around and swallowed hard, suddenly aware that she was out in the middle of the river with someone who was practically a stranger. Alex might have sailed around the Greek islands with him, but Polly didn't know if he could be trusted or not.

'Why?' she asked, staying exactly where she was.

'Come and take the tiller,' he said. 'Come on. Don't you want to have a go at steering?'

Polly wasn't sure if she did or not, but it would seem churlish if she didn't show some interest and so she walked towards him and placed her hands on the smooth wood.

'Oh,' she said a moment later. 'You have to be quite strong, don't you?'

'It's not as easy as a wheel,' he told her. 'Keep between the buoys. We'll just go a little further and then turn her around.'

Polly laughed. She couldn't help it. This was actually really good fun.

'Okay?'

She nodded because she didn't think she could speak whilst concentrating on what she was doing with this man's yacht. He had trusted her to take charge of it and, although he was standing right beside her and able to correct any mistakes she might make, it showed a great deal of faith on his part, and she appreciated that.

Sean took the tiller from her when it was time to turn around, guiding the boat back up river, passing the church and Pin Mill once more before returning to the marina where the *Oystercatcher* was moored.

'I had a lot of fun,' she told him after all the ropes had been fixed.

'Me too,' he said, giving that smile again that she was going to find hard to forget. 'Listen, come out with me again some time. Make a day of it.'

'A day?' she said. 'A whole day?'

'You need a whole day to make real progress down the river. We'll take a picnic, moor up somewhere and eat on the boat. What do you say?'

Polly wasn't sure what to say, but she found herself nodding and smiling.

'Here,' he said, taking a mobile out of his shorts pocket, 'let's swap numbers.'

Polly got her phone out. 'Prior, right?'

He nodded. 'What's your surname?'

'Nightingale.'

'That's pretty. But I'm not going to put that.'

'What are you going to put?'

He tapped into his phone and then held it up to her.

Pretty Polly.

She grinned.

'I'll call you.'

Georgia, who'd waved like a mad thing when she'd spotted them from the pub garden, came running down the pontoon now, ready to leap upon her.

'Ahoy there!' she yelled. 'Hi Sean. Hope you took care of my friend.'

'He did,' Polly told her, smiling as Sean held up his hand to wave goodbye.

'So,' Georgia said, linking arms with her and leading her away, 'did you give him your number?'

'I might have done.'

'I'd never met him before today,' Georgia said, 'but I've heard bits and pieces about him from Alex.'

'All good?' Polly asked and a tiny frown appeared on Georgia's face.

'Yes.'

'You hesitated.'

'No, no,' Georgia said. 'I mean, Alex once told me about a guy he went sailing with who had a bit of a temper, but that probably wasn't Sean.' She frowned again. 'No. I'm *sure* it wasn't. He is much too good looking to be bad-tempered, isn't he?'

Polly smiled. 'He was very patient with me. He let me steer the boat.'

'Did he?'

She nodded. 'And we're going out again. All day.'

Georgia squealed. 'Oh, Polly! I'm so excited for you.'

'It's just a day out. Don't go booking the church or anything.'

'Oh, you are funny! I'm not like that.'

'Of course you're not,' Polly said, turning around one last time to take a look at the handsome man who was watching her from on board the *Oystercatcher*.

Holding the little model boat in her hands now, Polly remembered that day with Sean like it was yesterday. The feel of the wind in her hair and the dazzling light on the water. She remembered how he'd shown her another world and how she'd been mesmerised by it. She really hadn't stood a chance especially when they'd moored on a private jetty and he'd kissed her for the first time, the spiralling song of a skylark making a romantic soundtrack high above them.

But what was going on with this little boat? It was too strange to think that he'd been hanging around the school waiting to give the gift to Archie. If he was truly back, why didn't he call her? Why play this strange cat and mouse game with a model boat?

For a moment, Polly remembered the way Dickens had barked at the back door. Had that been Sean? Had he been right there? She'd had the feeling once or twice before that somebody had been watching the house, but maybe that was just paranoia.

'Sean?' She spoke the name quietly as if testing it out. Maybe if he was really still alive, she'd feel something and know for sure? But she felt nothing. Nothing but fear, that was. It was awful to admit it, but she was frightened at the thought of him being back. It was now three and a half years since he'd gone missing and those years had been difficult and strange, but Polly had adapted. She was proud of herself for being able to cope as a single mother. She and Archie had had some rough times, but they'd always managed; they'd had each other and that was enough. But what if Sean came back? Archie didn't really know his father at all. How would he react if Sean came walking back into their lives now?

And Jago. What about Jago?

Polly felt tears threatening to spill. If Sean was truly back, what would that mean for her and Jago?

Jago was cleaning up after an early tea when his mum came home.

'You're late,' he said, greeting her with a kiss in the hallway.

'Stopped for some groceries,' she said and Jago took the bags from her to take through to the kitchen. 'You okay?'

'I'm good,' he said. 'Had a minor crisis with Briggs and the band, but it's all good now.'

'Briggs is always in a state of crisis, isn't he?'

Jago laughed. 'More or less.'

She turned to take her hat and coat off and Jago cleared his throat.

'Mum?'

'Yes?'

'There's something I want to tell you.'

She frowned. 'Sounds serious,' she said.

'It is,' he told her.

They went through to the living room and Maureen drew the curtains against the wintry night and put an extra lamp on.

'There, all nice and cosy,' she said, removing an ancient copy of *Woman's Weekly* before sitting down in her favourite armchair. Jago sat down opposite her. 'Now, what is it?'

Jago scratched his chin. 'I'm seeing Polly.'

His mother frowned. 'Polly Prior?'

'Yes.'

'From across the road?'

He nodded. 'Yes, of course from across the road. How many other Polly Priors are there?' He bit his tongue. He hadn't meant to snap. 'Aren't you going to say anything?'

She shifted uneasily in her chair and he didn't think it was because she'd found another magazine lurking there.

'What should I say?' she asked. 'It seems like you've made your mind up about it.'

'I have.'

'Well, then.'

He sighed. 'I'd like your approval.'

'You don't need my approval, son.'

'I know, but I'd like it all the same.' He watched his mother's reaction. His throat felt dry and he could feel himself tensing up.

How ridiculous was that?

'I can't give it,' she said at last.

'Pardon?'

'I can't give you my approval.'

He took a deep breath. 'Why not?'

'Because I think you should stay away from her.'

'But you like her,' he said. 'You've said you like her in the past.'

'I do like her. I also think that it would be ill advised to become involved with her.'

'What do you mean?'

Maureen Solomon shook her head. 'She's a married woman, Jago. A married mother.'

'You think she shouldn't be involved with anyone even though her husband's been gone for over three years? You think she should shut herself off from life?'

'I didn't say that.'

'No? Because it sounded like you said *exactly* that.'

'Please don't raise your voice.'

'Sorry,' Jago said, and there was a pause before he spoke again. 'I love her, Mum, and I want to take care of her and Archie.'

His mother's eyes widened at this. 'That's an awfully big responsibility to take on at such a young age.'

'I'm not exactly a boy.'

'I know,' she said, 'but you haven't even found your way in the world.'

'What's that supposed to mean? I can't fall in love until I earn x-amount of money?'

'I didn't mean that,' she said. 'I just think you don't know what you're taking on.'

Jago stood up. 'Polly and Archie – that's who I'm taking on. So you're just going to have to get used to it.'

CHAPTER 18

The first time he hit her, it was so unexpected, that Polly wasn't quite sure it had really happened. In fact, she'd laughed which had just made the situation even worse.

'What the hell are you laughing about?' Sean had cried.

'You – you hit me!' she said, her hand flying to the hot spot on her cheek. Yes, it was definitely stinging. She hadn't imagined it.

'You made me do it,' he said, his face full of remorse.

'What did I do?' Polly was perplexed. What on earth had she said or done to make him behave like that?

'I didn't want to do that, Polly,' he said, 'but you make me so angry sometimes.'

'I make you angry?' It was the first time she'd heard about it. As far as she was aware, she'd never made anybody in her life angry. Well, unless you included siblings when growing up, but that didn't count did it?

'You shouldn't say things like that.'

'What? What did I say?' she asked him. They'd just come back from lunch with Alex and Georgia who'd been best man and chief bridesmaid at their recent wedding. It had been a wonderful day full of laughing and reminiscing, but somewhere, somehow, Sean had turned. What had happened? What had she done?

'Sean?' she said. 'Tell me. What did I say?'

He looked at her, his blue eyes suddenly steely and cold, unrecognisable. Polly swallowed hard. She'd never seen him like this before and it scared her. There'd been a couple of times in the past few months when he'd been sullen and withdrawn. She'd tried to reach out to him at those times, but he'd refused to talk about it, choosing to go out instead, usually on his boat.

'You said that I spend all my time on the boat. That you're a boat widow.'

'What?' Polly said.

'You said that. You made me sound ridiculous.'

'But that was just a joke,' Polly said. 'We were having a laugh. You laughed yourself.'

'Yeah? Well, I didn't find it very funny.'

'I'm sorry. I didn't mean to hurt you.' She reached a hand out to him but, before it got to his face, he grabbed her wrist.

'Don't ever make me feel like that again,' he said, his eyes holding hers with a quiet intensity.

Polly nodded. 'I won't.'

Only she had. She'd made him feel like that over and over again, and each time was completely out of her control because she had no idea what the triggers were. It might be a look she gave another man – a totally innocent look that would wind him up, or something she said that he twisted and misconstrued.

That first time could have been forgotten, she sincerely believed that. A little misunderstanding. A marital blip. A lesson learnt. But the second time, the third and fourth, the fifth, sixth and seventh ...

Polly hadn't told anybody. What was there to say? Sean Prior was the perfect gentleman. He was handsome and charming. He worked hard for his family. He took part in community projects and was a total sweetheart to his parents who doted on him. It was so hard to reconcile the man whom everybody else knew with the one that Polly knew. The one she lived in dread of.

She'd thought about confiding in her mother, but she'd known what Eleanor would say. Leave him. Polly couldn't do that. She couldn't bear the thought of letting Archie grow up without a father and she still loved him too and wanted to help him. She truly believed that she could.

But then he'd gone. Vanished. The funny thing was, they hadn't fought for weeks. The police had asked her over and over again.

Did anything out of the ordinary happen between you before he disappeared? Did you fight? Were there any problems?

No, Polly had told them. And she'd omitted to tell them that there had been problems in the past because the past was the past. That was the thing with Sean's brand of abuse. It was all over and done with in a flash of the fist. Like a terrible storm after which the air was clear. A new day. A day of remorse and his remorse was always great. Flowers, gifts, heartfelt apologies. How often Polly had forgiven him, comforting him like a child.

It's okay. It's okay.

You still love me?

Of course I still love you.

But she'd feared him too. She loved him, but she would always carry around that little piece of fear for the man she'd married.

When Jago came round for Archie's next guitar lesson after school, Polly was still feeling jittery about the whole idea of Sean being around somewhere.

'Hey,' Jago said as he came into the house with his guitar, cupping her face in his strong hands before kissing her gently. 'You look tired. Are you okay?'

She nodded, willing herself not to cry at his gentleness.

'You sure?'

'I'm fine,' she said. 'How are you? How are things with Briggs?'

'Oh, he's okay. Crisis averted – for now.'

'Good,' she said.

He narrowed his eyes. 'You really do look tired.'

'Just the winter blues,' she said, moving away from him and walking into the kitchen. 'I hate these dark days.'

'I know what you mean,' he said. 'I miss summer evenings when I can go out on my bike.'

'What did you say?'

'I said I miss summer evenings when I can go out on my bike.'

Polly swallowed hard. She'd thought he'd said "boat". Oh, God, she was imagining things now.

'Polly?' he said, approaching her, but it was then that Archie came bustling in.

'Jago!' he cried.

'Arch!'

'I'm ready for my lesson,' he said.

'Good,' Jago said. 'And I've got some news on the guitar front. One of my students has a guitar for sale that would suit Archie perfectly. I've checked it out and it's in excellent condition. Save you a bit of money compared to buying a brand new one. If you don't mind second-hand, that is.'

'Not if you give it the thumbs up,' Polly said.

'I do. I actually think you'd struggle to find as good a one new.'

'Archie? Do you mind second-hand?'

'I've been playing Jago's and that's second-hand,' he said with great maturity.

'You're right,' Polly said with a proud smile.

Jago told her the price and Polly agreed to buy it.

'Thanks, Mum!' Archie said, flying across the kitchen to hug her. She kissed the top of his head, catching Jago's eye and mouthing a thank you. He smiled back at her and she felt a surge of gratitude that he'd come into their lives.

She left the two of them to it, listening to the now familiar sound of Jago's patient teaching voice and Archie's tentative strumming. She walked over to the kitchen sink and looked out of the window into the back garden, remembering how Dickens had barked the other day as if there'd been an intruder there. Could it have been Sean? And, if it was, why hadn't he called?

Polly could feel her heart racing at the thought of what might have happened if he had called. How would she have responded? And how would Sean have responded to finding her there with Jago? Terrifying thoughts chased around her head as she continued staring out into the darkness. She wasn't aware of time passing but a whole hour must have elapsed because, before she knew it, Jago was in the kitchen.

'Archie's still playing. I literally can't stop him.'

She turned and smiled at him. 'I've never known anything like it. I feel so guilty now that I nearly didn't let him have lessons.'

Jago crossed the room and held her hand. 'I think we should tell him.'

'What?'

'You know – that we're a couple,' he said.

Polly didn't say anything.

'Polly?' He squeezed her hand.

'I'm not sure it's the right time,' she said at last.

'But I thought you were all for it.'

'I – er – I'm not sure now. I think it might be too early.'

Jago frowned. 'But you said you thought he knew anyway.'

'I just think we should wait.'

'Wait for what?'

She shook her hand out of his and walked over to the kitchen sink. 'I don't want to talk about this now, okay?'

'No,' Jago said. 'It's not okay. Tell me what's going on. Why the sudden change?'

'There is no sudden change. I just–' she stopped. What exactly was she going to say to him? That she thought her missing husband might be hanging around, threatening to make an appearance at any moment? Was she going to tell him that she couldn't get involved with somebody else on the off chance that Sean might be coming back into her life? And did she even want that? Did she really want Sean back if he was still alive?

'Something's going on here,' Jago said, turning her towards him. 'Tell me.'

She shook her head. 'Nothing's going on.'

He placed a finger under her chin and tipped her head up towards him. 'Please don't lie to me.'

Her eyes widened. She didn't want to lie, much less be accused of lying to the man she was in love with.

'Jago,' she said, his name coming out in a strangled whisper.

'What is it?'

She took a deep breath before confessing. 'I think Sean might be back.'

'What?'

She walked over to the dresser and opened one of the drawers, taking out the model boat which Archie had been given.

'Archie brought this home from school the other day. A man gave it to one of Archie's friends, telling him to pass it to Archie.'

Jago took the boat from Polly and looked at it. 'I don't get it. What's this got to do with Sean?'

'It's the spitting image of his boat, the *Oystercatcher.*'

'You think Sean gave him this boat?'

'I don't know. But who else would do something like that?'

Jago shrugged. 'There are a lot of crazy people out there and I'm a bit disturbed that some of them might be hanging around Archie's school handing over gifts. But it's probably just a sad old guy giving out random things. We had a strange old woman who used to hang around our school giving away sweets. The headmaster marched her off one day, threatening to call the police, but she was harmless enough. Just lonely, I guess.'

'But this isn't just a random gift,' Polly said.

'Isn't it?'

'No. The man told Tiger to give it to Archie.'

Jago didn't look convinced. 'So you think Sean's back and that he's hanging around the school watching Archie?'

'He probably wouldn't even know what Archie looks like anymore

– that's why he gave the boat to another boy, see?'

'This is all sounding nuts,' Jago said.

'What about when Dickens was barking the other day?'

'He's a dog, Polly. Dogs bark.'

'There was somebody out there. I know there was.'

'It was probably a squirrel.'

She shook her head. 'I think someone's been watching the house too.'

Jago didn't look happy at this revelation. 'Are you sure?'

'I once thought I saw someone out on the green watching the house.'

'Why didn't you tell me about all this?'

'I'm telling you now,' she said. 'I'm worried. I think he's back.'

Jago folded his arms around Polly and hugged her to him. 'And that's why you don't want Archie to know about us?'

'Yes,' she said. 'I'm so sorry. I really don't know what to do.'

'It's okay,' he said. 'I understand. But promise me something?'

'What?'

'You'll let me be here for you. I don't want you going through all this on your own.'

She took a deep breath and sighed it out. 'I don't want to do this alone either.'

He stroked her hair and that's when Archie walked in. They hadn't realised that the strumming had stopped, but there he was, staring open-mouthed at them embracing in the middle of the kitchen.

'Have you two been kissing?' he asked.

'No, we haven't,' Polly told him, leaping away from Jago. 'Just hugging.'

Archie looked from one to the other as if not totally convinced.

'Your mum needed a hug,' Jago said, crossing the room and suddenly catching him up in a hug too. 'We all need hugs from time to time, don't we?' He started tickling him.

Archie laughed. 'Let me go!'

'Don't we?' Jago said.

'Yes!'

Polly watched her son, gauging his response. He seemed totally unfazed by the whole thing and then he surprised her by what he said next.

'It's okay you know.'

'What's okay?' Polly asked.

'If you were kissing,' he said. 'I don't mind.' And then he left the room, running up the stairs to his bedroom. Polly looked at Jago and he stared right back at her and then they burst into laughter.

'Your son is the coolest little lad on the planet,' Jago said.

'I know.'

'And if that's his view about the matter—'

Before Polly could say anything else, Jago was kissing her and Polly didn't stop him because she wanted him just as much as he wanted her.

'Jago?' she said, when they finally stopped. 'I'm scared.'

He hugged her to him and kissed the top of her head. 'I'm right here,' he said, 'and I'm not going anywhere.'

Polly clung to him, feeling some of her tension slip away. How lucky she was to have this man in her life, she thought. How very lucky.

CHAPTER 19

As the days turned into weeks and February sped by in a blur of rain, hail and snow, Polly began to forget about the incident with the model boat. Perhaps Jago had been right all along and it had simply been a loon at the school gate. The feeling of being watched had stopped too. She hadn't had that eerie feeling for a long time now.

It was the last Sunday in February and Polly was driving Jago and Archie to Campion House in the Land Rover.

'Are you sure your folks won't mind me turning up again?'

'Of course not,' Polly said. 'Mum specifically invited you.'

'Yeah?'

'Yes!'

'It's not too soon since Bryony–'

'That's all in the past,' Polly said as she slowed the Land Rover to allow a pair of partridges to take off from the road into a field.

'Why did Jago go out with Aunt Bryony?' Archie asked from the back seat.

'It was a mistake,' Polly said.

'Your mum set me up,' Jago said.

Polly gasped.

'Why did you do that, Mum? I thought *you* liked Jago.'

'She was in denial,' Jago said.

'What's that mean?' Archie asked.

'It means she didn't want to admit that she was madly in love with me.'

Polly thwacked Jago's leg.

'Ouch!' he cried, causing Archie to laugh.

'You two!' she said, shaking her head, but she secretly adored his banter and how he got on with Archie. Everything seemed so natural with Jago and she had to admit that she'd never been happier.

Parking in the driveway of Campion House, the three of them got out of the car together with Dickens. Jago dared to take Polly's hand, squeezing it tightly in his.

'Here we go,' she said as they knocked on the front door before opening it.

Out of all the people who could have greeted them first, it had to be Bryony.

'Oh, hi,' she said.

'You okay?' Polly asked, kissing her sister's cheek.

'Oh, you know,' Bryony said. 'Still selling books. Still single. Still looking for a bloke my sister won't steal from me.'

Polly's mouth dropped open in horror. 'Bry–'

'I'm joking!' she said. 'Come on – I couldn't miss that opportunity, could I?'

'I guess not,' Polly said as Bryony thankfully turned her attention to Archie. 'How's my favourite nephew?'

'I'm your *only* nephew!' Archie pointed out.

'Maybe not for much longer,' Bryony said with a naughty grin at Jago.

'Oh, God – is this what it's going to be like?' Jago said.

'For the first couple of years, I'd say,' Polly said. 'It might settle down a bit after that.'

And, sure enough, Sunday lunch continued very much in that vein.

'So, which one of my sisters are you dating this week?' Josh asked Jago.

A stunned silence greeted the question from around the table. Even Grandpa Joe didn't know what to say and then he gave a funny sort of chuckle which was followed by Frank joining in and, soon, everyone was laughing, the tension of the situation broken.

'I'm sorry if I've confused you all,' Jago said.

'You haven't,' Bryony piped up. 'You and Polly – well – you were meant to be together.'

'Can we please talk about something else?' Polly asked. 'Mum, these potatoes seem lighter and fluffier than normal. How did you cook them?'

'My daughter always takes an unnatural interest in vegetables whenever she's trying to avoid answering questions,' Eleanor said.

'I do not!' Polly protested.

Jago cleared his throat. 'I – erm – I'd like to say that I think Polly is a really special person. Well, I think you all are.'

'Don't try and date me next,' Josh said.

'Oh, for goodness' sake, Josh!' Polly groaned.

'What?' he said innocently. 'He does seem to be working up to something.'

'I just wanted to say thank you for inviting me here today,' Jago said. 'I understand if it's awkward.'

'It isn't awkward,' Eleanor said. 'I'm sorry if any of us have been teasing you.' She looked around at her family. 'But that's going to stop now, right?' Eleanor's stern gaze travelled around the table. 'Josh?'

'Yes, Mum,' he said with a reluctant sigh.

'Bryony?'

'What? I didn't tease him?'

'Not at the table, perhaps,' Eleanor said, 'but I'm sure you've had a little dig at some point.' She paused and it was as if everybody was waiting for her to pass judgement. 'So, we've all agreed that we're very happy to have Jago here today with our Polly.'

Nods of approval greeted her from around the table.

'Of course,' Sam said.

'Very happy indeed,' Frank agreed.

'Jago's great,' Archie added.

'I'm sure he is,' Eleanor said as she passed the dish of glazed parsnips to her right. 'How's the writing going, Callie?'

'Yes, when will you have another bestseller out for me to sell?' Bryony asked.

Polly noticed Callie blushing at the sudden onslaught of attention she was receiving. She still wasn't used to being part of a huge family, Polly thought.

'It will be a little while yet, I'm afraid,' Callie said.

'She's writing a brilliant book,' Sam said.

'Well, I don't know about that,' Callie said, her face positively aflame now.

'But her pig of an ex is being awkward,' Sam said.

'No, he isn't,' Callie told Sam. 'Not anymore. I'm working with my new editor now and she's great although she expects me to work at a pace I'm not used to.'

'Tell her to wait,' Sam said. 'Art can't be rushed.'

'But they've got deadlines,' Callie said.

'Deadlines should be arranged around the artist,' he said. 'They should be working around you not the other way around. Honestly, the whole publishing industry sounds crazy to me. I don't know how you put up with it.'

'Because I can't do anything else,' Callie said with a tiny smile.

'You could do *any*thing you put your mind to,' Sam said, leaning forward and kissing her cheek.

'Good grief,' Josh said from the other side of the table. 'Do we have to have this sort of thing at the dining table?'

Everyone laughed.

'You're just jealous,' Grandpa Joe said from the end of the table, 'but it won't be long before you're bringing a young lady here and mooning all over her.'

'I will never moon,' Josh said, making Sam and Bryony snigger. 'You know what I mean!' He shook his head in despair at his relatives.

'Jago, you write, don't you?' Frank asked.

'Just songs,' Jago said, 'nothing as complex as a novel, I'm afraid.'

'They're beautiful songs,' Bryony said. 'After all, he once sang one to me.'

'Bryony!' her mother said in a warning tone.

'Sorry. Couldn't resist,' Bryony said. 'Sorry, Jago. Sorry, Polly.'

Polly felt her cheeks heating up, embarrassed by the whole situation. Why, oh why had she ever encouraged Jago to go out with her sister?

'So, Jago,' Josh began, 'any more conga lines around Polly's living room?'

'Mum, I thought we said no more teasing Jago?' Polly said.

'I'm not teasing,' Josh said. 'I'm genuinely interested.'

'No,' Jago said, 'no more conga lines.'

Josh nodded. 'I think we should have one here, don't you?'

'A conga line?' Bryony asked.

'Yes!' Josh said. 'Right here – right now!' He pushed his chair out from behind him.

'Josh – we're still eating!' Eleanor complained, but Archie was already on his feet as was Grandpa Joe.

'Come on!' Josh cried. 'It'll be fun.

'No, don't!' Polly all but screamed. 'Archie – sit down and finish your lunch.'

But Archie had scampered round to the other side of the table where Bryony was also on her feet.

'We haven't got any music,' Bryony pointed out.

'Oh, yes we have,' Josh said, pulling a tablet out of his jacket pocket. Soon, the dining room was filled with the bold, brash notes of the latest chart topping song.

'What's happening?' Grandma Nell asked, looking confused.

'We're going to do the conga,' Grandpa Joe told her.

'Well, it's about time,' she said.

Grandpa Joe laughed and gently guided his wife out in front of him, placing his hands on her hips.

'Come on, son,' he said to Frank. 'On yer feet – give your mother something to hold on to.'

Frank shook his head in bewilderment, but got up nevertheless.

'I can't believe this is happening!' Polly cried, half-thrilled, half-mortified as Jago dragged her up from her chair. Sam and Callie got up too and Eleanor, who was the last one sitting, threw her napkin onto the table so she could join in.

A strange, wonderful couple of minutes ensued with the Nightingale family and their guests making a rather haphazard conga line around the dining room table.

'Josh – you've got no rhythm at all!' Bryony shouted over the music as she tripped over her brother again.

'You just can't keep up!' he shouted back.

Archie was laughing so much that he kept breaking the line and Grandma Nell seemed to forget what they were doing and tried to sit down to finish her lunch but was thwarted by Grandpa Joe who insisted that she joined in.

One, two, three, kick! One, two, three, kick!

'You should never have mentioned the conga, Archie!' Polly cried, but she couldn't help smiling at the sight of her family snaking around the table. The look on her grandmother's face was priceless and her father's red cheeks were a picture.

Finally, the song came to an end.

'Again!' Archie cried.

'No way!' Bryony said. 'I'm done in. I didn't realise how unfit I was.'

Grandpa Joe helped Grandma Nell back to her chair and everyone else collapsed into theirs too.

'We should make this a new family tradition,' Josh said, 'in between courses.'

'You've got to be joking,' Eleanor said. 'That's a sure route to indigestion!'

Sitting back in her chair next to Jago, Polly felt his hand reach out and squeeze hers under the tablecloth.

'Your family's brilliant,' he whispered to her.

She smiled at him. 'One of a kind,' she told him.

When they got back to Church Green, Polly made her and Jago a cup of tea while he lit the wood burner in the living room. Archie took Dickens out into the garden and the two of them came back with six muddy feet.

'Towel!' Polly shouted, watching as her son grabbed one of the towels that resided by the back door. He was pretty adept at cleaning Dickens's feet now and, when the task was done, they all went through to the living room together.

Jago was bent in front of the wood burner, watching the progress of the fire.

'Here's your tea,' she said, placing it on a little table behind him. It was then that something across the room caught her eye. She frowned. 'Jago?'

'Hmmm?'

'Did you move this photo?'

'What photo?'

'The one of me and Archie that lives on this shelf,' she said, picking it up from the next shelf down.

'I didn't touch it,' he said, standing up.

'Archie?'

'What?' he asked, looking up from a comic he was reading.

'Did you move this photo?'

He shook his head.

Polly returned it to its rightful place. She was still frowning.

'What's the matter?' Jago asked.

'Nothing,' she said, smiling brightly at him. She didn't want to voice her fears. 'I'm just popping upstairs, okay?'

He nodded and Polly left the room, climbing the stairs quickly. First, she went into Archie's room, but it was impossible to tell if anything was out of place in there because everything was always out of place no matter how many times she nagged him to keep things tidy. She crossed the landing into her own room. Her and Sean's room. She looked at the neatly made bed, the two little bedside tables either side of it, the wardrobe and the dressing table. Was it her imagination or had another photograph been moved? She walked towards the dressing table where a collection of photo frames lived. Polly was notoriously neat and everything was always in its rightful place and at the correct angle, but the gold-framed wedding photo of her and Sean which she kept in the bedroom looked slightly askew. She picked it up and examined it as if for clues, but it yielded nothing and so she replaced it, looking around the room again.

'Polly?' Jago's voice called up the stairs. 'All right if Archie and I play guitar for a bit?'

'Yes!' she shouted back. 'Go ahead.'

As she heard the first guitar notes coming from the living room, Polly walked back out to the landing and looked around, her breath coming thick and fast. She couldn't shake the idea that somebody – somebody who had once lived there – had been in her home.

CHAPTER 20

The March meeting of the book club came round faster than Polly could have imagined, but she was ready with her folder of notes for discussion points and was happy to support her brother at their first real meeting.

Having dropped Archie off at his friend Tiger's for tea and a film, Polly and Jago drove into Castle Clare, finding a parking space in Church Street, and walking together towards the shop.

'I love Castle Clare at night time,' Polly said. 'The streets are so quiet and it always reminds me of a film set with all the medieval buildings.'

'When I was in America, people would ask where I was from and I'd show them some photos of Castle Clare and Great Tallington and they couldn't believe how old the buildings were. One woman actually asked me how they made the buildings look so old!'

'She didn't!'

'She did. She really wouldn't believe that they *were* that old.'

'I don't think I could live somewhere like America. I'd miss all these half-timbered houses and narrow streets too much,' Polly said, and there was real affection in her voice. 'When you grow up somewhere like this, it becomes a part of you and you might go away like I did when I taught abroad or you did to America, but you'll always find your way back.' She looked at him. 'Do you think you'll stay now?'

He stopped walking and reached out to cup her face in his hands. 'Wherever you are, I want to be,' he said. '"*I love you far more than common.*"'

Polly gasped. 'That's what Gabriel Oak said to Bathsheba!'

'I know,' Jago said. 'I have read the book, you know.'

She smiled and then she realised just what he'd said to her. 'Oh, Jago,' she said.

He stroked her hair. 'You don't have to say anything.'

'But I want to,' she said, 'I want to tell you that I love you too. "Far more than common."'

'Now, that's my quote,' he said. 'You'll have to come up with your own.'

She looked thoughtful for a moment. 'I can't think of one.'

'What?'

'I really can't think of one!'

He shook his head in what she hoped was mock despair.

'My mind's gone blank,' she confessed.

'And you're helping to run a book club?' he said.

'Shocking, isn't it?'

He took her hand in his and they hurried towards Nightingale's, opening the green door to the merry tinkle of the bell and crossing the wooden floorboards to the back of the shop.

'Polly! Jago!' Sam cried as they entered the back room. The chairs had been arranged in a circle, the cushions on the sofa had been plumped and Callie was in the tiny kitchen.

'Hi Callie,' Polly said.

Callie waved back.

Over the next few minutes, the book club members began to arrive. Antonia Jessop was the first, naturally. Winston Kneller arrived next with his Labrador, Delilah, waving a hand in greeting but not bothering to remove his old felt hat.

'Winston – what's happened to your boot?' Sam asked and it was then that Polly noticed that it had string wrapped around it.

'Sole's flapping off,' he said, landing heavily on the sofa. 'Still lots of wear in it, but it does mean a wet right foot every day.'

'Oh, dear,' Polly said. 'Can't you get a new pair of boots?'

'I've put a special order in at the charity shop,' he said. 'I'm top of their list if some come in.'

'At least the weather's improving now,' Polly said, 'but it's been a filthy winter. I sometimes thought there was more mud in our house than outside. But that's what having a spaniel and a little boy does to your home.'

Winston nodded, recognising the scenario as most country people did. Mud was a part of everyday life in the winter.

It was then that Flo Lohman came in with a little basket in the crook of her arm. 'What are we all talking about?' she asked with a cheery smile.

'Mud!' Winston barked from the sofa.

'Don't talk to me about mud. My hens have wrecked the lawn this winter. It's a sea of mud. Nearly has me on my back every time I venture out there.'

'You must be careful, Flo,' Sam said in alarm.

'Oh, I'm careful, but what can you do when you've got animals? You can't keep them all indoors, can you?'

'I thought you did!' Winston said. 'The last time I came round there was a hen on the kitchen table and one on the draining board.'

'That was just Winnie and Ella. They have special dispensation. And that reminds me,' Flo said, lifting off the tea towel covering her basket. 'I've made us some cherry buns. I raided the freezer and found about three pounds of cherries from the summer.'

'And these were made in your kitchen?' Antonia said. 'With the hens?'

'Well, the hens weren't actually present when I made them,' Flo said with a little smile.

'I think I'll pass,' Antonia said.

Winston had no such qualms when it came to cherry buns and dived straight in.

Hortense Digger – or *Honey* as she liked to be known – was the next to arrive.

'I love her clothes,' Callie whispered to Polly. 'I'm always fascinated to see what she'll be wearing.'

'Me too,' Polly said and the two of them watched as Honey took off her coat to reveal a splendid royal blue jumper over a long cerise skirt. The two colours seemed to be at war with each other and were quite startling to behold and Antonia Jessop's eyes were out on stalks when she saw them. But it didn't end there. Never one to leave a single inch without colour or texture, Honey was also wearing a pair of chandelier earrings in gold and a big hammered gold cuff on her left wrist.

Lily Ann Taylor, who hadn't been able to make the first meeting, was the last to arrive. In her mid-fifties, Lily Ann was the complete antithesis of Honey Digger with hair that had never seen a colouring bottle and clothes that were neat and tidy, but were rather drab and uninspiring. It was as if she had given colour up one Lent and never bothered to find it again.

Antonia and Honey were now jostling each other in the tiny space of the kitchen.

'That's *my* plate,' Antonia said, taking hold of a pretty pink and white china plate on which she then placed her flapjacks.

'I always find flapjacks a little bit sickly,' Honey said.

'Do you?' Antonia said. 'Then you're obviously not making them right.'

Polly, Jago and Callie watched in amusement.

'It's battle of the biscuits time,' Polly whispered.

'I love it,' Callie said.

'I bet all this will find its way into one of your novels one day, won't it?' Polly said.

'It's very likely!' Callie said.

When Honey came out of the kitchen, she was armed with a plate of immaculate biscuits.

'Sam – these are from the book I bought from you,' Honey said proudly.

'They look marvellous,' Sam said as he bent forward over the table she'd put them on. 'May I?'

'Please do.'

Sam took one. It looked like a round piece of shortbread.

'Delicious!' he said.

'Aren't they? Just a hint of vanilla, but a very important hint.'

Soon, hands were flying forward to sample Honey's wares and Delilah's wet nose tried to get in on the action too.

'Oh, no you don't, old darling,' Winston said, his hand digging into his pocket and bringing out a dog chew for her.

Antonia looked at the plate of biscuits, her nose wrinkling a little as if a nasty smell had invaded it. 'They don't look properly baked to me.'

'I assure you they are,' Honey said. 'Now, I know you always like to *over* bake your biscuits, but these are meant to be pale.'

Antonia made a derisive noise.

'Well, I'm having another if I may,' Winston said, taking the biggest on the plate and munching appreciatively. 'Jolly good.'

'Why, thank you, Winston,' Honey said although she said it more to Antonia than she did to Winston.

'I'll be having one of your flapjacks next,' he said, sending a saucy wink to Antonia.

'Right then,' Sam said, 'have we all got a seat?'

Polly sat next to Jago and Callie sat next to Sam.

'I think we've all enough to eat for now with more than our share of Honey's delicious biscuits, and Flo's buns and Antonia's flapjacks so let's make a start,' Sam said. 'What did we all think of the novel? Anyone want to kick off?'

'Thomas Hardy, wasn't it?' Winston began.

'Erm, yes, Winston,' Sam said. 'You did read it, didn't you? *Far From the Madding Crowd?*'

'Oh, yes,' Winston said, 'just making sure.'

Flo Lohman shifted uneasily in her chair. 'I found it difficult,' she said.

'How?' Sam asked. 'The language?'

'The language, the subject, the characters. I mean, there wasn't really anyone likeable, was there?'

'That's an interesting point,' Sam said. 'What do we all think about that? Do we need to like characters in order to enjoy a book?'

'Well, I do,' Flo said.

'I think characters should be engaging,' Callie said, 'but not necessarily likeable. They should be sympathetic, though. A reader must be able to understand why they do things.'

'So who did we engage with?' Sam asked. 'Anyone?'

'Not that awful heroine,' Antonia said. 'Vain, stupid–'

'Not stupid,' Lily Ann interrupted. 'She was a good businesswoman, wasn't she?'

'But to turn down Gabriel Oak,' Antonia went on.

'Yes, but if she'd accepted him in those early chapters, there wouldn't have been a book, would there?' Callie said.

'Trust a writer to point that out,' Antonia said. 'So it's a plot device of Hardy's to make her stupid?'

'I think we established that she wasn't stupid,' Lily Ann said.

'Lilian, I have my opinion–'

'*Lily Ann,*' Lily Ann corrected. 'Not Lilian.'

Polly leaned in towards Jago. 'Never ever call her that,' she whispered. 'She hates it!'

'I'll do my best to remember,' he whispered back.

'The early rejection of Gabriel Oak makes it all the sweeter when they come together at the end, don't you think?' Polly asked.

'Oh, I do like a happy ending!' Flo said. 'It's just a shame that there were so many deaths along the way.'

'It *is* a Thomas Hardy novel,' Sam said.

'So depressing,' Flo said.

'But there's lots of humour in there too. Did you like the scene with the farm hands? When Bathsheba meets them all?'

'Chapter ten,' Callie said. '"Mistress and Men" it's called.'

'I *loved* that chapter!' Honey enthused. 'Especially the poor stuttering fellow.'

'Oh, I missed that bit,' Flo said. 'There's a horrible stain on my page eighty-five – look!'

The group looked at the disgusting reddish-brown stain on Flo's Pan edition which featured the young Julie Christie on the cover.

'Why do people have to bleed over books?' Antonia asked. 'It's a filthy habit.'

'They probably don't do it deliberately,' Polly pointed out.

Jago laughed. 'Yeah, like, "I've got a nice bit of Graham Greene to pour this paper cut over!"'

'Don't be foul,' Antonia said.

'Jago, what did you think of the book?' Sam asked, obviously in an attempt to keep things on topic, Polly thought.

'I liked it. I really did,' he said. 'I like the way Hardy's characters are all so closely linked with the countryside. I read somewhere that Hardy referred to his major books as "novels of character and environment"?'

'Oh, very highbrow,' Honey said. 'We have a brain amongst us!'

'Sorry, I didn't mean to sound–'

'No, it's wonderful,' Honey added quickly. 'It's just you'll put us all to shame.'

'Well, *you* perhaps, Hortense,' Antonia said. '*I* was aware of that, Jago.'

The conversation continued with the group taking it in turns to talk about their favourite scenes and the scenes that moved them the most and it was universally agreed that Troy was one of literatures most despicable characters and that he could never be forgiven for his treatment of Fanny Robin and that the scene in the graveyard in the rain was one of the saddest ever written.

'I mean that's the height of cruelty, isn't it?' Lily Ann said, 'for Troy to just disappear like that and not tell Bathsheba what was going on. How she could even contemplate getting back with a man like that.'

'It's hard to put yourself in that situation, isn't it?' Flo said. 'I mean, I've never had a husband leave me, but I couldn't imagine what Bathsheba went through.'

'It's the not knowing,' Honey said. 'Imagine day after day not knowing where he was or what happened to him.'

Polly looked across the room at Sam and he seemed to understand her.

'What do we think about Boldwood's behaviour at this time?' he said, but there didn't seem to be any hope of him changing the direction of the discussion.

'Just imagine that for a minute,' Honey said, 'the *agony* she must have gone through worrying about what might have happened to her husband.'

'It must have been unbearable,' Flo said, shaking her head sadly.

Suddenly, Polly was on her feet, her wooden chair scraping back noisily.

'Polly?' Sam said.

'I – I – I've got to go,' she stammered, grabbing her coat from the back of her chair and charging out of the room.

Polly had found the conversation about missing husbands unbearable even though she'd known that they were all talking about a fictional character and that they weren't talking about her situation at all.

She stood for a moment in front of the till, hearing the voices from the back room as she tried to gather her thoughts.

'I should have thought,' Sam was berating himself. 'We should never have chosen this book!'

'It wasn't your fault,' Callie was telling him.

'I'll go after her,' Jago said and Polly quickly wiped her eyes as he caught up with her.

'Hey,' he said gently. 'You okay?'

She nodded. Then she shook her head. 'No,' she said.

'It was the book, wasn't it? All that talk about husbands disappearing.'

'I shouldn't have let it get to me,' she said.

'It's okay.'

'I should go back and apologise.'

'There's no need. They'll understand,' he told her. 'Would you like me to drive you home?'

'I can manage,' she said. 'But you can come with me if you want to.'

He nodded. 'Of course I want to.'

They crossed the room to the door just as Sam approached.

'Polly?' he called softly. 'I'm so sorry.'

'I'm all right,' she assured him. 'Just being silly.'

'No you're not.' He was by her side in an instant and caught her up in a big hug. 'You're never silly.'

'I had no idea I was going to react like that. I mean, I read the book, I know the plot and everything. But hearing that situation being talked about like that.'

'We should have been more mindful,' Sam said.

Polly smiled up at him. 'Get back to your book club, Sam,' she told him.

'You'll be okay?' he asked.

'I'll make sure she is,' Jago told him.

He nodded. 'I'll call you tomorrow, okay?'

Polly and Jago left the shop, walking out into the silent street. She took some deep breaths of cold night air and tried to clear her head.

'I'm sorry,' she said at last.

'What for?'

'Dragging you into all this.'

'You didn't drag me. I plunged in.'

'*Plunged?*' she laughed.

'Very willingly!'

'I'm a mess. You'd be better off with somebody else. You know that, don't you?'

'You're not thinking of pushing me on poor Bryony again, are you? Because I don't think she'd take me back.'

She stopped walking and stared up at the great flint tower of Castle Clare's church which was floodlit at night.

'You can change your mind at any time,' she said without looking at him.

'I know,' he said.

'You can walk away whenever you want to. I won't mind.'

He moved to stand in front of her. 'You won't mind?' he asked. 'Not even a little bit?' He cocked his head to one side. 'I'm offended. You wouldn't miss me at all?'

'Of course I would,' she said. 'I'd miss you like crazy.'

They hugged one another.

'Polly, I don't know why we're even talking about this because I'm not going anywhere. I'm staying right here with you and we're going to work through this together.'

'It just seems so unfair that you're being put through—'

'Shush!' he said, stroking her hair in that way he had which instantly calmed her. 'I love you, Polly, and I want to be with you. No matter what happens, okay?'

She nodded and they kissed.

'Let's go home, shall we?' she said. 'Archie's not being dropped off for another hour and a half yet.'

'Really?' Jago said.

'That gives us plenty of time for something rather special.'

'Yeah?' Jago grinned.

'Yeah,' Polly said. 'We can start planning his birthday party!'

Jago laughed. 'You are full of surprises!'

'Good ones, I hope?'

'Oh, yes, always good ones.'

It was as they reached the Land Rover that Polly's mobile beeped.

'It's a text from Sam,' she said and then she started laughing.

'What is it?' Jago asked, but Polly couldn't stop laughing. 'Polly – *tell* me!'

'He says...' she laughed again and, for a few moments, seemed incapable of speech.

'Give me the phone and let me see what's so funny,' Jago said, but Polly shook her head, doing her best to recover herself. 'What's he say, Polly?'

She wiped the tears of laughter from her eyes. 'He says we left the shop in the nick of time. Winston's dog's just let one rip!'

CHAPTER 21

'So, when are we going to meet this Polly girl?' Briggs asked, flicking his hair back from his face and fixing his gaze upon Jago.

'She's not a *girl*,' Jago said.

'No, that's right,' Briggs said. 'She's your *older woman*, isn't she? What's it like being a toy boy?'

'Please don't use that term,' Jago said.

'I quite fancy having a cougar myself.'

'Or that one!' Jago said, shaking his head.

'We all want to see her,' Briggs said.

'Well, that's not your call,' Jago told him firmly, walking through to Briggs's kitchen and attempting to find a clean mug to drink out of.

To be perfectly honest, Jago didn't like the idea of sharing Polly with the outside world. Not that he didn't want to show her off a bit, but he had to admit that he was more than content with the time they spent together at 3 Church Green. They'd created such a wonderful little world together there and he didn't see the need to leave it just so that they could sit in some pub together. It was a safe, happy, protected world and they were all happy enough in it, weren't they? But maybe he was being selfish. Maybe Polly would like to go out sometime. He should really have thought about that and maybe taken her out to dinner or a trip to the cinema. He'd give it some thought later when he wasn't being hounded by Briggs.

Jago had never been happier in his whole life than in the last few weeks he'd spent with Polly and Archie. Who would have thought that he'd find true happiness with a mother and son? Perhaps it was the feeling that he'd walked into his own ready-made family – an experience that had been denied him as an only child from a very broken home.

'Hey, if you find another clean mug, make us a cup too,' Briggs said.

'You are such a slob,' Jago said. 'You've really got to learn to clean up after yourself.'

Briggs shrugged. 'I cleaned up last week.'

Jago shook his head in despair. 'You know I'll never agree to share a house with you unless you get yourself sorted.'

'So you're giving it some thought, then?'

'Sure. I can't live at home with my mum forever, can I?' Jago said. 'Hey – when are Mike and Davy due because I can't hang around forever.'

'Got to get back to the old ball and chain, eh?' Briggs said as he entered the kitchen.

'No, I'm giving a lesson in a local school.'

'Oh, cool,' he said, making a token gesture of putting a few clean plates back in their cupboards. '*Then* it's back to the old ball and chain?'

'Briggs, my friend,' Jago said, 'I can't wait until you fall in love – and I mean *really* fall in love. Not just flirting with the latest groupie.'

'You mean you're giving groupies up?'

Jago glared at him. 'I was never into groupies to begin with!'

'Maybe not, but they were into you!'

'And that's just the kind of talk I don't want around Polly. If I'm ever stupid enough to introduce you to her,' Jago said.

'Hey, man – I wouldn't say anything. Band of brothers and all that.'

Jago shook his head. He didn't hold out much hope of Briggs ever growing up, but Jago was awfully glad that *he* had.

After attempting to teach her students the difference between countable and uncountable nouns, Polly had driven in to Castle Clare. Things had been slow in Sam's bookshop, but it had been good to spend time with her brother. He'd filled her in on what had happened at the book club after she'd left with Jago. Everyone had been desperately worried about her and had passed on their love via Sam.

'I'm glad you've got Jago to look out for you,' Sam had said. 'He seems like a really good guy.'

'He is,' Polly had said. 'I feel so lucky to have him in my life. But please don't think I *need* somebody to look out for me. I can cope perfectly well on my own. I just had a little wobble the other night, that's all.'

Sam had nodded. 'I know,' he said. 'You're the strongest person I know.'

Polly had given her brother a hug just as a customer had walked in. Then, having embarrassed him quite enough, she'd dusted around the shelves, done some minor repairs to some of the second-hand books and put in some orders for customers before driving home.

Parking outside her house, Polly noted a small red car outside her neighbours' which she didn't recognise. There was a woman sitting in the driver's seat. She was pretty with straight blonde hair down to her shoulders and she looked no more than thirty.

As Polly got out of her car, she was aware that the woman was watching her. Perhaps she was lost, Polly thought, but she didn't maintain eye contact when Polly made to smile at her and so Polly opened her door and went inside.

She hadn't been in the house for more than a couple of minutes when somebody knocked on the door. Promising Dickens she'd be right back for his long-awaited walk, Polly went to open the door and came face to face with the young woman from the car. So she was lost, Polly thought. But she didn't ask Polly for directions.

'Who are you?' the blonde woman asked.

'Excuse me?' Polly said.

'I need to know who you are.'

Polly frowned. 'But *you* knocked on *my* door. Who are *you*?'

'I found your address,' the woman said. 'I'm looking for someone.'

'Who are you looking for?'

'Sean,' she said. 'I'm looking for Sean Prior.'

Polly almost buckled at the mention of her husband's name.

'Sean's not here,' she managed to say, her throat suddenly very dry.

It was then that Dickens ran into the hallway barking. Polly grabbed hold of his collar and turned him around.

'Quiet, boy,' she said, sending him back to the kitchen, and then something clicked in her mind.

'You've been watching the house haven't you?' she said to the woman.

The woman nodded. 'I didn't know what to do. I was hoping to see him. I haven't seen him in weeks. He just disappeared.'

'Weeks? You haven't seen him in *weeks*?' Polly said, thinking of the long years in which she hadn't seen her husband.

The woman nodded.

'I think you'd better come in.'

The young woman walked into the hallway. She looked awkward and nervous and Polly couldn't help wanting to put her at ease even though her own mind was racing.

'I'm Sophie,' the woman said. 'Sophie Randall.'

'I'm Polly. Polly Prior. Come and sit down,' Polly said, leading her through to the living room. She felt slightly removed from herself, almost as if she was floating somewhere above the scene before her and that it wasn't quite happening. 'Can I get you a drink? A cup of tea?' she heard herself asking.

Sophie shook her head. 'Just a water, thank you.'

Polly went through to the kitchen for two glasses of water. Dickens looked up expectantly from his basket, but Polly shook her head and he settled down again.

Returning to the living room, she noticed that Sophie hadn't sat down. She was standing by the shelves, looking at the photographs.

'You're married to him, aren't you?' Sophie asked, turning her bright eyes on Polly.

'Yes,' Polly said. 'We have a son. Archie.'

Sophie nodded. 'He didn't tell me.'

Polly swallowed hard. 'I think you'd better sit down and tell me everything you know.' She handed Sophie a glass of water and the two of them sat at either end of the sofa.

'How long were you married for?' Sophie asked.

'We're still are married,' Polly said. 'Listen – you *are* telling me Sean's alive, aren't you? That *is* what you're saying?'

Sophie frowned. 'Of course he's alive!'

'I mean he went missing. Three and a half years ago. He just disappeared and I haven't heard anything about him since. Look – when did you meet him? You said he's missing now, right? You've got to tell me–'

Sophie put her glass of water down and moved to sit closer to Polly, taking her hands in hers.

'It's okay,' Sophie said, her voice calm and soothing.

Polly realised that she was shaking. 'I need to know,' she said. 'I need to know what's going on.'

'I know you do,' Sophie said, 'and I'll tell you everything I know, okay? And you'll tell me your story too because Sean never spoke about you.'

There were tears in Polly's eyes now. Hot, stinging tears. Sean was alive! He was truly alive. But where had he been all these years? And what exactly was his relationship with this woman sitting on her sofa? She felt so confused and anxious.

Sophie cleared her throat and, still holding Polly's hands in hers, she began.

'I met Sean at Dell Quay–'

'Where's that?'

'Chichester Harbour on the Sussex coast.'

He'd sailed to the south coast?

'Was he in the *Oystercatcher*?' Polly asked. 'His boat?'

'He was in a boat, but it was called *Swan*.'

'*Swan*? Are you sure?'

'Pretty sure.'

Polly frowned. Had he sold the *Oystercatcher* and bought another boat? Or had he just renamed the old one? 'Go on,' she said. 'Please.'

'I don't know what to tell you.'

'Everything – tell me everything.'

'It's kind of awkward.'

Polly could feel her tears rising again. 'I need to hear it, whatever it is.'

Sophie nodded. 'He flirted with me,' she said. 'I'd just come out of a bad relationship and it was nice to be treated as special again. So I flirted back. He told me he'd been sailing around the UK for the last five years, but he was looking to settle down at last.'

'Five years? He told you five years?' Polly cried, astounded by the blatant lie.

'He said he'd never been involved with anyone special. That he was a real old sea dog.'

This time, Polly's tears did spill.

'I'm so sorry,' Sophie said. 'I had no idea that you existed. I'd never have got involved with him otherwise.'

'What happened next?' Polly asked. She wiped her eyes and did her best to brace herself.

'He moved in with me. I've got a little flat in Chichester. It's small, but he told me he'd been sleeping on his boat for years and that my flat was like a palace.'

'You lived together?'

Sophie nodded. 'For nearly two years.'

Polly tried to calculate her husband's movements. He'd gone missing in September three and a half years ago. Had he been living on his boat all the following winter and spring? How had he managed to live? Had he been working?

'Did he have a job?'

'I think he was doing some sort of consultancy work. He was always on his laptop in the evenings.'

'But the police looked into that,' Polly said, more to herself than to Sophie.

'He was working as Sean Parker,' Sophie said. 'He told me that was his name. I didn't find out it was Prior until I found a business card of his that led me to you here.'

'He changed his name?'

'I guess. Was Prior his real name?' Sophie asked.

Polly nodded. 'It's his parents' name.'

'They live nearby?'

'Yes,' Polly told her.

'I'd like to meet them, but they probably wouldn't want to meet me.'

'They would if you told them what you've told me,' Polly said. 'They're desperate to hear news of their son.'

'Could you arrange something?' Sophie asked.

'Leave that with me.'

Sophie sighed. 'I didn't know whether to come here. I wasn't sure how you'd react and if you'd want to see me at all.'

'You did the right thing,' Polly said. 'I'm glad you came.'

'Where do you think he is?'

'I don't know,' Polly said honestly. 'But I think he might have been here in the house. One day, when I'd been out, I noticed some photo frames had been moved. I had a feeling – the strangest feeling – that he'd been here.'

'But you haven't seen him?'

'No,' Polly said, her head spinning as she tried to process everything. 'And he said nothing about me and Archie?'

'Not a thing. He said he was single.'

Polly blanched at this, imagining Sean taking off his wedding ring at some stage and inventing another life for himself. What kind of a person would do that when he already had a wife and son, family and friends? Because it hadn't just been Polly and Archie he'd walked out on that day, it had been everybody who'd ever known him.

'After he'd been missing for a few days, I started to go through his things,' Sophie said. That's when I found the photo of him with you. A wedding photo. It was in a folder of paperwork on his boat and – well – I was just being nosy, I guess. That's where I found the business card too with this address on.'

'Yes, he used to work from home,' Polly said. 'When he started up his consulting company.'

'It was my only lead. I didn't know where else to go.'

'Did you go to the police?'

'No,' Sophie said. 'I didn't think I had much of a claim on him. He came into my life so unexpectedly and I thought perhaps that was the way he was going to leave it too. There was also a part of me that thought he'd come back at any minute.'

Polly nodded. 'Sophie,' she said, wondering how on earth she was going to ask this question.

'What?' She leaned in a little closer.

'Was he ever–'

Sophie frowned. 'Was he ever what?'

'Violent. Was he ever violent to you?'

Sophie swallowed and nodded. 'He hit me. Just the once, though. It was some misunderstanding we'd had. I'd said something and I didn't realise how much it had upset him. I apologised and he did too. He felt awful about it.' There was a pause. 'Did he hit you?'

Polly nodded and held the young woman's gaze. 'If I was you, I wouldn't try to find him. Go back to your life and forget him.'

Sophie looked genuinely puzzled, but she stood up. 'I – erm –'

Polly felt for her in that moment. Sean had reeled her in, hadn't he? He'd made her love him, but the violence would have got worse if he'd stayed, she knew that from experience, and she was determined to prevent that from happening to Sophie.

'Trust me on this,' Polly said. 'You don't want him in your life.' They walked to the front door together. 'Listen, have you got a mobile number for him?'

'His number's been disconnected,' Sophie said, 'but I'll give you mine, okay? And you'll let me know if you hear anything?'

Polly nodded. 'But you should go home, Sophie. Live your life. Without Sean.'

***

Polly didn't have time for a breakdown after Sophie left because she had to drive to the school in Castle Clare. She didn't tell Archie what was going on. Instead, she smiled as he babbled on about his day at school. All the while, thoughts were tumbling around her head. Sean was really alive. But he'd chosen to walk out on them. He'd been living with somebody else. He'd changed his name. He hadn't thought to get in touch and let everyone know he was okay. What kind of man did that to the people who loved him? Polly couldn't begin to understand although she'd seen glimpses of that Sean during her marriage to him – the man who could detach himself from others, the man who always put himself first.

'Mum!' Archie suddenly screamed from the back seat.

Polly braked hard, narrowly avoiding a cat streaking across the road.

Concentrate, she told herself.

She was mightily relieved to reach the sanctuary of home and did her utmost to put thoughts of Sean out of her mind as she buttered some toast for Archie. They took Dickens out together. It was a blessed relief for it to now be light until after five which meant they could enjoy a dog walk together after school.

They'd just made it back inside when Jago arrived for Archie's guitar lesson.

'Hey, Polly – I've got a great idea,' he said, following her into the kitchen as Archie went into the living room to watch some TV. 'How about I take you out for a night on the town? Just the two of us? We can get dressed up and I'm sure Mum would look after Archie–' He stopped. 'Are you okay?' Polly now had her back to him as she fiddled in the cutlery drawer. She felt his hands land heavily on her shoulders. 'Hey,' he said. 'Look at me.'

She turned around and that's when the tears began. 'S-somebody called here today.'

'Yeah?'

'Someone called Sophie Randall.'

'Who's she?'

'I only met her today,' Polly said, desperately wiping the tears from her cheeks.

'But she made you cry? What's going on, Polly?'

'She's been living with him.'

'Who?'

'Sean?'

'Sophie's been living with Sean?'

'Yes!'

'Then where is he?'

'I don't know. She – Sophie – doesn't know.' Polly started crying again. 'He's alive!

Jago looked as stunned as Polly felt.

'Did she show you a photo?' he asked at last.

'What do you mean?'

'A photo – a recent photo of Sean.'

'No. I didn't think to ask her for one.'

'Then we've got no proof.'

'You don't believe her?' Polly asked. 'Why would she make something up like that?'

'I don't know,' Jago said. 'I'm trying to be logical about this.'

'She had one of Sean's old business cards with this address on. That's what brought her here. And she talked about his boat.'

'And how many business cards did Sean hand out in his lifetime, huh? Quite a few, I imagine. I'm sure a fair few people knew about his boat too.'

Polly stared at him in disbelief. 'Why don't you believe me?'

'I believe *you*,' Jago said, 'I'm just not sure if I believe this Sophie.'

'Okay, then,' Polly said, grabbing her mobile.

'What are you doing?'

'I'm going to ask Sophie if she has a photo of him.' She quickly sent a text to Sophie and put her phone down, staring at Jago in defiance. The reply came back a few moments later. Polly picked up the phone and stared down at the screen.

'What is it?' Jago asked. 'What does it say?'

Polly sighed. 'She said she doesn't have one. Sean didn't like his photo being taken.'

'That's convenient,' Jago said.

Hot tears pricked at Polly's eyes again. 'Why aren't you supporting me in this?'

'I am, Polly. I *am* supporting you. I'm just not supporting this Sophie person.'

Archie chose that moment to come into the kitchen

'What's wrong, Mum?' Archie asked, obviously seeing her tears. 'Is it a headache?'

It was only then that Polly fully acknowledged the fact that her temples had been throbbing and she nodded.

'You should lie down. Let me get you upstairs,' Jago said.

'I'm okay,' she protested.

'No you're not. This is all too much for you. I'm getting you into bed.'

'Can I get you anything, Mummy?'

'Just water,' she said.

'Have you any tablets you can take?' Jago asked.

'In the drawer of the dresser,' she said. 'Archie knows which ones.'

Archie got the pills and a mug of water and followed them up the stairs.

'I'll take it from here, Arch,' Jago said after Archie had put the water and tablets down on the bedside table and Polly had sat down on the bed.

He leaned forward to kiss her cheek which brought yet more tears to her eyes.

'Take your tablets and lie down,' Jago ordered, easing her slippers off and unrolling the duvet.

'Jago, he's alive!' she said, once Archie was out of the room.

'We'll talk about it later,' he said. 'Get some rest, okay?'

'But Archie—'

'I'll look after him. Take these tablets,' he said, holding the mug of water for her. Polly took two.

'Now, rest.'

Polly finally gave in, allowing her head to sink into the pillow as Jago drew the curtains.

'I'll be downstairs. I'll come and check on you later, okay?' He bent forward to kiss her forehead. 'Yell if you need me sooner, okay?'

She reached out and squeezed his hand. 'Love you,' she whispered.

'Love you too,' he said.

Polly woke up in a panic. What time was it? She reached for the alarm clock and hit its light. It was after ten. *Ten!*

She leapt out of bed and then immediately regretted the action for, although the worst of the headache was gone, she felt horribly dizzy and dehydrated. She sat back down on the bed and drank the water and then went to the bathroom to wash her face in cold water.

She tiptoed across the landing and opened the door into Archie's bedroom, smiling as she saw the sleeping figure of her son. She moved towards him quietly, pulling his duvet up around him and kissing his cheek.

'Night, darling,' she whispered. He stirred, eyelashes flickering.

Polly left the room, venturing downstairs. Jago was sitting in the living room, Dickens by his feet. It looked as if he'd always been there, always been a part of life at 3 Church Green.

'Hey, how are you?' he said as soon as he saw her. 'Come and sit down. You're as pale as a particularly pale ghost.'

Polly joined him on the sofa, patting Dickens's soft head before snuggling into Jago's arms.

'I'm okay,' she said.

'Archie's in bed. He had a bath and did his teeth,' he said before Polly had time to ask.

'Thank you so much.'

'My pleasure.'

'What about tea?' Polly asked.

'Tea? Oh, damn. I knew I'd forgotten something!' He grinned. 'Only joking! We had a Spanish omelette.'

'Really?'

'Truly,' he said. 'Want me to make you one?'

Polly shook her head. 'I couldn't eat a thing.'

'Cup of tea?'

'I'm fine. I'm sorry I was out for so long. What have you two been doing?'

'We played some music really quietly, but we didn't want to disturb you with the guitar. We watched a bit of TV, took Dickens out the back, had tea and talked a bit.'

'Yeah? What about?'

'Oh, you know. Guy stuff.'

'Really?'

He laughed. 'Archie wanted to know about my band. I censored the details, don't worry.'

'The details like you getting it on with all the groupies?'

Jago leaned back from her. 'You think I'd do that?'

'I hope you wouldn't now,' she said, 'but I'm sure you did in your time.'

'I might have had a few passing flirtations with the fairer members of our audience,' he said, 'but you're the only one for me now.' His arms tightened around her and they sat in blissful silence for a moment.

'You think he's been here, don't you?' Jago said at last about the subject that simply couldn't be ignored. 'You think that was him at the school that time? That he gave the model boat to Archie?'

Polly nodded. 'I do.'

'Why didn't he just call round like a normal person?'

'I don't know. Because he's not normal? I mean, a normal person wouldn't just disappear for three and a half years without a word, would they?'

'What are you going to do?'

'I don't think I can do anything,' she said. 'He seems to be holding all the power, doesn't he? I can't do or say anything until he makes an appearance.'

'Have you told your mum?'

'No. I've only told you,' she said. 'It's all happened so fast. I couldn't think of anything more than just trying to process it all.'

Jago continued to hold her and Polly willed herself not to cry again.

'Have you thought about what you'd do?' Jago asked her.

'What do you mean?'

'I mean, if Sean comes back.'

Polly swallowed hard. It was the question she didn't want to think about. But what would she do if Sean suddenly appeared? He was her husband, wasn't he? Or was he? Did a man have the right to be thought of as a husband if he upped and walked out – or sailed out – one day? She'd got over Sean. She'd made a good, solid life for herself and Archie and, for the first time since he'd left them, she'd found some happiness of her own with Jago. What would happen to all of that if Sean came back? She was too scared to think about it and so she closed her eyes against it all, her head resting on the solid warmth of Jago's chest.

They sat there in silence a while longer, the fire slowly dying in the wood burner, and then Jago got up.

'You're going?' Polly said, dreading the moment when she'd be alone with her thoughts.

'Got to, I'm afraid. Early start at one of the schools I'm teaching at.'

She nodded and they walked through to the hallway which felt cold after the warmth of the living room. Polly shivered as she opened the front door.

'Don't stand there getting cold,' he told her. 'Get right up to bed, okay?'

She stood up on tiptoes and kissed him. 'Thank you for being here.'

'You're more than welcome,' he said. 'Call me if you need anything, okay?'

'Even if it's a cuddle in the middle of the night?'

'Especially if it's a cuddle in the middle of the night!' he said.

They kissed again and then he walked across the road.

'Jago!' she called softly as he headed into the shadows that engulfed the green.

He turned around and crossed the road back to her and she ran into his arms right there on the pavement.

'You'll get cold,' he said to her.

'Not when I've got you to hold.'

'You'll always have me to hold,' he told her.

'Promise?'

'I promise.'

CHAPTER 22

The school music room was a pretty uninspiring place, Jago thought as he sat down and waited for his first pupil. The walls were a sickly sort of yellow and covered in the remains of Sellotape corners and blobs of old Blu-tack, and there above the desk was a peeling poster of Beethoven looking particularly wild and scary. Still, at least they encouraged the children to play an instrument, he thought. So often, the arts were the first to suffer with budget cuts.

He looked down at the timetable he'd been given. He had three pupils this morning and, as he waited for the first to arrive, his mind drifted back to the night before.

How could he feel threatened by a man who'd been thought dead up until a few hours ago, he wondered? A man who, it seemed, had thought nothing of walking out on Polly and Archie. A man whom Polly had moved on from. Yet, that was precisely how Jago was feeling for what chance did he have if Sean was alive and he came back to claim what was rightfully his?

Jago got up and walked across to the window. It was a bright spring morning and the sky was a heartening blue with white wispy clouds, but it did nothing to lift his mood because he was terrified, absolutely terrified, that he was going to lose Polly and Archie.

He got his phone out of his pocket and sent a quick text to Polly.
Hey, Poll. You okay? J x
It took less than a minute for a reply to come.
Okay. Miss you. P x
So at least Sean hadn't made an appearance after he'd left last night, he thought. Or this morning. But Jago sincerely believed that it was only a matter of time.

'Mr Solomon?' a voice called from the door.

'Lucy?' he said, turning around to see a gawky girl of about twelve standing in the doorway. She nodded.

'Come in.'

'Sorry I'm late, Mr Solomon.'

'It's okay,' he said with a smile. He still wasn't used to being called Mr Solomon. It made him sound about a hundred years old, he thought. He'd once made the mistake of telling the pupils in a class to call him Jago and the supporting teacher's eyes had been out on stalks.

'You do that and they'll run rings around you,' she'd warned at the end of the session.

'Where's your guitar?' he asked Lucy now.

'At my mum's,' she said. 'I had to stay with my dad last night.'

'Oh, I see,' Jago said, wondering if children of divorced parents wheeled out that excuse on a regular basis. 'Well, it's lucky that I've got one you can use for the lesson, isn't it?'

She nodded and he handed her a guitar, trying to shut thoughts of Polly out of his mind as he concentrated on placing Lucy's bitten nails in the right place.

Bryony was watching her sister very closely as she moved like a sleepwalker around her shop. She didn't look right. She wasn't her usual business-like self, that was for sure. Finally, Bryony could take it no more.

'Where's your head at? she cried.

'What do you mean?' Polly asked, looking stunned by the question.

'I mean, you've just shelved *The Secret Garden* in amongst that new supernatural series.'

'Oh,' Polly said. 'Did I?'

Bryony put her hands on her hips. Today, she was wearing an indigo-coloured skirt with a silver-white blouse and black denim jacket. And that was something else she'd noticed about Polly today – her hair was a mess. A mess for Polly, at least. It was immaculate by Bryony's own standards. Had she had a fight with Jago?

'Polly – sit yourself down.'

'I'm not sitting on – or in – one of those bean bags.' Polly frowned. 'Which is it? Sitting *on* a bean bag or *in* a bean bag?'

'It doesn't matter,' Bryony said. 'I meant the stool anyway.' She gestured to the one adult seat in the shop.

'You've really got to get some proper chairs,' Polly said as she hopped up onto the stool just as the phone rang. Bryony answered it.

'Hello Mrs Steel. Yes, I remember. No, I'm afraid it's not in yet,' Bryony said. 'Would you like me to call you when it is? Okay, I'll do that. No. No. I'm not engaged to Colin. Where did you hear that?

Well, it's not true. Okay. I'll give you a call when the book's in.'

Bryony hung up. 'Can you believe that? There's a rumour going around that I'm engaged to Colin. *Engaged!* I only went out for a meal with him and the whole of Castle Clare's got us married off already.'

Polly laughed. 'You should be used to that sort of gossip by now.'

'Well, I'm glad it's cheered you up at least. Now, what's the matter? And don't tell me nothing because I'll not give up until you've spilt everything!'

Polly took a deep breath and began. Bryony listened and, for once in her life, she didn't interrupt.

'You think he's back?' Bryony asked when Polly finally finished.

'I really do,' Polly said.

'Oh, my God, Poll. What will you do?'

'I don't know,' she said. 'I've been up half the night asking that same question.'

'And what about Jago? What's he said about all this?'

'He hasn't said much, really. He didn't believe what Sophie said, but how does that explain the model boat?'

'That's weird,' Bryony said.

'It is, isn't it?'

'You should call the police.'

'And say what? That I think my missing husband's back, but I haven't seen him yet so I guess that still makes him missing.'

Bryony blew out her cheeks. 'You could tell them that this Sophie's seen him.'

'I guess,' Polly said, 'but I want proof myself before I do anything.'

Bryony nodded. 'No wonder you're a mess at the moment.'

Polly frowned. 'What do you mean? I'm not a mess!'

Bryony leaned forward and tucked a loose strand of her sister's hair back behind her ear.

'You're right. I am a mess,' Polly admitted. 'It was all I could do this morning to get Archie ready for school.'

'Have you told him?'

'What's there to tell? That a man he might not even remember *might* turn up out of the blue?'

'He didn't get a look at him at the school that day?'

Polly shook her head. 'I've asked him over and over what he remembers, but he didn't see anything.'

Bryony's head was spinning at her sister's news so she could only imagine how Polly was feeling.

'If Sean does turn up,' Bryony began hesitantly, 'if he wants to pick up where he left off, what will you do?'

Polly's dark eyes filled with tears. 'I don't know,' she said. 'I really don't know!'

'Oh, Polly!' Bryony hugged her close and let her cry. 'I wish there was something I could do.'

'I feel so helpless,' Polly whispered. 'Why's he doing this to us? Why doesn't he just show up instead of inflicting this slow torture?'

Bryony stood hugging Polly as she sat on the stool for a few minutes more and then Polly pulled away, moping her eyes with a tissue from her pocket.

'Will you let me know?' Bryony said. 'I mean, if he shows up.'

'Of course I will.'

'We'll get through this,' Bryony said.

'That's what Jago keeps saying,' Polly said. 'But I can't stand all this waiting for something to happen. I feel as if my life is on hold.' She took a deep breath. 'I just wish it would all begin so I could make a start on getting through it.'

Jago was waiting for them when they arrived home from the school run that afternoon.

'Jago!' Archie shouted as he leapt out of the car outside their house.

'Guess what I've got?' Jago said, holding up something that looked suspiciously guitar-shaped.

'Is it my guitar?' Archie asked, looking from Jago to his mum and back again.

'It certainly is,' Jago said. 'I picked it up this morning, given it the once-over and it's all yours!'

'Let's get inside before he opens the case right here on the road,' Polly said.

They bundled into the house in an excited heap, running through to the living room as if it was Christmas morning.

'Can I open it?' Archie asked as Dickens ran into the room to see what all the fuss was about. Jago handed Archie the guitar case.

'Go on,' he said.

'Wow!' Archie said a moment later. 'Is it really mine?'

'It sure is,' Jago said.

He looked at it in awe for a moment before pulling it from its case and holding it next to his body in a funny kind of embrace as if he never meant to let it go.

'I never saw you cuddling your piano,' Polly said.

'That was never mine,' he said.

'Yes it was,' Polly said.

Archie shook his head. 'It was Dad's and Granddad's.'

'Well, this is yours, my darling,' Polly said, kissing the top of his head.

'Thanks, Mum! Thanks, Jago!'

'You're welcome,' they both said together.

Polly watched her son as he strummed his first notes and then she left the room, walking into the kitchen followed by Dickens. Jago joined her.

'Hey,' he said. 'You okay?'

She nodded. 'I thought I'd leave you to enjoy the moment.'

'I don't think Archie would notice if I was doing handstands,' he said.

Polly laughed. 'Thanks so much for finding it for him.'

'One of life's greatest pleasures is to match the right instrument to the right person,' he told her.

'What a lovely notion,' Polly said.

Jago moved an inch closer to her. 'But not as lovely as matching the right person to,' he paused, 'the right person.'

Polly smiled. 'That's a pretty good notion too.'

'It is, isn't it?'

Polly gazed into his slate-grey eyes and ran her fingers over his wide mouth. He was wearing a cute black waistcoat today with the buttons all undone and it made her want to kiss his neck.

'What is it?' he said when she withdrew her fingers from his mouth. 'Where'd you go? That was just getting interesting.'

'I think I might know where Sean is,' Polly said, thoughts of waistcoats and sexy necks flying from her mind.

'Where?'

'Woolverstone Marina,' she said.

'What makes you think that?'

'It was a favourite place of his and, if he's living on a boat, it might well be there.'

'Okay,' Jago said cautiously, 'and what do you want to do?'

'I think I should go there.'

'What – just turn up and check out every single boat?'

'We check his old mooring first,' Polly said. 'I don't know if he's still using it, but it's got to be worth a try, hasn't it?'

Jago didn't look convinced. 'I don't know if that's such a great idea.'

'Why not?'

'Surely if he wanted to see you – I mean if he's even in Suffolk–'

'He's in Suffolk. I know he is and I can't just hang around and do nothing. It's driving me crazy, Jago!'

'Okay, okay,' he said. 'We'll check out this marina place.'

'You're coming with me?'

'Of *course* I'm going with you. I've got a lesson, but that's easily rearranged so we'll go as soon as you drop Archie off at school tomorrow, all right?'

Polly nodded, feeling a little easier now that she had a plan in place.

The morning was cool and bright when they arrived at Woolverstone Marina. They parked the Land Rover and got out, walking towards the water.

'Blimey, this place is huge,' Jago said. 'I've never seen so many boats in my life.'

'I think Sean said there are over two hundred berths here,' Polly told him.

'That's a lot of boats,' Jago said. 'I hope you know where it is. It's like a city of masts down there.'

It was a daunting yet inspiring sight with the wide river and the great expanse of the road bridge which crossed high above it. She'd used to love coming to the marina with Sean in those heady, early days of their relationship. Before he'd first hit her. Bright spring mornings, blue-skied days of summer and crisp autumn afternoons – all had had their own particular magic when out on the water. Now, however, it was a cold, grey March morning. A bitter wind was coming off the river and there were some heavy clouds scudding along the horizon. It wasn't a day to be out on the water, she thought, but would Sean be on his boat?

'The mooring place for the *Oystercatcher* was down there,' Polly said, nodding across at a row of boats. Suddenly, her nerves began to kick in. She'd managed to keep them in check all morning as she'd got on with the usual routine of getting Archie ready for school, and Jago had kept her mind off things with a funny story about one of his pupils. But there was nothing to distract her now.

Jago took her hand and squeezed it gently. 'You sure you want to do this?'

'I'm not sure *want* is the right word,' she said. 'But I *need* to.'

Jago nodded. 'Lead the way.'

She took a deep breath and, together, they walked down amongst the boats. Even though it was the middle of the week, there were a few people around, eager to make the most of the spring day by doing routine maintenance work before the sailing season ahead.

'I think it's this row,' she said a moment later as they walked along a pontoon lined with fabulous white boats, their sails folded away and their masts reaching skywards.

On they walked until Polly stopped.

'Is it here?' Jago asked. 'These all look the same to me.'

Polly looked around. She had to admit that the boats all looked the same to her too, but she was pretty sure that she was in the right place.

'I thought it was here,' she said. 'But this boat's a much bigger one than the *Oystercatcher*.'

'It's also called *Mirage*,' Jago pointed out.

'Yes,' she said.

'And that one's *Happy Days*,' Jago said, looking at the boat to their left, 'and this one's *Sea Quest*.'

'It's not here,' Polly said, feeling both deflated and relieved at the same time.

Jago put his arm around her. 'You tried,' he said.

Polly looked along the line of white boats and back towards the car park. 'Wait a minute,' she said.

'What is it?' Jago asked.

'It's over there,' she said. 'Not here. It's the next pontoon along. Come on!' She took off at a great pace, her energy renewed.

'Slow down!' Jago called after her. 'I don't want you ending up in the water.'

Polly relaxed her pace a little not because Jago had asked her to but because she'd reached the right pontoon at last.

'Here!' she said. 'This is it.'

They walked down the pontoon together, passing gleaming white boats bobbing gently on the water. Finally, Polly stopped and examined one boat in particular.

'Is that it?' Jago asked.

'I think so,' Polly said.

'Listen,' he said, 'have you really thought about this?'

'I've thought of nothing else,' Polly said.

'I mean, what are you going to say? And how are you going to introduce me?' Jago's tone was deadly serious and his face was pale and anxious.

'I – I don't know,' Polly said, and it was true. Although she'd thought of very little else since Sophie Randall had walked into her life, Polly didn't actually know what she'd say to Sean if and when she came face to face with him. She had been so focussed on finding out whether it was true that he was alive that she hadn't thought much beyond that. But Jago was right. How was she going to explain his presence there?

Hi Sean. Good to see you after all these years. Meet my new boyfriend, Jago! She shook her head. That wouldn't do at all, would it?'

'Is that even the right boat?' Jago asked and Polly looked at it again.

'It looks like it.'

'Yeah? Well, to my eye, that one looks just like this one, and all of those over there too.'

'Look for the name,' Polly said, peering around the boat without actually stepping onto it.

'Here,' Jago said. He'd walked along the length of the pontoon and found the name on the back. Polly joined him and read it.

Swan.

'It's the name Sophie told me,' Polly said.

'Is it the *Oystercatcher*?'

'It looks like it,' Polly said, 'but I'm no expert.' She made to step aboard.

'What are you doing?' Jago cried in alarm.

'I didn't come all this way just to look at her,' she said.

Jago looked up and down the pontoon as if expecting an alarm to go off or the police to show up. One thing seemed sure, he wasn't going to follow her on board, Polly thought.

She stepped down into the cockpit and looked at the door into the cabin. If anybody was aboard, the door would be open, but it was resolutely closed. Locked too, she discovered a moment later. Still, she couldn't stop herself from knocking on it.

'I think we should get going,' Jago said from the pontoon.

'Give me a minute,' Polly said, not quite sure what she was waiting for, but then she turned around and, with Jago's hand stretched out to take hers, stepped out of the boat. Once back on the pontoon, she turned back towards the boat, trying to see into one of the portholes, but they were so tiny and it was dark inside the cabin.

'What do you want to do?' Jago asked.

'I don't know,' Polly said, suddenly feeling quite lost.

'Let's walk back to the car, shall we?' Jago said, putting his arm around her as if taking control. 'Hey, I've just had a great idea.'

'Yeah? Because I could use a good idea about now,' Polly said with a weak smile.

'We're not far from Ipswich. How's about we pop into town and visit a party shop I know? Pick up a few things for Archie's do. What do you think?'

Polly looked up at him. 'I think you think of the sweetest things!' she said, standing up on tiptoes to kiss him.

CHAPTER 23

The best birthday present a boy of seven can have is finding that his birthday falls on a Saturday. Of course, that meant that Polly didn't get her usual extra half an hour in bed. Still, it wasn't every day that you were seven, Polly thought, as she swung her legs out of bed and drew open the curtains. It looked like a wonderful spring day and Polly smiled as she saw that the daffodils on the village green were now open, their yellow throats wide as if they were about to launch into a flowery rendition of "Happy Birthday". Polly's own modest garden had been filled with snowdrops earlier in the year but Polly always thought that it was the yellow of the primroses and daffodils that heralded the real arrival of spring.

'Mum? Are you up yet?' Archie called from the landing.

Polly opened her door. 'Happy Birthday, sweetheart!' she said, kissing his cheek and hugging him to her. 'Why don't you go and play your new guitar whilst I get dressed?'

'Okay,' he said.

An hour later all of Archie's presents had been opened. There was a new football from Uncle Josh, a box set of books by a new adventure writer from Aunt Bryony, a selection bag of evil-looking sweets from Aunt Lara, a waterproof digital watch from Uncle Sam and a Meccano model set from Grandpa Frank and Grandma Eleanor. Great Grandpa Joe had given Polly some money towards the party on behalf of himself and Nell.

Polly had chosen some new computer games for him and a skateboard.

'Which is *only* to be used when I'm around to supervise!' she warned him.

'Thanks, Mum!' he cried, launching himself into her arms.

Jago came over mid-morning, bringing with him a huge present wrapped in shiny blue paper with a large silver ribbon.

'Happy Birthday, Arch!' he said as Archie opened the door to him. 'I won't sing. Well, not yet anyway!'

'Thanks, Jago,' Archie said, taking the gift from him. They went into the living room where Dickens was sniffing around the discarded wrapping paper, no doubt hoping to find something edible amongst it all.

'What is it?' Archie said.

'Open it and see,' Jago said.

Archie tore into the paper, the ripping sound making Dickens so excited that he started turning circles and barking.

'Oh, wow!' Archie said.

Polly blinked in surprise. 'What is it?'

'It's a guitar stand,' Jago said. 'When you're playing and you just want to put your guitar down for a moment, you don't want to keep putting it in its case. Plus it's great to just look at in your room. Makes you think about it.'

'Thanks, Jago,' Archie said, giving him a hug.

Polly blinked back the tears as she watched the two of them. It was such a wonderful moment full of tenderness.

'I've put a couple of music books in there for you too. We can go through them together.'

'Thanks!'

'Thank you, Jago,' Polly said. 'It's an amazing present. And the guitar of course. We mustn't forget the guitar.'

'Hey, I only found it for you.'

'Jago?' Archie said.

'Yes?'

'Can I join your band one day?'

Jago grinned. 'If you keep practising and improving, sure you can.'

'Cool!' Archie said and Polly laughed.

The noise made by ten six and seven-year-olds had to be heard to be believed. Polly should have spent less time shopping for party poppers and more time researching ear defenders, she thought, as she dived back into the throng in the living room. She was glad she'd had the foresight to move her beautiful velvet cushions upstairs because Tiger had spilled his lemonade and little Tommy Manders was now jumping on the sofa.

'Off from there, Tommy!' Polly said, doing her best not to shout as she removed Dickens from the fray in case he decided to join in.

Jago was in the thick of it all. He'd been playing both the guitar and the piano and Polly thought she might have to put him on the payroll as an official party entertainer. The children adored him.

The trip to the party shop in Ipswich had been a great idea of Jago's and they'd got all they'd needed to fill the party bags for later. Polly had also made a cake in the shape of a guitar which she was particularly proud of.

'I hope I get one of those for my birthday,' Jago had told her when he'd first seen it.

'Don't fret about it!' she'd joked.

'Very funny,' he said, pulling her in for a kiss. Polly had truly never been kissed more in her life than in the last week and she had to admit that she liked it.

Now, she took a moment to look at the spread of buffet-style food that had been prepared by her, Jago and Eleanor who had nipped over just before the party had kicked off and delivered heaps of sausage rolls and iced buns.

She barely heard the knock at the door and nearly ignored it, but it sounded again. An early parent, she thought, looking at the clock, but it was very early at just gone five in the afternoon. The kids hadn't had their tea yet. She brushed her hair back from her face with the back of her hand and checked the front of her dress for bits of crisps and jelly. She was good to go.

'Coming!' she cried over the din of small children, closing the kitchen door to prevent Dickens from getting over-excited. She took a deep breath and opened the front door, but her smile soon vanished as she saw who was standing there.

'Sean,' she said, the word exiting her mouth as if it had been shot out.

At first, he didn't say anything, but just stared at her with those startlingly blue eyes of his. And Polly stared right back, not knowing what to say although there were about a thousand thoughts flying around her head. Three and a half years' worth of unanswered questions, for a start.

'Aren't you going to invite me in?' he asked.

'What?' she said. He hadn't even said hello yet.

'I want to see Archie,' he said. 'It's his birthday, right?' He gave a kind of smug smile as if he expected Polly to congratulate him on having remembered this little fact.

'Sean,' she began again, 'we thought you... we thought you might have died.'

He gave a little shrug. 'What can I say? I'm still alive!'

His flippant tone riled Polly. 'You've been missing for three and a half years!' she told him in case he'd forgotten. 'And now you just turn up on our doorstep and expect me to let you in?'

'I want to see my son, Polly. Don't make this difficult for me.'

Her eyes widened. 'You're accusing *me* of making things difficult?'

'I'm back now. Isn't that the main thing?'

Polly almost choked. 'Are you serious? You're back! You've just decided to *come back*.'

'I thought you'd be happy to see me,' he said, making a move towards her. 'Polly–'

Polly backed away from him. 'No,' she said, shocked by how frightened she was.

'Polly,' he said again, 'come here.'

Suddenly, his arms fastened around her and she found herself in his embrace. She could barely breathe and her heart was racing wildly, making her feel as if everything was spinning out of control.

'Sean,' she cried, and there were tears coursing down her face. 'Sean!'

'It's okay. I'm here now,' he said, holding her tightly.

'I didn't know what to do.'

'Shush,' he said.

'I tried to find you. I tried *so* hard,' she said. 'Why didn't you call me? What happened?'

'It's all right,' he whispered. 'I'm here now. That's all that matters, right?'

Polly felt too confused to answer. She also felt lightheaded and as if she might faint at any moment and, all the while, Sean kept telling her it was all right. But it wasn't all right, was it? He hadn't so much as said sorry or even tried to explain where he'd been. It was as if he expected her to accept the fact that he could disappear for more than three years and have god only knew what kind of adventures whilst she was left to prop up the remnants of their life together, terrified that each knock on the door or telephone call would bring news of his death.

'Are you going to let me in?' he asked her again. 'Can I see my boy?'

'Archie,' Polly said as he finally relaxed his hold on her.

'Yes, Archie,' he said with a little laugh, but Polly wasn't laughing. She didn't quite know what to do. 'I'll come in, okay?'

She couldn't stop him. He had pushed her gently to one side and was through the door. As soon as he entered the hallway, Dickens raced through from the kitchen barking. Archie or one of his friends must have been in there and left the door open.

'Woah! You got a dog?' Sean cried in alarm.

'Yes, we got a dog,' Polly said.

'You know I hate dogs.'

Polly stared at him. 'What?'

'Why did you get a dog when you know I hate them?'

Her mouth dropped open. 'In case you'd forgotten, you've not been around.'

He shook his head. 'I can see you're not going to let that go easily, are you?'

Polly was literally dumbstruck. When she'd been told by Sophie that Sean was alive, she'd tried to imagine their first encounter and it hadn't been anything like the one before her. She'd thought he'd apologise. She'd thought he'd explain. There'd even be tears of remorse for what he'd put her through. But there was none of that. Instead, the old arrogant Sean was now in her house, remonstrating over the decisions she'd made in his absence.

A couple of Archie's friends ran from the living room into the kitchen and then back again in some sort of game.

'Looks like a fun party,' Sean said.

'It is,' Polly said. 'It was.'

It was then that Jago popped his head around the living room doorway.

'Who is it, Polly?' he asked.

Polly turned to face him and saw the smile drop from Jago's face as it obviously dawned on him who it was standing in the hallway. He looked at her as if to gauge what she wanted to do, and what she wanted him to do.

'Jago,' she said hesitantly, 'this is Sean.'

Jago stared at the intruder, a cautiousness in his eyes.

'Jago?' Sean said, repeating the name. 'Children's entertainer?'

'No,' Jago and Polly both said at once and Polly felt the full weight of Sean's gaze upon her.

'You didn't waste much time, did you?' Sean said.

'Just three and a half years—'

'Oh, here we go again with the three and a half years,' Sean said.

211

'Hey!' Jago said, moving towards Polly and putting a protective arm around her. 'What did you come here for?'

'You're asking me what I came here for? This is my home!.'

Before she could stop him, Sean had pushed passed both her and Jago and was in the living room.

'Sean – no –' Polly cried, but it was too late.

'Archie? Which one of you is Archie?'

Polly was standing behind her estranged husband when Archie turned around, a huge smile on his face. The room fell quiet. Perhaps the kids thought that Sean was someone hired to entertain them.

'I'm Archie,' Archie said.

'And do you know who I am?' Sean said.

Archie shook his head.

'I'm your father,' Sean continued.

'No you're not,' Archie said without a beat and Polly watched as Archie ran out of the room and tore up the stairs. A moment later, they heard the sound of his bedroom door slamming.

'I think you'd better go, Sean,' Jago said as he came into the room.

'I beg your pardon?' Sean said.

'Nobody wants you here,' Jago said.

'And who are you again?'

'It doesn't matter who I am.'

'Oh, really?' Sean said. 'You think you have the right to tell me what to do in my own home?'

'Yeah, I think I do. Because this isn't your home anymore, pal. This is Polly and Archie's home.'

'Please leave, Sean,' Polly said. 'This isn't the time.'

Sean stared at her as if she was mad. 'I'm not going anywhere,' he retorted. 'I came here to see my son.'

'Get out,' Jago said. 'You're upsetting everybody.'

'Archie!' Sean called, going to the foot of the stairs.

Polly followed him, grabbing his arm.

'He's upset,' Polly said. 'Please leave – let me talk to him.'

'*Archie?*' Sean shouted again.

'This isn't the way to do this!' Polly cried.

Sean turned to face her. 'Don't tell me–'

'Hey!' Jago said. 'This isn't doing anybody any good. There's a room full of children here in case you hadn't noticed, and you're scaring them.'

Sean glanced towards the living room. Several of the youngsters were standing in the doorway, eyes wide as they watched what was happening.

'This isn't over,' Sean said at last in a low voice.

'No? Well, it is for today,' Jago said, escorting Sean down the hall before shoving him through the door and closing it in his face.

By the time Jago walked back to Polly, she was shaking. He leaned forward and hugged her.

'How's about we serve the tea, eh?' he said.

Polly looked up. His grey eyes were full of warmth and love and she nodded. 'But I have to talk to Archie.'

'I'll go and get him,' Jago said.

'What will you say?'

'I'll say it's his birthday and it's time to cut the cake.'

'But what about Sean?'

'I'm not going to talk about him, and you're not going to talk about him. Not yet. Not today. Okay?'

'Okay,' she said.

'Today is Archie's birthday. It's about presents, cake and friends. That's all.'

He gave her a quick kiss on her forehead before going upstairs.

How Polly managed to get through the next hour, she didn't know. When Archie finally appeared at the kitchen door, his face looking a little paler than normal, she was filled with relief that he'd rejoined them and she watched in delight as his face brightened at the sight of the guitar-shaped cake lit with seven candles for him to blow out.

There'd then been a mad scramble for plastic plates as food was grabbed by eager little hands, and the smile which Polly had forced onto her face after Sean's departure soon became a real one.

Finally, when the knocks on the door began for the children to be taken home, Polly and Jago handed out the party bags and Archie said his goodbyes. The house was horribly silent when the last guest had left and Polly and Jago exchanged glances as Archie disappeared upstairs.

'You okay?' Jago asked.

'I don't know how I got through today without a complete meltdown,' she said.

'Because you're the best mum in the world.'

She smiled. 'I don't know about that.'

'Yeah, well, I do.' He hugged her to him. 'Do you want me to stay?'

'That's sweet of you,' Polly said. 'But as much as I'd like to have you with me, I think it needs to be just me and Archie.'

Jago nodded. 'What are you going to tell him?'

Polly closed her eyes for a moment. 'I don't know,' she said. 'I really don't know. But I'll answer his questions if he has any. Reassure him.'

'You know where I am if you need me.'

She leaned forward and kissed him on the mouth. 'I couldn't have got through all this without you.'

'Yes you could,' he told her.

'Well, maybe,' she said, 'but I might have spiralled into insanity before Archie had blown his candles out.'

She walked with him to the front door.

'Call me – soon!'

She nodded and, closing the door, took a deep breath before going upstairs.

Archie's bedroom door was shut and Polly stood outside on the landing, her hand hovering before knocking softly.

'Archie?' There was no reply. 'Arch? Can I come in?' She opened the door slowly. Archie was sitting on the floor, his back up against his bed. 'I thought you'd want to play with your toys.'

He shook his head and Polly walked into the room, squatting down to sit beside her son. She couldn't remember the last time she'd sat on the floor of her son's bedroom and she took a moment to take in life at Archie-level. For a start, his carpet could do with being replaced, she thought, cringing at the murky thinness of it. She shook her head. Now wasn't the time to think about carpets. She was just trying to delay the inevitable.

She cleared her throat. 'You okay?' she asked. He nodded. 'You sure?' He nodded again but, when he looked up at her, she could tell he'd been crying. 'Oh, Archie,' she said, hugging him to her. 'Don't cry, darling. Please don't cry. It's your special day.' She let his tears fall, allowing a few of her own to join them before she spoke again.

'Do you want to talk about it?' she asked him gently.

'Was that man really my dad?' he asked, wiping his eyes with the sleeve of his jumper and sniffing loudly.

'Yes,' Polly told him, handing him a clean tissue from her pocket of never-ending tissue supplies.

'But I don't remember him.'

'I know, darling,' Polly said. 'He left a long time ago. That's why it was such a shock to see him today.'

'Did he know it was my birthday?'

'He did. He remembered,' Polly said kindly.

'Will he come back?'

'I think so,' she said. 'He'll want to see you.'

'Even though I ran away from him?'

'He understands,' Polly said, squeezing him against her. 'You got scared. You weren't expecting to see him. Neither of us were so it's been a big shock, hasn't it?'

'Everyone was asking me questions afterwards.'

'Were they?'

'Well, Tiger was.'

'And what did you say?'

'Nothing. I ignored him and gave him another iced bun.'

'A good solution to any problem,' Polly said with a smile.

'Why can't Jago be my dad?' Archie asked.

Polly sighed. 'Because he's your friend.'

'I wish he was my dad.'

Polly sighed. 'So do I, darling. So do I.'

CHAPTER 24

For the first time in years, Polly thought about ringing her mother
and saying she couldn't make Sunday lunch at Campion House. She
could so easily say she had one of her headaches. Her mother would
be sure to believe her for Polly never told lies, but Jago persuaded her
not to.

'You need to talk about this,' he told her.

'I've talked to Bryony.'

'Yes, but to your whole family. You guys are close and, if you get
this thing out in the open, you'll feel better.'

'Will I?' she asked.

'I guarantee it. You've been carrying it around on your own for
too long.'

'But I've had you to talk to.'

'Yes, but I'm not your family.'

'It feels like you are,' she said, kissing him.

'I hope not,' he said with a grin.

'You know what I mean,' she said. 'You–' she paused, wondering
if she was ready to say this.

'What?' he prompted.

'You complete me. Us. Archie and me.' She heard him take a deep
breath.

'You guys complete me too,' he said. They hugged each other.

'Okay,' Polly said at last. 'We'd better get ready.'

'It's the right thing to do,' Jago said.

'I know.'

'They'll want to know what's going on.'

Polly nodded. 'You're right.'

There'd been a hard frost that morning and the grass in the shade
at Campion House was still silvery and sparkly. The daffodils and
primroses may well be flowering, Polly thought, but the warm days of
spring and summer were still a long way off.

Polly, Jago, Archie and Dickens all bundled into the house, glad to
be in the warm. A fire was blazing in the living room and they joined
Sam, Callie and Josh who were also thawing out there.

As Archie was thanking everyone for his presents, Bryony walked
into the room and took Polly to one side.

216

'You look tired,' Bryony told her.

'Do I?'

'Yes.'

'You try handling a seven-year-old's birthday party,' Polly joked.

'Is that the only reason?' her sister asked.

Polly looked Bryony square on. 'No,' she said. 'It isn't.'

'I thought not. What's been happening? *Something's* happened, hasn't it?'

'I'll tell you, I promise,' Polly said. 'I'm going to tell everyone, okay?'

'Polly!' Eleanor cried as she walked into the room. 'And Jago *and* the birthday boy.' She caught her grandson up in a hug. 'How was your party?'

'Brilliant!' he said. Polly watched him warily. She'd told him not to say anything about his father's arrival and had explained to him that she'd be telling the family about it herself. But she needn't have worried as he genuinely seemed to have forgotten about it as he told his grandma about the games they'd all played and the food they'd eaten.

By the time they all sat down to Sunday lunch, Polly was a bag of nerves. Jago seemed to sense this and kept hold of her hand under the table until it was absolutely necessary for her to use it for eating.

She found it increasingly difficult to join in the usual Sunday banter. But it was even more difficult a task to heap her fork with food and eat it, even though it was all delicious, because she knew what was coming. She was going to have to let her family know that Sean was back.

Home-made rhubarb crumble and heaps of happy yellow custard followed the roast. Polly had the smallest bowlful which didn't go unnoticed by her mother.

'Not hungry, darling?' Eleanor asked.

'Not very.'

'Too much birthday cake yesterday,' Jago chipped in and Eleanor nodded, but Polly could see that her mother didn't look convinced.

The conversation droned on around the table. It was the usual talk about books and life's little dramas, but even Lara's lurid tales of university life couldn't engage Polly.

'Polly?'

Somebody had called her name. She looked up. It was her mother.

Of course it was her mother.

'What is it?' she asked, seeing her mother's anxious expression.

'Your custard.'

Polly looked down and saw that she'd dropped a huge blob of custard onto the tablecloth.

'Oh, no,' she said, whipping her napkin from her lap and dabbing at it. 'I'll get a wet cloth,' she said, making to stand up, but Eleanor stopped her.

'Don't worry about it. Put your napkin down and tell us what's going on.'

'What do you mean?'

'Something's obviously on your mind,' Eleanor said. 'You've not heard a word any of us have said this entire meal, have you?'

'She hasn't,' Jago assented.

'Dad's back,' Archie blurted.

'Archie!' Polly cried.

He looked at her with huge, innocent eyes. 'Sorry,' he said.

'It's okay,' she assured him. 'I was going to tell them.'

'What's this?' Frank asked from his end of the table.

'It's Sean,' Polly said. 'He's back.'

'What do you mean?' Grandpa Joe asked.

'He was at Polly's yesterday,' Jago said, squeezing Polly's hand. She seemed to be suddenly unable to communicate. 'He's been in the area a while, we think.'

'What?' Eleanor said. 'You knew about this?'

'Not for sure,' Jago said. 'A few things have happened and–'

'And you didn't think to tell us about them?' Eleanor said.

'We didn't really know what was going on,' Jago said. 'We didn't want to alarm anyone.'

'Where is he now?' Bryony asked from across the table.

'We don't know,' Polly said, finding her voice at last. 'He's moored at Woolverstone Marina.'

'He's living on his boat?' Frank asked.

'Who's living on his boat?' Grandma Nell asked.

'Sean,' Grandpa Joe said. 'Polly's husband.'

'Polly's married again?' Grandma Nell asked, obviously confused.

'No, this is the husband who went missing,' Frank said.

'I thought he was dead,' Grandma Nell said.

'Yes,' Grandpa Joe said. 'We all thought that.'

'What did he say to you?' Eleanor asked. 'How did he explain himself?'

'We didn't really give him a chance to explain,' Jago said. 'He arrived in the middle of Archie's party.'

'Oh, heavens!' Eleanor said.

'What did he look like?' Lara asked. 'I mean, did he look the same?'

'Yes, pretty much,' Polly said.

'He didn't look like he'd been in some accident and had amnesia for three years?'

'You watch too many silly films,' Bryony told her younger sister.

'You can learn a lot from films,' Lara said.

'Maybe, but not about Sean Prior,' Bryony said.

'How do you know he's come back?' Eleanor asked. 'I mean, what if he disappears again?'

'He won't. He wants to see Archie,' Polly said.

'And how do you feel about all this, Archie?' Eleanor asked gently. Archie gave a shrug of his little shoulders. 'Don't know.'

'Has he been in touch with the police?' Frank said. 'Has anyone been in touch with the police seeing as he's no longer a missing person?'

'We haven't been,' Jago said. 'I don't know what Sean's stance is on that.'

'He's been working under a different name,' Polly said.

'What?' Sam said. 'Isn't that fraud or something? Polly, you can't be involved with somebody like that.'

'Just in case it's slipped your attention, I *am* involved,' she said, nodding to Archie whose solemn gaze was somewhere at the bottom of his pudding bowl.

'Sam's right. You've got to get rid of him,' Josh continued.

'Josh, please,' Polly said. 'This is Archie's father and he's back.'

'I don't care if he's the Dali Lama,' Josh said. 'The way he's treated you – *everyone* – is despicable.'

'I agree,' Bryony said. 'Unless he's been at death's door for over three years and couldn't contact you or had some sort of amnesia like Lara's suggested, he had *no* excuse not to get in touch.'

'Or if he's been held prisoner in a jungle and made to read Dickens to a madman,' Josh said.

'*A Handful of Dust*,' Grandpa Joe said with an excited wave of his fork. 'Wonderful book.'

Eleanor held her hands up. 'I think we all need to calm down,' she said. 'This is a problem that isn't going to be solved by us all shouting our opinions at one another. It's a private matter between Polly, Jago, Archie and Sean. We're all here if you need us, you know that, don't you?'

'Yes, Mum,' Polly said. 'I know that.'

Polly didn't go on the afternoon walk with the family. Jago took charge of Dickens so he'd get his exercise and Archie went along with him, Sam and Callie, Bryony, Lara, Josh, their father and Grandpa Joe.

Grandma Nell was having forty winks in her favourite chair in the living room, the fire having just been given a new lease of life by Frank before he'd left the house, and Polly wandered through to the kitchen to help her mum.

'There's not really a lot to do,' Eleanor told her. 'Go and sit down.'

'I'd rather not,' Polly said. 'I'll just wash these glasses.' She could feel the full weight of her mother's anxious gaze upon her as she poured hot water into the sink. 'I'm okay, Mum,' she said without turning around.

'Are you?'

Polly looked out of the window across the garden towards a clump of pretty yellow and purple crocuses which were doing their best to banish winter and herald the spring.

'No,' she said at last. 'I don't know how I feel, but it's about as far from *okay* as a person can get.'

Her mother sighed. 'I never thought this day would come,' she said. 'I mean, I've wondered what would happen if he came back, but I think I gave up any hope of it actually happening some time ago.'

Polly turned to face her. 'When?'

'When what, darling?'

'When did you give up hope, Mum?'

Eleanor looked pensive. 'I think when it came to the one-year anniversary of his disappearance.'

'Really?' Polly said, genuinely shocked that her mother would have given up hope so soon.

'I guess I thought that he must be dead because surely nobody would walk out on their wife and young son for that length of time. Not without some sort of explanation at least.'

Polly nodded.

'And you said he didn't have any reason for leaving,' Eleanor went on. 'I mean your relationship was good, wasn't it? You hadn't argued or anything, had you?'

'No, Mum,' Polly said. 'We hadn't argued.' Not on the day of his disappearance at least. But she wasn't going to tell her mother that arguments with her husband were far from rare.

'I wonder what he'll have to say for himself,' Eleanor said.

But Polly knew that she wouldn't get any sort of explanation out of Sean. He'd left because he'd wanted to. It had suited him at the time. Now, it seemed, he wanted to come back. He was nothing more than a selfish, thoughtless, heartless individual, and Polly had no intention of sharing that with her mother.

There was a car waiting outside their house when they got back and Polly instinctively knew it was Sean before she even saw him. It was time. There was no hiding behind a children's party today. She was going to have to talk to him and she was going to have to let him talk to Archie.

'I'll come in with you if you want,' Jago said.

'Best not,' Polly said.

'You sure?'

'No, I'm not sure!' she said with a tight laugh as she parked the Land Rover opposite Sean's car. 'I've got to do this on my own.'

'Have you thought about what you'll do next Sunday?' Jago asked.

'What do you mean?'

'I mean, which one of us will you take to Sunday lunch at your parents?'

'Oh, Jago! Don't tease me.'

'I'm not teasing you,' he said.

'I can't even think about what the next hour's going to bring let alone next Sunday.'

'I'm sorry,' he said, quickly taking her hand. 'I just had a horrible image of us all arriving together.'

'That will never happen,' she said. 'I'm going to let him see Archie and let him say whatever he's got to say.'

'What if he wants to move back in?'

She shook her head. 'The house is mine. Well, as much as a rented house can be. He lost his rights to it being his home when he walked out.' Polly looked closely at Jago. 'You do believe me, don't you?'

'Yes, I believe you.'

'You think I'm going back to him, don't you?' she said in a low voice, aware that Archie was sitting just behind them. He may have looked absorbed with his tablet, but it was possible he was listening to everything they were saying.

'Well, I can't say I'm happy about this situation,' Jago told her.

'Neither can I,' she said. 'But it's happening and we've got to get through it.'

Jago squeezed her hand. 'Call me if you need me.'

'I will.'

'Bye, Archie.'

'Bye, Jago.'

She watched as he got out of the car. Sean was watching too, she noted. 'Ready, Arch?' She turned to the back seat.

'Is that Dad?' he asked.

'It is.' She waited for his response but he said nothing. 'He'll want to see you, sweetheart. Is that all right? Will you talk to him?'

'Will you stay with me?'

'Of course I'll stay with you!' she said. She was definitely *not* planning on leaving Sean alone with their son lest he attempted to leave with him for another three and a half years. She certainly wouldn't put that idea past Sean.

They got out of the car together. Polly took a tight hold of Dickens's lead which was just as well as he started to pull and bark as soon as he saw Sean getting out of his car.

Sean glowered at the dog. 'You should get that thing under control.'

'He *is* under control,' Polly told him, 'and his name's Dickens.' She stared at her husband for a moment, taking in the brilliant blue eyes and the short sandy hair. He was still the handsome man she'd fallen in love with, but she felt absolutely no love for him now. The only feelings she felt were curiosity, hurt and fear.

'Are you going to invite me in or are we going to stand out here on the cold pavement all evening?' Sean asked.

'You'd better come in,' Polly said.

'Got a hello for your father?' Sean asked once they were all in the living room.

Archie looked up at him. 'Hello,' he said in a small, barely-there voice.

'I got you something,' Sean said, reaching into his jacket pocket and bringing out a small package and handing it to Archie. 'I tried to give it to you yesterday, but you took off.'

Archie slowly unwrapped the gift and looked up at his mum as he saw what it was. 'It's a model boat.'

Polly looked at it. It was similar to the one Archie had been given in the playground.

'You got my other one?' Sean asked.

'A man gave my friend a boat to give to me,' Archie said.

'That man was me,' Sean said. 'I couldn't see you in the playground so I asked a boy to give it to you.'

Polly was so tempted to accuse Sean right then and there of not being able to recognise his own son, but she bit her tongue.

'Mum's got it now,' Archie said and Sean glanced at Polly.

'Why did you take it?' he asked her.

'We had no proof it was from you,' she said.

'Well, of course it was from me,' he said. 'Who else would it have been from? You did recognise it, didn't you?'

Polly nodded. So much inside of her wanted to scream at him, but she wasn't going to do that in front of Archie.

'Yes, I recognised it.'

'The other was just a model,' he told Archie now, 'but you can put this one in water.'

'Thank you,' Archie said.

'Have you ever been sailing, Archie?'

Archie shook his head.

Sean turned to Polly. 'You've never taken him sailing?' His tone was accusatory.

'No,' she told him. 'We've been kind of busy for the last three and a half years. What with it only being the two of us to do everything.' She sighed. She hadn't meant to say that, but it was pretty hard to keep all the years of pent up emotions from blurting out. 'Archie, I think it's time you went up to your room so I can talk to your father, okay?'

He looked up at her and nodded and left the room.

'He's a great lad,' Sean said.

'Yes, he is,' Polly said. 'He's the sort who deserves to be loved every single day of his life.'

'I've never stopped loving him, Polly,' Sean said, his voice low.

'Oh, really? You don't even know him!' Polly said, closing the living room door. 'I don't understand, Sean. Why didn't you just call me? Why wait like this, spying on me, breaking into the house?'

He stared at her, dumbstruck. 'How did you know–'

'Do you think I'm stupid?' she said. 'Did you think I wouldn't notice that you'd shifted things around?'

'Well, I didn't break in. This is still my home and I've still got my key,' he said.

'This is not your home,' Polly said. 'You gave up the right to call it that when you walked out and stopped paying the rent.'

'Polly–'

'It was cruel of you,' she went on. 'To let me know that you were around, but that you weren't getting in touch.'

'I had things to do,' he said. 'Things to sort out.'

'Things like Sophie, you mean?'

'How do you know about her?' Sean all but screamed.

'I know about her because she visited me,' Polly said, watching the look of shock that passed over his face.

'Typical of her to poke her nose in where it isn't wanted,' he said in a vicious whisper.

'Where it isn't wanted?' Polly asked incredulously. '*I* wanted to hear what she had to say.'

'How the hell did she get this address anyway?'

'She found an old business card of yours.'

'She snooped through my things?'

'Sean – you were hiding the fact that you had a wife and son from her and you're worried about her snooping through your things?'

'She means nothing to me anyway,' he said.

'You were just living with her, were you? Using her like you used me.'

His mouth dropped open. 'I never used you, Polly!'

'No? Are you sure? Sure you didn't just get a bit bored of playing husband and father one day and decide to go off on another adventure?'

He looked uneasy at her words and she felt like she might have hit a nerve.

'She wanted to see your parents, you know,' Polly confessed, wondering whether she was wise to do such a thing.

'Sophie?'

'Yes, Sophie.'

'Why the hell would she want to see them?'

'Hmmm, let me hazard a guess here. Because she was in love with you?'

'What's that got to do with anything?'

Polly couldn't quite believe what she was hearing. 'She wanted them to know that you were alive, Sean.'

Sean shook his head and left the room, stalking through to the kitchen where Dickens immediately began to growl at him.

'Can't you put this dog out in the garden?' he said.

'No I can't. This is his home.'

'Oh, so this is the dog's home but not mine?'

'That's right,' Polly said. 'Dickens has been loyal and faithful ever since we got him.'

She watched as Sean opened one of the cupboards to fetch a glass. So he remembered which one, Polly couldn't help thinking as he poured himself a glass of water.

'Be nice if you offered me a cup of tea,' he said.

'Oh, would it?'

'Polly – for God's sake – how long are you going to keep this up for?'

'I don't know,' she said. 'Maybe three and a half years!'

'Jesus!'

He shook his head and walked across the room, stopping at the dresser.

'What's this?' he asked, picking something up. It was Polly's folder for the book club. She watched as he flicked through the papers. 'Castle Clare Book Club,' he read. 'Are you in charge of this?'

'I help,' she said, wishing he'd put her things back down.

'You always were one for making lists and rules about everything, weren't you?' He shook his head. 'You and your books. I never did get that.'

'No, you didn't.'

Suddenly, the tension seemed to have calmed between them as quickly as it had flared, but Polly felt as if she was still on tenterhooks, waiting for it all to kick off again.

'I've got to get something,' Sean said at last, leaving the room.

As she heard him open the front door, a part of her was desperate to close it and lock it behind him and call the police, but what could they do? Arrest him for shouting? Maybe they could arrest him for wasting police time for having so convincingly staged his own disappearance. Polly didn't rightly know.

But she was too slow and, before she could do anything, Sean was back in the house again and Polly had to control every fibre of her being not to react at what he was holding in his right hand.

It was a suitcase.

CHAPTER 25

It was driving Jago crazy not knowing what was going on at Polly's house. He wasn't happy with the situation at all. From the little Polly had told Jago about Sean, he didn't like the idea of her and Archie being alone with him. But what could he do? This was something that she had to sort out herself, he knew that. Still, he couldn't help wanting to go over there to make sure everything was all right.

He picked up his phone, thinking that maybe he could get away with a quick phone call instead, just to make sure all was well, but he changed his mind. Just as he was about to put his phone down, he thought about somebody else he could ring and found the number.

'Hello?' he said a moment later. 'Bryony?'

'Jago?' she said, sounding surprised. 'Is everything okay?'

'Yes,' he said. 'Well, I don't know. Sean's here.'

'Here *where*?'

'At Polly's.'

'Oh, God!'

'He was waiting for her when we got home.'

'Should I come over?' Bryony asked.

'Probably best not. Polly said she needed to do this on her own.'

'Blimey, Jago, I don't know what to say,' she said. 'Are you all right?'

'I don't think I'm the one you should be worrying about,' he said.

'She really loves you, you know,' Bryony told him, 'and I don't know what Sean's story is going to be, but whatever he tells Polly isn't going to change her feelings for you. I'm sure of that.'

'Are you?' Jago said.

'I really am. I've never seen her so happy as when she's with you. I know we've been teasing you both mercilessly, but you're like one of the family, Jago. You really are. And I hope you don't feel threatened by Sean coming back like this.'

Jago took a deep breath. 'It's pretty hard not to.' There was a moment's pause before Bryony began again.

'You know, there was always something a bit ... *off*. With Sean, I mean. I could never quite put my finger on it,' she said. 'Oh, he was

charming and handsome and he genuinely seemed to adore Polly, but
– I don't know – there was something about him I never felt a
hundred percent easy about. Does that make sense?'

Jago sighed. 'Listen, I'd better go.'

'Keep an eye on things, won't you?' Bryony asked.

'Of course,' he told her.

Hanging up, Jago stared out of the window across Church Green.
It was dark now, but he could see the lights on at Polly's and he
couldn't help wondering what was going on over there.

Polly watched as Sean casually walked upstairs with his suitcase and
started to unpack in her bedroom. *Her* bedroom!

'Sean,' she began, 'I really don't think this is–'

'We'll talk later, Polly,' he said sharply. 'Just give me some space,
okay?' He turned to face her for a brief moment and she saw the
iciness in his blue eyes and she simply nodded. The old Polly, the
compliant Polly, taking over once again.

'I'll be downstairs,' she told him.

As she walked out onto the landing, Archie came out of his
bedroom.

'Is he staying?' he whispered as she approached him.

'I think so,' she said, stroking his hair.

'Did you ask him to stay?'

'He wants to stay with us,' she said, evading the question. 'That's
nice, isn't it?'

Archie gave a little shrug and went back inside his room.

'Archie,' Polly said, following him and pushing his door behind
her, 'your father and I need to talk. We might spend a lot of time
talking tonight. Is that okay?'

'What shall I do?'

'You don't need to do anything,' she said, 'but it might be a good
idea if you stay in your room. Adults sometimes need a – a little bit of
privacy.' She swallowed hard.

'Okay,' he said.

'Good boy,' she said, bending to kiss him.

She went downstairs. Dickens was pacing around the kitchen
looking unsettled, fully aware that there was a stranger in the house
and liking it about as much as Polly did. But what could she do? Sean
had flashed her one of those looks that she remembered so well and

she'd completely backed down. It was a survival tactic that she had learned.

When he came downstairs, he stood in the doorway of the kitchen glaring at Dickens who glared right back at him.

'I'm probably allergic to dogs,' he said.

'You'd be sneezing by now if you were,' Polly told him.

'I don't want him in this house.'

'Dickens is part of the family.'

'Not part of *my* family,' he said.

'You walked out on your family,' she said. She couldn't help it. The last thing she wanted to do was to rile him, and yet there was this fundamental need to get back at him for the upset he'd caused her and her family, and the fact that Archie had been growing up without a father.

'How many times do I have to say sorry?' Sean asked.

'Once would be nice,' she said, 'because you haven't apologised yet.'

He frowned. 'Yes, I did.'

'You didn't, Sean. You just turned up and barged your way in here. That wasn't apologising.'

'Yeah, well, I'm sorry.'

She stared at him as he pulled a chair out and sat at the kitchen table. 'You are?'

He put his head in his hands and, for a moment, looked so much like Archie whenever he sat doing some impossible piece of homework that it quite took her breath away and she found herself reaching out to him, gently placing a hand on his shoulder. And that's when the crying began. Not hers; his. Big, body-shaking sobs that made Dickens start to whine.

'Hey! It's okay. It's okay,' Polly said, her arms completely around him now.

'I'm sorry. I'm sorry. I'm sorry,' he said over and over again.

'It's all right. You're here now.'

Later that night, after they'd all had tea together and talked for hours, and after Polly had tucked Archie up in bed and taken Dickens out, they went upstairs together. When Sean asked her for a towel, she went to the airing cupboard and handed one to him. When he came out of the shower, he walked around the bedroom as if he'd never left. She noted that he was still in good shape. He obviously still worked out. He'd always taken a pride in his body, Polly remembered, and she'd felt the result of all that strength on several occasions and had worn the bruises to prove it.

As she was thinking these thoughts, standing still in the middle of the room, he beckoned to her with a movement of his finger.

'Come to bed, Polly,' he said, and there was something of both ice and fire in his voice which filled Polly with fear and made her nod and slip into bed beside him.

'So,' he said, his voice seeming loud in the quiet darkness as his fingers pressed sharply into her flesh, 'this Jago—'

'Is just a friend,' Polly said, closing her eyes as Sean began to kiss her.

Jago cancelled his Monday morning appointment with a pupil. He couldn't concentrate. Simply put, he couldn't think of anything other than Polly. He hadn't wanted to appear stalkerish but he couldn't help watching as Polly left to take Archie to school that morning. Was it his imagination or did she seem subdued? He really couldn't tell from all the way across the green and he didn't think she'd want him approaching her to find out as Sean's car was still parked outside.

So, he'd stayed the night, Jago thought. But had Sean spent the night on the sofa? It was driving Jago mad not knowing.

His mum had left for work earlier that morning and, as soon as Polly drove off with Archie, he started pacing. He'd give her ten minutes to drive into town and drop Archie off and then he'd ring her. He couldn't wait a single minute more than that.

Exactly nine minutes and fifty-three seconds later, Jago rang Polly's mobile.

'Hey!' he said.

'Jago? I can't talk now.'

'Why not?' he said. 'Sean's not with you, is he?'

'No,' she said, 'but I'm coming to see you later.'

'You okay?'

'I'm fine.'

'You don't sound fine,' Jago said.

'I'll talk to you later, okay?' She hung up.

He raked a hand through his hair and sighed and managed to get absolutely nothing done as he waited for Polly to call round to his house.

She arrived half an hour later and he answered the door on her first knock.

'Hello,' she said, her voice barely above a whisper. 'I need us to – to ...' she didn't finish.

'Come inside, Polly.'

'No, I can't,' she said.

'What do you mean?'

'He's watching.' She turned to look back across the green at her home. Jago looked too, but didn't see any sign of Sean.

'He spent the night, didn't he?' he said. 'Didn't he?'

'Yes,' she said, almost as if ashamed to admit the fact. 'I couldn't say no.'

'No?' Jago said, frowning. 'Why not? Why couldn't you say no to the husband who walked out on you and your son?'

'Because we needed to talk.'

'And what did he have to say? How did he explain his absence for the last three and a half years?'

'He – erm – he's sorry.'

'Oh, really? Is that all he had to say?'

'He was confused and–'

'Confused? What, like he woke up one morning and thought, "What on earth was I doing getting married and having a kid? I'd better get out of this fast!"'

'Jago, please!'

'No, Polly, I really want to know what's going on with this guy you've let back into your life.'

'He's Archie's father.'

'Biological father, maybe, but Archie certainly doesn't seem to know him.'

'They talked last night,' Polly said.

'That's nice. A father who talks to his son every few years.'

'And we talked as well.'

'Give the guy a medal!' Jago said, unable to hide the anger from his voice.

'Why are you being like this?' Polly asked.

'Like what?'

'You're all sharp and defensive.'

'I'm being like this because *you're* not!'

'I've got to give him a chance, Jago.'

'You're kidding, right?'

'I'm not kidding. He's Archie's father.'

'You keep saying that as though it gives him a right to mess your lives up.'

'He knows what he did is wrong and he's sorry for it. And he's my husband and I loved him once. I've got to give him a chance, Jago. Can't you understand that?'

Jago stared hard at her. It was as if the Polly he'd known and fallen in love with had somehow vanished in the night because he hardly recognised the woman standing before him now.

'He's brainwashed you, Polly. He knows exactly how to reel you back in. He's a nasty manipulative-'

'Stop it!'

Jago sighed in frustration because he just wasn't getting through to her.

'Is this what you really want,' he asked. 'What you really truly want?'

'It's the right thing to do.'

'Has he hurt you? Because, if he has, I'll be over there so fast-'

'Please don't,' she said quickly. 'This isn't your battle. And – no – he hasn't hurt me.'

There was a pause.

'What about Archie's guitar lessons?' Jago asked. 'I can still come over for those, can't I?'

'I don't think that's a good idea.'

'I see,' Jago said. 'And what about us? Is that it?' He saw her eyes fill with tears.

'I'm sorry,' she said.

He shook his head. 'Don't do this, Polly. Please don't do this.'

'I have to give Sean a chance,' she said and, before he could say anything else, she turned and ran across the green back towards her house.

Jago was a nervous wreck by the time his mum came home from work.

'I told you not to get involved with her,' she said once Jago had blurted out what was going on. 'I had a bad feeling about this from the start.'

'Mum, saying "I told you so" isn't going to solve anything.'

'Well, at least it's over now. Better sooner than later, that's what I say.'

Jago sighed in exasperation. 'This is far from over.'

'What you mean? You're not going to involve yourself in this, Jago. I think it's time you backed away.'

'I can't do that.'

'You *will* do that,' she told him.

He shook his head. 'I only met this Sean once, but you know who he reminded me of? Dad.'

Maureen paled at the mention of her estranged husband. 'You're being fanciful and overdramatic,' she said, walking through to the kitchen and busying herself with putting the shopping away.

'I can see exactly what he's like,' he said, following her. 'He's not to be trusted, Mum.' He stared hard at her and she seemed to understand him.

'You think he'll hurt her?' she asked, her voice low and fearful.

'I don't know what he's capable of,' Jago said, 'but I love her and I love that son of hers and I'm going to be there for them whether they want me or not.'

CHAPTER 26

As soon as Polly had returned from the school run, Sean asked her to sit down.

'What is it?' she asked anxiously.

'I called my parents.'

'Oh,' Polly said, surprised by this news. 'Are they okay?'

Sean shrugged. 'Mum was crying,' he said as if this was very odd behaviour indeed.

'I'm not surprised,' Polly said seriously. 'Sean, you put her through hell—'

'Don't start!'

'I'm not starting,' she said. 'It's just you seem surprised that she would cry.'

'Women are weak.'

'Sean!'

He started pacing the room. 'I'm back, okay? I don't see what all the fuss is about.'

Polly gave him a moment to calm down. 'Are you going to see them?' she asked.

'*We're* going to see them. Right now.'

'Now?'

'No point in prolonging the agony,' he said, and she felt quite sure that he was referring to his own agony rather than that of his parents. 'Come on.'

They went in Sean's car and drove the country lanes in silence. Polly still couldn't believe that he was really back, that he was really *alive!* The evening they'd spent together had been tense and bizarre, but she had also seen little glimpses of the Sean she'd fallen in love with. The Sean who had been so charming, so loving.

But, try as she might to overcome her feelings, she knew in her heart that the situation she now found herself in wasn't normal. *He* wasn't normal. To be able to do what he'd done to his family, to simply walk away without explanation or apology, to cruelly have them wonder if he was even alive. What kind of a person did that? Yet here he was, seemingly trying to make a go of things, and did she really have the right to deny him that and to deny her son his father?

Maybe Sean had changed too. When he'd broken down and

apologised to her, it seemed as if he truly saw the agony he'd caused her and Archie and was genuinely remorseful. Maybe they could forge some sort of future together. Was that possible? Polly wasn't sure. She felt so confused and conflicted by what was happening.

She looked out of the window as they raced past high hedges and she thought about Jago, his kind face filling her mind. Only it hadn't been so kind when she told him she was leaving him. She didn't think she would forget the hollowness she'd seen there and the hurt which had filled his eyes, those beautiful slate-grey eyes which had never been filled with anything other than love and kindness.

She clutched her hands together in her lap to stop them from shaking and blinked away the tears that threatened to spill. She had to pull herself together if she was going to face her parents-in-law.

Anthony and Alison Prior were both standing at the front door when they pulled into Constable View and Polly watched as Sean got out of the car and his mother ran into his arms, tears streaming down her face.

Polly gave them a moment before joining them.

'Come inside,' Anthony said, 'come inside.' He seemed aware that his wife was making a spectacle of herself and that sort of thing just didn't happen in a nice little cul-de-sac like Constable View.

There were more tears inside and Sean did his best to calm his mother down.

'We didn't know where you were...'

'I know.'

'We thought you were dead!'

'I'm sorry.'

'Why didn't you call, Sean? Why did you let us go on thinking—'

'I'm here now, Mum. I'm here,' he said, just as he'd said to Polly. It was all the explanation he was going to give and it was no explanation at all. He hugged his mother close to him so that she was unable to say anything else.

It was a good half an hour before things calmed to something approaching normality. Alison Prior had actually had to leave the room at one stage and Polly guessed that she was washing her face and composing herself in the bathroom. When she came back into the room, she looked at Sean with tear-bright eyes and then she shook her head.

'This woman turned up, Sean. Sophie something or other.'

'Randall,' Anthony said.

'That's right,' his mother said. 'Young, pretty. She said she knew you, darling.'

Sean shifted uneasily on the sofa next to Polly and he shook his head. 'Not really,' he said. 'We worked together.'

'She seemed worried about you,' Alison continued.

'Yep. Always was a worrier, Sophie,' he said with some levity. 'I'm sorry she bothered you. I'll have a word with her.'

Polly sat watching her husband's face. He was completely unmoved by the plight of this young woman, wasn't he? He had met her, made her love him, and left her. She didn't matter to him. The fact that she'd followed him from the south coast to the east, desperately trying to find out what had happened to him, meant absolutely nothing to him.

Alison glanced at her husband and they exchanged a look which seemed to say that this was a subject best left alone. Polly knew that Sean's mother felt that something wasn't quite right about it all and oh, how Polly wished she had the courage there and then to stand up and shout, "Your son isn't normal." She wanted to scream and throw things around the room. She felt so angry that this man, her husband, thought he had the right to turn everybody's lives upside down and then to just come waltzing back and expect everything to slot into place without so much as a few tears. And, more than anything, she wanted him to pay for what he'd done. It wasn't fair that his parents should accept what he told them, but hadn't she done exactly the same thing? She wondered if he managed to manipulate his parents just as easily as he'd manipulated her.

So Polly didn't shout or scream. She remained sat on the pristine white sofa, her hands clasped in her lap as though this was the most normal situation in the world.

When Alison went through to the kitchen to make tea, Polly went to help her, keen to leave her husband's presence if only for a few moments.

'Did you know he was back?' Alison whispered as she pushed the kitchen door behind them for some privacy.

'I wasn't sure,' she said. 'I had some suspicions.'

'You should have told us.'

'I didn't want to build your hopes up.'

'And this Sophie business. What do you make of that?'

Polly swallowed hard, not knowing what to say. 'I'm not sure what to make of it, but I think she's gone now, hasn't she?'

Alison nodded. 'She looked in a terrible state, poor girl. We didn't know what to do with her.'

The two women stared at each other and Polly could see that Alison was shaking.

'Let me do that,' Polly said, taking over the tea things. If there was one thing Polly was good at in any situation, it was getting the tea made.

'I can't believe he's really here,' Alison said, leaning on the sink for support. 'My son.'

Polly saw the elation in Alison's eyes, but she could see the fear and anxiety too.

'Archie must be thrilled,' Alison said, and Polly thought of the way her son had sat on the floor of the living room, listening to his estranged father without really looking at him, gently accepting the words which were being spoken. Polly wondered what on earth had been going through his mind.

They took the tea things through to the living room and a strange half an hour past during which questions were asked but not always answered. Sean was the master of deflection, turning the conversation in any direction he wanted. Was Polly the only one who could see that? His mother and father seemed to be completely under Sean's spell and Polly really wasn't surprised when he had them both laughing at some joke which she didn't find very funny at all.

Finally, he got up to go.

'Can't you stay a little longer?' His mother begged, as if terrified that he was going to vanish again.

'Things to do,' he said enigmatically and Alison nodded, accepting this.

'Of course, darling.' She leaned in and kissed him and Sean shook his father's hand, accepting the awkward back slap that followed.

'I hope you'll be staying now, son,' Anthony said and Polly noticed the stern tone of voice and the serious look on his face. 'You gave us quite a turn just disappearing like that.'

Sean did a funny kind of shuffle and made his way towards the door without saying anything.

'Do you think we should go to my parents now?' Polly asked once they were back in the car and had waved their goodbyes. She didn't really savour the idea of a visit to Campion House, but it seemed only fair having visited Sean's parents.

'We're not going to visit your parents, Polly,' he told her as they drove out of the village and into the country lanes.

She frowned. 'Why not?'

Sean slowed the car down, pulling over in a passing place.

'What is it?' Polly asked, suddenly anxious.

He switched the engine off and unclipped his seatbelt and then he turned to face her, grabbing her right wrist in his hand.

'I can't believe you gave Sophie my parents' address?'

'Sean—'

His grip was vice-like and his eyes had that steely quality again. 'Sean, *please*, you're hurting me.'

'And you think you haven't hurt *me* by giving my parents' details to *that woman*?'

'She was worried about you. I texted her the address. I'm sorry, okay?'

'It's not okay, Polly. It was none of your damned business to interfere.'

'None of my damned business? I'm your *wife*, Sean! Another woman who you'd been living with came to our home wondering where the hell you were, and you say it's none of my damned business?'

Keeping hold of her wrist, he pulled her closer towards him and then flung her back so that she cracked her head on the window of the passenger door.

'Your loyalty's to me, Polly. To *me*! Not to Sophie Randall!'

He fastened up his seatbelt and started the car again and Polly stared at him, Her hand inched back towards the passenger door. If she was quick enough, she could get out and run, just run. Across the fields, through the woods, leaping wintry ditches, she didn't care. As long as she got away from Sean.

But she wasn't quick enough. With a skid of tyres, Sean pulled out into the lane and drove them both back home.

A tense week went by with Polly spending as much time in Sam, Bryony and Josh's shops as possible and taking on an extra class at her school, explaining to Sean that that was her normal timetable.

Her siblings had all been questioning her, of course, and her parents had been in to the bookshop to see her whilst she was working, asking when Sean was going to pay them a visit. Polly had managed to deflect their questions with vague answers, and her father had told her mother that Polly and Sean obviously needed time to get to know each other again before they all descended on him. Polly had smiled and nodded her assent, but her mother had probed her with those questioning eyes of hers and her father had looked anything but happy about the situation and she couldn't blame him for that. They were all obviously anxious about Sean's reappearance.

Sean had been working on his boat, fixing it up now that the weather was improving, and he'd been getting home some time after six in the evenings which at least meant that Polly had a couple of hours to spend alone with Archie. He'd been uncharacteristically quiet since Sean's arrival. But, then again, hadn't she too? Both of them seemed to have slunk away deep into themselves as if trying to ride out a storm and, all the time, Polly was cursing herself for getting her and her son into this situation.

It was Friday night when Sean finally snapped. Archie was sitting at the table eating his tea. Well, he wasn't really eating it, Polly observed; he was just kind of rearranging it on his plate. Sean was sitting opposite him watching and Polly saw the precise moment that the indulgent smile left his face to be replaced with a dangerous frown.

'Archie – go to your room,' she told him.

'Let him finish his tea,' Sean said. 'The boy needs to eat.'

'He's not hungry.'

'Eat your tea, Archie,' Sean said, his voice raising. Dickens gave a low growl from his basket. He hadn't stopped growling at Sean all week and Sean hadn't stopped glaring at Dickens.

'Quiet, boy,' Polly said, giving the dog a warning look.

'Shut up!' Sean snapped at Dickens. 'Or I'll kick you out right now.'

Archie glared at his father and then got up from his chair.

'Go and do your homework, darling,' Polly said. 'I'll be up in a moment.'

When Polly heard Archie's bedroom door close, she got up to clear his things away from the table.

'Leave it,' Sean said.

'I just want to–'

'I said, leave it.' He was on his feet in an instant, his hand gripping Polly's wrist once more in that vice-like way of his.

'Let go of me!' Polly cried.

'Why do you defy me?'

'What?'

'I tell you to do something and you blatantly ignore me.'

'I was just clearing the table,' she told him.

'It doesn't matter what you were doing. I told you *not* to do it.'

'You're not my boss, Sean,' she said. 'I'm not yours to command.' Her heart was racing now and she knew that the words she was speaking had the power to rile him, but she simply couldn't stop herself. Seeing Archie's pale face at the dining table had been more than she could bear. This simply couldn't go on. Sean had to leave.

'You're my wife, Polly,' he told. 'You took a vow.'

'I took a vow to love you, not to obey you. No modern woman with any sense says those words anymore. In fact, I've had enough. There was a time when I thought I wanted you back. I wanted Archie to have his father and I wanted the Sean I'd fallen in love with. But he never really existed, did he? There were glimpses of him now and then but he was lost inside this other cruel man, and I won't have him back. Not in my house. *Not* with my son.'

'What?' he snapped, his hand still tight around her wrist. 'What are you saying?'

She stared him straight in the eyes as she spoke. Her words calm and clear. 'I want you to leave,' she said. 'I want you to go upstairs and pack your things and I want you out of this house – right now.' Even as she said the words, she knew what was coming. It was fully expected.

But it would be worth it.

Maureen Solomon had just drawn the living room curtains at 7 Church Green when there was a knock on the door

'You expecting someone?' she asked Jago.

'No,' he said, going to the door as a second round of knocks sounded. 'Archie?' he said a moment later.

The young boy looked up at him, his eyes large and full of fear. 'It's Mummy,' he said. 'She needs your help.'

Jago took Archie's hand and the two of them ran across the green together just as they saw Sean pulling away in his car.

240

'Where's your mum?'

'In the kitchen!' Archie cried as he opened the front door before running down the hallway.

When Jago entered the kitchen, Polly was on the floor near the dresser amongst broken glass and crockery, her knees drawn up into her chest and her arms over her head, Dickens by her side looking distressed.

'Polly!' Jago gasped, instantly on his knees beside her. 'Look at me.'

Polly lifted her head. Her beautiful dark eyes were full of tears but there was something of triumph in her expression and she began to laugh.

'What is it?' Jago asked. 'Are you okay? Did he hurt you?'

Tears spilt down her reddened cheeks. 'Dickens went for him!' she said.

'What?' Jago said as Polly held her arms open to Archie and he fell into them.

'Dickens defended me. My hero,' she said, stroking the dog's long silky ears. 'And you, darling Archie!'

'I heard him shouting,' Archie said. 'So I came downstairs.'

'It's okay. He's gone now.'

'And you two are not staying here a minute longer.' Jago told them.

'But this is our home. He's not scaring us away from our home.'

'I'm not leaving you here. You're coming back with me right now. Pack a few things together and we'll get you out of here.'

'He won't come back. Not after what Dickens did,' Polly said.

Jago shook his head. 'We're not going to take that chance. Pack your things,' he told her again.

Maureen was waiting by her front door when they crossed the green together.

'I can't put on your mother,' Polly said.

'Yes you can,' Jago told her, his arm around her shoulder. 'She'll want to help, trust me.'

'Oh, my dear!' Maureen said as Polly entered the house followed by Archie, Jago and Dickens. The bruise on her cheek was beginning to deepen and her ribs felt sore too. 'Let me get you fixed up.'

Polly nodded. She felt numb now and she allowed herself to be taken care of.

'I'm ringing the police,' Jago said.

'Not yet, Jago,' Maureen said.

'But we need to-'

'We need to take care of Polly. We'll sort things out with the police later.'

Polly didn't protest. She just wanted it all to go away.

'Archie – why don't you and Dickens sit by the fire? Have a strum on my guitar there,' Jago said.

'Really?' Archie's face instantly lit up and Polly smiled as she watched her son pick up the full-size guitar.

'Come on,' Maureen said, 'you're coming with me.' She guided Polly up the stairs to her bedroom and Polly sat on the edge of the bed. There then followed a quiet few moments during which Maureen bathed Polly's face.

'You've got broken glass in your hair,' Maureen told her, taking care to pick it all out.

'He's not a very good shot,' Polly said with a grim laugh. 'It could have been a lot worse.'

Maureen shook her head as she continued to work in silence.

'Thank you,' Polly said to her after a moment.

'You don't need to thank me.'

'Yes I do,' Polly said. 'I need to thank you for Jago.'

Maureen gave a tiny smile. 'I told him not to get involved with you.'

'I don't blame you.'

The two women looked at each other.

'I shouldn't have told him that,' Maureen said.

'You were protecting your son. I would have done the same thing'

Maureen pursed her lips before speaking again. 'You see, I've seen this before. With Jago's father,' she told Polly. 'My Murray used to hit me. Got clever about it too. Only striking in places which wouldn't be visible.'

Polly felt tears pricking her eyes. 'The first time Sean hit me was on the cheek, but he got wise to that too. There must be a guidebook somewhere for men like them. *How to hit your wife without being found out.*'

'Yes,' Maureen said. 'But they can't make you hide that look in your eyes. That haunted look that women like us have.'

Polly looked at her questioningly.

'Oh, yes,' Maureen said. 'You have it too. I recognised it as soon as I met you.'

'But nobody's ever guessed.'

'Are you sure about that?'

'Well, nobody's ever said anything.'

'That's not the same thing though, is it?' Maureen said. 'I bet your mother knows or at least suspects something.'

Polly thought about it. All those times her mother had asked her if everything was all right. Had she suspected something? Had she only kept her distance out of respect for her daughter's privacy?

'Sean's worse than I remembered,' Polly confessed now. 'I'm not sure what I was expecting. But I really thought he might have changed. Isn't that stupid of me?'

'They don't change,' Maureen said. 'It's something deep down inside them and you'll never root it out.'

A wave of emotion hit Polly and she began to cry again.

'It's okay, my love,' Maureen said, holding her gently. 'He's gone now and we'll make sure you only ever see him again in court.'

CHAPTER 27

'I'm taking you straight to the hospital,' Maureen told Polly after she'd winced for the third time at the breakfast table the next morning.

'I'm just sore,' Polly insisted.

'Better to know for sure,' Maureen said, 'and we'll go straight to the police station after that. You need to report this, Polly.'

The Priors and the Solomons had been unofficially watching 3 Church Green throughout the preceding evening and all of that Saturday morning, but there was no sign of Sean for which everybody was grateful.

Jago stayed at home with Archie and Dickens whilst Maureen took Polly out and, once everyone was safely back in the afternoon and had had a light lunch, Jago and Polly went for a walk with Dickens.

'How are you feeling?' Jago asked as they walked down the lane behind the church.

'Nothing's broken,' she said.

'I'm glad to hear it,' he said, 'but that's not what I meant.'

Polly climbed a stile after Dickens had shot over it, pulling a face as she did so. There were no bones broken, she thought, but there were bruises galore. Deep, painful bruises.

'I'm okay,' she assured him.

'He'll pay for what he did to you,' Jago said.

'He'll be long gone by now.'

'How can you be sure?'

'Because he's good at that. He's good at disappearing.'

'As long as he never shows his sorry face here again,' Jago said as he followed her over the stile. 'I won't let him get close to you again, Polly, you can be sure of that. I saw what my mum went through with my father. She told you about him, didn't she?'

Polly nodded.

'Well, I won't let that happen to you.'

The field opened out before them in shades of green that always astonished Polly each spring, and a cool wind caressed them. It felt good to be outdoors. After spending the entire morning in the hospital and then the police station, she was glad to be breathing in fresh air and glorying in simple sights like the sky-reflecting puddles that littered their path.

Jago took her hand and smiled at her and tears instantly rose in her eyes at his sweetness.

'Sorry,' she said.

'It's okay.'

'I feel a bit strange.' She wiped the tears as they fell.

'You don't need to apologise. You've been through hell.'

She took a deep breath. 'I thought I could make things work. I wanted it to work for Archie. I wanted Archie to have his father.'

'He doesn't need a father like Sean.'

Polly nodded. 'No, you're right. I saw that straightaway too. Archie was terrified of him. He wouldn't even look at him. And I don't think Sean was really interested in being a father anyway. I don't know why he came back.'

'Let's hope he's gone for good now,' Jago said, 'but we need to make that legal, right? You need to talk to people about this. You have to protect yourself and Archie.'

'I know.'

They walked on across the field, their boots now covered in shiny mud. The trees were still bare but the sun was shining and Dickens was finding plenty to enjoy with the animal scents he was following.

'It was my fault,' Polly suddenly said.

'What was?'

'The attack. It was my fault.'

'How can you say that?'

She shrugged. 'I don't like the person I become when he's around. He changes me. I feel anxious – as if I'm waiting for things to kick off and I'm trying to appease him all the time. Either that or I'm baiting him and I couldn't stop last night. I kept picking at him, goading him. I think I was trying to make him hit me so I could throw him out. I needed something final. Does that make sense?'

'Nothing that man did to you was your fault, Polly. You know that, don't you?'

They stood still for a moment beside a long hedgerow white with blackthorn blossom.

'I know,' Polly said at last.

Jago ran a hand through his hair. 'I want to be with you, Polly,' he said. 'I think I *should* be with you. How about I stay with you and

Archie at yours?'

'No.' She shook her head. 'I need to be with my son for a while. Just us.'

'I don't like the idea of you at that house. The thought of Sean turning up whenever he wants is freaking me out.'

'We're going to stay at my parents',' she announced.

'Won't that be the first place he looks for you if he comes back?'

'Probably. *If* he comes back, but I don't think he will and at least I'll feel safe there.'

'You know you're more than welcome to stay with us for as long as you want.'

'We can't do that. You'll begrudge us if you have to spend another night on the sofa.'

'No I won't. I like knowing you're nearby.'

'We'll only be at Campion House. It's not too far away.'

'It won't be the same,' he told her.

'I know.'

'Do you want me to come with you and help you pack some more things?'

'We'll be okay.'

'You sure?'

Polly nodded. As much as she dreaded going back into the house, she knew she had to face it and it would be better if she did it on her own.

They walked around the edge of the field, following the circuit back to the village and popping Dickens on his lead once they reached the church. They walked in silence and Archie ran to greet them as they entered the hallway.

'We've made cookies!' he shouted as Polly grabbed hold of Dickens to rub him down with a towel which Jago had ready by the door.

'Aren't you clever?' she said, luxuriating in the wonderful smell coming from the kitchen.

'He's a natural, you know,' Maureen said. 'Proper little cook.'

'You can help Grandma in the kitchen,' Polly told him. 'We're heading over there now.'

'You're going?' Maureen said.

'But we've just made cookies!' Archie cried.

'Yes, you can't go now,' Jago said.

'Have a cup of tea and a cookie first, okay?' Maureen said.

Polly was feeling tearful again and felt like she needed to get away. She thought of her bedroom at Campion House and how her mother had always kept it the same. It was always there for whenever she needed it like when she'd come back from university and after she'd been teaching abroad. She hadn't needed the room recently, but she wanted it more than ever now. She wanted to walk through that familiar door and close it behind her and sit on the bed and cry.

'Polly? A cup of tea and a cookie?' Maureen repeated and Polly nodded.

'Do we have to go, Mum?'

'Yes, darling.'

Archie gave a great sigh as he sat down in the living room. 'I want to stay with Jago.'

'Don't you want to see your grandparents and great-grandparents?'

'Yes, but not just yet. We'll see them tomorrow, won't we?'

'We're going to see them today, Archie,' Polly said, her voice firmer now.

'Here you are,' Maureen said as she handed out the cookies and went to make the tea.

Before Jago sat down, he looked out of the living room window. 'All quiet,' he said.

'I wish you'd stop doing that,' Polly said. 'It's making me nervous.'

'It makes me nervous *not* doing it,' he told her.

'I don't want him to come back,' Archie said.

'He won't,' Polly told him.

'He hurt you, Mummy.'

Without warning, Polly shot up off the sofa and left the room.

'Polly?' Jago called after her, following her as she ran upstairs. 'Hey!'

She ran into his room and then turned back, confused, her eyes filling with tears. 'I shouldn't be here. This is your room.'

'It's okay,' he told her.

She shook her head. 'I need to go.'

'Okay.' He reached a hand towards her.

'I need some space. *Please.*' Without looking at him, she returned downstairs. 'Archie, we're going.'

Maureen was by her side in a moment.

'I'm sorry,' Polly said.

'It's all right. Listen,' Maureen said, 'I know what you're going through. You've got to be with your boy. Put him and yourself first and don't worry about anybody else. We're here for you if you need us.' Maureen opened her arms and embraced Polly and it was all she could do to hold herself together.

'You've been so kind to us.'

'No need for any of that. It's what anybody would have done,' Maureen said.

'Tell Jago I'm sorry,' Polly said.

'He understands.'

Polly called Dickens to her and sent Archie upstairs to collect their things together. She heard him talking to Jago but he came downstairs on his own a moment later and for that she was grateful.

'Ready?' she said.

He nodded but he didn't look happy.

'Thank you,' Polly said to Maureen before leaving the house and crossing the green towards her own.

Her hands were shaking as she popped the key into the lock, but she was determined not to show her fear in front of Archie. She had to be strong.

'Pack as if you were going on holiday for a whole week,' she told him as soon as they were inside.

'When are we coming back?' he asked.

'I don't know,' she said honestly as she walked into the kitchen. Archie followed her and gasped as he saw the mess. There was broken crockery on the floor and paper everywhere. Archie bent down to pick one of the papers up.

'Careful!' Polly shouted. 'There's broken glass everywhere.' She got hold of Dickens's collar and sent him into the living room before he cut his paws.

'It's your book club papers,' Archie said when she came back, handing the piece of paper to her and she remembered the look of pure hatred on Sean's face as he'd taken her well-ordered notes and started ripping them up.

'Why did he do that?' Archie asked.

'He was mad.'

'At you?'

'At me. At life. At everything.'

They looked around at the devastation before them and, in that moment, Polly knew that leaving Church Green was the right thing to do. But where would she go? She'd lived there ever since she'd got married, but the thought of staying there now was quite unbearable. Every time she'd walk into the kitchen, she'd see Sean standing over her, ready to strike her, and she hated the idea of spending even a single night in the bedroom they'd shared.

Archie put the piece of paper on the table and gave his mum a hug which brought fresh tears to her eyes.

'Let's go, eh?' she whispered to him.

Polly had rung her mother before they arrived at Campion House and told her what had been going on, and Eleanor Nightingale was on the doorstep to greet them, wrapping them both up in a huge hug and showering them with kisses.

Archie took Dickens out into the garden together with Hardy and Brontë and then Eleanor led Polly into the living room.

'Why didn't you tell us?' Eleanor asked as soon as they sat down. Her face was pale and anxious and Polly could tell that her mother had been crying.

'I was trying to work things out,' Polly said.

'You shouldn't have struggled through this on your own,' Eleanor said.

'But it was my marriage, my problems.'

'Polly! We're a *family*. Families help each other through problems. You know that. That's my job as your mother – to help you.'

Polly looked down at her lap, suddenly feeling ashamed at having shut her family out.

'It had been going on for a while, hadn't it?' Eleanor asked. 'Was he violent from the very beginning?'

'Not before we were married,' Polly said. 'There were flashes of anger, but he seemed to be more in control of it then. But not this time. It was as if he had years of resentment built up inside him and it all unleashed at once.'

Her mother nodded and reached out a hand to gently stroke Polly's cheek. 'Look what he's done to you!'

'I'm okay.'

'You've seen a doctor?'

Polly nodded. 'I'm fine, Mum, really. I just need to be quiet for a while.'

'I've made your bed up. I've put Archie in Sam and Josh's old room.'

'Thank you.'

The door to the living room was pushed open as her father and Grandpa Joe came in. Polly got up to greet them.

'My own darling Polly!'

'Grandpa! Hey, Dad!'

They all embraced and Polly felt so incredibly lucky to have these wonderful men in her life with their safe arms to fall into whenever life got tough.

'I can't believe it. I simply can't believe it,' Grandpa Joe said as they all sat down together.

'If he ever dares show his face around these parts again—' Frank began.

'You will do nothing,' Eleanor interrupted. 'Nothing but call the police, that is.'

'Where's Grandma?' Polly asked.

'In the bedroom,' Grandpa said.

'Is she okay? I mean, does she know?'

'We told her,' Eleanor said, 'and she seemed to understand.'

'*Seemed* to?' Grandpa Joe said. 'She called Sean a nasty brute and said he should be horse-whipped!'

Polly smiled at that.

'You look exhausted, darling,' Eleanor said. 'How about taking your things up to your room and I'll make us a cup of tea?'

'That sounds perfect,' Polly said.

Her father helped her bring her things in from the car which included two suitcases, a dog basket and Archie's guitar.

'I'll leave you to settle in,' her father said as he gave her a gentle hug before leaving the room. Polly closed the door after him and walked across to the window, looking out at the view of the garden which she had grown up with and loved so much. The sweep of lawn led down towards the fruit trees at the foot of the garden under which a wonderful display of crocuses was blooming with yellow, purple and white blooms all jostling for attention.

Turning back into the room, Polly looked at her old bed, freshly made up with pink and white *toile de jouy* bedding and a heap of pretty white cushions. Her mother had picked a bunch of daffodils and had placed them on the bedside table. Polly sat down on the bed now and looked around her. As the eldest, she had had the luxury of her own room. Bryony had shared with Lara, and Sam and Josh had shared the one Archie would be staying in.

Beside the daffodils, Polly noticed that a copy of Rosamunde Pilcher's *The Shell Seekers* had been left out. It was one of Polly's favourite novels. Her mother's too. They used to talk for hours about it and it was sweet of her mother to leave it out for her now so that she could dip into that safe fictional world and escape the horrors of the real one. Polly might well be a mother in her thirties, but she would always be a daughter too, and her mother would always be there to look out for her.

A gentle tap on the door roused her from her thoughts.

'I've brought you a cup of tea,' her mother said as she walked into the room.

'Thanks,' Polly said as she took hold of the pretty china mug.

'You settling in okay? Got everything you need?'

'You mean like a good lawyer?'

'Oh, Polly!' Eleanor said, sitting down on the bed beside her. 'I guess it's something you'll have to think about. What's happening with the police?'

Polly sighed. She'd had a call just as she'd got in the car to drive to Campion House.

'They went down to the marina to look for Sean's boat, but it had gone,' she said. 'They found his car, though. It was only hired. So they've not really got much to go on.'

'We'll get some legal advice,' Eleanor told her. 'Don't you worry – we'll make sure this is all sorted.'

'You mean a divorce?'

'A divorce and legal custody of Archie.'

Polly nodded. It was the right thing to do, of course, but it was still a shock to think that she was getting divorced.

'How will it work if we can't find Sean?'

'Polly, I don't think there's a court in the land that wouldn't grant you a divorce after your husband walks out on you and your son and, when he comes back, he behaves like a beast.'

Polly closed her eyes. She was very near to crying again. Her mother seemed to sense this and placed an arm around her.

'You're going to get through this,' Eleanor told her.

'I know. I just feel as if I've made so many mistakes and I hate myself for them.'

'Don't hate yourself, darling. You've been so brave.'

Polly shook her head. 'No I haven't. I've been stupid. I should never have let Sean back into our lives. I should have turned him away the minute he knocked on our door, but I couldn't. I just couldn't!'

'You mustn't upset yourself, Polly,' Eleanor said, her voice calm and soothing.

'I should never have exposed Archie to him, but – but – there was a part of me that thought he might have changed – that his time away might have made him different.' She pulled a tissue out of her pocket and mopped her eyes. 'Stupid. *Stupid!*'

'Not stupid,' Eleanor said. 'You wanted to give him a chance which is more than I would have done. Nobody can accuse you of not giving him a chance to be a good husband and father.'

Polly nodded.

'Polly?'

'Yes?'

'Did Sean–' she paused.

'What, Mum?'

'Did he ever hurt Archie?'

She shook her head. 'No. Never. If he had, I'd never have let him near us again.'

Eleanor breathed a sigh of relief. 'I wish you'd told us what was going on all those years. But I should have known things weren't right between you. I mean, I got little glimpses every now and then, but I had no idea it was so bad.'

'That's because I was very good at hiding things from you.'

'*Too* good, Polly,' Eleanor said. 'You should have come to us right away. As soon as he first hit you. We could have helped you.'

They sat quietly for a moment.

'The worst thing about all this, though,' Polly began, 'is that I shut Jago out. I've been so cruel to him. I pushed him away when he was trying to help me. Why did I do that?'

'He'll understand.'

'Will he? You didn't see his face when I told him I was going back to Sean. I really hurt him, Mum! And I don't think he'll ever forgive me for having let Sean come between us.'

'Of course he will. He loves you. I've never seen a man more in love,' Eleanor said, 'and he'll be there for you when you're ready to see him again.'

Polly shook her head, torturing herself with the same questions. 'Why did I let Sean back in? I knew I didn't love him anymore. There was absolutely nothing left in my heart for him. I knew that and yet I still let him in.'

'But he's gone now,' Eleanor said, 'and you've got to put this behind you. Give yourself some time. Rest, eat well, sleep late, take the dogs out and walk, read, watch a funny film or two. And let us take care of you and Archie. I'll take him to school and pick him up.'

'You don't need to-'

'I *want* to do it,' Eleanor said, 'so you're going to let me.'

Polly gave a tiny smile.

'Right?'

'Oh, Mum,' Polly said, nestling into the warm embrace of her mother.

'It's all right. You're home now. Safe and sound.'

CHAPTER 28

The days turned into weeks and Polly did as her mother had told her: she rested. She allowed her parents to dote on Archie, to wake him up and give him his breakfast, to make his packed lunch and to take him to school, all whilst she slept. It wasn't easy to rest at first. It wasn't in Polly's nature. She was the sort to start tomorrow whilst it was still today. But, the peace and familiarity of Campion House soon encouraged her to rest – to really rest, and it felt pretty good.

During the day, she took long walks with the dogs, wrapping herself up against the cold winds of early spring whilst taking heart at the slowly lengthening days. And, with the help of her mother, she got some advice about her and Archie's future and how she could move forward.

Polly could have stayed in the safe cocoon of Campion House for the rest of her life, but she knew that she and Archie had to leave at some point and get on with their own lives and that meant finding somewhere to live.

It seemed like an age since she'd left Church Green and there'd been no word from Sean and no news from the police about his whereabouts. Once again, he had disappeared.

There was somebody else she hadn't heard from too. Jago. Polly had dropped him little texts to keep in touch, but his replies were no more than one word. Over and over, she'd said how sorry she was, how she should never have let Sean back into their lives, and how much she regretted pushing Jago away.

Okay.

That was all the reply she could get out of him and she couldn't blame him. Not really. But still she kept on with her one-sided conversations, telling him little stories about the dogs and sending him silly photos of them. She'd tell him about her country walks, and about the muddy footpaths and the beautiful sunsets. She'd give him little updates on the garden – which plants were coming up and which seeds were going in and, slowly, Jago's replies became longer and more frequent until she was receiving several messages a day.

Then Polly shared something with him.

I need to find somewhere new to live, she texted him. *I have to move on.*
That's good, he texted back.

It was after Polly had come back from teaching her class in Bury St Edmunds one morning that she found her mum in the kitchen preparing lunch.

'I don't suppose you want to go and fetch your father, do you?' she asked as Polly walked into the kitchen.

'Where is he?'

'In the garden,' Eleanor said.

Polly nodded. 'Of course. Silly question.'

'Think he's doing something with some chicken manure a neighbour gave him.'

'Oh, lovely!' Polly said with a grin.

Polly took her neat little shoes off and popped on a pair of wellies before whistling for the dogs and heading out into the garden. It didn't take her long to find her father. The six raised vegetable beds were Frank Nightingale's pride and joy and there he was, fork in hand, as he worked, a robin eyeing the proceedings from the hedgerow.

'Polly!' he said, looking up as she approached.

'Hi Dad. How's it going?'

'Soil's warming up,' he said. 'Always a heartening time of year, isn't it?'

Polly looked around the garden, trying to imagine it in all its summer finery and longing for those blissfully warm days when the French windows would be open and the family would take their tea outside.

'How was your morning?' Frank asked.

'My students are struggling with the past continuous tense.'

Frank shook his head. 'I don't know how you have the patience to teach.'

Her eyes widened. 'I always thought I got my patience from you, Dad.'

He shook his head. 'Oh, no,' he said. 'Your patience comes from your mother. She's the one who brought up five children without once losing her cool. Not me.'

'Rubbish!'

'Why do you think I took up gardening?'

Polly frowned.

'If ever it all became too much, I'd escape out here and dig a trench or something,' he said.

Polly laughed. 'Mum's asked me to tell you to come in for lunch.'

Frank stuck the fork deep into the ground before wiping his hands down the front of his trousers and the two of them walked across the lawn together.

'Dad?'

'Yes?'

'I'm going to Castle Clare later. To the estate agents. There's a little house on the Great Tallington Road that's up for rent.'

'You ready for that?'

'I can't go back to Church Green. It wouldn't feel like home anymore.'

Frank nodded. 'What does Archie think?'

'If he's got his guitar with him, I think he'll settle anywhere. And it's time we made a fresh start.'

'And does this fresh start involve Jago?'

They stopped walking and turned to face each other.

'I hope so,' she said. 'One day. When we're both ready.'

Her father opened his arms and Polly snuggled into them. He was so wonderfully comforting in his big tweed coat which smelled of bonfires and the earth.

'Oh, Daddy!' Polly cried. 'It's all such a mess.'

'No it isn't,' he told her. 'Well, maybe just a little bit.'

Polly gave a little laugh. 'It is, isn't it?'

'Nothing you – we – can't sort out. Starting with this new place of yours. Do you want me to come and see it with you?'

Polly shook her head. 'Thanks, but I'd rather go alone.'

'Okay. Let us know how it goes.'

'I will,' she said, and the two of them went into the house for lunch.

Now that the idea was in her head, Polly couldn't wait to get to Castle Clare and, after parking, made straight for the estate agents. She couldn't see the little terraced house advertised in the window and so went inside to enquire.

'You mean Lilac Row?' the young man said. 'I'm afraid that property's not available.'

'Not available?'

'It's already rented. Yesterday as a matter of fact. Went very quickly.'

'Right,' Polly said, furious at herself for not having moved quicker. Properties in Castle Clare were always sought after and she should have realised that she didn't have the luxury of time.

'There's another on the other side of town. Nice Victorian semi. Four bedrooms. I can get you the details.'

'Oh, no thank you,' Polly said quickly, knowing that she wouldn't be able to afford a place with four bedrooms. The three-bedroomed Lilac Row had already been pushing her meagre budget.

She left the estate agents feeling very glum. She hadn't realised it until that moment but she'd rather fallen in love with the house on Lilac Row from the photos she'd seen online of the pretty white-washed home with the sash windows. It had been easy imagining her and Archie there together, and its enclosed cottage garden would have been ideal for Dickens and, being right on the edge of town, it was handy for myriad footpaths into the countryside.

'There'll be others,' her mother told her when she got home with Archie.

'I know,' she said.

'And, in the meantime, we're happy to have you here.' Eleanor beamed her daughter a smile.

It was just after Polly had collected Archie from school the next day when she got the call from Jago. It was the first time she'd heard his voice in weeks.

'Hey,' he said when Polly answered. 'You in town?'

'Yes. I've just–'

'Picked Archie up from school? Good! Meet me by the church, okay? I've got something to show you.' And he hung up.

Polly frowned. 'That was Jago,' she told Archie. 'He said he's got something to show us.'

'Excellent!' Archie said from the back seat.

Polly drove from the school into town, parking near the church and walking to where Jago was sitting on a bench near a yew tree. He didn't spot them at first. He was looking at something he was holding that Polly couldn't make out.

'Jago?' she said, feeling ridiculously nervous at seeing him again.

He looked up, popping whatever he was holding into his pocket as he got up from the bench and walked towards her, a hesitant smile on his face. Archie broke the awkwardness of the moment by running into his arms.

'Arch! How are you?'

'I missed you!' Archie said.

'I missed you,' Jago said and then he looked up at Polly. 'Missed you too.'

'And I missed you,' she said. 'I'm sorry for every-'

Jago shook his head. 'No need for that.'

'But I-'

He took a step forward and picked Polly's hands up in his and held them. 'I want to show you something.'

'What is it?' Archie asked.

'It's down here,' Jago said, leading the way out of the churchyard, but still keeping hold of Polly's right hand.

'Where are we going?' she asked.

'Just a short walk,' he said.

It wasn't until they were on the Great Tallington Road that Polly began to get suspicious.

'Jago?'

'Nearly there,' he said.

'What are we doing?'

He didn't answer her and didn't say anything else until they were standing outside the house on Lilac Row: the one with the sign outside which now read 'Let'.

'Briggs has asked me to move in with him,' Jago said.

'I see,' Polly said. 'So you're renting this place with him?'

Jago shook his head. 'He's a slob and–' he stopped.

'What?'

'And – rather crucially – I don't fancy Briggs.'

'I never suspected you did.'

Jago laughed and then reached into his jacket pocket for the item he'd placed there in the churchyard. It was a set of keys.

'Have you rented this, Jago?' Polly asked.

'I have,' he said. 'I wanted to show it to you.'

Polly stood by the gate he held open for her.

'What's the matter?' he asked.

'I was in the estate agent's yesterday asking about this property.'

'You were?'

'She was,' Archie said, nodding solemnly.

'But somebody beat you to it?' Jago said with a wink.

'Yes,' Polly said with a little smile, 'they did.'

'Well, come on in and see what you missed out on.' Polly watched as Jago opened the front door. 'It's a great house. Nice cosy rooms, lots of period features. The kitchen's a bit small, but the garden's a good size for a townhouse and the bedrooms are too.'

Archie ran ahead of them, bombing around the bare rooms, his voice echoing as he called back to them. Jago was right. The house was great and, although Polly was thrilled for Jago, she couldn't help feeling a little sad that she'd missed out on it for her and Archie.

It was when they ventured upstairs that she saw it.

'Your guitar!' Archie cried as they entered the master bedroom at the back of the house. It was propped up against a wall next to a pretty Victorian fireplace.

'That and a mattress and an overnight bag are the only things I've managed to move in so far,' Jago said. 'It feels a bit strange being here on my own.'

'You'll get used to it,' Polly told him.

'You think?' he said, taking a step towards her. 'Because I don't think I will. I mean, not on my own.'

'You can always give Briggs a call if you get lonely.'

Jago grinned. 'Not going to happen.'

'Or we can visit!' Archie said.

Polly turned away, but she could feel Jago's eyes upon her.

'I'm hoping you'll do more than visit,' Jago said. 'I was kind of hoping you'd want to live here with me.'

'Jago!' Polly cried as she turned to face him. 'Really?'

'You, me, Archie, Dickens. What do you say, Polly?' he asked. 'We could make a good life here. A *new* life.'

Archie looked at his mother and then at Jago and then back at his mother.

'Say yes, Mum! Go *on!*'

A sudden laugh exploded from Polly. 'You're *serious?*'

'Completely. I want to be with you and Archie more than anything else in the world, and I know we haven't known each other long, but I can't imagine life without you two now. Does that make sense?'

'But—'

'But what?'

'This is crazy!'

'Why? Tell me why it's crazy.'

'Because I'm getting divorced and everything's a mess and I'm – I'm so much older than you, Jago!'

He shook his head. 'No you're not. You're perfect. Absolutely perfect. And whatever mess there is going on in your life, we'll sort it out – *together*. Just give us a chance, Polly. Say yes. Say you'll live here with me.'

Polly gazed into Jago's eyes. They were so full of love and expectancy that there was only one answer she could give him, but she had to check with somebody first.

'Archie – you really think this is a good idea?'

'I think it's the *best* idea in the whole world!' he said

Polly nodded and then turned to Jago. 'Yes,' she said. 'Let's do it!'

'Really?' Jago cried. 'You'll move in with me?'

'We'll *all* move in with you!' Archie shouted, launching himself into Jago's arms.

Jago laughed and Polly felt tears misting her eyes.

'Come here!' Jago said and Polly joined them both, ready to embrace their new life together.

The Book Lovers

VICTORIA CONNELLY

Book one in *The Book Lovers* series.

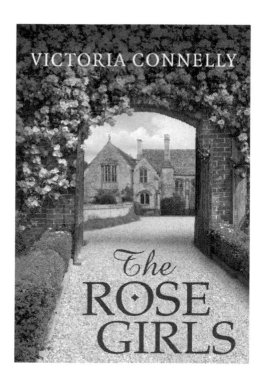

Thirty-year-old Celeste Hamilton's life is at a crossroads: she has just left a disastrous marriage, and her estranged mother has recently died, leaving the family's rose business in jeopardy. Reluctantly, Celeste returns to the family home, a moated manor house in Suffolk, to help her two younger sisters sort out the estate and revive the business.

Having endured the fallout from her mother's Narcissistic Personality Disorder when she was younger, Celeste is filled with self-doubt and crippling insecurities. But she must find the strength and courage to take charge and make some tough decisions to keep the old house from falling down around them.

The Rose Girls is an uplifting, tender and romantic story of courage, perseverance and the healing power of family.

ABOUT THE AUTHOR

Victoria Connelly was brought up in Norfolk and studied English Literature at Worcester University before becoming a teacher. After getting married in a medieval castle in the Yorkshire Dales and living in London for eleven years, she moved to rural Suffolk where she lives with her artist husband and a Springer spaniel and ex-battery hens.

Her first novel, *Flights of Angels*, was published in Germany and made into a film. Victoria and her husband flew out to Berlin to see it being filmed and got to be extras in it. Several of her novels have been Kindle bestsellers.

To hear about future releases sign up for Victoria's newsletter at: www.victoriaconnelly.com

She's also on Facebook and Twitter @VictoriaDarcy

BOOKS BY VICTORIA CONNELLY

The Book Lovers series
The Book Lovers
Rules for a Successful Book Club

Austen Addicts Series
A Weekend with Mr Darcy
The Perfect Hero
published in the US as Dreaming of Mr Darcy
Mr Darcy Forever
Christmas with Mr Darcy
Happy Birthday, Mr Darcy
At Home with Mr Darcy

Other Fiction
The Rose Girls
The Secret of You
A Summer to Remember
Wish You Were Here
The Runaway Actress
Molly's Millions
Flights of Angels
Irresistible You
Three Graces
It's Magic (A compilation volume: Flights of Angels,
Irresistible You and Three Graces)
Christmas at the Cove
Christmas at the Castle
A Dog Called Hope

Short Story Collections
One Perfect Week and other stories
The Retreat and other stories
Postcard from Venice and other stories

Non-fiction
Escape to Mulberry Cottage
A Year at Mulberry Cottage
Summer at Mulberry Cottage

Children's Adventure
Secret Pyramid
The Audacious Auditions of Jimmy Catesby

Printed in Poland
by Amazon Fulfillment
Poland Sp. z o.o., Wrocław